A Touch of Aether

An Urban Fantasy Anthology

Three Ravens Publishing
Chickamauga, GA USA

Table of Contents

Urban Fantasy

By: Charity Ayres

Sometimes, a character's voice reaches out to you from the darkness. It glides through the dark of night to whisper in your ear about the great adventures that await if you'd *just* walk alongside them. Perhaps you take their hand and follow the siren's song of adventure, boarding a train filled with fae and vampiric creatures to dance the night away. Or new voices add to the whispers until you find that you've entered a realm alongside Urbana, peacefully hidden until you touch an innocuous object that is anything but.

Worlds wait when you dance with darkness, light, or rainbows. Magic is like that. Writing is like that. For some, they are one and the same.

Storytelling in worlds of modern mystical mayhem is like touching the live wire of our perception of magic. It's heady and powerful.

I was hooked the first time I opened a book that melded what I knew of the world with beings who wove new colors into the cloak of darkness. I date myself when I tell you I found most of those books mixed only in the romance section. To my misfortune, I had finished all of my *Dragonlance* books, but the bookstore on base had no other fantasy that sounded appealing. It was a one-room shop with maybe ten book stacks and mostly empty wall shelves.

My fellow sailors took every opportunity to point out the "girl" books I was reading as though I should be ashamed. I was at first. Please realize that this was the era of bodice-ripper romance and colorful euphemisms for genitalia. I didn't want to be associated with *that* sort of story as though the book we read could somehow influence our abilities to function in a military capacity. Magical creatures in conflict? Sure! Busty women wearing flowy gowns pulled up around their hips? Only in behind-doors military "training" videos.

I couldn't stop, though. The allure of magical beings in my world beyond vampires and werewolves was exhilarating and new. What if worlds like fairy realms or dimensions of complete societies of accepted magic truly existed, but we didn't see it? How amazing could it be to see the overlap on a sleepy Sunday afternoon? Or to see the mermaids that still adorned so much of the nautical designs that nearly overlapped my military branch of choice?

It was the "what if" of it all. That's a powerful phrase: What if. As an author, I know that's when you have your audience. The moment your reader pauses and wants to believe what you've written in small or large expanses, you've connected to them.

Despite my eventual acceptance, mixing fantasy with the "real" world in my writing didn't happen right away—even though the potential of it in what I was reading had snared me. I stuck to fantasy. I wanted my stories to be found in the *Sword and Sorceress* anthologies or by Mercedes Lackey or the effervescent duo of Weis and Hickman.

It had to be *Pure Fantasy*. Not something muddled with the bodice rippers and the stigma of the time. I wanted to be a classic, not a dime store buy, read, and discarded. Fantasy icons were impactful artists in writing. I wanted that.

Years later, after my military service, I worked in a bookstore. It was here that I started to see things differently. Some of the authors I'd read for years who lived in the romance section were suddenly being reshelved, and the sci-fi/fantasy section was now split into two different sections. It was the early years of the Boy Wizard and the following that would change the face of fiction.

I was excited. My favorite genre was bursting at the seams, and my stories began to change. I managed to get my first short story published in a tiny, short-lived publication. It revolved around a group of elves protesting their mistreatment only to find out that the primary person subverting them was an icon—and one of their own kind.

Those tiny voices in my mind that wanted to play with magic in a world I knew had found their place on paper—and someone actually wanted to read them.

I had created a world for characters and a story I would have wanted to find on the bookshelves. I got my first sale and was recognized for my writing ability. I was hooked on the layering beauty of urban fantasy. I was overjoyed that I could twist known elements easily seen and described with a magical realm's free-form, no (or almost no) rules.

And the characters! They flooded my mind like a mob of children promised candies and kittens. They were adorned with strange appendages or linked to various cultural mythological beings and every power I could imagine for them. We danced together in the playground of my mind because we knew the stories could go anywhere we wanted (and anywhen).

The power of "what if" that had drawn me to the stories I read now powered my own writing. They permitted me to be whatever I wanted so that I could create the stories I wanted to read. "What if" drove me to push the bounds of tricksters that could exist through the will of humankind. "What if?" let a roguish pirate whisper in my ear about her displeasure with a walrus-based crewmate that she desperately wanted to tie to a cannon and drop overboard. "What if" permitted me to dream up new worlds that were simply nesting dolls inside our known world.

The power of being a writer attached to their genre is heady, to say the least. It means that the boundaries we start with are only stopped by a lack of will. Creativity thrives in our ability to think beyond those bounds, where we forge new paths for ourselves and those who will come next.

In Urban Fantasy or any genre, as a writer, you are only stopped if you let yourself be.

An Eye for Royalty

A Nimble and Scales Mystery
By: Matthew Olaranont

Griffe Hardlocke paced small Gnomish steps clockwise around the top half of a dead dragonborn's body in time to the waves lapping against the pier. He tilted up his fedora with a single finger before putting his hands into the pockets of his trench coat, examining the scene with care. The bottom of what was left of the torso was burnt to a crisp, leaving nothing below a scaly, ridged sternum. The wood beneath the corpse was untouched, the same worn browns as the rest of the docks. The night patrolman had found the body an hour after the beginning of midwatch. The deputy sheriff had finally arrived with his men at the witching hour. It wasn't long before sunrise now that Nimble and Scales were on the scene and nothing was getting any fresher.

"Our friend seems to have lost his footing." Griffe said to his partner.

"And his leggings, and his ability to remain… hip." Urlthor Xendrax spoke stoically, the low rumble of his voice punctuated by exhalations of smoke upward through his nostrils. Though he stood stock-still and imposing against the sea breeze like a dragon shaped monolith in the fog, the Dragonborn detective's yellow slitted eyes darted around the remains in a cloverleaf pattern, searching. Griffe knew the smouldering as a sign of muted anxiety, but it was easy to read it as annoyance.

The Gnome knelt down at the crisp end, the smell of stark carbonization carrying over the salt smell of the sea air.

"And you said you found him this way?" Griffe asked over his shoulder to the watchman—a squirrely, scrawny man dressed in dockworker's clothes.

"Y-yeah, twernt no flames nor fire neither. Jus' smoke 'n' ash."

Griffe reached a cautious hand down next to the burnt end, holding it just far away enough to see if it was still warm.

"Any ideas on what could do this, Url? Normally you guys are mostly fireproof." He touched the tip of a finger to the carbonization. It crumpled, long since cool to the touch.

"All of the things which do come to mind—you wouldn't like." Url stepped a large clawed foot to the side and began to pace widdershins around the corpse. The dead drake's expression was one of surprise, mouth slightly open and vertical slit eyes narrowed to near pinpricks. Griffe stood up, dusting off his hands on his coat and pulling down on the brim of his fedora to put it back where he wanted it.

"Stupid magic crap." The Gnome muttered under his breath. The body had one arm pointed toward the distance, the other down by what was left of its side. Griffe scanned the area around them, noting most of the spot being bordered by a sheer drop into the sea. The sound of the waves hung in the air punctuated by signal bells and the lapping of water against the iron sides of the Aethero-magical ships. There weren't any obvious signs of what might have caused any of this beyond the burn marks, but dead drakes told no tales.

"Did you move the body at all?" Url turned back to the deputy with a swirl of his black coat, towering over the human.

"Nossir," The young man was obviously out of his element, fingering the badge on his tabard like it would spare him the dragon's questions, "Watchman told me he was here an' I came straight over. The-the sheriff always spoke about you two whenever he couldn't figure out who the criminals were so I-I thought it best to send for you two."

Urlthor exhaled another small cloud of black smoke from his pyrolytic gland. Other dragons had better control over the color, but Url could've used an antacid.

"Url, why don't you give these fine folks another run down while I hoof it around here? I don't think we're going to get much more off the body but we probably shouldn't move it yet." Griffe squeaked from just above Url's knee height. His much larger partner just nodded.

The Gnome walked back over to the body, standing perpendicular to it and staring down at the dead dragonborn's shiny auburn scales. He couldn't tell if the coloration meant anything, or if its sheen held a clue to the situation at hand. He followed the line of the outstretched arm, looking down the docks in the direction it was pointing. The line ended toward the doors of a warehouse, green glass windows reflecting in the freshly broken dawn and cutting through the fog.

Griffe turned to look at a warehouse closer to them on the docks and then back down toward the one the body was pointing at. Back and forth one more time to make sure. The one down at the end of the docks was missing a window. It might've been nothing—but it was also the only thing that stood out from normal.

"Hold down the fort, will ya Url? I'm gonna see a man about some gams."

Url turned over his shoulder and gave Griffe a nod, a questioning look on his face but no protest voiced. Griffe took off at as speedy of a walk as his little legs could carry him, shoes tapping his rhythm over the boardwalk. Up close it was obvious the window had been shattered inward. Shards of glass still clung to the outer frame but no obvious pieces on the ground outside of the large sliding cargo door. The ground beneath it had the subtle mark of a burn indented into the wood, the gaudy black splotch a sign of something's passing. The Gnome detective looked down at the blotch, up at the window, and back down again. He heaved a heavy sigh at the implication, putting a hand out over the mark and feeling a few hairs perk up on the back of his hand. He grumbled and shoved both of his hands into his trench coat's pockets and stomped over to the warehouse door in a huff. Trying the handle, the human sized door was unlocked, but stuck.

"Elms and stones." Griffe cursed under his breath and began to shove his shoulder against the door underneath the handle. With a grunt and a wail, he forced the door open into a dark warehouse, tumbling inside after losing his balance to the free swinging door.

The sound of his messy entrance echoed through the otherwise silent warehouse, the noise fading back into the sound of the waves until his mind began to ignore that as well. The large wooden crates in the warehouse cast long, stark shadows in the light of the rising sun; motes of dust playing in the bright beams piercing down through the greenish glass save for the single rod of pure daylight coming through the broken hole above the cargo door.

The shards of what remained of the busted window glittered on the floor beneath it like the fractal reflection of the sun on calm seas—whatever had landed inside after the action had left a splash of blood not too far away from the glass. Griffe whistled at the results, walking over to the rusty brown patch of dried blood, looking around the room near it before seeing what he was looking for.

Caught on the edge of a mostly closed crate was a toe claw from a dragonborn, pointy end jammed into the wood and the bloody stump from where it had been ripped from the foot was the same ruddy brown as the patch on the floor. Griffe pulled over one of the smaller boxes nearby and used it as a stepping stool, reaching his hands underneath the partially pried up lid and opening it the rest of the way.

"That was a hell of a two-step there, pal." He said to himself as the light hit the contents of the crate. On top of the packing material the bottom half of the dragonborn from the pier looked like it had shoved itself inside the crate using its legs to do all the action before curling up with the burnt end facing the opening and a pool-cue sized ball of iridescent glass resting in the spot where his stomach would have gone. The ball was a sight to behold, catching the brilliance of the dawn with the same prismatic intensity of a rainbow peeling apart white light. Griffe narrowed his eyes and leaned down toward it, a trick of the light giving off a fuzzy image of something at the core of the glassy globe.

"*Jour de Joie!* Hark fair stranger who hath rescued me!" A voice yelled out exuberantly from inside the sphere. Griffe tumbled off his makeshift stool in surprise, only just managing to catch his hat before it tumbled off his head.

"What in the—" Griffe scrambled back up to his feet, spinning around wildly to make sure he was still alone.

"*Bonjour! Voilà, Ici!* Hail and well met!" The sphere called out to him again, more softly this time. Griffe recognized it and narrowed his eyes before dusting himself off and muttering,

"Stupid magic crap."

The detective climbed back onto the crate, reaching out a shaky hand toward the sphere, pausing before actually touching it.

"You're not going to kill and/or maim me, are you?"

"*Bonté divine!* You are my savior. Though, *s'il vous plait*, do not tell the constabulary that I am here." Griffe recoiled his hand from the sphere at the wrist.

"Why? What's your game here, pal?"

The colors inside the sphere shifted around—no longer a kaleidoscopic rainbow, but a milky, pearlescent shadow.

"Please, we cannot speak here. There are many eyes," the image in the sphere shifted to something akin to a Dragon's eye—poison yellow with a jagged slit in the center like spilt ink, "seen and unseen."

Griffe hesitated.

"I beseech thee, monsieur. Anywhere but here. Anyone but the authorities."

Griffe pulled his hand back and reached into the pocket of his coat, pulling out a canvas sack and using that to scoop up the sphere without making skin contact with it. From within the bag, the sphere cried out,

"*Mon Dieuuuuu,*" as he faded into silence, like tossing something down a very deep well. With a few more perfunctory looks over the scaly legs and abdomen shoved inside the crate, Griffe dismounted the box and headed back to the dock where Url was now arguing with the city sheriff.

"—asked you here. You two think you can just show up without a writ?" The sheriff was already into his usual complaints about who was responsible for what.

"I would like to remind you that the terms of our warrant extend directly from the governor, sheriff." Url was polite to a fault as always, humoring the much smaller man. The sheriff had mistaken his restraint for weakness.

"Yeah—only if I call you for help! And did you receive a summon from me?"

"We got called in by one of the boys from your office." Griffe joined in, jabbing a thumb at the nervous looking deputy who was doing his best to go unnoticed. It was enough to get the heat off of them. The sheriff was apoplectic, turning his fury over to his subordinate while the unlikely duo conferred.

"Did you find something in that warehouse?" Url asked, keeping his voice low.

"Yeah, but not here. We can talk about it over coffee." Griffe said and stretched his arms above his head, fingers interlocked and palms facing up. Url grumbled assent.

Griffe finished his stretch and shoved both hands into the pockets of his coat and started to walk away.

"Hey! You two can't leave! I'm not done with you!" The sheriff yelled after them when he caught Url walking away in the corner of his eye.

"Yeah, but we're done with you and your half a friend there. You want us, you can come get us at the office." Griffe waved over his shoulder without turning around to look at the man.

"What about witnesses?" The sheriff yelled back.

"Have you tried talking to your deputy?" Url replied in a voice like thunder.

Back at the office after grabbing breakfast, Griffe dumped out the deflated canvas pouch into an ashtray on his tabletop before sitting down into his chair and putting his feet up. Griffe's half of the room was built to his size—a small desk and coat rack that matched his stature, the only thing that was sized regularly was the ash tray that now held the glassy sphere that he had found in the bowels of the dead dragonborn.

The espresso machine was on Url's side of the room—everything on that half sized upward to match his proportions. It gave the whole place the feeling of an Ames room.

"I didn't realize we were in the habit of collecting shiny trinkets like those feathered Kotengu." Url voiced his concerns over the hiss of the steam coming from the machine.

"This isn't just some crystal ball, Url, this is a witness." Griffe pulled an engraved cigarette case from his drawers and lit one up with a match before setting his feet back down on the floor where Url walked over with his cup and saucer—the double shot of espresso cafe au lait was large in the Gnome's hands.

"For a witness, it's being quite silent." Url dragged his chair over from the other side of the room and sat down kitty-corner to Griffe at the desk, the table barely coming up to the bend in his knees.

"Hmph!" The sphere huffed, the color inside shifting from perfect clarity to a reddish brown. Url raised an eye ridge mid sip. The ceiling fan above them creaked slow circles.

"You want to start talking there, pal? You're the one that begged me to talk somewhere else. So here we are, somewhere else." Griffe ashed the cigarette into the tray beneath the sphere.

"Hmph!" The sphere huffed again, the swirl of colors more vibrant now.

"Is there something we could do to encourage you to talk?" Url asked, setting his cup back down on its saucer.

"Zut! At least tell your miniscule companion to stop sprinkling ashes on me!" The sphere finally spoke to Urlthor. The dragonborn reached one enormous hand over and placed it between Griffe's reach and the ashtray.

"Alright alright, no need to be so insulted." the Gnome ashed the cigarette into the saucer at the base of his cup, "Now I have to wash this."

"Insulted? INSULTED?" The sphere seemed to have a flash of lightning within, "When I asked for your assistance I did not expect to be thrown into a dark hole so laissez faire!"

"Perhaps you should apologize to our new… friend." Url suggested. Griffe sipped his coffee and smoked the cigarette from one corner of his mouth. The sphere simmered like a roiling sandstorm.

"Alright, alright, I'm sorry I put you in the bag without warning you. Happy?" Griffe spoke up when he finished his coffee, stubbing out the cigarette into the small pile of ash in the saucer.

"Hmph. A disgusting habit." The sphere judged him.

"I do always tell you that it'll be the death of you, Griffe." Url chided him without malice.

"Yeah, well I'll deal with it when he gets here."

"If you're speaking now, would you like a coffee? Maybe it would help you recount your story." Url offered.

"Hon, hon! You I like, fellow dragonkin!" The sphere exclaimed, "but alas, I am unable to enjoy the pleasures of life as I once did."

Griffe mouthed the word, "Fellow?" at his friend, but said nothing aloud.

"Then perhaps we should start at the beginning—who, or what, are you?" Url continued.

The colors in the sphere swirled about, reforming to a ruddy earth tone with a sanguine dragon's eye overlaid.

"I am the Eye of Pivonax!" The sphere declared, practically glowing, "Witness of ages! Record of the forging of the Aegis!"

Urlthor's eyes widened at the declaration—if dragonkin could break out into a cold sweat, this would be the moment for it.

"The eye of whose-a-what-now?" Griffe asked.

"Pivonax." Url said.

"—of legend!" The sphere added.

"What'd he do?" Griffe asked, still confused.

"He was an ancient hero to the Northern Dragon tribes. I don't know many of them—my clan is from the west—but even then his name is well known among most dragonborn." Url explained.

"Then what's this thing?"

"It is said the Eye of Pivonax is a record made by an ancient mage to capture the essence of his soul so that all of dragonkind would have guidance into the future."

"So stupid magic crap." Griffe offered.

"I'm afraid so." Url agreed.

"I AM NOT CRAP!" The sphere yelled.

The two detectives looked down at the crystal ball in the ashtray.

"So, how'd you even end up here?" Griffe asked the Eye.

The images within turned to stormy seas and more flashing lightning, dark clouds over a foreign land that morphed into a ship rocking—Aether powered engines struggling to keep it right in the storm.

"The time is right for me to seek the exiled heir!" The sphere spoke, "the lost princess of the Covenant of Frost must inherit my wisdom. My steward was told that she had been sent to this fair city to be raised safely away from the treachery of assassins and bureaucrats. It is my shame that she was not able to receive me here."

"Your steward is the one I found you in the crate with?" Griffe asked.

"*Oui*, alas, he was of righteous spirit."

"I'd say his opinion's split."

"Who told him that the heir would be in this city?" Url cut in.

"The bloodline of Pivonax is strong! We have many such allies throughout the land and many relatives amongst the common kin."

Griffe lit another cigarette. Urlthor drummed the tips of his clawed fingers against his leg, rippling the pinstripe pattern of his black pants.

"So what happened last night at the docks?" Griffe asked.

"Treachery! Betrayal! The infinite curses of dragonkin on those that betray their own!" The sphere declared, pulsing to red, incandescent in its own anger.

"Yeah, but what *happened?*" Griffe reemphasized his point.

The eye pulsed like it was counting to ten to calm itself down.

"It would—it would be easier to show you. *C'est facile.* Place your hands upon me."

Url reached a hand up over the orb, but Griffe groaned.

"*Qu'est-ce que c'est?*" The eye asked.

"It's going to be a vision, isn't it? I hate visions." Griffe said, reluctantly reaching his hand out to the side of the sphere.

With a jolt, it was a dark night drenched in fog, the heavy air of the port outshined by the inner fire of a roiling pyrolytic gland. Griffe guessed this was how Url felt when he was nervous—it was like heartburn and hookah smoke all at once. The connection between the orb and the steward was strong enough to tell it was the dead dragon they had found at the docks—

ostensibly still in one piece. A group of dragonfolk shaped shadows appeared out of the mist near one of the warehouses, a voice addressing their point of view.

"Welcome to the ville." The drake's voice was of the city, yet tinted with the same inflection as the Eye's accent.

A more slender dragonborn stepped out at his side, the higher pitch of her voice and more refined stance giving her away,

"*Bonjour,* fair steward." She said, but took no step forward until the first drake pushed her gently.

"Greetings fair lady," the steward said with a bow, "I trust you know that the time has come."

There was a pause and a searching look from the princess.

"Yes," she spoke after an offbeat silence, "I—I'm ready to receive the knowledge of the clan."

The steward stepped forward, his clawed hand reaching into his coat and wrapping around the Eye. The princess held out a hand, just far enough that it gave the steward pause. The first drake in the entourage gave the Princess another push forward—something seemed off. The steward looked between them as the Princess reached her hand out unsteadily, an expression on her face even Griffe could read. In a breath, the masque broke and the Princess yelled,

"Run! You must take it away! They-" A rough pair of hands from one of the others in the entourage grabbed her and the first drake began to step forward, intent on grabbing the Eye.

The steward turned to run, taking the glass sphere and shoving it directly into his mouth, swallowing the orb whole in a single adrenaline fueled gulp.

"Get him!" The lead drake yelled, falling into the chase.

The steward ran, but the weariness of his journey held him back.

"Please," the steward begged, "Grant me some of your power!" addressing the Eye of Pivonax.

"*Bien sûr!*" The sphere replied, beginning to glow.

A flash of light put the pieces together for Griffe, followed by the fleshy thump of the steward's torso hitting the ground behind them. At the base of the warehouse doors, another bright flash led to the feeling of wind and the crashing of broken glass that told the rest of the tale.

From inside the hastily hinged crate the orb watched the other two dragonkin who had been chasing it burst through the entrance, cursing all the while. The darkness of the warehouse concealed everything but the few crates in the weak beam of moonlight shining through the broken window.

"We gotta go. *Allons-y!*" One of the pursuers said to the other over the sound of the Princess's screaming. The door slammed shut behind them a moment after.

Griffe came back to reality with the feeling of falling flat on his ass into the office chair. Urlthor had managed to do so with a little more grace.

"*Ben, c'est tout.*" the sphere concluded, "A tale of betrayal and kidnapping most vile!"

"Sure seems like it," Griffe retrieved his still lit cigarette off the floor and took a drag, "also seems like you're the one that killed our John Dragon."

"Oui, a most unfortunate mistake. He could not handle the raw energy. His *poumon de feau*, it was… *petit.*"

"Those kidnappers seem familiar, Griffe?"

"Seemed like it was the inner city scaly types. The kind from the quarter across the river."

Url grumbled, trying to sip something out of the empty cup he had set down before putting the cup back on the saucer with an audible clink.

"So… what will you do? The princess is in dire need." The sphere entreatied.

Griffe sighed, stubbing out the cigarette next to the previous one.

"I don't like it, Url." The Gnome said with an air of finality.

"The circumstances do seem undesirable." Url agreed.

"*Mes amies*, have I misjudged you?"

"I never said that. But, ol' knife ears always told me messing with dragon cases was a quick ticket to the grave." Griffe reached for the cigarette case again, but set it back down without opening it. Url tsked pensive puffs of smoke from his nostrils in time to the drumming of his claws on his leg.

"We could bill the city double." the dragonborn suggested.

"But would it be worth it?" Griffe tapped the edge of the saucer with the tip of his finger.

"Eternal glory! Tests of Valor! What more could one want?" The Eye tried to be helpful.

"The bounty on whoever is behind this might pay for some of your vices." Url said with a sidelong tilt of his head.

"Well—" Griffe started.

"Coffee is getting more expensive these days." Url added, clearing his throat into his fist.

Griffe let out something between a sigh and a groan, "I guess we'll have to go save ourselves a princess."

"*Merveilleux!*"

The plan was simple—with a positive ID on the dragonborn that had kidnapped the princess, the only thing left to do was to shake the trees and see which one he fell out of. The northern Dragon quarter was across the river, a canton that was in the open specializing in a river walk that was part of the industry that spanned the length of the waterway that was in town. The length of the River District was separated into microcosms of clans and ethnicities as a holdover from the compact ghettos that had once corralled all of the war refugees.

Url recommended starting their squeeze at a dive named "*La course de l'aile*" closer to the eastern city center than it was the riverwalk. It was the kind of place matron drakes warned their hatchlings about. Staffed by worse dragons than their clientele, the crew that owned it made sure their crooked customers knew the length of their leash. A trolley ride later and an hour before noon the wayward sleuths were walking down the back stairs to the regulars lounge with Url leading the way carrying the Eye of Pivonax in his breast pocket. The air in the bar and lounge hung heavy with smoke from cigarettes, houri bloom spliffs, and dragon's fire. Nobody batted an eye to Url's entrance but the mood shifted considerably when Griffe stepped in behind him. The Gnome didn't bother removing his fedora, keeping a steely eyed glare on his face and scanning the room.

Business was good, and the only seating left was at the bar. Griffe climbed up onto a tall stool next to Url, catching the patron on his other side eating the local dish of fried potatoes with gravy and cheese curds on top of it. Griffe couldn't stand the stuff.

"What'll it be?" The dragonborn tending bar asked them, giving most of his attention to Urlthor.

"I'll have a Wingspan. Straight up." Url ordered the house drink—a cocktail popular with the dragon folk that mixed in a liquor that was as strong as undistilled Aether. The last time Griffe tried it, a sip had almost punched a hole in his stomach. He had been laid up in bed with a pounding headache sipping on an Elven decoction for days .

"What about you, tiny?" The dragon addressed him with as much reverence as he had for the worn out dish towel in his hand.

"Whiskey, neat. The Human stuff. Two fingers." The dragon behind the bar scoffed.

"Yours or mine?"

Griffe leaned forward and tilted up the brim of his fedora,

"What about Jax Kalifax's?" He tapped two fingers on the bartop like he was asking for the next card.

The bartender snorted a small jet of flame into the flagon he had been cleaning and walked away polishing the heated glass. The way he figured, Griffe would have to play hardball to get any answers. Kalifax was one of the more well known mobsters in the dragon's dens—smuggling, racketeering, prostitution, the list went on—but one thing he didn't like was people disrespecting their ancestors.

The barkeep dragon returned a few minutes later with their drinks, Griffe's in a lowball that was too big for his hand and Url's in a traditional wide, high flute glass.

"Want me to do it?" The bartender asked when he set the glass down in front of Url.

"No, thank you. I can manage." Url said before exhaling the smallest jet of flame into the drink and setting it alight. The drink burned with a clean blue flame. If it had been mixed just right the flame would eek out in two directions like the name implied before fading away. The blue shifted to green and spread outward over opposite edges of the rim, catching the sugared edges and caramelizing it with a hiss before burning itself out.

"Good mix." Url commented before taking his first sip.

"Clean fire." The bartender returned the compliment before turning back to his duties.

Griffe drank and watched everyone else in the room, taking in the crowd. He was the smallest one there but stood out the most. The whiskey was decent imported stuff with a peppery finish that was popular with dragonkin. It wasn't the first time he had to get answers in the Dragon quarter.

"Word on the street is that there's a princess in town." Griffe got straight to the point with the barkeep.

"Rumors are cheap. I get too many on a daily basis." The bartender said dismissively, squeaking towel in glass.

"Except this is not rumor." Url backed up his partner, "we have it on good authority that there *is* a princess in town and that she's dealing with some… unsavory types. Artifact smuggling, murder, blasphemy. Those kind of people."

The bartender looked up from his polishing, yellow slits sliding along to stare at Urlthor.

"You two some kind of constables?"

"Not if we get the information we need. We just want to help the princess—smuggling's not really what we mess with." Griffe said over the rim of his glass.

"Keep drinking." The bartender said, pouring each a new one before disappearing behind a door in the back and heading upstairs. The two detectives took the invitation to stay—Griffe spinning around on the stool and taking in the view of the room to make sure no one was walking up to them unnoticed.

"*Que fais-tu?*" The ball asked Url from inside the pocket.

"Waiting on an invitation to see the dragon that runs this place."

"*Excelsior!* Then we challenge him to honorable combat, oui?"

"No, he's not the one we want. I bet he has the information on your mystery kidnapper." Griffe whispered into Url's coat. The Eye grumbled something impatient before going quiet again.

Half a glass of whiskey later the bartender reappeared from behind the door and hissed at them to get their attention, producing a narrow jet of flame out of the corner of his mouth that didn't quite reach the floor. The two investigators stood and went to him, Griffe following behind Url again. Going down the outer stairs had been one thing, but following dragonborns up dragonborn sized stairs proved to be difficult to accomplish at a reasonable pace. A few steps up, Url had taken note of his friend's difficulty and paused, letting the overhang of his long black coat sit still for a moment. Griffe used the time to climb up his friend's back and hold on to the epaulets of the duster, feet braced against the back of the dragonborn's belt—vaulting up in a smooth, practiced motion that didn't even alert the bartender.

On the landing at the top of the stairs, Griffe dismounted without a sound and walked to the side to see the bartender tossing the towel up to rest on his shoulder so he could open half of a set of double doors. The two entered at his behest, adding a little bit of distance between their paces to make sure there was room to react in case of a trap. The office beyond the doors looked like it had been transplanted from a palace treasury—opulent gold filigree carved into dark, rich woods accented the black and gold marble floor in a way that expressed the lap of luxury but put the hairs on the back of Griffe's neck on end.

"*De que c'est?* Who are you two?" The dragonborn in tailored pinstripe behind the desk asked them—obviously the one in charge. He was flanked by two other dragonnesses that Griffe assumed were pretty, but dressed for business. You could never tell if a lizard lady was a trophy wife or a trophy assassin in this business.

"Nimble and Scales Detective Agency. Pleased to meet you?" Griffe left a pregnant pause at the end.

"Kalifax. Jax Kalifax. You asked for me. So which—"

"I'm Scales. He's Nimble." Griffe answered, jabbing a thumb at Url in the process. Kalifax tilted his head and narrowed his eyes—more confused and intrigued than upset.

"*Tire une bûche.*" Kalifax said after a moment's thought, one hand indicating the two chairs in front of him and the other taking the cigar from his mouth and placing it onto the ashtray on his desk.

The two sat down, Griffe taking off his hat and placing it on his knee.

"I was told you insist that there was some kind of heresy going on in my part of town." Kalifax said with an air of seriousness that betrayed his commitment. Griffe let Url do the talking—this was dragon business.

"There's an heiress in town. She's a princess from the Northern Khaganates. If you haven't read the papers yet, there's a dead kin on the pier that just arrived from there the other night."

Url started without giving away the game; Kalifax listened with an impassive expression.

"The meet went wrong. A dragonkin kidnapped the heir—someone with the resources and the power has taken her. We're looking to get her back to safety."

Kalifax brought the cigar back to his mouth and took a contemplative pull on it, exhaling the cloud of smoke upward through his nostrils—the cloud swirled with the hint of enhancement like a dragon flying a small circle before dissipating into the rest of the smoke in the room.

"How do you two know this? What makes me believe you?" The boss asked.

"They were trafficking something that needs to get to the princess." Url started, "Something even I've heard of that carries importance to the Northern bloodlines."

"What is it? Those are my tribes you're talking about Sunsetter."

"I am of legend!" The Eye yelled out from inside Url's coat. Urlthor took the sphere out with a disgruntled, smokeless sigh.

"*Bonjour! Comment allez-vous?* I AM THE EYE OF PIVONAX!"

Url held it out in his hand, palm up. The colors in the sphere swirled in their best intimidating shades.

Kalifax's eyes widened in their sockets, the pupillary slit almost round for how wide it was.

"The… the prophecy." Kalifax intoned the last word in a reverential whisper. The cigar fell to the floor somewhere forgotten and the attendants with it into deferential prostration.

"*S'il vous plait*, tell my chevaliers where we may find this evildoer."

"I—yes, of course mon Seigneur." Kalifax scrabbled about in a drawer and pulled out a notepad, plucking the dip quill from its stand and scribbling notes and addresses.

"One I'd point my finger at is Flaubert Thereuax. Young kid for what he's got. No respect for tradition."

Griffe took the page of notes from Kalifax, looking it over to see a handful of addresses, but Kalifax held fast to the end he held.

"Promise me that you'll get her gone, I don't care what it takes. Her and the Eye could burn this place to the ground."

Url placed his hand atop Kalifax's burgundy scales, an understanding between them.

The older dragon let go.

They looked up the addresses in a directory book kept back at the bar the most likely candidate out of the few that were provided was a warehouse in the industrial zone outside the Dwarven district— somewhere you couldn't hear a princess's screams over the sound of forges and machinery. But noise worked both ways—Thereuax probably would be lying low while he was convinced the town constables were looking for him and wouldn't try to move the heiress until after dark.

A share-cab ride later and they were a few blocks down the road from the address, dismounting the vehicle in the Dwarven part of town and walking the rest of the way over where the precisely chiseled stones changed into old fashioned cobble. It was midafternoon and most of the buildings were still occupied—leaving the safehouse the only one on the block that didn't have the doors open or the windows cracked.

"Kid's getting sloppy. Closed door stands out a mile." Griffe noted.

"Indeed. What approach do you want to take?" Url paused outside the wrought iron fence surrounding the warehouse grounds. There wasn't a large distance between the fence and the main building but the open ground between the two left them vulnerable.

"Same as usual. I'll go high, you go low. I'll tap if I see anything and I guess you can throw a rock or something to get my attention."

"Our battle will be glorious!" The Eye yelled.

"No, no. You need to shut up so our battle can be as quiet as possible. We don't know what this guy will do to the princess if he gets wind of us being here." Griffe countered.

"The cad! Has he no honor?" The Eye said.

"If he did, we wouldn't be here." Griffe said offhandedly while buttoning his coat. He finished his preparations by taking off his hat and holding it in both hands.

"Ready?" Url asked.

"For what?" The Eye asked.

"The ol' razzle dazzle." Griffe said with a nod to Url. The Dragonborn lifted his partner by the waist in one hand, grabbing his lapel with the other, rocking him back and forth above his head.

"One… Two… Three!" On the third count, Url hurled Griffe up high over the fence and onto the warehouse roof, the Gnome doing a flip mid flight and landing with barely a sound, sliding down the angled sheet metal to belay his momentum. Once he was stable, Griffe undid the buttons on his coat and put the hat back on his head before looking around. One of the skylights was propped open, giving a half decent view of the situation below.

The interior was cavernous darkness punctuated by the warm orange pools of filament bulbs pointed to the ground. A pair of guards were walking back and forth between ends of the room while the rest sat around a table playing a game with a set of green-backed cards. Griffe looked up and waved both arms to get Url's attention before he entered the grounds. The Gnome clapped twice before he was cut off by the shrill hoot of a factory steam whistle next door.

On the ground, Url acknowledged the warning with a single wave of his arm before crouching low and leaping the fence with nimble grace, landing into the midnight depths of a long shadow in the late afternoon sun and disappearing like a drop of ink back into the well. It was pure trust to know that the dragonborn would make his way inside soon without being caught.

Griffe waited, feeling a drop of sweat slide out from beneath the brim of his hat and glide its way down to his chin. The sign came when one of the guard dragons set a foot outside the light of one of the bulbs and was pulled into the darkness with a muffled sliding and the sound of constriction. Griffe tucked his head into the skylight and grabbed onto the boneworks of the roof, scaling his way down the beam and taking note of a second floor office with its lights on just beyond the table where the guards were playing their game.

The second guard disappeared from his patrol and the winner of the card game finally looked up.

"Hey!" The winning guard yelled at the emptiness, expecting a reply, "you guys still down there?"

One of the other guards got up and moved toward the door, running for a large switch that looked like it was for the larger warehouse lights. As soon as he set foot into the shadows surrounding, the sound of parallel footsteps cut him off with a noise like something bodily slamming into the floor.

"What's going on out there?" Their leader had shown himself, stepping out from inside the office and yelling down at the guards from under the spotlight of a bulb. Griffe noted the silhouette of someone else in the office and started to clamber his way over toward the roof of the second floor room.

"Someone's in here, boss!" The winning henchman yelled up.

"Show yourself, you *lâche!*" the other standing guard yelled.

"Go turn on the light, you idiot!" Flaubert yelled down to his minions. Both scrambled over each other to head for the main switch, but ran wide apart to avoid being caught. One of the guards disappeared into the dark immediately and was dispatched the same way as his cohorts, but the other was toppled by the glassy orb crashing into the side of his skull.

In the meanwhile, Griffe had climbed over the railing, caught a rope down to the catwalk above the office and hopped down next to a vent. He ripped it from its fittings and jumped down into the well lit room with the hostage while Flaubert yelled,

"Get him! Get him! It's the Eye!"

The Princess was chained to a chair and padlocked in a way that would've made it impossible for her to pick it herself or melt with her own fire even if she hadn't been gagged. Griffe held up a finger in front of his mouth and said,

"Shut up, Princess. We're here to rescue you."

"*En Garde, vache chien!*" The Eye of Pivonax yelled from somewhere outside. Griffe got the padlock open with a pick when the warehouse lights came on with a snap, bright and clear—leaving him silhouetted against the outside.

"Hey!" Flaubert yelled before running back toward the office—a pistol in his hand now obvious in the light. The mob boss made it back to the doorway before Griffe could get the Princess fully free from her chains, the dragoness only just managing to stand when Flaubert filled the entryway and pointed his pistol at her and then to Griffe.

"Who the hell are you?" Flaubert asked as everyone froze. The sound of a punch and a grunt came from down on the warehouse floor.

"A Gnome that ain't afraid of iron or dragons." Griffe said, standing defiantly.

"Get outta here ya—" Flaubert raised his pistol to fire but before he could there was a loud cry from outside that was a blend of two voices— Urlthor and the Eye—a shout of incomprehensible fury that was followed by an extraordinary heat and a flash of light that blinded Flaubert with its intensity. The glass windows of the office melted instantly, running down in a searing dribble that left the skin on the back of Griffe's neck feeling like he had spent a full day under the sun.

"Princess, tag team!" Url's lone voice yelled up from the floor.

"Comment?" She said in polite surprise—turning to Griffe while Flaubert blinked both his inner and outer sets of eyelids trying to get his vision back.

The Gnome was already on it—turning around toward the now open windows in time to catch a vibrant glass orb imbued with the image of an angry xanthous dragon's eye. It was uncomfortably warm in his hand and only growing hotter.

"Monsieur Griffe, I shall use you to enact my wrath!" The Eye declared.

"No you won't! That'll kill me worse than the steward!" Griffe yelled, "You take it Princess!"

"Non! I cannot!" She declared.

"Of course you can!" Griffe yelled back.

"It is not—" She started, but Griffe was done playing with the burning sphere.

"Take it, lady!" Griffe played hot potato and lobbed it at the freed hostage.

"*Mon Élue!*" The Eye declared as it flew toward her.

"Shit." said Flaubert.

The Princess barely caught the ball in its tossed arc, but the effect was instantaneous. Griffe dove away from her and pulled his hat down over his eyes as the same intense light filled up the room like someone had rented the sun for an afternoon social.

The sound of sizzling and hissing followed by Flaubert's scream spelled the death knell for the evening's activities—the Eye proclaiming, "*Victoire!*"

But Griffe didn't move until Url's familiar voice said,

"You can open your eyes now." with a gentle shake of his shoulder. The little Gnome pulled his hat back up and rolled over, opening his eyes to see Url's extended hand and the Princess standing behind him cradling the Eye of Pivonax like an egg.

"Thanks, pal. You make it through in one piece?" Griffe asked. Url's black coat barely hung on him, a ragged hole burnt across the shirt underneath.

"Monsieur Urlthor was a conduit most excellent!" The Eye declared. Url burped up a black cloud of smoke politely into his other fist.

"It was not an entirely unpleasant experience." Url said.

"So what happened to Flau-" Griffe caught the smoking pair of shoes and what was left of the upstart's pants left in the doorway, snapping his mouth shut when he saw the aftermath.

"Princesse Jeanne was wonderful, no?" The eye was beaming with pride over her work, "She has put an end to the conniving vache."

The Princess looked down and away for a moment before turning back to extend a hand to greet the two,

"What are the names of my saviors?" She asked.

"Urlthor Xendrax."

"Griffe Hardlocke. We're the Nimble and Scales Detective Agency."

"Enchante." The Princess gave a neat, if flustered, curtsy with her greetings, "I am Jeanne Sertonax, heir to the wisdom of the blood of Pivonax. How was it that you knew of my woes?"

"Lady, do we have a story for you."

The Princess turned to give one last wave to the two detectives escorting her before boarding the Aether-liner bound for somewhere as far as they could convince her to go. It was a whirlwind argument between all parties involved convincing the Princess that she needed to leave town between the Eye threatening to challenge her adversaries to trial by combat and all of them coming to the casual conclusion that Flaubert's very sudden disappearance both from the city and the mortal coil might be more trouble than it was worth to stick around.

Eventually, Griffe's insistence to the request they had received from Kalifax brought the Princess around to the idea of taking an extended vacation so she—and the Eye—could lay low for a while.

Griffe and Url stood dockside until the ship powered up and began to steam away, the characteristic purple glow of Aether burn under the waterline disappearing as the ship faded into the fog.

"So what'd you put on the invoice?" Griffe asked as the last of the warm glow disappeared into the haze, the red glow of his cigarette, the brightest thing left in the mist from underneath the top of the railing.

"I billed them double. One for solving the murder, and the other for taking care of Flaubert." Url said.

Griffe leaned on the support next to him and ashed into the waters below.

"Who took the fall?"

"I told them that the dead steward had been smuggling a highly magical artifact and that Flaubert had wanted it at all costs." Url replied. Griffe took a drag on his cigarette while the dragonborn leaned both elbows on the railing.

"Not an outright lie—I like it."

"And then I told them that when we hunted Flaubert down he tried to use the artifact on us and it backfired."

"And that's why we're only getting a third of his bounty."

"Because they don't believe a dragonborn could spontaneously combust, Griffe."

"No Princess?"

"Not a peep."

"Kind of a shame. She seemed like a nice kid. Hopefully Kalifax keeps his mouth shut."

Griffe exhaled smoke out of his nose in the best impression of his friend he could do. Url smiled a sharp, toothy smile.

"I'm sure he will, Griffe. A Drake like him keeps secrets like treasure."

Dead Wolf

By: Jesse James Fain

Shadow of Intent slammed from my headphones as I mended the six-inch gash poor Jimmy had cooked up for himself. I've healed more than my share of nasty wounds in my time. This wasn't going to kill Jimmy, but I knew that even on a seasoned warrior, this cut would hurt like a son of a bitch. The kid had taken a wrong turn on a hill, and skateboarded into a construction zone. He'd slashed his side on the rubble's exposed rebar. Thank god the wounds were shallow, having just grazed him, instead of him hitting head on, or we would have had a much more lively night in trauma surgery for my last patient. I'd given him some lidocaine to help, but no amount of numbing would take all the sting out of a patching.

I had given him one of my earbuds so he could listen too. Jimmy seemed to be a budding Deathcore fan. Even through the piss poor experience, He was a good kid.

Jimmy's mother, Sylvia, did not appreciate my demeanor as I bounced to the heavy metal and stitched her kid. I felt for her as Jimmy's mom, but I was fixing a serious injury in minutes. So, respectfully, she could blow her trepidations out her back-end. I work how I work, and I'm damn good at it. Nobody knows flesh like me.

I know I'm not what anyone expects in a proper Healing Technician or doctor, but if she took issue with me, she obviously hadn't taken a thorough look at half the staff here. Nearly everyone here had tattoos under their lab coat sleeves and drank like sailors in their off hours. Don't get me wrong, I work with kind and generous people, but the hero image people paint onto medical professionals, just like soldiers, doesn't take into consideration we're human, just like everyone else. I kept the rant to myself, though, and just finished stitching the poor kid.

"Okay buddy. That's it for the stitching, the rest of the work is magic. This is going to burn some, probably itch too, but it'll save you walking around with that cut for weeks. So take a deep breath for me and let it out slowly. Try to count to five between breathing out and breathing in. When you exhale, I'm going to start. Focus on keeping that breath slow and steady for me. It helps a lot, I promise."

Pain meds didn't work on magical healing. It moved too fast. Forced the regeneration of tissues too quickly, and it just burned the meds out. If you wanted it healed fast, you had to take the pain head on. I'd seen that pain make grown men piss themselves for larger wounds. I'd pissed myself one time getting a gunshot healed. We had to be careful with elderly patients because it could trigger a damn heart attack. This was going to be a lot for a kid to handle.

I reached for my magic then, the side of me that felt so at home in the swirl of cosmic energies and demiplanes of existence; drawing power and energy to myself, and pouring it into the mending of Jimmy's flesh. My magic shook itself with floppy ears and yawned. This was boring fanfare, but it metaphorically licked the wound to healing.

Jimmy, bless him, followed instructions like a champion. Tears and slow, steady breaths carried him as I watched the stitched line of flesh heal itself. I couldn't be more proud of him. He let out one sob as the stitch cord fell out into my hands. I gave him my brightest smile then, and clasped him warmly on the shoulder once I tossed out the cord.

"All right Jimmy-Roo, all patched up like new!" I said, tussling the teary-eyed kids' hair. "If you go ask Ms. Wanda at the front desk, she'll have snacks for you. Maybe even some candy, if your mom is OK with it."

I sent the kid out of the exam room and down the hall. Accelerated healing took a lot from the body, and if he wasn't already hungry, he would be soon. My magic provided some of the energy needed, but the body still paid a price.

"He's good to go, Mrs. Carnes. Don't be surprised if he is extra hungry for the next day or two. He will need extra fluids as well. Water if you can get him to drink it. A little bit of lemon also helps with the cravings after the procedure. You just need to sign with Wanda. The insurance copay should only be about twenty bucks."

Mrs. Carnes gave one more look at me, my black and green tiger stripe scrubs, and tattoos. She seemed thoughtful for a moment. Something like approval registered on her face. Then, without a word, she turned and followed her son. That worked just fine for me. I was tired in the way only a twelve-hour shift at work can produce.

Jimmy was my last patient for my shift, so I dipped back to the locker room, changed out to my jeans, Slaughter to Prevail shirt, and leather jacket, and headed out through the ER. It was a quiet night, thankfully. Minimal disasters had befallen our fair city's citizens, so I was actually heading home on time. I thought I might even call Adriana, see if she wanted to go out for dinner. She seemed to be too busy for me lately, but the beauty on a motorbike at least answered my calls.

The crowd of nurses is what first caught my attention on the way out. Some clearly tearing up. That was a hell of a thing. It takes a lot to make an ER nurse cry. Seeing Death every day, battling against the Dark Lady's kiss, either broke or hardened the men and women that worked this job. They sat right outside one of the triage rooms, slowly cleaning a crash cart, and licking emotional wounds.

I eventually found Gianna's gaze amid the sea of blue scrubs, a thousand-yard stare even as our eyes met. I'd watched Gianna heal severed limbs, shove a man's guts back into his body, and save countless lives with her powerful magic. She was gassed out, barely standing. This case must have been catastrophic damage.

When I approached her to say something that would somehow cut through the misery here, I heard the sobbing. Sobbing that carried all the weight of the price of love. The tragedy that comes at the end. Someone had lost everything just now. Had their world shattered by the Long Walk.

If the curtains had been drawn, I would have just kept walking, but when you have my gift, you learn how to read Death, or generate it. I'd done a lot of both and stayed sane…ish. So instead I did something great or stupid depending on how you looked at it, and peeked inside.

The scene before me was too familiar to an ER. A fit man, uniform ripped and cut away, lay torn to shreds in final sleep. Over him, still bloody, wept a young woman. She barely noticed my entry, and I didn't disturb her at first, looking over the victim instead. I looked over the wounds and locations and knew pretty quickly this officer had run into something nasty. Basilisk maybe, or a Honey Isle Mauler. Not enough ragged tears and missing chunks for a lycanthrope. He was ripped up, but not chewed up. Multiple vital organs were damaged. I could see the hole in his liver.

"What's his name?"

She looked at me then, wiping her bloodshot green eyes and using her nails to fix brunette hair.

"Darryl. His name is... *was* Darryl." The 'was' caught a sob.

"Boyfriend? Brother?"

"Husband." Again, the quiver was impossible to fully hold.

"I'm sorry for your loss. My father was PD. Duty doesn't make sacrifice any easier, but it does make it a lot more noble. I'll add his name to the wall myself."

We had a monument in the hospital gardens for men like Darryl. Men like my dad, who'd stepped up when something nasty came out, and gave all they could to stop it.

"Thank you, but who are you?"

"I'm Leonidas Vanagandr. Leo for short. I'm one of the Magic Techs here at the ER. Like Gianna. Tell me…" I stopped to gesture at her for her name.

"Rebecca Sanders" she supplied.

"Tell me, Rebecca, was he a good man?"

"The best." She answered fiercely. "He was the best man I had ever met. Paid for everything working overtime so I could be a writer. God, I didn't even get to tell him all the good news today. I'm getting published, and… and… he… he was going to be a father." New tears came now. New sobs. If I hadn't seen it so much, I'd have been in trouble trying not to join her in lamenting. Real grief from a loved one to another is a pure emotion that can be contagious. It made sense why the nurses were so upset. There was purity and power in Rebecca's mourning.

I nodded gravely to the widow, and looked to Gianna, then to Helena, the charge nurse, outside. My posture asked a silent question. I had an opportunity here to use my… unique talents for good. I wanted to gift this woman something, but there was some risk in interfering. It was my risk, and I was licensed, but the two women were good judges of character, and I wanted their opinion.

The two women nodded and closed both the curtain and the doors to the trauma room.

"Do you want to talk to him? One last time?" I asked the grieving widow.

"What?" Her response was incredulous.

I peeled my jacket and shirt away, revealing the Legion 13 tattoo and the skulls that formed an 18 inside a Delta symbol.

"I was Special Forces Medical Sergeant Leo Vanagandr, once. A Demon Delta. Healing was part of our mission. The other was making the enemy pay for our dead by reanimating them. I mastered the magic of Death. That was my specialty."

The recognition of the controversial military unit dawned on her. "You're a Necromancer!" She hissed. Necromancers, in general, are despised. Hated for all the stories, both true and false, about what we could and would do. We were the classic villain of every adventure and movie. My magical brethren were reviled and feared.

"I am, and Darryl is close enough on the other side of Death's door that I can pull him back for about five minutes. Let him talk to you. You can tell him your good news; that you got to fulfill your dream, that his bloodline will carry on. I cannot save his life—he is dead—but I can give you five minutes to say everything you need to say for both of you to accept the end of his life with closure. It's not enough, but it's all I can do. I also ask that you never speak of this outside this room. I'm legally Gifted and even have a degree from Miskatonic University, but that doesn't stop people from hating Necromancers." I paused a moment to let her consider, and then asked her once more. "So, do you want to talk to him?"

Rebecca took a deep breath and then nodded. "More than anything. Yes, please."

I reached to my other magic, whispering words of dark power. The force of my gifts and will flared my rune tattoos to life along my spine and across my knuckles. My magic stretched and shook, and with its long muzzle full of teeth I reached down the dark river between dimensions that the souls of the dead travel. I grabbed Darryl from his seat on Charon's Ferry, and plopped him back into his body. The corpse opened its eyes and took a half breath. The lung damage would limit his ability to speak.

"You have five minutes to talk before you are back to your fate." I said to the corpse's bewildered look. "Don't waste them crying." I said to both of them and stepped out of the room.

I waited. I could have left and let the spell hang, but if I got miles and miles away from my work, it might cut out. So I stayed and got Gianna some food from the cafeteria, then helped the nurses with some simple cases. After I'd fixed a few broken toes, I finally stepped out to head home. I was next to my bike when Rebecca walked out, and wrapped me in a hug.

"Thank you!" She said exhausted in the way only she could be. In the way only Death can take from you.

"It may have only been five minutes, but I can't repay you for that. We got to have them only because of you."

She released me.

"Are you sure you want me to keep quiet about this? People might change their minds when they hear what you did."

"I'm sure. It doesn't matter sometimes if you are good or bad. Spend enough time with Death and people attach your name to it."

I gave Rebecca my card. "Let me know when the book is out. Get some rest, and make yourself eat something. Grief can rob you of yourself. Darryl wouldn't want that."

I gave her one last nod, tossed on my helmet, and hit the road home.

Adriana rejected my call, but shot me a text that she couldn't talk right now and she would call me soon. That was as fair as I could expect. The woman was hell on wheels, quite literally when she rode with her father's motorcycle club. She was probably in the middle of a club meeting or brokering some deal. She had every right to her time, to not answer, to live her life, but sadness and loneliness seeped into the corners of my mind. A black cloud that I couldn't shake off.

I chewed over every thought I could to fight off the depression. In the service I hadn't had time to be lonely. Time to think about building a family, or a career, or what I was going to do with the next seventy years if nothing killed me. I'd been home a year, patching up kids and saving lives. There was a fulfillment in it, but a part deep inside of me missed the mission. The fight. The feeling of winning, and the unshakable loyalty of the men and women next to me. I'd not always loved that I was a walking nightmare, but the magical hum of a thousand dead marching to my will was something I missed. My magic had not been tested for too long, and the little taste of letting Darryl and Rachel speak for the last time had only brought memories of the time I was ...*more*.

With no date and knowing my few friends were tied up with work or family, I took off into the Dallas night and started heading towards home. Fortunately the rumble, and the wind could chase away my melancholy for the forty-five minutes home. This was my Zen state. My sweet Lara, a BMW SR1000RR, carried me into the darkness with the growls, and screams of my favorite playlist. Black, blue, and green; I'd paid a mint to have her beautiful soul illustrated in grave dust and cremation powder. The spirits of the damned ran wild across the black void of her paint. Mind, music, machine, and my magic melded into my blissful trance. More than anything, this was my first love. I roared through the turns, no validation paid to the speed limit or the looks of the drivers I passed. I could RIDE. Ride like my life depended on it, as it sometimes had. Alas, my Zen was interrupted halfway home when Master of Puppets suddenly interjected into my bluetooth. I picked up the call.

"Fast Break Billiards, we rack em, you clack em." I said, a joke I often cracked when I didn't know who was calling, or if I actually wanted to be myself to the telemarketers.

"It's been ten years Leo, at least find a new joke," my best friend grumped. Jason Balboa, and I had known each other since middle school, had discovered our magic together, and served together. He's been my Weapons Sergeant in the Legion. We'd fought and bled with each other for twenty years. After leaving the Legion, we had both come home. I went to the hospital, Jason went to the PD, eventually making Detective. Having known him so long, I didn't like his tone, or the fact he was calling me on duty.

"You're in a sour mood." I let the implied question hang. The statement was enough of an invitation for him to speak on what had pissed in his cereal.

"Any chance you've sic'd a zombie on somebody in the last twenty-four hours?"

"No, but that can change if someone's really bothering you..."

"I've got a particular Captain I wouldn't mind seeing shamble into a foundation pour, but no. Sadly it's someone who shouldn't have been killed instead of someone who needs it. I need you to meet me."

"Do I need to come heavy?" There was no question that I was coming. That's what we did. The question was did I need to come with a rifle and body armor ready to snatch souls?

"Not yet, but it might come to it. Every day carry should be fine unless we have any more walking dead. Come to the Fast Trip on Mockingbird Road, by the Triple Bush Inn. Look for the blue lights."

"Copy that, Sarn't" I said in a half serious tone like we were back in the Legion.

"Just get your ass over here, Leo."

I pulled into the Fast Trip parking lot, dropping my helmet onto a handle bar. The uniformed PD must have had a good description of me from Jason, because all I got from the gruff looking Corporal was "You Leo?" and a nod was enough to get me in among the carnage.

The place had all the trimmings of a firefight, though the bullet holes were a bit anemic. Blood sprayed across the glass doors and shattered front windows. Three corpses were scattered like sadistic bread crumbs by the front door. One in the telltale yellow polo that matched the eye-bleeding paint-scheme of the Fast Trip.

"Fuck a duck in the muck." I muttered, trying to plot a course without stepping through the gore. "Should have worn my damn Lowas." I loved my combat boots, and they were both waterproof, and a fuck of a lot easier to clean than my sneakers. I'd been tip toe to elbow in blood and guts before, but it had never been a fun process for me. Could do it, and want to do it are different things, even for necromancers.

"Hold it there Leo. We need more photos, and evidence tags before I have you back here, anyway." Jason and two other men carefully navigated their way out the front of the FT, blue latex gloves and rubber foot coverings making sure they didn't contaminate anything, and didn't get gore covered if they moved wrong.

Jason was a tall, broad man with sun darkened skin. He had a piercing brown eyed stare and sharp, hawk-like features. He kept his almost black hair shorn close and just out of Legion regulations. His black mustache looked like a giant, Ethiopian poisonous caterpillar had attached itself to his upper lip. Like me he was covered in tattoos for the Legion, his family, and his passions. They were hidden under the dress shirt and police jacket he wore on duty. He tossed his protective gear into a trash bag, and then embraced me warmly.

"Thanks for coming. I've already gotten your paperwork through, and you are officially hired as an investigative consultant for your specialty field. Danton, Morris, This is Leonidas Vanagandr. He's as solid as they come, and one of the world's leading experts in necromantic arts."

"Holy shit, this guy's Dead Wolf?" Morris said in a heavy New York accent. "This is the guy that put your leg back on in the sandbox?" Morris was medium height with wide cheekbones and ginger hair. Everything about him screamed Irish besides the accent, Notre Dame pin on his collar and all.

"And flooded that valley with zombies when you were outnumbered twenty-five to one?" Danton added on. Deep dark in complexion, Danton had jovial coffee eyes and neat waves in his clean cut hair. He carried a joyful charisma that was at odds with being a homicide detective.

"And ripped that Taliban guy's soul out when he was trying to stab you to death?" The corporal that had let me in added from where he was enjoying a cigarette.

I gave a barking laugh. While most of that was true, talking about it only distracted us from the work at hand, and I didn't want a legend. It would help me with this crowd, but every mother in the world would make her kids cross the street if she saw me coming. I'd rather people didn't know the Valley of the Damned had been my doing. We were supposed to be silent professionals even if that cat was already out of the damn bag..

"I see Wildfire has been telling stories." Referring to my friend's old moniker, as the men had used mine. "Well, he left a few details out. Mostly the multitude of times that he saved my life or someone else's with a fireball or lightning bolt. That whole time I was fixing his leg from that RPG, he was raining hell on the platoon that was attacking us. It was the dead from all his attacks that I sent down the valley."

I shook both men's hands. "We can swap war stories after we figure out what in the hell happened here."

"Zombies happened here. That's why I called you. I'd recognize the way they move in my sleep thanks to our experience together, it's clear on camera. One using teeth, the other with a wicked knife. The teeth one is on the ground by the door. Shot by one of the civie's inside. Got a lucky headshot. The knife-wielding shambler got to the clerk, and stabbed him to death." Jason shivered when he said it. I couldn't blame him, my kind of magic is hard on the mind and the soul. It didn't keep me up at night, but that was because of my natural talent for it. For the rest of the world, dealing with the power of the Abyss and the touch of the grave was a nightmare.

"I was hoping you could talk to the dead clerk over there and get more details, then watch the footage and tell me if it's an accident or a murder."

Despite what people normally thought, necromancy and the undead do occur naturally. It's not common, but vampirism and ghoulary are sometimes just the result of being a big enough bastard, or getting buried in the wrong place. Either through a long-standing curse, malady of the soul, or some other terrible circumstance, a necromancer isn't needed. It also doesn't take diabolic influence for a necromancer to raise the dead. I made no dark pacts with demons for my power. It was ancestral. Going back to my family's roots in Scandinavia.

I walked over to the Fast Trip employee, and flared my magic. Poor kid couldn't have been twenty-five; just trying to pay for school or get started on his career. He was skinny, and messy. Being given the Ceaser treatment didn't help his cleanliness. The neck wound was the straw that bled the camel's hump, if I had to guess. Whoever did this, zombie or not, was a lot more frenzy than focus.

Once more my runes flared with light and life when I reached into the underworld for him…to find nothing. I slammed the spiritual door closed, panic filling me. If this poor child's soul was not on Charon's Ferry, it was being held by someone else. That was not natural. Soul taking, destroying, or devouring was not part of the natural order. It was something only demons, necromancers, and the occasional angel could do.

"Wildfire! This is a murder, and that wasn't a zombie. His soul isn't where it's supposed to be."

"The fuck you mean?"

"Fucking what?"

"Holy Hell?"

Danton, Morris, and the patrolman all answered at once. Jason, more educated on my line of work, just nodded. "Can that be done remotely, or would the perp need to be close by."

"I could do it from line-of-sight in an emergency, but it's taxing. Would be a lot better to do it by hand, but that's for a human or humanoid. If we have a Rakshasa or some kind of supernatural being involved, then it gets a lot more variable. I need to examine the bodies. Depending on the magic used there will be signs, but something besides a natural undead killed these people. Only intelligent undead and sentient creatures would violate the sanctity of the soul." I shivered then, knowing that this murder was going to be something far beyond the bodies on the ground.

"Show me that security footage, Jason."

Three days later, I sat reading over the autopsy report and rewatching the security camera videos. Watching our perp stab Frank Swilly to death for about the tenth time. He looked like a zombie, pale skin, and ragged clothes, but it didn't add up. There's subtle but tangible differences between the living and the undead, even the vampires, and liches that can talk and walk. The mindless dead move with fluidity if the necromancer is good, but they still don't hold themselves right. They don't balance right, don't remember to breathe, or lack thought in their posture. Everyday people miss it because they are so rare a threat, but when you live in the world I do, you can tell even from a distance or on a grainy security video.

This murderer was breathing, posturing, and doing his best psycho impression the way a human would. He even got tired. The weapon was unique. The single-edged blade was long and thin, about the length of a man's forearm. The handle was shaped in what might be the precursor to the "pistol grip" modern manufacturers used. It was old though, even with the poor-quality video, I could see the ancient craftsmanship.

"You recognize that type of blade?" Jason asked me.

"Barely. It looks like one of those Khyber knives from Afghanistan. I don't remember what the locals called them, they sold them at the markets sometimes. I always thought they were more ceremonial than practical."

"I looked it up. It's a Pesh Kabz, they were used even before the British invaded. That's an old design. They're made to punch through padding and chain mail."

"That's an old-ass knife. Looks like it got used in a fish market for a hundred years."

"Well, our guy made it work for him on a lot bigger fish. The zombie body had matching wounds in the lower back, according to the medical examiner. So our mystery killer stabbed him in the back, killed him, and then drove his corpse into the Fast Trip for an evening snack. Then, while his shambler ate the customers, he chased the clerk out and went slasher-movie villain on him."

"What a dickhead." I supplied, only briefly noticing the desk sergeant tore past us at mach-Jesus, darting into the chief's office like a cartoon coyote after a roadrunner. I hadn't seen that kind of urgency since our time in the desert.

Afghanistan had been a nightmarish second-home for our operational detachment. The 13th Legion spent a lot of time hunting terrorists in the sandbox. After Osama Bin Laden and Al Qaeda had unleashed hell on the

World Trade Center, we returned the favor, blasting anyone who'd even sold them groceries. It was while walking through the rocky mountains and rugged landscapes of the Graveyard of Empires Jason and I had earned our names as sorcerers and warriors.

The Chief emerged from his office while I pondered our old war, looking as pale as a tablecloth. He gazed over the room once, and then his tired eyes landed on us. "Balboa, Vanagandr. I need to speak with you both." Short in both stature and temperament, the Chief had the distinct look of a man that was locking his emotions down and doing a really bad job at it. You could see the sweat starting to break out.

When the two of us sat in his spartan office he didn't waste a second in getting to the point.

"I've just been informed by the security sergeant that we have an entire horde of zombies outside, and one of them just knocked on the door with an envelope addressed to you two. I've quietly ordered everyone to start arming up, but there are at least a hundred bodies milling around out there. Who did you idiots piss off?"

"Nobody that we know of." I spat, got to my feet and hustled downstairs. Sure as shit, there was a shambling mob outside. A single corpse, a rather dapper gentleman, if you ignored the stab holes and bloodstains on his jacket, reached out with a heavy envelope. Opening the door just enough, I took the yellow paper package from the messenger, and resecured the door. *Balboa* and *Vanagandr* were written in sharpie on the front, it was even spelled right, which felt ominous, given my name. Given the dire state of things, I took the stairs; not wanting to wait on the elevator.

I opened the envelope as soon as I was back in the Chief's office, revealing a cheap burner cell phone. Jason and the Chief hovered over my shoulder as I unlocked the screen with a swipe, and started to dig through the device. Moments into my search, a video call started up. We glanced at each other for a moment before I shrugged and answered. The call put us face to face with our Brutus from the Fast Trip. He'd clearly washed off the blood from that night, and shaved. Pale, skinny and sullen eyed despite his youth, he gave me a smile that could shatter glass. The man could have fit in almost anywhere that lighter toned skin was part of the population. Black hair and brown eyes, a change of clothes could have dropped him anywhere besides China or Hawaii and called him a local. His eyes darted around the screen briefly as he registered who was watching.

The chuckle was worse than the smile. Full of venom and abyssal in its lack of mirth.

"Mr. Vanagandr, how nice to meet you, finally, and with Mr. Balboa in tow. How perfect." His tone was anything but nice, and despite his paleness and nondescript features, his accent hinted at middle eastern roots.

"My name is Din Hazmat, and I have waited a very long time to speak with you two. Close to a decade in fact. I've been very excited to meet the men who made their names butchering my father, and uncles with a wash of flame and dead friends. You know... I always imagined you would be taller."

"I get that a lot." Jason deadpanned.

The laugh that Din answered with was manic, too fast, too deep, and the sheen of lunacy was all to clear.

"We will see how long your humor holds Mr. Balboa. See if you are still so laconic when my ocean hits your shores, like the tide of the dead washed over our valley. I'll check your merriment when my ghouls are ripping your liver from you while you still live."

"If you just wanted us dead, Din, then why call us? Why wait till we spoke? Why now, when we have friends, guns, and shelter. I can't bring your family back. Not any more than you clearly can. That's an impressive number of shamblers out there, Din. That took talent or practice." I spoke before Jason could come off the hip with another banger line to antagonize the maniac with the undead masses outside. He lost a lot of diplomacy when the threats started. This was when we would have been shooting people back in the Legion.

"What do you want from us?"

"I want you to think you are strong, Leonidas. How fitting that you will make a last stand holding off superior numbers. I want you to look at your comrades, and brothers next to you, and think you can fight any enemy you need to. I want you to have your guns, and your magic, and your friends all with you when the end comes for you. Just like the fighters in my village did. Just like my father did. Unlike them though, I want you to know who killed all of your mentors, all of your hope. I wanted you to know it's coming. I wanted you to know it was me!" He laughed again then. That terrible, mentally broken laugh. A cartoon villain laugh packed with true malice.

"But, you won't have to watch the women beg, and walk for miles for help, or fall dead from dehydration or starvation weeks later. You won't have to dig desperately into the sands and rocks hoping to find something of value, so your sister doesn't have to sell her body, or your mother plead for shelter. You won't have to sell your soul to the Djinn for the power to protect them. You won't see when I skin your families alive. You will just have to die."

Silence hung for a moment, the three of us staring back at the young man who must have been a child when his father and uncles tried to make war with us in a rock-strewn valley on the other side of the world. Ten years ago, we had been hunting in a large valley trying to track down an infamous bomb maker that supposedly lived in one of the two villages nearby. The Taliban fighters of those villages must have been paying great attention or gotten tipped off, because they met us full force with an ambush as we snuck in. Jason had been hit by shrapnel from an RPG round that blew most of his upper leg to shredded meat. Half his femur had been turned to dust, and most of his quad muscles were gone. It wasn't a full amputation, but it might have been kinder if it was. In the opening chaos I was in a good place to drag him behind a boulder, and try to put him back together. There were two large villages of men shooting at us, at least one hundred fighters, as we tried to hide behind anything we could and shoot back. The firepower was overwhelming. Leaning out to return accurate fire was near suicide even with the protections of the small irrigation ditch, and sporadic boulders we tried to shrink into. Scrambling, our Engineer, Charles, had dug us deeper in with his earth magic, but it would take time we didn't have to survive that way.

Sure, we were outgunned, but that didn't mean the Legion was out of options though.

Jason exploded with fury, and I stretched my healing powers to the limit to mend his gushing artery and pulverized bone. His eyes flaring with fathomless hatred and maddening pain, he turned into a one-man mortar squad. Truck-sized balls of flame formed in his hands before he sent them roaring through the sky, washing the mountainside in constant waves of incendiary death. Men screamed in high-pitched torment running as the flames chased them, sticking to them like napalm. The fires couldn't be smothered or rolled out. Hungry magic and wrathful curses fueled the conflagration as it spiraled from my injured companion. Jason's bleeding stopped, and I joined the fight again as the enemy burned and died.

A wonderful thing about pairing a pyromancer and a necromancer. The damage the flame does is normally more pain than structural issues. Organs shut down before the muscle burns off completely, which means It takes a long time and a nightmarish amount of heat to render a burn victim into an ineffective zombie.

Their dead, most of them still aflame, stopped screaming, and came to their feet again to start shooting, tackling, biting, and clawing their former allies. The enemy broke then, half the survivors fleeing into the rising sun. Din's family must have been the brave ones that stayed. We rushed forward then; my magic howling to the setting moon, snapping its teeth at fleeing prey and slaying all it could. We combined spellwork with shooting, moving, and communicating, putting down any still screaming men with a rifle round to the head.

Then we swept down the valley, hitting one village, then the other. We killed anyone that fought back. My burned minions lead the way, every dead man another ghoul added to the bullet sponges and back breakers. It was a war. I cared nothing for the nightmares of my enemies, for the sanctity or honor of the men trying to kill me. I cared nothing for their sons, daughters, and wives at home. Only that we lived and they died. Jason got a Silver Star, I got a Bronze with V for Valor in the face of the enemy. When it was all said and done word spread. We became infamous and famous.

We fought more. We killed more, and life went on. Years passed, enlistments done, sick of war and sick of administrational bullshit, we discharged and came home. Jason made a career and a family. Tried to stop bad guys on home soil. Sick of being a walking nightmare, I went to the hospital to try and find redemption in healing the sick and the injured. The Valley of the Damned was just something we did. We were fired upon first. We defended ourselves. Case closed. We had fought and killed before that day, we fought and killed a lot afterward, but that valley made us famous to both allies and enemies. The fatigue of destruction would take years longer to set in. I wasn't proud of the death, but I was proud of my courage and my strength.

Now, I was faced with the unseen hand of that battle. The consequences of raining death on the enemy of my country. It was staring right at me with crazed eyes and expectations of slaughter. I knew what was coming; The gunfire and death, The pure chaos. I'd tried to leave that behind, but

I wasn't scared of war. A deep part of my spirit loved war. I also felt a bizarre kinship to the orphan turned killer.

I could have been him. If my home was invaded. If my power was all I had to right what I saw as injustice. I'd have hunted me across a decade. I'd be monologuing my revenge now. That wasn't the worst part though. The worst part was I could have saved him. Mentored him in his powers. Made sure humanitarian aid made it to his village. Made sure his mother and sister could eat. I could have helped this loyal son become a powerful man instead of a powerful monster. I spoke to him as that thought zapped through me, ending the weighted pause.

"I'll walk out to you, Din. I'll come out right now, and stand before your judgment. You're right. You deserve it. I'll face you, man to man, necromancer to necromancer. It was my ghouls that flooded your village. Don't make all these people die like your father did. Don't create that nightmare for fifty more children. Don't put other innocent kids through the hell you suffered. You didn't deserve it. They don't either."

For a moment, just a brief second, something like remorse flashed across Din Hazmat's face. My words had struck something. Then the fires of madness leaked back into his eyes, and he drew that long, thin knife into his hand. It pulsed for a moment with a puss yellow light.

"I have power, Leonidas. Power and purpose that never would have been in my grasp if not for what you did. You tell me that this will force others to feel what I have felt? To panic, and scrap as I have panicked? Then I say to you… Good! Let the weak perish and the strong conquer. Let them suffer, and die or grow."

The call cut then, and glass shattered as the dead began their assault.

Jason and I arrived downstairs with little fanfare compared to the sounds of shattering glass and gunfire. While not exactly a fortress, the station had been designed defensibly, and Din's little conversation with us had let the thirty odd detectives and officers empty the armory, and ready any personal weapons. The one thing we hadn't had enough of was fucking ear protection, and thank god I had a spell for that or the incessant sound of a broken TV on max volume would have driven me to madness long before a shambling corpse assaulted me. Tinnitus is no joke kids, practice shooting responsibly. Danton and Morris, Creator bless them, were hot on our heels with patrol rifles and spare magazines.

On the ground floor, corpses slammed and tore at the walls and windows; while the more aggressively minded officers fired from the second and third-story. Basic necromancy like this used magic to fuel the corpse mind, and body with energy to puppet the built in strings of the nervous system. It made zombies keep going long after catastrophic wounds, but the brain still made up the pilot system. Therefore, a good old 5.56mm round to the dome was enough to put most shamblers down. Nastier undead like Vampires and actual Ghouls wouldn't like it either, but the much more powerful, and complicated magics would let them heal and shrug off nightmarish amounts of damage. Enough bullets would kill anything, but I was grateful that Din's magic seemed to so far be just basic and powerful. It gave me something to exploit.

Hitting the glass box that served as a security entrance, I saw the dead had massed in the entrance, easily breaking through to the foyer, but they struggled with the bulletproof, and reinforced doors before the sergeant's desk. My magic awoke with a metaphysical howl, snarling and snapping its teeth at the prospect of prey. This was what the Dead Wolf wanted. What the primordial chaos attached to my soul craved. Runes and tattoos flaring, I lashed out at the connection between Din and his minions and found my second magical surprise of this wild case. The thing gripping these bodies was no mortal.

Seething with slimy hatred and dark, unclean power, some unholy thing held these cadavers in sway. The beast inside frenzied then, hungry to destroy the wrongness that was seeking to take what was ours from us. To take pack and territory from us. Wild magical fangs tore at the connection to the dead itself; freeing the bodies from this monstrosity, and allowing me to turn the tide of control. Eyes flaring with blue and green power, I reached for the corpse's and gave them more than just life. Old Norse pouring from my lips, bidden by my will and birthright, they transformed.

Teeth became fangs, nails became claws, muscles and tendons swole with dark energy, and as more of the enemy undead tried to force themselves forward into the fight, my own minions rose again.

"Rip their fucking heads off! Make us a hole!" I roared to my Draugr, whom even the mighty Berserker's had feared. Stronger than any mere corpse, and capable of great regeneration, they were the nightmare that had stalked the cold nights in Norse legend. They wasted no time, twenty-five of the enemies' own now slicing into the charging mass. Jason and I tore out the door as soon as the space cleared.

I'd spent over a year of my life avoiding what came next. I'd grown tired of soldiering. Tired of blood and brutality and being a thing that nearly all the world hated. What had once held purpose had become burdensome. All talk of glory and honor had washed away in blood long before I'd killed my last man and hung up my rifle and body armor. I had wanted to heal, not harm. I expected that Peace would fix things, and for a while it had, but the cost of the peace was suppressing a part of me as well. I'd given up one half of my soul for the other, still leaving me incomplete.

When Jason and I put steel and magic to work in that moment though, something broken in me felt whole again. This was the Dance of Death. We had sweat and bled for years to be the best. Men had died for this knowledge. We carried the lessons of hundreds of years of war.

I opened up with my shotgun, the Beretta A300 set up specifically for combat, double-aught buckshot tearing great holes in the zombies if I missed a headshot. Jason turned into nothing but fury and thunder as he hammered round after round out with his personal Sig Spear, set up to match his old service rifle; besides opting for an Aimpoint red dot instead of a low power variable optic. Leaning to the side to shoot around my scything Draugr, a devastating clap lashed out as his magic blasted lightning out into the horde.

Blinded by the flash, I shoved more shells into my shotgun by feel two at a time, hands too shaky and my adrenaline too high for me to risk quad loading like I had been practicing on the weekends. Danton and Morris came out on my heels, taking only a handful of shots in the confines of that entry turned slaughterhouse.

"Mag change!" Jason called and dropped back among the twice-slain at the door; using the wall and smashed doors for cover out of a long ingrained habit. My Draugr stalled just outside the shattered entrance, outnumbered and outweighed even if the dumber and weaker zombies couldn't stand against them in smaller groups.

I stepped up, physically shielding Jason and letting loose into the mass to our left and right sides, blasting them off of windows and walls. Morris in the lead, our partners stepped up to the other corner and rained as much devastation as they could.

"I'm up." I could hear the bolt slam forward and the safety click off as we swapped places, stepping awkwardly over bodies.

"Reloading!" I loved that fucking shotgun, but, as much as I had to shove shells into it, my fingers would bleed for a week if we survived.

Jason's fire amped up and then slowed, and suddenly his support hand was shooting forward, multiple bolts of electricity arcing through the dead with a cacophonous assault. I reached into the Abyss and tore more of the dead from the horrific grasp of whatever bastard thing piloted them for Din's revenge. Jason's electricity could maim and destroy, but the flow of electricity did something far more important. It disrupted the enemy necromancer's grasp.

My magic flashed malice and bloody teeth, viscous and eternally hungry as I bound more meat puppets to my control. Gods and Stars I had forgotten how it felt to flex those muscles. We pushed forward again then, out into the enemy, into the courtyard, risking encirclement to hunt the real problem. Part of me wanted to find a solution to this besides the death of the young man whose life we had unknowingly ruined, but even if I wanted to lie down and die for it, Jason had a family that I would never let Din take him from, or take from him. If he would stop this. Stop the slaughter, then maybe we could do something, but if not, rabid dogs have to be put down, even if it isn't their fault.

So we strode out, firing, and fighting for all we were worth as my eyes hunted for any sign of the wrathful young man. We didn't have to wait long. I was in the middle of ripping another body from the nightmare's control when they went still, and something that sounded like a ten thousand pound bear bellowed from behind the mass of zombies. They parted and Din strode forth. Sickly yellow magic danced around him, his eyes consumed by the glow, and that long, sharp knife clutched in his hands like to part with it meant death. I ordered my undead to halt. Could this be the chance to save him?

"YOU." The voice that came from the young man was more than any one thing could produce, seeming to be made of every tone and volume, from whisper to scream.

"You dare to steal from me? To take FLESH from me? I have devoured armies of souls. Seen the fall of empires and the rise of kingdoms. I have whispered in the ears of Emperors and claimed all my desires from men who stood as gods!" The thing that was driving Din had finally revealed itself. That malevolence that I felt controlling the zombies he sent for us.

I felt stupid afterwards. Din had told me he sold his soul to the Djinn, or genie if you only have only ever watched Aladdin and never touched a book. I'd stung its pride, stripping its magic hands from its puppets, and turning them against it.

"Bold talk for a glorified personal assistant." I cracked the joke offhandedly, waving an errant hand to Jason before letting loose again.

"You think he talks this way when he isn't hiding behind a mob of minions and the child he groomed?"

"I Am Ankargahn! I Hide From No Man! I Will Strip Flesh From Your Bones Until You Weep At Death's Door, And Then I Will Devour Your Soul To Fuel My Conquest And Vengeance! Face Me Sorcerer And Tremble At My Might!"

"Then face me Ankargahn. So ferocious and powerful. Meet me alone on the field of battle and show you can fight your own battles instead of relying on war orphans and the backstabbed." I turned to Jason, and the other detectives.

"Hold the door with my undead and cover me. If he brings anyone else into this fight, go back to killing. If I go down, my Draugr will follow my last order, but will be wild afterwards. Use fire, and take their heads. Burn the corpses or they will come back on the next full moon." I turned back to the monster now piloting Din Hazmat, "Do we have a duel, Djinn?"

"We do, Seidrmadr."

I passed my shotgun off to one of my minions, then my jacket, and my Khublai Khan TX shirt; till I was just tattoos, jeans and boots. My left hand floated to my waist, drawing the seax knife from my beltline. Etched in the same runes as my skin, the blades' familiar handle settled home in my hand. Steel in hand, I reached deep into the darkness between worlds and pulled. My magic howled in elation, finally unleashed. Sucking heat from the air and light from the setting sun. The souls of the devoured screamed on the suddenly violent, whipping winds. Power, electric and ethereal lashed about me like a neon tornado. The normally invisible strands of magic now supercharged and clear to the naked eye. I gazed again not to Din, but to the malevolence that the cursed blade had brought to him.

"Waiting on you, Secretary."

With a roar of fury, the yellow clad young man rushed forward. Pestilent lightning leading the way. The Djinn lashed out at my soul with his sick power, great spells of pure demonic energy. They hunted my heart and soul, looking to twist or corrupt me if not rip the life from me. My cold winds rushed to meet the curses, crackling blue and green with eldritch fury. Hungry neon winds smashed against the diseased yellow lightning. Ankargahn was a power to be feared, but not a power I would fear.

Rage had fully taken me now. The battle song that flows in the blood of warriors eternal vibrated through my magic and my soul. Most sorcerers and wizards could not have withstood an onslaught like that. Jason could have burned it away, his flames from deep in the furnaces that forged not just planets but our reality itself, but I didn't need to overwhelm this sickness. I simply opened my birthright and devoured it.

Forced to exert more as Din and I closed our final steps, I could now see the wretched visage of Ankargahn. The djinn was a mass of muscle and boils, with a wide snarl and long greasy black hair. Nauseating yellow flames filled his eye sockets. He stank, like rotten flesh and deep pits of shit. The demonic thing hovered over Din like polluted smoke as the man lunged at me with his long knife. I slapped the blade wide and added my own roar and howl to the chorus of a few thousand years of the eternally eaten. My magic pulsed once more, and the blue lashing in the winds coalesced into my own monstrosity above me. Magic forming vengeful lupine eyes that tracked the djinn with unmatched malice as great jaws drooled green energy to the concrete. The thick neck of my inner beast clanking as broken chains lashed about between its fur. For a brief moment we hung there. Din's eyes locked to mine, Ankargahn glaring hatred at my magic spirit.

My seax snapped out, power flaring as I carved into Din Hazmat's mutating arm, eliciting a gasp from both man and monster. I whipped a low front kick out in the distraction, stumbling the younger man backwards as his knee threatened to hyperextend. I laughed then, feeling the bloodlust, the desire to conquer, and the pure desire to destroy my magic invoked.

Ankargahn attacked again with his corrupted power, and my wolf simply opened its electric green maw and snapped it down to the Abyss. Then I saw it, the tear, not in Din's eyes, but in the eyes of that ancient and evil thing that had promised him revenge and taken over him instead.

"What are you!" it squealed and roared and sang and hissed all at once. Knife still raised, I stalked forward and snarled.

"I am Leonidas Vanagandr! I am the terror hunting in the night. Son of the Ravager, Grandson of the Fens and the Ironwood. Last of Loki's mortal line! I am Blood of the Chain Breaker, destined to consume the world and the Gods. Pride of Angrboda!"

I paused for just a moment, relishing in the boast. Then I added one final detail.

"I am The Dead Wolf, Bane of Ankargahn."

"N—" was all that escaped the demon as my magic snapped forward with razor teeth and began ripping him to shreds down to his very essence. With my own roar, I struck half of Din Hazmat's right hand from his body with my seax, parting the cursed blade from him in a bloody crash of metal and fingers.

Both man and demon wailed then, one in great pain and another in deepest terror, and the walking dead dropped like puppets suddenly severed from their strings. With Ankargahn slain, I centered myself, and slowly my magic came to heel. No longer manifested outside, I felt it settle in and begin to groom the blood from its fur and lay down to rest. I was suddenly cold and sweat soaked as the battle fury faded. My hands trembling slightly and eyes tearing from the adrenal crash.

I looked at the wounded and sickly young man on the ground. Watched as he slowly became himself. He found his mental anchors and moaned in pain. He seemed to regain an awareness of himself, followed by a look of fear as his eyes met me with my bloody knife. The gaze trailed a moment later to his own magic dagger on the ground and his ruined hand.

"It's time to make a choice Din. It's a hard one. You don't have to do this. You can blame it on the Djinn. He possessed you. I can testify to that. You can be evaluated and cleared. They will see the monster's scars on you. I can't make up for your family Din, but I can give you a future, I can teach you to wield power. To be a force for good, and to make sure orphans of war have help. You can be a good man Din, and I will do all I can to help you. Jason and I both."

We stared at each other for a long time. I tried to measure him. He measured me, and the mad gleam in his eye turned inward. I hollered for Jason to bring a med-kit; turning my head slightly, but keeping my peripherals on the broken man. I saw him go too still, his left hand going for his knife.

It couldn't be helped. I spun around and gave Din Hazmat the Ceaser treatment. Pinning him. Stabbing him. Again and again. In this world, Even the hungriest wolf could have loyalty. Rabid dogs, though, have to be put down. It doesn't matter that it isn't their fault.

Daughter of Love and War

By: Melissa Olthoff

There were days where I wished I had more to go home to than an empty apartment after a long day at a thankless job. Days where I wished there was somebody waiting for me, even if it was just a cat.

And then there were the days like today, where all I wanted out of life was a cookie.

I opened my mouth to take a bite of fresh-baked heaven—and my phone rang. With a whimper, I reluctantly set aside my cookie, swiped my phone off the side table, and rolled my eyes at the caller ID.

"Perfect timing as always, Dad."

"What? Did I interrupt a hot date or something?" Hep asked.

I smiled at the gruff, familiar voice. "Yeah, with a cookie."

He cleared his throat. "You know, as your dad, I'm probably not supposed to say this—but you need to get out more, Nia."

I laughed so hard I nearly fell off the couch. "This, coming from the original hermit? When was the last time you left your garage?"

"I'll have you know I just got back from the store," Hep replied triumphantly, a loud creak undercutting his words. I could almost see him leaning back on his old bar stool next to his workbench, beer in hand.

I snorted. "Beer runs don't count."

Silence. Then, voice unusually serious, he said, "Sweetheart, in case you haven't noticed, I'm old. I've lived my life. I just want you to live yours."

I opened my mouth, but nothing came out. Familiar anxiety rose up and gripped my heart in an iron fist. I grabbed onto the pendant hanging around my neck like a lifeline and let the cool metal seep into my soul. I cleared my throat and tried again.

"I know, but—"

"Hold on," he said sharply. "Somebody just pulled in the drive."

I frowned. It was late for visitors and he lived way out in the country. Also, nobody ever visited him.

"Who is it?"

Wariness threaded through his voice. "I don't know, they've got their headlights in my face."

I heard the muffled thumps of several car doors closing. Apprehension tightened my gut. Hep's next words were cold, hard, and clearly not directed to me.

"Can I help you?"

"You had your chance to help, old man." The voice was faint thanks to the cell phone, but distinctly male and decidedly unfriendly. "We even offered to pay for your services. Too late now."

Hep snarled a curse.

"Listen carefully, Nia," he rushed out. "Call your Mother, tell her I've been taken."

"*What?*"

"Grab him!" the same man shouted.

My fear spiked. "Dad? *Dad?*"

There was a clatter, as if the phone had dropped to the ground. The last thing I heard before the call cut out was shouting.

"Dad!"

My hands shook as I tried calling him back. No answer. My anxiety spiraled so high I sat there frozen, wasting precious seconds to the fear. The annoyed beep of my phone snapped me out of it and I did the only thing I could think of—I dialed 911.

The operator patiently listened to my story, extracted the information she needed, and promised a patrol car would be sent to my dad's house. I sat with my phone clenched in white-knuckled fingers and waited for the police to call me back.

The minutes crawled past in aching silence, each like an eternity. When the phone finally rang, my hands were shaking so badly it took three tries to actually answer it.

"Ma'am, this is Officer Carmichael, Larson County Sheriff's Office," a deep, oddly annoyed voice rumbled. "We just did a safety check on your father, Hep Vulcanus. He's fine."

"Thank goodness." Relief hit so hard I slumped forward, as if my fear had been the only thing keeping me upright. With a deep breath, I forced myself back up and attempted to focus. "What about the guys who tried to kidnap him? Did you catch them?"

"Ma'am, those were just some friends that stopped by."

"Those didn't sound like friends," I said slowly, a scowl forming at the condescension dripping from his voice. "Since when does my dad have friends? And what happened to his phone?"

"His phone broke because he dropped it. He said everything is fine, it was all just a misunderstanding."

Somehow, I managed to keep my tone polite, but it was difficult when the officer spoke to me as if I were a child in need of soothing. "I want to speak with him. Please."

"I'm sorry, but we've already left your father's residence. He said he'll call you once he gets a new phone and not to worry."

My breathing grew choppy as I struggled with an impending panic attack. "That doesn't sound like my dad *at all*. Are you sure you were at the right place? I'm telling you I heard—"

"Ma'am, we have actual work to do," he interrupted, voice sharp with annoyance. "Your father is fine. Have a nice night."

I listened to the dial tone in stunned silence. How the hell had I misunderstood what was going on? And even if I did, why hadn't Hep borrowed the officer's phone to talk to me? He had to know I was frantic with worry. I replayed the call with him in my mind and froze.

Hep hadn't said to call 911. He'd said to call my mother. His ex-wife. The person he'd said on more than one occasion that he'd rather stab himself in the eye than talk to. But he'd specifically said to call her.

I tried to figure out the time difference between Ohio and Germany, but gave up after a frazzled couple of seconds and just stabbed at her name in my contacts. I listened to the phone ring ten times and was disconnected without reaching her voicemail. I tried again and again, until finally, the call connected.

"Darling daughter," a sleep muzzy, velvety contralto voice murmured. "Do you have any idea what time it is here?"

"Mother, Dad's been kidnapped" I blurted, back in full-on panic mode. I spilled out the whole story, including the bizarre conversation with the cop, and waited for her reaction.

I knew they didn't get along—at *all*—but an annoyed sigh wasn't what I expected.

"Again?"

"What do you mean *again*?" I demanded shrilly.

"Darling, you might not remember, but Hep used to be quite the renowned—" There was a muffled sound, as if she'd covered the speaker for a moment. "Oh, your father would like to speak with you."

The General? Oh goody.

"Daughter."

I drew in a deep breath and blew it out slowly. Getting emotional never worked with my father. I had to stay calm. I gripped the intricate metal pendant my *dad* had made for me and fought the panic back until I had it locked down tight. Only then did I speak.

"Father. Hep has been kidnapped. Something weird is going on, and I need help." I paused and unlocked my jaw. "I need *your* help."

His voice was cold when he responded, but then again, I'd never heard it warm up in my entire life. "Do you remember what I taught you?"

I squeezed my eyes shut, concentrating on long-ago lessons. "Assess the situation. Attention to detail..."

Come on, come on, what's the last thing he always harped about?

My eyes snapped open. "And always bring backup."

"Good," he replied shortly. "What will you do, if you find Hep gone and the police unhelpful?"

"I'll find him myself," I snapped without stopping to think.

There was a brief silence that sounded of shock. Or at least mild surprise, which was one heck of a reaction from the emotionless bastard.

"If this was all it took to spur you to action," he finally muttered, "I would've had the old hermit kidnapped years ago."

Great, now both my dad and my father were commenting on my lack of a social life. It might be the first thing they'd agreed on in years. Or ever.

"Daughter... be careful."

I blinked. That was unusually sentimental for the General. "I will."

"You still need backup," he said briskly. "I'll send someone to meet you at Hep's workshop."

I groaned. "Please tell me you're not using this to try to set me up with another meathead soldier of yours."

My father chuckled, not an ounce of humor in the cold sound. "Two birds, one stone."

As deep in the countryside as it was, it usually took a solid hour to reach Hep's place. I made it in forty minutes.

The garage door to his workshop stood open, spilling light onto the gravel drive. I jumped out of the car, ready to rush in, when the General's cold voice echoed in my mind.

Assess.

I froze with one hand on the car door and listened intently.

A few minutes slowly trickled past where I heard nothing more sinister than crickets. Hep's truck was the only vehicle in the driveway. The cops had already been here. There was nothing to be afraid of, except… Hep always came out to greet me, no matter how badly his leg hurt.

"Dad?"

There was no answer.

I strode up the driveway and into an absolutely trashed workshop. The bottom dropped out of my stomach as I took in the level of destruction. My gaze skipped from his precious woodworking tools scattered over the floor, to his solid oak workbenches flung aside as if they were cheap card tables, to the large chunks of drywall torn out of the walls—but it was the walking stick lay abandoned on the floor that sent a bolt of terror into my heart.

He never went anywhere without that walking stick.

I crouched and brushed the fine layer of drywall dust from the smooth wood with shaking hands. A low whistle startled me. I rose and spun around, walking stick raised defensively. I'd always joked the thing could double as a weapon, and after seeing my dad's ruined workshop, I was more than willing to use it.

"Sorry, didn't mean to startle you." The unfamiliar man standing in the driveway held up his hands. "Nia, right? General Thrace sent me."

He was roughly my age, brown hair neatly trimmed, fit, and reasonably handsome if you were into the meathead soldier look. In short, exactly the kind of backup my father would send. I almost relaxed. Almost. But that cold voice echoed in my mind again.

Trust, but verify.

"You stay right there," I snapped and whipped my cell out of my back pocket. "Name?"

"Captain Nathan Washburn," he replied politely. He deliberately kept his hands open, empty, and visible, which I appreciated.

I gritted my teeth and called my father directly instead of going through my mother like I usually did. And unlike my mother, the General answered immediately. In short order, he confirmed Nathan was legit, complete with photo identification and his qualifications. Both professional and personal. I sighed and hung up on my father mid-sentence.

"Sorry, I've had a rough night," I said to Nathan by way of apology. I kept the walking stick though. The feel of the smooth wood beneath my fingers was comforting.

Nathan snorted as he looked around the workshop. "I'm guessing it wasn't half as rough as Hep's."

"The cops said he was fine, but…" I leaned on the walking stick and fought back the urge to hug it like a safety blanket. "This is obviously *not* fine. I've got to find my dad."

"Isn't General Thrace your dad?" he asked, head tilted in confusion.

"No, he's just the bastard who knocked up my mother. *Hep* is my dad."

Nathan drew back as if I'd personally insulted him. "You should show more respect—"

"Why?" That old rage rocked through me, the mental walls I used to compartmentalize slightly thinner than usual under the strain. "He's a freaking Army general, not God's gift to war. Seriously, are you here to help, or suck up to my father?"

Nathan's jaw visibly tightened. "Have you checked the house?"

"No, not yet." At his exasperated frown, heat washed over my face. "I only got here a few minutes before you did."

The soldier grunted and carefully picked his way through the wreckage to the battered screen door that led into the house. I followed him into the kitchen and swiped my free hand over the light switch. The old fluorescent strip lighting flickered to life and illuminated another mess almost as bad as the one in the workshop.

I sucked in a sharp breath before resolutely searching the house. Since it was actually smaller than the workshop, it only took seconds to verify what I already knew.

Hep was gone.

Nathan broke his silence when we were back in the workshop. "Any idea who would want to take Hep? Or why?"

My chest tightened as the fluttering wings of panic battered at my heart. "I don't know. I guess he used to make weapons, but all he's done for years are simple woodworking projects."

I crouched down next to one of the overturned workbenches and held up an unfinished cutting board for his inspection.

"That's nice, but not worth kidnapping someone over," he replied cautiously.

He probably expected me to yell at him again.

I brushed sawdust and drywall powder off the board and gently set it back down. It gave me a great excuse not to meet his eyes.

"Thank you for coming to help. You didn't have to."

Nathan laughed, a surprisingly contagious sound, and I looked up to see him grinning at me. He had a good smile.

"I don't think you understand how the military works. General Thrace gave an order, and I followed it." His voice deepened just a touch. "But you're welcome, Nia. Now, how about we look for any clues they might have left behind?"

We methodically combed through the mess. As the minutes dragged on with nothing to show for our work, despair rose in a choking wave that strangled the breath in my lungs.

Desperate for comfort, I grasped my pendant with one hand and clutched the staff with the other in a white-knuckled grip. The dual sensations of cool metal and warm wood soothed the misery before it bloomed into a full-on panic attack, and I remembered Hep's lessons.

I closed my eyes and took a deep breath. Another. I kept up the slow, methodical breaths until my racing heart slowed and I could think clearly again.

I opened my eyes on one last, slow exhale.

They landed on the battered sword that usually took pride of place over his main workbench. It was discarded on the floor like worthless trash. I pried my fingers off my pendant and bent to pick up the old sword. My fingers barely brushed the worn leather sheath when a shout jerked me upright again.

Nathan strode up the driveway. "Looks like Hep put up a bit of a fight. Found this where the gravel was all churned up."

He dropped a keychain bottle opener in my outstretched hand. I flipped it over to read the words etched on the back.

I frowned doubtfully. "It's a local bar. It's probably my dad's."

"Maybe, maybe not," Nathan replied, running a hand over his close-cropped hair. "Look, we've been at this for over an hour. It's the best lead we've got. Why not ask around, see what we find out?"

I hesitated, but I really didn't have any better ideas.

"Fine," I sighed. I squinted past the glare of the workshop lights and into the darkness. "Where's your car?"

"A friend dropped me off," he replied easily. "Mind if I catch a lift?"

He gave me a genuine smile with just a touch of sheepishness. If I wasn't so desperate to find my dad, I *might* have noticed he was actually kind of cute. I shoved down the momentary attraction. I needed to focus, not drool.

I jerked my head at my car. "Let's go."

Charlie's Country Bar was about as busy as you'd expect on a Friday night, with every local yokel from a ten-mile radius drinking and dancing to a live band playing the latest country pop song. It took a few minutes of determined wriggling to make our way to the bar, and another five to get the bartender's attention.

I held up my phone. "Excuse me, do you know this man?"

The grizzled bartender squinted at the image. "Old Hep? Yeah, I know him. Comes in a few times a month for cheeseburgers."

Hope bubbled up despite my best efforts to squash it down. "Have you seen him tonight?"

"No," he said, popping my little bubble of hope with a sharp scowl. "And I'll tell you the same thing I told those other guys—I'm a bartender, not an informant. Now buzz off."

"Wait, what other guys?" I asked desperately, but he stalked off to the other end of the bar without answering.

"Wow, what a friendly guy," Nathan muttered.

I slumped against the bar. "Now what?"

Nathan plucked my phone out of my hand. "Now, I'm going to go flirt with some waitresses."

"I'm sorry, you're going to *what* now?"

"We know people were asking about Hep. I'll see if the waitresses know anything."

He disappeared into the crowd before I could object or offer to go with him. With nothing better to do, I hopped onto the nearest barstool and leaned my elbows on the slightly sticky bar. It wasn't that I didn't understand he was going to try to charm the waitresses, which would go better without me hanging on his arm. It was that I didn't want to be left with too much time to think, and as the minutes ticked past, I had *far* too much time to think.

My panic came roaring back.

What if I can't find Dad in time? What if… what if they…

Desperate for a distraction, I looked up at the giant mirror set behind the liquor bottles. My gaze immediately fell on a young man standing across the room. My lips parted in appreciation. That was one hell of a distraction. With his tousled reddish-blonde hair and muscular arms bared despite the autumn chill, he was easily the hottest guy I'd ever seen in real life—and he was staring right at me.

Unfortunately, he wasn't checking me out. He was glaring at me with undisguised hatred, and I had no idea why. I'd never seen him before in my life, and a girl did *not* forget that kind of face.

When he kept glaring at me, I frowned back.

Who pissed in your cheerios?

I twisted around on my barstool, but the crowd surged and I lost sight of him. I was still searching for him when Nathan came back.

"Looking for me?" he asked with a teasing smile.

"Uh, yeah." I gathered my scattered thoughts. "Find out anything?"

His smile faded. "No, sorry."

My hands tightened into fists. The sting of my fingernails biting into my palms grounded me. Barely. "What do we do now?"

"I…" He scowled and shook his head. "I don't know. Go back to Hep's?"

Once again, I couldn't think of anything better to do. I huffed out a sharp breath and berated myself. If our situation were reversed, I knew Hep would burn down the world to find me. All I was doing was flailing helplessly and drooling over hot guys in bars. I really didn't think this was what he'd meant by getting out more.

Even so, I couldn't help but search for the guy on our way out. There was something about him that called to me. I rolled my eyes at myself as we walked into the crisp night air. Something called to me all right—all those muscles wrapped up in a yummy package.

Nathan's phone rang before we reached my car. He glanced at the caller ID and narrowed his eyes. "Excuse me for a minute, Nia."

I watched him wander off into the parking lot. I had to admit, he was different than the usual meatheads the General threw my way. More relaxed, maybe. Was it weird that my father kept trying to set me up on a date? Yes. Yes, it was. But maybe this time it wasn't a bad thing.

I leaned against the cold metal of my car but soon got impatient. I weaved my way through the parking lot and finally spotted Nathan pacing the far edge, phone pressed tight to his ear.

"…agreed?" Nathan asked as I walked closer.

The voice on the other end was loud, and I thought I heard him say *bring her*. Gravel crunched under my foot and Nathan's eyes snapped up to mine. He didn't seem upset at my eavesdropping.

He just grinned that charming grin and replied, "Of course I'm going to bring her. This is the best lead we've gotten all night. Hopefully we'll find her dad soon. Thanks for your help, I owe you one, man."

He slipped his phone into his back pocket and raised his eyebrows at me expectantly.

"You got a lead?" I asked cautiously, afraid to let hope get the better of me again.

His smile softened. "We've got a lead."

"Yes!" I punched my fist into the air, my own grin escaping. "Let's go!"

I raced across the parking lot and jumped into my car. I had the engine started and popped into drive almost before my seatbelt clicked into place.

"Well, where to?" I demanded impatiently as Nathan *finally* slid into the passenger seat.

He pulled up a map on his phone. "Turn left out of the parking lot."

As I followed his directions, I shot him an impatient look. "Spill it, soldier boy. Who were you talking to? What did you find out? Where are we going?"

Nathan snorted. "*Soldier boy*? Really?"

"It's better than meathead," I muttered before I could think better of it. I winced, but to my relief, he roared a laugh.

"I'm going to give you a pass on that one, seeing as you're under a bit of stress," he said as his chuckles died down. "I was talking with a buddy of mine on the local force. I called in a favor earlier before we met up, had him checking traffic cams near Hep's place around the time he was taken."

I blinked. I didn't know there were any traffic cameras this far out in the country.

"Lucky for us, traffic was light and he was able to give us a few leads to follow. We're going to the most likely one first."

I swallowed the rest of my questions and followed his directions to the miniscule industrial section of town. I slowed to a crawl as we drove down a service road, warehouses looming large on either side.

"One of these things doesn't look like the other," Nathan sang off-tune as he pointed out a shiny muscle car. It stuck out like a sore thumb against the backdrop of an especially rundown warehouse. There were no other cars. I drove past without slowing until I was several warehouses down the line.

My breath shook with nerves as I parked behind the shelter of an off-white semi-trailer. "What do we do? Should we call the police?"

"And tell them what?" Nathan countered. "There's a suspicious car? We need to take a closer look and see if he's even there. Then we can call it in."

He slid out of the passenger seat, but ducked his head back inside the car when I didn't immediately follow. "Are you coming or what?"

I didn't like the scorn in his voice one bit, but it was the look in his eyes, as if I'd disappointed him, that really got me. One hand wrapped tightly around Hep's walking stick, the other around the cool metal of my pendant. Soothing, grounding. I drew in a deep breath for courage—and got out of the car.

"Let's go find my dad."

We circled around to the back of the warehouse and made our way back up the row to the one we wanted. Most of the lights were burned out or shattered, leaving pockets of deep shadow, and our pace slowed as we dodged battered dumpsters and nasty puddles from yesterday's rain. I tripped over a rusted bumper and would've face-planted if not for Nathan's quick reaction. He kept his hand on my upper arm after that and steered me around the tripping hazards.

Apparently, soldier boy's night vision was better than mine.

We reached the back of the correct warehouse where a single flickering security light illuminated a padlocked door and a loading bay. After giving the door an experimental tug, Nathan hopped up onto the chest-high loading bay. He leaned back down, grasped my wrist with warm fingers, and hauled me up after him.

I wobbled from the unexpected strength of his assist, and he caught me around the waist to steady me. For a breathless moment, I was pressed against his muscular chest and absolutely enthralled by his intense gaze. Then I blinked rapidly and pulled out of his arms. *What the hell am I doing?*

Embarrassed and certain my face was as red as a volcano, I jerked my head at the corrugated rollup door. "Should we give it a try?"

For just an instant, there was a hint of regret in Nathan's expression. But he gave me a quick smile and turned to the door.

"Sure." He grasped the rope handle in both hands, impressive shoulders bunching as he strained to open it. He shot me an exasperated look when it didn't budge. "A little help, princess?"

My cheeks flared hotter. "Sorry."

I wedged my smaller hands into the handle next to his and set my feet.

"Count of three," Nathan instructed.

On three, we both pulled. Nothing happened for a long, torturous moment. Then, with an ear-piercing squeal, the door rolled upwards a few feet before getting stuck again.

I winced. "Think they heard that?"

Nathan shot me an incredulous look. "You're kidding, right?"

He crawled beneath the door and disappeared inside, leaving me no choice but to follow. It seemed like that was all I'd done tonight. Follow and hesitate and do fuck all to actually help. I clutched the walking stick a little tighter and ducked under the door before I lost my nerve.

Inside, the cavernous warehouse was a vast expanse of soft gray shadows interspersed with the darker rectangles of shipping crates. As I crept further into the room, I could see light seeping out of the blind-covered windows of an office at the far end.

Nathan and I exchanged a glance. With his warm hand on my upper arm guiding me through the shadows, we stole across the warehouse floor to the windows. But no matter how I angled my head, the dusty blinds refused to allow even a glimpse inside the room. Nathan pointed to the door to my left. For once he was the one to follow me, my eagerness overriding my caution and speeding my steps.

I grabbed the doorknob, half-expecting it to be locked, but it turned easily in my hand. Praying this door wasn't as obnoxious as the last, I eased it open. Light flooded through the door and momentarily blinded me. I froze and tightened my grip on the walking stick.

A sigh of relief gusted out when there was no immediate outcry, and I blinked my eyes clear. A maze of cubicles and stacks of dusty filing boxes filled the room, thrown into sharp relief by cheap industrial overhead lights.

Voices murmured from somewhere deeper in the maze. I eased a few steps into the office and tilted my head as I listened intently. I didn't recognize the first speaker, but the second was undeniably Hep.

Overwhelmed with relief and excitement, I grabbed Nathan's arm and met his eyes with a wide grin before reaching for my phone. It was past time to call in the cavalry.

The door slammed shut behind us. I whirled around and swallowed a shriek at the giant of a man blocking the doorway. He was taller than Nathan and easily twice as wide, all bulky muscles and scars from countless fights. He strode forward at an unhurried pace, each step revealing more muscles, more scars, and an implacable expression on his granite-hewed face.

Fear rose up and swallowed me whole. It felt like I was drowning in it, and no matter how hard I kicked I couldn't reach the surface. Trembling, I shrank away from the giant stalking ever closer and pressed into Nathan's side.

The man grinned at my obvious fear before he shifted his gaze to Nathan. "What took you so long?"

"She drives like an old lady," Nathan said with a derisive snort. "Took us forever to get here."

I jerked my gaze up to him. "*What?*"

I backed away from them both and patted my back pocket frantically.

"Looking for this?" Nathan asked with a grin as he held up my phone. His smile wasn't nearly as charming now, and I itched to scratch it off his smug face. "Aw, don't be like that, Nia. You wanted to find your dad, didn't you? He's right this way."

Nathan tucked my phone away and strolled deeper into the office, leaving me alone with the menacing giant, who jerked his head for me to follow. I hesitated, but then he took a long step closer and a fresh tidal wave of fear crashed over me. I swallowed a scream and scrambled after the lying bastard. It seemed like the safer alternative at the moment.

I followed Nathan through the cubical maze, teetering between the urge to beat him over the head with Hep's walking stick and having a full-blown panic attack. Before I could tilt one way or the other, we spilled out into a large central area.

"Dad!"

I sprinted across the room, completely ignoring the third man in my haste to get to Hep. He was sitting in a chair with his bad leg stretched out in front of him, sporting one hell of a shiner and bloody knuckles. I let out a shuddering half-sob of relief and threw my arms around his neck.

"Nia!"

He patted my shoulder reassuringly before he pushed me back to glare at the men who'd kidnapped him. All of a sudden, he didn't seem old or helpless. A shiver walked down my spine at the volcanic rage lurking just beneath the surface of his craggy face.

"You touch her, and all the gods in the heavens won't be able to find your broken bodies," he said in a voice soft as steel. "I promise you that."

The third man laughed and I stiffened in recognition. This was the man I'd heard over the phone.

"Relax, old man. She's just here as insurance. No one will touch her so long as you give us what we want."

"What you want is stupid, Thrasos," Hep growled in frustration. "And not possible."

Any amusement fled Thrasos' face, replaced by a grim sort of warning. "You are the master craftsman of the gods, Hephaestus. I know what you are capable of."

I was torn between terror and confusion. Even more so when Hep didn't refute the ridiculous statement.

"I don't think you do, boy," Hep said quietly. "Let my daughter go—"

"But she's not your daughter, is she?" Nathan interrupted with a smirk.

"Yes. She is."

Silence fell at the dangerous growl and the flash of heat that seemed to accompany it. I wiped at the sweat on my face. It was definitely getting hot in here.

Thrasos smiled, undeterred. "Where are my manners? We haven't properly introduced ourselves. I am Thrasos, god of daring."

Nathan bowed with a flourish. "Dolos, god of trickery, at your service."

When he straightened up, he looked like a completely different person. Blonde instead of dark, golden tan instead of pale skin, and brown eyes now an impossible shade of green. Dolos winked at me, and then he looked like me. Exactly like me. He laughed in my voice before he changed into Hep's identical twin.

A lightbulb beat me over the head. "You're the reason the cops thought everything was fine!"

"Guilty as charged," he said in a gruff voice.

"I do *not* sound like that," Hep muttered in a gruff voice, but I was too busy staring at the supposed god to so much as glance at him.

My mouth hung open as a dozen questions clashed in my head. Important and relevant questions. What actually fell out of my mouth was neither of those things.

"I thought Loki was the god of trickery."

Anger flashed across his face and he shifted to the green-eyed blonde again. "Loki wishes he was as good as me. Stupid movies."

"What happened to the real Nathan?" I asked, one of those relevant questions finally making it past the snarl in my brain.

Nathan—no, *Dolos*—waved away my concern. "Ares' little messenger boy is just taking a little nap. I'm not suicidal."

My voice came out a hoarse whisper. "Ares?"

The last man heaved an impatient sigh as he moved to flank Thrasos. For a moment, I couldn't even breathe. The fear became so strong and all-encompassing that rational thought fled and left only base instinct behind. I wanted to run even as my legs threatened to give out.

"Deimos, god of dread," he said in a deep rumble. "Son of Ares. And your brother."

"This is insane," I said, fully aware that my voice had gone up an octave and far past the point of caring. As I backed away, my hand brushed Hep's shoulder, and I recoiled from the heat coming off him. "None of this is happening. And you are definitely *not* my brother."

Deimos smiled. Somehow, it was worse than his scowl.

"Aphrodite and Ares haven't let me or my twin around you since you had your little mental breakdown. They worried we'd push you over the edge. Doesn't look like you needed our help, *Nia*."

"Poor little goddess," Dolos added with a mocking grin. "Everyone knows your story. How you fell in love with a mortal and tried to follow him into death. You're the cautionary tale we tell little gods and goddesses."

"Insane," I repeated in a whisper as I trembled.

Thrasos grabbed my arm and yanked me up against his chest. I had to crane my head back to meet his scornful gaze. "What's insane is pretending to be a human when you're actually a god. Why would you want to be weak?"

"She's not pretending. She *forgot*."

I tried to jerk around at Hep's soft confession, but Thrasos didn't loosen his hold. He threw back his head in a belly laugh, and his eyes danced in merriment when he looked back down at me.

"You drank from the river Lethe. Foolish and weak," he declared, pushing me away.

I stumbled backward and fell on my butt. Through a fresh wave of laugher, I looked up at Hep, silently pleading for him to tell me it was all a bad joke. I had a good education on the classics. I knew of the river Lethe and its waters of forgetfulness and oblivion, but it wasn't *real*. It couldn't be, any more than gods were real.

"Dad?" I tightened my grip on his walking stick when he didn't answer, didn't even look at me.

Shame drowned his gaze when he finally looked up. "Better for you to forget than to die."

I gaped at him. This was insanity. Hep was one of the smartest people I knew. He couldn't be buying into this crap.

"I'm sorry for a lot of things in my life, Harmonia." A measure of steel returned to his voice. "But I will never be sorry for saving you."

I jolted. It had been so long since anyone called me by my full name. Hep held my gaze for a heartbeat before he turned back to Thrasos. He hesitated, drew in a deep breath, and rolled back his shoulders as if ready to face his own execution.

"Let her go, and I'll give you what you wa—"

"Wait!" I clambered to my feet, angling the walking stick across my body like the staff it so desperately wanted to be. I'd never heard that level of fear and defeat in Hep's voice. It scared me.

Deimos growled.

"No more waiting. Craft us a weapon capable of taking down Zeus, or we'll break you one piece at a time." His arm snapped out, so fast my back was pressed against his over-muscled chest before I knew what was happening. His next words were breathed into my ear. "She can watch."

I struggled even as dread rushed through me. "Leave my dad alone!"

Deimos tightened his arm across my chest and chuckled, something I felt as much as heard. My breath shuddered and my heart raced along so fast I wondered if it was possible to die from fear alone.

Dolos smirked. "What can you possibly do to stop us? You're the goddess of *harmony*."

I was the goddess of what *now?*

I couldn't deny the title struck a chord deep within, but I brushed it off. Whatever was going on, I'd figure it out later. After I saved Hep.

Deimos' breath tickled my ear as he laughed along with Dolos, and I took my chance, slamming my head backward as hard as I could. I was rewarded by the crack of his nose and a bellow of pain. I ducked under his loosened arm and spun around to face him. He glared at me through watering eyes as blood gushed out of his nose.

I drew my foot back and he automatically dropped his hands to cover his crotch. Instead of kicking him in the family jewels like he expected, I jabbed stiffened fingers into his throat. He crashed to his knees, gagging and choking. I took a split second to savor the fear on his face as he struggled to breathe, even as my own fear swelled into abject terror.

With a snarl, I swung the walking stick into the side of his head.

The dread vanished like a popped balloon, leaving only adrenaline and ordinary fear behind. I watched the creepy giant topple like a tree. Out cold. Or at least, I hoped he was just unconscious.

"What in Tartarus was *that*?" Dolos blurted.

Hep laughed. It wasn't a nice sound. "She's the daughter of Love and *War*. Did you really think Ares didn't train her?"

Dolos' eyes snapped to mine. "I thought he was just the bastard who knocked up your mother."

Sometimes, I knew exactly what to say to get people to work *with* me instead of against me.

"Yeah, but I'm still his daughter. He's still my father." I smirked. "I hear he's the vengeful type."

Dolos paled. "You never said anything about pissing off the freaking *god of war*, Thrasos. I'll repeat, I'm not suicidal."

"Dolos—"

"Nope." Dolos cut Thrasos off with a rapid shake of his head. "So much nope. I'm out."

With a ripple like a mirage melting away, Dolos vanished. A few seconds later, a door slammed shut, proving he hadn't actually teleported. I snorted. As if being able to make himself invisible was any less terrifying. I was going to spend the rest of my life wondering if I was actually alone in a room. *Ugh.*

Thrasos glowered, all alone. No. Not alone. Leaning up against a desk in the shadows was the hot guy from the bar. Good lord, how many people did I have to beat up? The back of my head throbbed from head-butting

Deimos. I didn't want to fight anymore, didn't want to have to save anyone. I just wanted a cookie.

"Can we call it even and all go home now?" I asked Thrasos somewhat plaintively, deciding to ignore the hot guy.

"Sorry, Nia. Old Hep here isn't known for his fighting prowess. You've lost the element of surprise. And unlike Dolos, I'm no coward." Thrasos drew a short sword from a back sheath I hadn't noticed. I froze, but he merely gave me a small yet genuine smile. "Lucky for you, I'm also no monster."

Thrasos stabbed the blade into an unfortunate desk as easily as if it were made of butter instead of wood. I tried not to think of how easily that could've been me.

The god of daring spread his arms wide in invitation. "Fight me, little goddess. If you win, I'll let you and Hep go free, never to bother either of you again. If you lose, Hep builds me my weapon."

Hep snapped his head up, fire in his eyes. "You're making it an official challenge?"

Thrasos dipped his head into a bow. "Yes."

"Good. We accept," he replied before I could stop him.

I spun to him, flinching at the heat he was still throwing off. I belatedly remembered Hephaestus was the god of fire as well as crafting. *Great, now I'm buying into the god crap.*

"Are you crazy?" I hissed, eyeing Thrasos with justified trepidation. He had about fifty pounds on me and a longer reach. The General had personally trained me in self-defense, but I was rusty. "He doesn't need a sword to kill me!"

"An official challenge has rules, Nia. The fight goes to unconsciousness or yield. Not death."

"Oh, that makes me feel so much better. Thank you," I replied sarcastically.

"You're welcome." His eyes twinkled as he silently laughed at me. "Now go beat the little prick so we can go home."

I held out the walking stick to Hep, but Thrasos decided to be generous. Or overconfident. One of the two. "Keep it, little goddess."

I cautiously circled around Thrasos, staff held protectively in front of me. It was surprisingly easy to fall back into old training habits. My father's lessons echoed in my head. *Sidestep, keep the weight balanced, watch the torso for movement.*

Thrasos snapped a low kick and attempted to knock my leg out from under me. I blocked it with a hurried sweep of the staff. He hammered a punch to my face, going for the quick knockout. I blocked with the staff again, smoother this time. I followed it with a stomping kick to his thigh, putting all my weight into the downward motion. His leg buckled but he recovered quickly.

He grinned.

The flurry of kicks and punches that followed proved he'd only been testing my reflexes. I blocked some, but plenty got through. A punch to my side set my ribs on fire. A roundhouse kick ripped the staff out of my hands, jagged pain lighting up my wrist. A blow to my face snapped my head to one side.

Before I could recover, a sweeping kick dropped me on my back and the air punched out of my lungs.

Thrasos pinned me easily and his hands gently wrapped around my throat. I gripped his arms and dug my nails in hard enough to draw blood.

"Yield, little goddess." His hands squeezed, just enough to let me know he had no problem choking me into unconsciousness if that's what it took to win.

My hands scrabbled on the floor, searching for anything to break his hold. My eyes locked onto the walking stick, but it was out of my reach. The hot guy walked over to it and glanced up. There was something there. A familiarity. He gave me the slightest nod and kicked the walking stick toward me. Then he vanished. I had the feeling that, unlike Dolos, he was truly gone as soon as he faded from sight.

I didn't have time to think. I snatched the staff up and smashed it into the side of Thrasos' head. The blow didn't have much power, but it was enough to knock him off me. I rolled with him and jammed the staff across his throat, pressing down with both hands.

"Yield," I snarled in a voice I barely recognized as my own.

Thrasos stared up at me in surprise before a slow smile spread across his face. "I yield."

The tension fled his body, and he relaxed beneath me. Interest burned bright in his intelligent eyes, as if I were the most fascinating thing he'd ever seen, and I couldn't look away. I wasn't sure if it was because I was afraid it was a trick, or if I simply didn't *want* to look away.

"Dad?" I was proud that my voice didn't waver. It was still fierce, still unfamiliar… but still mine.

Hep limped up next to me and gazed down at Thrasos with a savage grin. "You can let him up now, Nia. It's over."

Several hours later, my butt was parked on an old stool in Hep's workshop. The night had given way to the gray light of a pre-dawn sky, but I didn't need sleep. I needed answers. Hep gave them to me.

Gods and goddesses were real. The myths and legends were distorted by time and fallible storytellers, but they were based on real events, real people. People like Hep. People like me.

"Is what they said true?" I finally asked as he took a slow sip of his latest beer. In his opinion, being kidnapped was thirsty work.

"Which part?"

I gave him a pointed look and he sighed.

"Ah, that part. Yes, you fell in love with a mortal. Married him, had good years together. He died, as all mortals do. You loved him so much you wanted to die with him. You even tried, but we're difficult to kill." He gave me a pained smile. "You're a clever girl, Nia. I knew you'd eventually figure out a way to join him."

That familiar anxiety rose up, nausea competing with a dull ache in my chest. I grabbed my pendant and breathed through the pain. I didn't doubt his words anymore. I felt the truth of them in my soul.

And in my heart.

I lurched up abruptly and stalked over to the beer fridge. Dad watched with sad eyes as I completely drained one bottle and opened a second. I wiped my mouth with the back of my hand and dropped back onto the stool. I would've paced, but we hadn't even begun to set the workshop to rights and I was afraid I'd trip over something. Again.

He spread his hands and gave me a pleading stare. "I'm a selfish old man, Nia. I couldn't let you do it. I gave you the waters of forgetfulness. I watched as your memories faded. I kept you from dying, but I couldn't make you live."

I sighed and rubbed at my tired eyes. This was a *lot* to process. And I still hadn't gotten my damn cookie. My jumbled thoughts bounced all over the place. I decided to ignore the big things for now and focus on the trivial.

"Why did you tell me to call my mother? You hate her guts."

Hep snorted a laugh. "I was hoping she'd piss you off enough to get you to act. To be honest, I would've had myself kidnapped years ago if I knew it would wake you up like this."

"Funny," I shot back with a grin. "Father said the same thing."

He rolled his eyes but couldn't hide his relief. "He would."

We were silent for a moment, simply enjoying the fact we were together and relatively unharmed. We had matching black eyes, which was kind of funny. I'd snapped a selfie of us earlier and texted it to my mother. Father had replied with a thumbs-up emoji. That was the closest thing to praise I'd ever gotten from the General.

Hep set his empty bottle down with a faint clink. "Your memories aren't gone forever, you know. You can get them back. If you want to."

I tapped my fingers on my beer bottle for a moment. "How?"

"It would involve a quest or two. We're Greek gods after all. It's kind of our thing."

As I thought about what the hell kind of quest a Greek god of fire and metalworking might send me on, Hep slid off his stool, leaning heavily on his walking stick as he limped across the workshop. He scooped up the old sword I'd noticed earlier and held it out to me.

"You might need this."

I took the sword from him, my lips quirking up in a little smile at the familiar feel of the smooth leather sheath. I tried to think of the last time I'd seen the blade uncovered and couldn't. It had hung untouched over Hep's workbench for as long as I could remember.

"It used to be yours," he added gruffly.

I snapped my gaze up. There was no trace of levity in Hep's face. His eyes were solemn but there was also hope shining through like the embers of a banked fire ready to burst into flames.

"You've slept for a long time, Harmonia. Are you ready to wake up?"

I tugged the sheath down, baring an inch of shining steel to the light. I traced a finger over cool metal before I grinned up at Hep.

"Can I have a cookie first?"

The Drowning Town

A Bureau of Magical Threats story
By: Peter McKay

He needed new wipers. More specifically, the department needed to issue new wipers to their cars. Thax made a mental note of that, trying not to blink in sync with the blades. The debriefing had mentioned heavy rain in the area. An entire storm centered on one town by the coast and showing no signs of drifting off.

Frank sniffed, "Can't smell a damn thing," his partner muttered.

"Should have told me you were sick." Thax reckoned the bureau might have pushed another team onto the case. The orc had no desire to fly out all the way to the coast and get soaked by an everlasting torrent. He hoped it was something being blown out of proportion. That people were just panicking over a little extra rain in a town used to it. The rain crashing down right on the borders of the town dashed that idea. In his experience, rainstorms weren't stationary.

He watched at the edge for five minutes, just to be sure.

"I'm not sick," the man in the passenger seat echoed defensively. "It's just hard to smell in the rain. Washes away the scents."

The orc readjusted his glasses before tilting his head toward his partner. "Even those scents?"

"Yeah," Frank nodded, "Just 'cause it's magic doesn't mean its scent isn't subject to… well, you know."

"Uh huh." The tension in the orc's voice was palpable. Magic, the great frustration of his life. People had been slinging spells for centuries, and despite modern knowledge, there were too many holes in theories for a solid understanding. He'd dealt with it enough that Thax could teach entire courses on magical theory.

Maybe he should do that with retirement? Get a degree in teaching and explain to all the young wizards, witches, warlocks, or various spell slingers the actual dangers of tricking reality into looking over its shoulder. Or he could just buy a decent house and stay free, relaxed, and bored.

"Hey Frank, what are you gonna do for retirement?" His partner opened his mouth to speak, but quickly shut it and leaned back. Frank was old, too old for field work. Sure, he didn't need to worry about breaking a hip, and he could still swing his sword with enough force and precision to lop off heads. But people his age were usually behind desks, delegating tasks to hungry agents. His experience alone qualified him for promotions up the chain.

"You know better than to ask about that." Frank smiled, "Especially right as the job is starting. I don't want 'two weeks from retirement' on my gravestone."

Thax shook his head with a smile. "You aren't two weeks."

"It's an expression." Frank ran his hands through the short gray hair across his scalp, scratching at an itch.

"More like a superstition." Thax pulled into the lot of the mayor's office. First step in any job was to talk to the person in charge of the affected area. School principal, CEO, floor manager, the more specific, the better. The broader? To the top. "How much you wanna bet the mayor's in on it?"

"Now you're just being stereotypical." Frank balled up his hand and put it forward. Thax did the same, and with three shakes of their fists, they decided who spoke first. "Scissors cuts paper." The man wiggled his two fingers like a scissor in his victory.

"Just don't get too chummy." Thax rolled his eyes and balled his fist into his pocket. "We're here to get information, not ask about the latest game between the Swarm and the Goats."

Ten feet in, and Thax felt he'd walked through a wall of water. The puddle at his shoes looked more akin to a lake. Across from the double front doors sat a single secretary with a beaming smile and a lavender dress with cat paws dotting the collar. Lining her desk were little clay sculptures of cats in uniforms, from firemen, police, post workers, and even a farmer. "Can I help you, gentlemen?" She asked, green eyes open with an inviting shine that drew themselves to Frank.

In unison, they pulled out their badges. "Special Agents Huddleson and Rex, Ma'am." Frank bowed his head politely. "We're from the Bureau of Magical Threats. Had a call from your mayor about a rain problem, as it were?"

With pursed lips, she leaned in, brown braided hair tipping over her shoulder. "The BMT?" Frank nodded. Thax made an effort to look around, noting the small little fliers and news clippings around the town hall. He read that this was a fishing town, but there was a lack of nautical themed adornments. Whether that was because of generational changes or trying to spruce up a new image, he didn't know. "Well, I can't imagine we have anything like a werewolf problem," the secretary said. Thax rolled his eyes. "Mallory Glemmings, by the way," she raised her hand to meet them. "Friends call me Mal."

"Lycanthropy's actually far down out list of concerns, Mrs. Glemmings." Frank took her hand softly. "Lots of folks are born with the condition nowadays, and it's hard enough to live with it without us breathing down their neck. In fact, the director's a lycanthrope. First one to hold such a position in our branch." He spoke with that warm southern charm that, for whatever reason, always garnered trust in whoever they spoke with. Thax knew his partner wasn't a wizard, but he didn't rule out one blessing the old man's tongue. "Anyway, not that I don't want to explain more. We do got a meeting with Mr… Tumbles, is it?"

"Tumblestool. Mayor Tumblestool, and please don't call me 'Mrs'. I haven't been one since my husband passed." She laughed quietly and brushed her hand away, returning to type at her keyboard, "Let me just see if he's busy. Oh, looks like he has a meeting now."

"Yeah," Frank winked, "that'd be with us."

"Oh, of course." The woman had a quacking giggle at the old man's confidence, nearly knocking over one of her clay cat statues as her office chair swerved. "I'll patch you on through."

Mayor Tumblestool was a portly, short and, ultimately human, male with thinning hair. The lighting in the mayor's office gave his skin a wet, almost amphibious look. He huddled behind his desk with dozens of empty water bottles strewn about, currently guzzling one as they entered. "H—Hello, you must be the agents. Did you have trouble getting here?" The mayor asked, waving to the seats for them to sit.

"Bit loud with all that rain. Didn't hear any thunder either." Frank smiled as he took his seat. "I figured that's why you called? The odd weather." Mayor Tumblestool nodded. Thax sensed relief on his face, but also a bit of uncertainty in that quivering lip. How much of this was his fault, he wondered. Or was this simply an unprecedented event in an election year? He'd have to look that up later. Thax didn't think too much on local politics even back home. Regional politics were stressful enough.

"Yes, the weather is why I called." The loose bits of his thinned hair waved back and forth with every nod. "It's been causing too much destruction. It started as normal as ever three months ago. Some heavy bursts of rain. The oddest thing about it was that it happened twice a week,

Monday and Friday." Thax took note of that, clicking his pen to copy his own thoughts on the matter. "It started to...well…" the mayor gulped and looked over to Thax, "W—What are you writing down, son?"

Thax stopped and subtly breathed deep before answering, stripping the last word from his memory. "Just taking note of our investigation, Mayor." He smiled, his tusks pointed and sharp. Either the greasy-skinned man was focusing on those, or Thax's green skin. Didn't matter which, they were always the center of attention in towns like this.

"Standard protocol," Frank assured him. "My partner here's the best note-taker I've seen. If I was in school during his time, they'd probably be sending me his notes for extra help." His hand joyfully fell on Thax's shoulder, easing any growing tension in the room. Thax let out a small chuckle, one he'd practiced enough to look natural. Tumblestool etched an awkward smile across his face and leaned back.

Hopefully, he'd stay like that.

The mayor went on to explain how the rain increased rapidly over time. What started with twice a week turned to four times after two weeks, then six days after three. For two months they had rain nonstop, leading to flooding and land erosion. "So, what would be the cause of this here rain?" Frank asked.

"I… I thought you'd know?" The mayor blinked, staring at them as though neither Frank nor Thax paid any attention. "You're professionals, after all."

Frank kept his eyes steady on Mayor Tumblestool as he spoke, hands together and hanging from his thigh. "Even doctors need more than symptoms. What you've described could mean any number of things."

"Such as?" The mayor leaned in, his girth tipping over empty plastic bottles, "Surely, you must give me something?"

"Don't call me Shirley." No one laughed at Frank's joke. No one but himself. He shook his head and sighed in disappointment, mumbling about the loss of classics. "Sounds like a curse, and the trouble with curses is that almost anything can cause it to happen."

"Well, we haven't exhumed any bodies lately." Now it was the mayor's turn to laugh alone at his joke.

"That's just one," Thax said, flipping his notepad shut. "Curses are created by extremely petty people who don't care about long-lasting consequences. They could create a trigger that activates years, decades, hell, even centuries after they die. Longest known curse trigger was about… five centuries, Frank?"

"Five, five and a half, give or take." He balanced his hand in the air for emphasis. "Thankfully, curses can only latch to around three things: People, Places, or Parcels. The three Ps."

"Parcels?" The mayor asked.

"He means objects," Thax corrected. "In the industrial age, it wasn't uncommon for the modern witches, warlocks, and wizards to send their curses through the improved mailing system."

The mayor's eyes went wide in thought. "But not anymore?" His fingers nervously tapped the plastic water bottle. "Should I be sending my mail to a wizard?"

"Well," Frank scoffed, "Not as effectively. Thanks to better security at the post office." The two had their fair share of postal related curse cases, but none of that matter beyond scaring the mayor. And Thax had no desire to scare people. "So the rain's been nonstop for about two months? Anything else unusual?"

Mayor Tumblestool raised his brow at the question. "How do you mean?"

"Well, like say, strange noises, wildlife being, um…" Frank snapped his fingers with the word lost on the tip of his tongue, "Funky? Yeah, funky or weird. Oh!" He pointed to the mayor. "Any list of demands being sent?" The mayor shook his head, which ruled out the idea that the curse giver was living or mortal. At least based on Thax's experience. Petty spells are slung by petty casters, and petty people love to make demands. "What about before the rain? Anything odd happen then? Like, you didn't have a fisherman drag up some sort of ancient artifact or a couple of kids disrespecting a burial ground, did ya?"

The greasy man grinned softly, but folded when Thax's partner leaned in. "I can't be certain. Even as mayor, I don't know every little thing that goes on in this town. People only come to me when things are a big problem, or if it's bothering them personally, though," He slumped into his chair with a deep sigh, "I usually hear about those when I'm shopping in my off hours."

"I see." Frank nodded along. "And who told you about the rain?"

"No one did." The mayor stated. "Made that call myself."

Thax stopped taking notes. "So, you don't know if this rain is magical?" The redundancies in his line of work forced him to question the obvious.

"Well, yes?" He kept his eyes focused on the orc, as though Thax said something stupid. "The patterns are too odd to be otherwise, right?"

"And how do you figure?" Thax asked, not realizing the aggressive cadence in his voice. "Did you just look up magical threat symptoms? Or do you have an actual wizard on staff?"

"Now, now, Thax," Frank rested his hand against his partner's shoulder, "Even I can see this is a bit odd. Mayor Tumblestool, we'll take a look over the next few days and see what we can find. Heck, the rain might even stop then. Who knows?"

"Will you be staying in town?" The mayor asked.

"We found a motel on the outskirts. We'll keep in touch." Thax stayed silent as they left, leaving Frank to wish Mallory a goodbye and thanks for her service. Silence pressed between them once in the car, broken by the constant pounding of raindrops. With a sigh, Frank looked out his window, then back to the orc. "Do I *need* to find a pile of bullshit just so I can toss you in and hope you build up a tolerance?"

"That's a roundabout way of saying it." Thax flipped through his notes. The pattern did lead to a curse, but being asked to come by without actual evidence was a waste of resources. Budget cutbacks already took away the good coffee maker. "I think it's a place curse."

"One continuous weather pattern localized around a given area nonstop? Next, you'll tell me that dragons love the stock market." Cracking a grin, Frank drove them down the road and passed Thax a map of the town. "Pawed this pamphlet on my way in. Find us the local library. We got some research to do."

"All nighter?" The orc asked.

"Probably." His partner sunk into his seat. "We'll need to get some coffee for sure."

Thax groaned. A small town like this probably didn't know how to give him a good mocha.

Amazingly, the town did have a Novabrew. Not even a small coastal town was safe from corporate overreach. Unfortunately for Thax, it was closed. Better for Frank, who wanted to try the local cafe instead. Thax tried to hold his disappointment, hard to do after hours of scouring through town records and finding nothing.

"They need to get a mage to scan their documents. Make them easier to search through," He muttered on his way inside. It was a small shop with only three tables to sit and relax by. Only one person stood behind the counter, an elf girl with a face full of piercings, hair split between crimson red and neon green, and a focus on her personal orb.

She didn't look up when they reached the counter. With a bored tone, the elf muttered, "No, Jeb, I'm not interested in going-" She blinked, casting a wide glance on both agents. The tip of her pointed ears turned red. Clearing her throat, she spoke up with a straight face and tucked her orb away. "Oh. I'm sorry, never expect newcomers around here." Forcing a grin, she added, "Welcome to Honeydew, sweet as can be. How can I help you today?"

"One black coffee, mind the sweetness." Frank ordered, casually nudging his partner in the arm before Thax said something sarcastic.

"No cream?" She asked.

Frank tipped his head. "No sugar either. Watching my health. Thax, you want your usual?"

Thax nodded, taking a seat in the corner as Frank ordered the orc his mocha. He looked out from the rain pelted window to see the heavy clouds above. His finger tapped rapidly against the table, eyes failing to pierce the gray sacks in the sky. The orc gave up and checked his watch, discovering they'd been searching through the library records for half the day. And what did they have to show for it? Fishing records, needless town events, and old minor curses that had been resolved.

Maybe he should ask for a sandwich, too. Being hungry didn't help the job.

"Coffee will take a bit," Frank said, sitting down across from his partner. "Sink's not working. So she's gotta use imported water."

"Imported?" Forgetting his hunger, He looked over and found the barista opening bottles of water to pour into the machine. "Huh… with all his rain, I figured that wouldn't be an issue." A thought hooked in, taking him back to the plastic water bottles in the mayor's office. "Think the mayor's pipes were broken?"

Frank shrugged. "He did look a little greasy. Like he hadn't showered in a few days."

"And she's using bottled water." The gears slowly clicked. The bathrooms at the library were closed for repairs, leaving outhouses outside. Peering out the window, Thax found two more outhouses in the front, raindrops bouncing off the plastic roofs and pooling at the ground. "Constant rain, but no running water. Connection looks obvious."

"Could just be a coincidence." Frank pointed to the barista. "You might as well ask her about it."

"Me?" He balked. "Why don't you ask?"

Frank sported a small, devilish grin. "'Cause you have terrible people skills."

"All the more reason for you to ask," Thax complained.

Frank shook his head. "Nope. All the more reason for you to get better with them. I can't be the face forever. Not with every wrinkle I get." Knowing how stubborn Frank could be in his 'lessons', Thax sighed and headed over to the counter. He thought about how best to start it, running several opening lines in his head and what kind of smile he could make. She's not gonna judge you, he thought, sure she's seen plenty of orcs. Not like you're a rarity.

"Excuse me, miss?" He pulled out his notepad. "Do you mind if I ask you a few questions?"

"It's Carly, for one." She raised one finger, then another, "And sure, but only if you answer some of mine." He nodded, letting her ask away first. "So, you guys after aliens or something?"

He fought the urge to blink while processing the question. "What?" He asked, hoping his jaw didn't hit the floor.

"You know, aliens." Her green eyes didn't waiver. "Dudes from space and the other realms. I figured that's why it's raining so much."

"Do you...do you actually believe that?" Thax questioned, dropping his professionalism at the absurdity of it all.

She laughed, "No, not really. But it'd be cool, right? If I remember my professor right, space is infinite, so there's gotta be life. But there's no reason for little gray dudes with bulbous black eyes to come visit this small town."

"Can't say I'd agree. Small towns like this make excellent cover. Cities are too populated to sneak around in." Pushing the movie tropes aside, he cleared his throat and asked. "So, is the whole town having a water problem?"

"The worst." Carly rolled her eyes back and groaned, holding onto the counter to not fall backward. "Pipes have been damaged for a month. My mom keeps buying bottled water to keep the shop going, hoping customers will flock over with Novabrew closed." She leaned in and whispered, "I've had to shower with buckets. Like in the Saddle Ages. It's frustrating."

Thax flipped to the next page. "And the whole town has this problem?"

She nodded. "Yeah. We're told not to flush any toilets, run any sinks, or really use anything related to the pipes. Only hot water I've been having is from coffee." Thax noted everything down. The entire town drowning in rain but unable to use their water? One solid connection, but he needed to establish it.

"So, who gave the order on that?" He pointed the back end of his pen to her, like a mic for confessions. "The mayor?"

"Mr. Gelp." Carly said. "Guy in charge of the water purification plant."

That didn't add up. Town looked too tiny to have a plant. "This town has its own plant?"

She shook her head. "No, but the plant for the county is based here. Figured the rest of the county was having similar issues, though. Why?"

Thax did not know if they were. He and Frank hadn't stopped by anywhere outside the town when they arrived. "Thank you for your time," He said, putting his notepad away. Sitting back with Frank, he retold his conversation and explained his growing hypothesis.

"Don't you mean theory?" Frank asked.

"No. A theory is already backed by data. All the evidence we have is circumstantial."

Frank looked out the window, noting the drenched landscape. "Looks like an obvious connection. But," He sighed, "Reports don't work on the principle of 'trust me' like they used to."

"Oh no, they actually *require* evidence to convict. The horror." Frank laughed at his partner's sarcasm. Thax didn't join in. The BMT had a history they needed to make better. "Whatever the case, Mr. Gelp is our next suspect."

"Maybe Mr. Gelp knows a thing or two about aliens." Thax narrowed his eyes at his partner, earning only a smile in response to the daggers pointed at the old man. "Oh, relax and enjoy your mocha when it comes. You get too cranky without sugar."

He wasn't wrong, not that Thax would admit it.

The water treatment plant was a good fifteen minutes out of town, letting Thax enjoy a clear sky as they drove off. The rearview mirror showed the clouds overhead the town, hovering still over it as though frozen in place. Their brief respite from the storm didn't last, as the people in the plant were confused about why the town had no water coming to it.

"We just got orders from the top to keep Vilik Bay dry," Said Daryl, one of the operators at the plant and the skinniest dwarf that Thax had ever seen in his life. His bosses weren't available—something about bad chili at the last potluck. They were able to get his address for later.

"Any reason why?" Frank asked, having won the right to question. "Surely they gotta give a reason."

"Something to do with a faulty pipe. But I haven't heard anything about replacing it." Daryl scratched under his chin. Or at least where his chin should be. The beard was so bushy and unkempt that Thax had trouble even seeing a mouth. "Not like I'm not asking either. My brother-in-law keeps harping on me about when he'll get his water back."

"How long has he been askin'?" Frank asked with friendly, but ultimately fake, concern.

Daryl paused and pondered, looking between both agents through his bushy eyebrows. "Bout half a month now? Freddie's usually pretty good at keeping his cool, but I can't blame him for being impatient now. Hells, I'm impatient. My utility bills have been going up since I've been letting him and his family do their laundry at my home. And then there's the showers."

Frank nodded along, listening while keeping a close eye on Thax's note taking. The dwarf passed along his boss's address and wished them good fortune on their way out. "So as far as we know," His partner said back in the car, "The pipes are fine."

"You don't have a realistic excuse?" Thax asked, "Like the company to replace them has been late or something?"

"No," Frank scratched his head, "It's possible, and incredibly unprofessional, but experience is telling me that our evidence is connected. One last thing to check, to be sure." One quick search, and they found the head of the treatment plant's house. Smaller than Thax imagined, but given the area, the manager's salary couldn't be much to work with. And it had more space than his own apartment.

Five minutes after they rang the doorbell, Frank took a heavy sniff to the air. With a grimace on his face, he pulled out a credit card and asked

Thax to keep watch. "What are you doing?" He asked under his breath while watching the road. "We can't just break in."

"Something smells off." He said with sincerity.

"Off?" He motioned to his hidden sidearm. "Magic off?"

"No. Dead off." Two feet in, and Thax saw what his partner could smell. A body laid out on the tiled kitchen floor. "Well, shit." Frank stopped at the edge of the kitchen and made sure Thax didn't cross. No point in contaminating the crime scene. "Looks like we got a murder on top of a curse."

A call to the local station and after a few questions they resolved with their badges, the agents were inside the coroner's office to learn all they could of the deceased Mr. Gelp. There, they learned that the water treatment manager died of drowning. But there was no evidence of water at the scene. The coroner theorized that whatever water didn't go down the sink drain just evaporated. Thax found it solid enough, but neither he nor Frank found any sign of a struggle. "Think he drowned himself?" Frank asked.

The sun had set by now, and Thax stretched out his arms. "No way. Could have pissed off a witch. A waterless drowning spell seems pretty on the note for them."

Too tired to do anymore research, the two had booked their motel room and settled in. Two beds, a single TV, and a leather lounge chair that Frank quickly tossed his jacket over. "I'll have to put in a call for a background check, then. Or you could." He kicked his feet up against the bed and flipped on the TV. "Maybe?" Thax shook his head, unconvinced. "But it might be someone inborn."

"Inborn magic is too simple." Frank finally stopped on a channel depicting the Great Lich War in all black and white splendor. "Curses are too complex. Lots of moving parts and triggers."

"Nothing stops an inborn user from learning codified magic." Thax sighed. "Besides, codified magic users can go undocumented all the time. That's a big reason for our department." The myriad of reasons why the Bureau of Magical Threats existed was a subject that Thax was too tired to rant about. At the end of the day, they were needed, and he made sure to do good work. "Whatever," he yawned. "I'm gonna have a quick shower before bed."

"Most people shower when they wake up." Frank didn't look away from his program.

He rarely had a choice in the matter. "It helps me sleep." Thax already started stripping away his tie and jacket, tossing them carelessly on his way to the bathroom. Waterless drowning, a town beset by constant rain, and an order to keep the pipes off in that area. He set his glasses down by the sink and ran the shower, letting heat and steam rise as he pondered the evidence presented.

Water was the key connection. A druidic curse, maybe? He'd need to get a consultant for that, and druids were notorious for being difficult to find unless they wanted to be. Besides, druids had limited control over the elements, being closer to nature. Conversely, shamans had a strong elemental connection, but the practice of shamanism was banned long ago. Why two similar schools of primal magic were so separate he didn't understand, and the urge to slap whoever decided it was ever present.

"Hey Frank!" He called out, "You sure you didn't smell any magic at the crime scene?"

"Positive!" His partner turned up the volume, "Though my nose felt a little stuffy, like in the town." Thax could hear the crackle of arcane lightning from the TV.

Like the town. But it wasn't raining at the manager's home. Thax stepped inside the shower and pondered, letting the warm water stream down upon him. Water, water, water, it was the main connection, but Thax couldn't grasp it. It was almost as if water itself was the culprit.

"Oh—" The warm water pooled around his head before Thax could utter another word. He scrambled at the bubble, but the steady stream flowing from the showerhead left his attempts laughable. Screams turned to gurgles of frustration, the last remnants of his air abandoning him.

He kicked at the curtain and flailed his arms wildly for the towel rack. Noise. He needed to make noise before the bubble enveloped him whole. Looping his fingers around the steel bar above him, Thax let his bodyweight tear it down. The momentum carried him hard against the floor. The water didn't break, coiling around him with purpose.

"What in the Sam hill are you—" Frank poked his head in and immediately ran out, returning with his sword drawn and ready. Liquid tendrils shot out after him, forcing his partner to slip behind the door frame and wait for an opening. Kicking his legs off the wall, Thax pushed himself far enough to grab the doorframe and pull himself forward. His vision blurred, seeing only a hazy figure raising a sword high above their head.

Sweet, delicious air burned the orc's lungs. He coughed painfully, letting Frank pull his naked body across the bedroom with strength his old body betrayed. "You can cough when we're safe!" Clear tentacles slithered out from the steamy bathroom and gave chase. He scrambled out to the front door and down to the lot, not giving head to anyone seeing his green ass as he popped the trunk.

"Where is it?" Thax muttered angrily, sifting through their supplies. Every mission came with at least one emergency pack for unexpected scenarios. From spare silver manacles and wolfsbane tranqs for lycans, garlic infused smoke grenades for vampires, dragonfire shells for trolls, and salt shells for ghosts. Without his glasses he had to squint to find the one box for elementals, opening it to reveal it split into four sections for the basics. He needed to have a talk with someone about expanding that later, thinking over the exact words as he loaded six sponge shells into the shotgun.

A torrent of water burst from the windows, carrying Frank and the shards of shattered windows off the second floor and into the motel pool. Thax hopped over the gate and brandished his weapon at the forming mass of water heading over to them. The living wave surged over the railing, and took the form of a wave that walked.

Accurate enough without his glasses, Thax fired the first slug center mass. It expanded upon impact, absorbing water inside its fibers and leaving a soggy ball behind the elemental. The watery mass broke apart and reformed, smaller but determined in its approach. He kept firing, shell after shell turning into wide, soggy orbs. He only seemed to impede it.

"The shower," Frank coughed, crawling out of the pool soaked and clutching his chest. Thax figured his partner had broken a rib or two. "Gotta turn off the source."

"Thought you did that." He fired another shell into the mass. It didn't stop, seeping through the gate bars like gelatin.

"Tried. Damn thing packed a punch." Frank raised his sword, the enchanted steel at the ready. "I can keep it busy."

The orc watched his partner, the pool, and the violent wall of water heading towards them. "Can you keep it out of the pool?" Thax asked.

He didn't smile. "I said keep it busy. Now go!"

Frank's sword kept the elemental from lopping off Thax's head. Quickly reloading, he fired shell after shell up the steps, turning tendrils into splashes. By the time he was back in the bedroom, he had one shell left.

It wouldn't be enough for the living water tank their room had become. Holding his breath, Thax dived in and swam to the bathroom. The water didn't try to kill him immediately, so Frank was doing his job in keeping it busy. Now all he had to do was turn a knob. That would have worked, if the showerhead hadn't been torn clean off.

Seeing a quick temporary solution, Thax fired his last sponge shell into the exposed pipe. The sponge expanded, but held. It'd have to be enough to cut off the elemental. The warped biome collapsed around him, carrying Thax out to the railing where he held on for dear life. Gasping back air, he sputtered out blobs of water and pulled himself back onto the floor, fighting for his second wind.

Judging from the rising tide in the pool, Frank hadn't had the best of luck. The old man dodged, weaved and sliced through what he couldn't in the torrent of liquid slams. By now people were out of their rooms, watching in confusion and terror.

"Sorry, government business." Thax grabbed one of their personal orbs. "This the police station?" The person on the other end started a tirade. He hung up and dialed the local law enforcement. "This is agent Thaximus Rex of the Bureau of Magical Threats," He answered to the emergency responder. "There's currently a large water elemental trapped in the pool of Motel 666 on Brandy Avenue. We need cryo-kits down here, pronto."

Officers arrived before he hung up. Dropping his gun, Thax raised his hands up for local law enforcement as several of them pointed pistols his way. Two pulled up gas grenade launchers and fired into the pool, freezing upon contact. The harsh cries roaring from the elemental scratched the back of his eardrums as it succumbed to its icy prison.

"Down on the ground!" One of the officers shouted, quickly drawing his sidearm from its holster.

Thax reached for his badge, only to find that it and the rest of his clothes were still in the motel room. He raised his hands. "Don't shoot! I'm a special agent. My badge number is—"

"On the ground!" The same officer roared, pulling the hammer back on his revolver. The gravel against his knees was a pillow compared to a bullet to the chest. "Not your night, huh?" Another officer sneered, roughly locking cuffs behind his wrists. "Gonna go streaking when an elemental is on the loose? Probably shouldn't have picked a place across the street from the station." Thax looked across the way, to the back of an unassuming building. He must have missed the police cruisers.

"I told you, I'm—"

The officer yanked him up before he could finish. "Shut up. Godsdamn pervert."

Thax found himself unceremoniously shoved into the backseat of the closet cruiser.

"Now stay here while we deal with a real problem."

With a slam of the door, Thax exhaled and took three deep breaths to keep calm.

"Just a random cop." His voice slowly rose, "Deep inside some coast hick town and… no, no, no," He softened his voice and straightened up. "Don't give in. That's what they want. You are a professional." And he'd be having that officer work behind a desk for a year if he could help it.

Leaning his forehead against the window, he watched in silence as the officers helped Frank out from the splash radius of the ice. He smiled when Frank looked over to his cruiser, his mouth moving wildly and finger pressing again and again against a cop's chest. With another breath, Thax closed his eyes and waited for the door to open. "Couldn't even grab a pair of underwear?" His partner asked with a weak smile.

"Just get me out of these cuffs," Thax demanded, the words deeper than he'd intended.

After being freed, he learned his clothes were drenched. The badge was safe, and as much as he'd like to shove it in the face of the cop who cuffed him, he took a towel instead and took the coffee his partner offered.

"Well, guess that explains why I couldn't smell it." Frank took a spare towel and dried his blade, leaning against one of the police cruisers. "Figured the rain was washing away the scent, not the actual scent itself."

Thax nodded, realizing that all that rain wasn't local. No, it had to be connected to the elemental plane of water. "Someone in that town pissed off a water duke."

"Got any idea who?" Frank asked.

Trying not to burn his tongue on the coffee, Thax shook his head. "Nope."

The actual evidence didn't line up, and the motives didn't show. Thax looked over his notes again and again for the next three hours, thankfully with dry clothes, a spare pair of glasses, and a nice mocha at his side. His first pair, unfortunately, broke in the scuffle with the elemental.

The local PD had the elemental contained, if only barely. Instead of proper containment facilities, they used several water jugs and kept the entity separate. Knowing elementals, forming a body was disorienting enough, so having it split would keep it indisposed.

For now.

A brown paper bag landed heavily against the table, shaking him out of his stupor.

"Hungry?" His partner asked, pulling out a paper wrapped delicacy and handing it over.

Despite everything, Thax was indeed hungry. That and maybe a little food might help him properly string his notes into a coherent case.

"What'd you get?" He asked while unwrapping it. White meat mixed with lettuce and tomato and a thick white sauce. "What is this, chicken?" Thax took a bite. It wasn't chicken.

"Swordfish." Frank unwrapped his own.

Swordfish? Thax looked up to his partner as if the man had a death wish. "Both of us nearly drowned, and you decided to grab a fish sandwich?"

Frank shrugged. "Went to a shop and took what they said was their best local dish. It's a little fitting if you think about it. Whenever they killed dragons in the old days, local villages would subside on their meat for weeks, months maybe depending on the size. With the killers getting the best cut."

"Pretty sure the best cut was the dragon's hoard." Thax had heard of people enjoying dragon meat, so much so that it was banned in much of the known world after the Great Lich War. Dragons didn't appreciate being hunted just to be served on a silver platter, and would-be dragon killers caused a lot of property damage both directly and indirectly. He pushed the sandwich aside and went over his notes. "Did you get a specialist?"

"Yeah. Morgal the Wrinkled." Frank took another bite, as though he didn't drop another headache.

Fighting the urge to sigh, Thax failed and tossed his notepad against the table. "Morgal? They're giving us that asshole?"

"He's not an asshole." Frank shrugged, "He's more…"

"Racist." The orc stated.

"Woah, woah." Frank raised his hand. "I was gonna say, 'set in his ways'. He's been in the game longer than me, so it's hard for him to change."

Another reason wizards sucked; the refusal to die when everyone else does. Thax leaned into his chair and rethought everything; the rain, the dead head of a water treatment plant, unfaulty pipes, and the water elemental. Was this a curse? Too many moving parts, but then again, he might be looking at the wrong parts, making the wrong conclusions. "How much time 'til he arrives?"

"A wizard arrives when he pleases." The absolutely most nasal and cranky voice scratched Thax's eardrums. He looked over to the door, finding an old man with an unkempt beard, a loose robe that carried dirt and dust from the ground, and a single badge pinned to his chest that stated his department and occupation. BMT: Wizard.

Despite the smile he carried across his wrinkly face, Morgal spoke as though everything outside of magical affairs was beneath him. This included social interactions with his coworkers. "With what task have you summoned the great Morgal?" He demanded, Thax hearing the wizard's spine crack, straightening himself up to stand closer to six feet. "I was busy decoding an old elvish recipe when I got word."

"Water elemental," Both Frank and Thax said in unison.

The old wizard raised his busy brow, so puffy that Thax swore the man needed to invest in a comb or a good barber. "An interpreter? They couldn't send anyone else?"

Frank shrugged, taking another bite out of his sandwich and chewing slowly, letting Morgal twitch like an impatient dog. "You're the closest," he said, "Specifically with that short range teleportation magic."

"Yes, and I have a spare scroll to get back to my house after this. Now what's the situation?" After explaining the previous events, Thax noticed Morgal's face twisted in disgust whenever he brought up the Vilik Bay. "Of course it had to be for this town."

"Something about it?" Frank asked, sitting next to Thax.

The wizard shook his head. "Just an old pride thing. My hometown and Vilik Bay never got along. Competing business in the fish market. It's silly, but when you're raised to not like people it's hard to get it out of your system." That'd almost sound introspective to Thax if Morgal didn't immediately follow with, "Grod, can you hand me your notes? I'd like to double check."

Thax did not. He stared at Morgal with the intention of sending flames from his eyes to burn the wizard down instead. Sadly, he was not capable of that, and the old cantankerous buffoon looked at him as though Thax misheard him. "Grod? Your notes."

"Thax," Thax said.

Morgal blinked, "Oh. Right. Sorry. Bad with faces. Can I see your notes?"

He passed them over and stepped out of the spare room the local police department offered, more to take a breath and rethink his next move. Pulling out his personal cellular orb, he made a quick call to the records department.

"Hello, this is Bliztmicktash, or Bob for the lazy." The other voice on the end spoke with an echo, as if two mouths were speaking at once. "How may I help you?"

"Bob, it's Thax." He walked down the corridor as he talked, passing local officers who were called in. They were all nudging and pacing, eyes jittering toward the interrogation room door. This time, he knew his badge was the reason. These people were used to dealing with petty crimes, not water elemental attacks. The chief probably called in extra just to be safe. "I need you to run some background checks on a few individuals."

"That's part of my job. What'll it be?" Thax gave Bob a quick list of everyone they'd met so far. He didn't have any key suspects, not with good proof, but it was better to be safe than sorry.

With Morgal on hand, interrogating the water elemental became almost safe. One wave of his wand, and the wizard had what he claimed to be the essence of the elemental clasped into a single foam cup. Despite the assurance, Thax preferred to stand away from the table when the questions flew.

"So, let's start easy." Frank locked his fingers together and leaned into the table. "What's your name?"

A single bubble rose from the cup. "Their name is Baron Hydrox of the Shimmering Court." Morgal translated, sitting next to the cup.

"Their?" Frank's eyebrows squished together, his gaze on the cup, then to Morgal. "Not his?"

Morgal rolled his eyes. "Elementals do not have a concept of gender."

"Yet they use a gendered title." Frank said.

"No," the wizard shook his head. "That's just my best translation of it."

Frank nodded, "Right, right. So, tell me, Hydrox-"

The cup bubbled again. "They want you to use their full title," Morgal explained.

Thax stepped in. "Well, I didn't want to almost drown, but here we are."

"Woah, woah," Frank raised his hand to keep Thax back, "Chill. We're all cool here, chilly."

He wasn't, not in the slightest. But professional courtesy kept Thax from walking out the door of the interrogation room. That, and the standard good cop, bad cop, routine that Thax loathed but pulled off thanks to Frank's charm. "Ok, Baron Hydrox of the Shimmering Court," His partner said, twirling his pen between his fingers, "What are you doing on our plane?"

The cup shook with popping bubbles, threatening to topple over. Morgal leaned back, eyes stiff at the display. "Well, that's quite a… colorful sentiment." The wizard cleared his throat and translated. "Baron Hydrox of the Shimmering Courts is not here because of choice, but of duty. It seems that over the past few years, members of their court have been going missing. Specifically, in their… what's the best word?" He snapped his fingers as if the sound would spark remembrance, "The baron's aquarium."

"His fish tank?" Frank asked, perplexed.

"*Their* fish tank," Morgal corrected.

"Right," Frank nodded, "Right, their. Wait, so this elemental is here because of missing fish? The plane of water is literally an endless sea." That they knew of, Thax would say, but he chose to remain quiet this time. "Why's he, uh, they bothered by a bunch of missing fish?"

The cup bubbled furiously, leading Morgal to shake his head. "Apologies, your grace. We mean well, but you must understand that the rules of sapience are different here."

"Where have they been disappearing from?" Thax stepped over to the table, hand holding him stable against it. "Is it one place, or a multitude of missing fish reports?"

Another bubble and Morgal nodded, "To the… diversity hire—their words not mine." Thax didn't believe that for a second but let the wizard continue, "One spot in the aquarium, so deep that they had not noticed it for years. Their sudden entrance to our plane has been a more rash decision than they realize, as they are not sure who caused it."

"They're not sure?" Thax asked. "So they attacked us and killed at least one other person without surefire reasoning?"

Thax didn't even care for the next few bubbles. He had every desire to toss the jugs of water into an open desert and watch it all evaporate. But that wasn't his call, and one look from Frank told him that nothing anywhere close was gonna happen. Because now this was an interdimensional incident, one that they couldn't let go public. "Do they know what caused the portal? Is it just an accidental tear or mortal-made?"

"They do not," Morgal said after one bubble. "I suppose I'll have to decipher that as well." The wizard sighed, as though his job was simply an inconvenience. After returning the Baron to their holding jug, Morgal slumped into his chair and muttered, "I suppose I'll have to sample local cuisine again."

"The swordfish isn't bad," Frank said, checking over his notes of the session.

"What?" Morgal pulled his head up, one bushy brow raised in confusion.

"The swordfish," Frank said. "I had some, pretty good."

"The water here is too cold for swordfish," the wizard stated.

The following pause between the three men felt like an opaque glass jar cracking. Its pieces falling to the floor and fitting into something else completely. "You're sure?" Thax asked, interposing himself into the conversation with a voice trembling on the edge of the truth. "You're *positive* that swordfish aren't a local fish?"

"I was born in Gurtleburg, fifteen miles down the coast of Vilik's Bay." Morgal straightened his shoulders, as though insulted by his coworker's lack of knowledge in his personal life. "Lived there for twenty years before I wised up, and my father was a fisherman. Not once," He raised one bony finger, "Not once, did I see swordfish as a local delicacy. Because it can't be. The water isn't the right climate."

"Hydrox did say their fish had been going missing," Frank said, tapping his pen against the small notepad of scribbles and two-word sentences. "And, while my knowledge of the plane of water is limited, I reckon it's got a lot of fish."

"An understatement." Morgal rolled his eyes. "The plane of water is a vast ocean where all aquatic life can live in harmony. Saltwater, freshwater, it doesn't matter. You can have cod and carp swimming in the same place without worry. The 'how' is still being studied."

Thax didn't need to know the 'how', just the fact that they could. It only further vouched the elemental's story, but it opened other questions. The most notable being how long this had been going on for swordfish to be considered a local favorite. "Three months," Thax said to himself, earning a stare from his compatriots. "The Mayor said the rain started three months ago, and had worsened since. Let's assume Hydrox arrived three months ago, and the rain was his–"

"Their." Morgal corrected.

"Whatever." Thax continued, "Let's assume it was Hydrox's doing. The elemental has been causing havoc for three months, and only recently started attacking people. So what's that tell us?"

"That they're getting impatient." Frank sniffed, his face twisting as if the air grew bitter. "Means we gotta find the wizard responsible."

"Hold on," Morgal said, "How do you know it's a wizard? Wasn't your working theory that this was some kind of curse?"

"It was," Thax said with a nod, palming his cell-orb as he felt the ball vibrate in his pocket, "But now, I think we can gather this was an unintentional side effect of an intentional magical act." One message from Bob. Thax smiled widely as he panned over the background checks. "And I think we got our wizard."

Despite the rain stopping, Vilik's Bay still had a drenched and dilapidated look to it. Thax found it fitting from the driver's seat. Constant rain was on architecture and roads. He expected the sun to help dry it all away, but the cloudy gray sky proved unwilling to let the ball shine down upon this fishermen village.

At least this time, it was for natural reasons.

Parking at the Mayor's office, the two agents prepped their gear. Frank with his sword, one both hoped he wouldn't have to draw, and Thax with his 9mm. "Are the scents clearing up?" Thax asked his partner.

Frank sniffed the air. "Just about. Rain's still heavy, but I can get a whiff of that conjuration magic from behind the doors." When he saw his partner get nervous, he added, "It's faint, don't worry. We shouldn't expect a fireball."

Thax tested his underarm holster just in case. Not as easy to draw from as from the waist, but it paid to be subtle. Satisfied, he cleaned his classes one last time before the two headed inside. They found the secretary behind the front desk. Miss Glemmings smiled at their approach. "Lovely day, ain't it gentlemen?" She said, "Clouds are still here, but the rain stopped. Why, the mayor was so happy I swear he could kiss both of you on the lips." Thax looked for any look of concern, but found none.

The next part was never easy. "Mallory Gemmings." Her face dropped with Thax's neutral tone, eyes falling toward the badge he flipped out. "For suspicion of interdimensional interference, we're placing you under arrest."

The silence in the room wasn't real silence. The soft blow of the air conditioner, the jingle of the handcuffs Frank pulled out, and the soft roll from the plastic wheels of her chair. They might as well have been mute with the shock across Mallory's face. "Pardon?" The secretary asked, keeping steady at her desk. Thax was sure she was debating her next move, whether to run, fight, or surrender.

Please, he thought, please pick option three.

"Excuse me?" Everyone present turned to the confused voice of the mayor, who stared out with his bulbous eyes wide. "What is the meaning of this?"

"We have reason to believe that Mrs. Gemmings is responsible for your rain problem. As well as indirectly responsible for the death of at least one person, and the assault of two federal agents." Thax kept his face indifferent as Mallory let his partner cuff her. He didn't want any smile to be taken as joyful. He was just happy he didn't need to draw his gun.

"Are you mad?" Mayor Tumblestool interposed himself between Mallory and Thax. "She's just a secretary, and a single mother. What makes you think she's responsible for a curse?"

"She ain't," Frank said, adding, "Cause it wasn't a curse."

The mayor blinked. "What?"

Putting his badge away, Thax explained, "Last night, a baron from the elemental plane of water attacked us. The baron explained that several of their inhabitants have gone missing over the years, and located a portal in their personal home. We have a team of specialists locating and examining the portal as we speak. If the signature doesn't match, she's free to go. Barring that, they don't find any illegal items in her home, or any other evidence linking her to the plane of water."

"But she doesn't know magic!" The mayor balled his fists, his outrage exuding more presence than the small and moist man seemed capable of mustering. "Not once in the ten years that I've known this woman has she cast a single spell. I don't know many wizards, witches, or warlocks, but I understand they love to show off their magic."

"She graduated from Harken University in 1583." The mayor's features softened as Thax continued, "She went on to grad school at Pellick, specializing in planar theory, and wrote several papers on the subject. Her works even impressed our resident wizard."

"Oh my lord, they still have those?" Mallory said, hanging her head to hide her blush. "So many errors."

"Point is, she's over a hundred and specialized in conjuration magic. Anyone with her skills and knowledge could open up a portal. This, combined with the fact that your local delicacies are made from fish that couldn't survive in these waters, and we've got reason to suspect that she is the culprit." He pulled out a slip of paper from his coat pocket, handing it over to the mayor, "And yes, we do have a warrant. We aren't tyrants. You can also expect more agents shortly, as we'll need to clear up if you were aware of this and the ecological impacts on the ecosystem."

"Mallory, tell me this isn't true." Mayor Tumblestool tried to push himself past Thax, but a solid foundation of muscle stopped him. "I swear I'll get you the best lawyers I can find. My cousin is a fantastic one. She'll do it for—"

"Johnny boy," Mrs. Gemmings lips curled like a sweet old lady meeting her grandchild. "It's alright. My late husband loved this town, and I only wanted to save it. But," she shrugged, "You know what they say about good intentions."

Good intentions or otherwise, Thax had to respect that she came along quietly. By the end of the evening, Mallory was in lockup and Morgal had confirmed her signature to the portal. "It should be closed by tomorrow morning." Frank stirred the coffee pot, yawning to himself.

"You can go," Thax said, eyes focused on the orb in front of him. "I can fill out the paperwork for both of us."

"Nah," Frank shook his head and sat down. "I won't leave until you do. That's what partners are for."

While he didn't argue, Thax did find himself thinking back to Mrs. Gemmings' reasoning. "Her husband died decades ago, and she was still in that town."

"Hmm?" Frank said, mid-sip of his brown brew.

"It's just… why not move?" He asked, running reasons in his head. "She's a wizard. She knows how to live longer than most. If you're gonna outlive your loved one, why not move on to somewhere else? Why stay?"

"Why not?" Frank asked, crossing his legs, "I mean, a lot of people just wanna settle down in their old age."

He looked deadpan to his partner. "Like you?"

The old man laughed, wiping whatever remnants left of his drink off his beard with a clean sleeve. "No, no. This," He tapped the table, "This is my settle. I dread the day I retire and need to find new things to keep me sane."

Thax wanted to say that Frank would change his mind. But he kept his mouth shut and focused on his work. Maybe he'd better understand it when he was older, but as of now, all he could see was the detriment of staying too long. Mrs. Gemmings indirectly killed a man and nearly doomed a town because she stayed and tried to fix things.

Hopefully, Frank would be different.

Borrowed Time

By: David R. Birdsall

The winter storm raged around Devyn as he leaned against his old Cadillac. The warmth from his cigarette seemed to be the only thing that kept him from freezing to death as he waited for his reluctant partner in this case.

He would have preferred to wait in the car, but she wouldn't show up unless she could see that he was alone. She insisted on him always waiting outside for her. Something about the steel and iron of cars bothered her.

The wind whipped the snow in cyclones around him as he pulled his trench coat collar up and his fedora down. The howling wind drowned the sound of her owl-like wings out, making it impossible for him to hear. Fortunately, he didn't depend solely on his five senses.

From a young age, he realized that by quieting his mind, he could hear whispers within. They offered guidance and advice on everything from mundane decisions, like what to eat for dinner, to life-or-death situations that proved life-saving. During his youth, it enabled him to excel at school, and as an adult, it aided him in locating those who couldn't be found.

By chance, he'd found a profitable purpose for this gift. He learned about the real-life existence of things that bump in the night. Demons, monsters, and the sort were real. The whispers would lead him to where they were hiding and how to dispatch them. When confronted, most would cut a deal with him. He would demand their service for not killing them when they slept. The arrangement stated that innocent individuals were off-limits, but they could target criminals and they needed to aid him whenever he requested it. It always helped to have a supernatural back up in solving missing persons cases.

While he took a long drag from his cancer stick, the thing his ex-wife called his coffin nail, a whisper glided through his mind, *"She circles… scorned spirit… cloaked deceit…"*

He smiled to himself as he tossed the butt of his cigarette into the snow. He raised his hand and waved to an unseen being amidst the storm and fading sunlight. The other hand he slipped into his coat pocket and gripped the snub nosed thirty-eight. It only had five rounds, but they were all blessed silver bullets.

The owl witch gracefully floated to a landing next to him. Her wings folded and assumed the shape of a long, oversized poncho.

"Thank you for meeting me, Tuco," He said as he tipped his fedora toward his partner.

"I have little choice. Given our agreement." She replied, "Why am I here again?"

"A young girl is missing. She's an orphan, but her older sister is caring for her and has hired me to find her. The trail led me here." Devyn nodded toward the abandoned home they stood in front of.

Boarded over Gothic windows, it looked like the house had closed its eyes in sleep. The rhythmic swaying of the wooden screen door added to the appearance of rest despite the snowy turmoil occurring around it. The only sign of occupation was wisps of smoke coming from the chimney.

"What is the sister's name?" Tuco asked.

"It's not important." He replied.

"Isn't it?"

For some reason, he couldn't remember her name. She contacted him and met him at his office. She gave him a picture of her little sister, along with a favorite toy, before she paid in cash and left. He remembered being given a name, but he couldn't recall it.

"It's not important to you. Unless you want to give me your real name." Devyn said.

"Tuco, Tuco…" the whispers chimed.

She smirked at him. "You will not trick me into giving you that type of power over me. Although I would like you to stop calling me Tuco."

"I can't go around calling you Owl Witch or La Lechuza in front of people. Now, can I?"

She only shrugged.

"Well then Tuco, it will remain until you give me something better."

"We'll discuss a different name later."

Both the man and the beast stood briefly in the swirling snow.

"How does any of this relate to me?" she asked. Her avian features of larger than usual eyes, white hair, sharp nose, and chin gave her a unique and complex beauty.

"Given your reputation for having a taste for young children, I wanted to find out if this," he motioned back towards the building, "had anything to do with you."

"We have an agreement, one that I'm not fond of, but still an agreement." She answered, "You don't hunt me or draw the attention of other hunters to me, and I do not follow my inclinations or desires to harvest the children of this town."

"She Lies…" the whispers hissed.

"Although," she continued, "I believe if you would lighten that up, you'd find that my purpose, my desires to take out the disobedient children would benefit this city. Remove the criminal element before it's a problem. I think everyone would benefit from a little culling."

"Now we will not get into this again Tuco." Devyn said, "You don't feed on children in my city. Period or I'm coming after you. And you know I can find you no matter where you hide."

"True, it's a gift given to you that makes life difficult for the rest of us. However, we have an agreement."

"In the meantime, you can aid me in finding out what happened to the child," Devyn replied. "My leads bring me to this location, and my gift tells me you've been here as well."

"True. I spent time on the upper floor, but only to rest. I've never fed here except for the occasional stray."

"Half-truths…"

"You're talking about animals, right?" Devyn asked, "Or are you pulling a devious technicality on me? Calling an orphaned child a stray."

Tuco shot Devyn a wicked grin. "I adhere to my agreements as they're intended."

"Dire Fact…"

Devyn realized he had a stranglehold on the grip of the revolver. The whispers reinforced his doubts about the pacts he'd been making. It began well, but he could feel things getting out of his control.

"Let's just go in and see what's up," Devyn said.

With that, the two unlikely partners strode up the snow-covered walkway to the porch.

The two paused on the porch. Devyn held the screen door open and reached for the doorknob when he heard the faint sounds of a stringed

instrument, like a guitar, over the whistling wind. Freezing in place, he settled his mind so he could hear the whispers, but they were silent. Despite the cold, sweat formed between his shoulders and his skin crawled at the unaccustomed silence.

Pulling his hand back from the doorknob, he looked at Tuco, confident that her owl hearing would hear the music. To his surprise, he saw puzzled concern written across her face.

All he could utter was, "Do you know," before Tuco flung open the door.

Upon stepping inside, they encountered a small living room. The only light in the room came from the open door and a small fire in the fireplace.

To the right of the fireplace, sitting in a tattered wingback chair, was an old dark-skinned man wearing a red trimmed black vest and pants. Wispy white hair curled out from under the black top hat that perched atop his head at an angle. Across his lap was a three-string cigar box guitar.

"Why are you here?" Tuco asked as she folded her arms across her chest.

"Come now, child," the man replied, "is that anyway to address me?"

"Beg your pardon, Papa Legba," Tuco said as she gave a deep curtsy. "You are far from your bayou home. Surely the touch of frost and snow doesn't agree with your warm blood."

"That is true, La Lechuza," he answered. "This cold certainly doesn't suit me."

"I ask again, why are you here?

Papa gestured to the opposite side of the fireplace. "This young one cried out to me."

Across the fireplace, shadows merged into a young child's shape, complete with pigtails and a black ruffled dress. The child's head turned towards Tuco. Its dark face splits to show a brutal smile, complete with pearly white teeth.

"Before she passed away, her mother showed great devotion to me and the Lwa." Papa explained, "Her sister now has embraced Hoodoo. I cannot allow what you did to this child to go unanswered."

Tuco's form shifted in a flash. Gone was her human visage and before them stood the Owl Witch in her true form. Large owl wings arced overhead, Talons erupted from her hands and feet. Her head rounded, a sharp beak replaced her nose and mouth. Feathers emerged from her body in a wave as a deafening screech pierced the space.

Devyn glimpsed runes blaze to life on a brass tube that Papa wore on one of his fingers. Papa Legba plucked the guitar on his lap and slid the metal tube down the fretboard. The strings caused a high-pitched sound to reverberate through the house.

Tuco screeched and abruptly dropped her head to the ground, covering her ears with talons from her front arms.

Shocked by the noise and the reaction from Tuco, Devyn spun towards Papa and drew the thirty-eight from his pocket. "Stop."

Papa whistled and from the depths of the fireplace burst two shadowy black hounds. They snarled and growled at Devyn.

He fired off two quick rounds at the creatures. The bullets passed through the spectral beasts, leaving only wisps of shadowy smoke trails as they exited and lodged harmlessly into the masonry of the fireplace.

The hounds cleared the room in two quick bounds. One's jaw clamped down on the hand, holding the small revolver, causing him to lose his grip on the weapon. The other slammed into his chest and knocked him to the ground.

Before Devyn could react, the one that had knocked him from his feet stepped onto his chest with both of his front legs. The weight of the animal was immense and forced the air from his lungs.

He tried to push the beast from his chest with his free arm, but his hand passed through it like he was trying to push air. The animal clamped to his arm jerked his arm, causing his head to shift, but it must have been enough because the one on his chest dropped its head to his exposed throat and clamped down as well.

Devyn expected to feel a sharp pain as the teeth pierced his skin before ripping his throat out, but the dog showed amazing restraint. The jaws clasped only hard enough to cut off the blood flow to his head. A dark tunnel formed around his vision.

Tuco continued to screech as the sound of the all too familiar twelve-bar blues chord joined the noise that filled the room. Out of the corner of his eye, he saw her attempting to force herself up while still clutching the sides of her face.

She braced her wings and legs to lunge towards Papa when another figure he hadn't seen rushed across the room, screaming something he couldn't understand and swinging what looked like a metal rod the size of a broomstick. When it struck Tuco, a sizzling sound and an avian wail of pain joined the cacophony of battle. The nauseating smell of burned feathers and flesh rolled through the room.

Tuco scurried away, still clutching her ears, trying to block the sound as Papa played on. The figure Devyn noticed was the older sister who had hired him to locate the missing child. She fiercely swung at Tuco. Screaming the same word with each strike, every blow that connected with the club caused an eruption of sparks and flames from Tuco's body.

Finally, out of apparent desperation, Tuco spun, extended her wings, and knocked the sister to the ground. With the path to the door opened, Tuco sprinted through the doorway.

The last Devyn saw of the owl witch as the dark tunnel of his vision closed in was her spreading her wings and taking flight into the snowstorm.

A searing pain and a hard pounding to his chest ripped Devyn back to consciousness. The head of what looked like a square headed nail jutted from his chest.

He found himself pinned to the floor. The spectral beasts held him there. Each one grasped a wrist in their iron-like jaws. The fireplace's burning glow was visible through the hellhounds.

"You see, Devyn," Papa Legba said as he walked back into view, holding another nail in his fingers as if he was showing Devyn something important, "this is a coffin nail."

Papa kneeled next to him and dipped the tip of the nail into the blood pooling on his chest. "In fact, it is the last nail for your coffin."

Devyn asked, struggling against the dogs, "What's happening?"

The dogs pressed meaty paws firmly onto his shoulders. After they stood, their combined weight on his upper arms held him to where he knew his struggles were in vain.

"Aren't they amazing creatures," Papa said as he passed his hand down one of the ghostly visage's back, "they are the spirits of Fila Brasileiro, a dog bred to catch and hold people like me until the master came to claim them. Now they serve me to hold you."

"You still haven't answered me," Devyn said. "What are you doing?"

"That's a most interesting question, Devyn. Do you know me?"

"Tuco called you Papa Legba. I only know of one Papa Legba, and he's a voodoo priest."

"Child, you know so much and yet so little. Despite being known by many as Papa Legba, I am far from a mere voodoo priest. I am the intermediary between mortals and the divine. I stand at the crossroads to greet those who wish to commune with the powers that be."

Papa walked over to a rickety wooden coffee table. On top of it sat an ancient-looking hourglass and a rusty hammer.

"Speaking of names," Papa continued, "Devyn is not your true first name, is it?"

"How did you know that?" Devyn asked.

"The divine speaks to me much in the same way it speaks to you. Your real name is Marthanach Devyn. Correct?"

"Yeah, I still don't understand how you could have known. I changed it years ago."

"Really child?" Papa laughed. "With all you've seen. All you know, you still don't understand. Pity. Do you know what your true name means?"

"It meant no one could pronounce it, so everyone just teased me or made up their own name for me. That's why I changed it to just Devyn as soon as I could."

"That's a shame. I recommend you look up the meaning of it. It's a powerful name and quite fitting, I would add. Did you know your parents?"

"No. Family Services said some animal killed them on the boat that brought us here from Scotland."

"Ah, and you have no family here, I suppose."

"No. And before you say ask, they couldn't find any in Scotland that would claim me, either. That's why I spent my life in the foster system until they finally just sent me to the boys' home. Now answer me. What are you doing with me?"

"To answer that question. You need to answer another of mine," he said as he placed the tips of his fingers on his own chest.

"What's your question?" Devyn said through gritted teeth.

"Do you know exactly what this is?" Papa asked as he lifted the hourglass from the table. The glass was opaque with age. The frame held the hourglass in place, formed by merging small, twisted chains into a ridged cage.

"An hourglass."

"Oh, come now, child," Papa replied, "I know you possess the gift of knowing." What some of you mortals call a sixth sense. You've used it before. Use it now. Please tell me what this is."

Devyn focused on the hourglass and took a deep breath while letting his subconscious open. He felt a wave of dread sweep over him as the whispers flooded in. Screams of a multitude of voices he didn't recognize echoed in his mind. His mind drowned in the torrent of chatter in his mind until the familiar whisper pulled him from the maelstrom.

"Lives bound. Eternal Servitude. Alive, unliving. Endlessly fragile."

"Why are you doing this?"

"Ah, so you know now," Papa said as he set the sand timer down and picked up the hammer before he walked back to where Devyn lay pinned to the ground.

With one fluid motion, Papa drove the iron coffin nail the rest of the way into Devyn's chest. Pain seared through Devyn's body as the nail pierced his heart. His breath seized in his lungs.

While Devyn's body arched and writhed in pain, Papa walked back to where the hourglass sat on the coffee table. Papa secured the second blood-dipped nail in the hourglass and then turned it over, causing the sand to pass from the upper chamber to the lower one. The pain left Devyn's body when the sand began moving.

"You see, this is the Memento Mori Hourglass. If you do not speak the old tongues, it roughly means "Remember that you must die." Here, it measures the time of twenty-four hours instead of a single hour. I have forever linked your life to it. If sand passes from the upper to the lower you will live but if it stops,"" at this Papa turned the glass on its side, stopping the flow of sand.

Pain seized Devyn's body again as his heart and lungs stopped working.

"You can live forever," Papa said, tilting the glass, "as long as the sand keeps flowing. If it breaks or doesn't get turned back over before it runs out, you'll die.

Devyn gasped and questioned, "Why did you do this?"

"Why, you ask?" Papa laughed. "The divine gave you a powerful gift, and you squandered it."

Papa motioned toward the wingback chair.

Devyn's eyes followed his direction.

In the chair sat the sisters. The ghostly younger one sat on the lap of the older.

"You were supposed to use it to protect the innocent. Instead, you used it to gain wealth and power. Your greed cost these two more than you can ever repay."

A heaviness that far outweighed the hellhounds settled on his chest.

"I planned to, shall we say, to use a permanent solution to this problem, but the Lwa wanted to give you a chance to redeem yourself."

Papa walked, sat on the coffee table, and looked between Devyn and the sisters.

"They left it to me to decide how best that could be done." He picked up the hourglass and held it in his hand. "I chose to use this." He gazed into the foggy glass for a time, "Just like a life it is fragile, if it breaks you will die, If you fail to turn it over before the sand runs out you will die," with that he turned the hourglass on its side again.

Devyn felt the pain of death again.

Papa glanced back at the sisters and turned it back, so the sand flowed. "You have ample lives to make amends for this."

He rose and crossed to where the sisters sat in the chair and handed the hourglass to the older sister. The sister nodded as she took it. Then she handed the bar to Papa.

Papa crossed back to where Devyn lay pinned to the ground by the spectral hounds.

"My friend will hold on to the hourglass until you hunt down and dispatch her sister's murderer."

The child's spirit slipped down. Getting to their feet, the sisters made their way to Devyn's location.

The young ghost stroked the side of his face. Searing cold pain streaked across his skin with her touch.

"You have twenty-four hours unless she is merciful and flips the hourglass for you." Papa said.

The older sister stooped and backhanded him across the mouth. Then spit on his face.

Papa chuckled, "I wouldn't hold your breath for that."

Hand in hand, the sisters walked into the night.

Papa kicked the revolver across the floor to Devyn. "Blessed silver bullets will harm La Lechuza," Papa said and then tossed the metal rod to the ground at his feet, "this will serve you better. It's iron. Say her true name when you strike her."

"A lot of help that'll do," Devyn growled. "I don't know her true name."

Papa picked up his guitar from the floor. After taking another look at Devyn, he crossed the living room to leave as well.

Briefly, he paused at the door, glancing over his shoulder at Devyn. "The gift revealed its true name to you." You just didn't know how to speak it. It's spelled Tuco, but the "C" sounds like a "K". Put an emphasis on the "K" sound when you speak it.""

With that, Papa whistled. He and the hounds all evaporated in tendrils of smoke.

After Devyn regained his strength and wits, he stumbled out of the abandoned house. The night had settled completely, and the storm had somewhat diminished.

Using the iron rod as a walking stick, Devyn made his way to his Cadillac. Opening the door, he slid his gifted weapon into the backseat before climbing into the front and closing the door.

With shaking hands, he tapped out a cigarette and lit it. He took a slow drag on the cancer stick. The burning in his lungs was comforting. Soon the nicotine invaded his bloodstream, further calming his nerves.

"Okay, now I can think," he said to himself, "I've got twenty-four hours to find Tuco before my time literally runs out." He chuckled at his own joke and sighed.

"It looked like she got hurt bad, so she'll either need to feed or rest. But which one?"

"Boys' home…" the whispers answered.

"Enough said," he replied to the whispers as he started the car and shifted it into drive. Its wheels spun for a moment and the rear end veered to the side before the tires found traction on the snow-covered street.

It took time to maneuver down the slick streets, but eventually he made it to the all too familiar boys' treatment home. On the way, the storm had subsided, all the clouds parted to reveal a clear sky. The sky showed the earliest signs of the coming dawn.

The home had changed names and owners more times than he could remember over the years. Now he believed that someone had given the home the name the Home Of Divine Mercy, but he couldn't be sure. He spent most of his childhood within its walls. Years have passed since he called it home.

The bedroom windows were dark behind the bars that covered them. The treatment workers, or I guess they're called house parents now, were turning on lights in the living room and kitchen. He could see their silhouettes projected against the cheap mini blinds.

Devyn pulled his iron bar from the back seat, took one last drag from his smoke before throwing it to the ground and grinding it out under his wing tip. Grasping the unconventional weapon in both hands, he stalked around the perimeter.

It'd been years since he lived here, but he doubted things had changed much. They installed the bars when he lived there. Probably his frequent escapes in the middle of the night may have been what prompted them to install them. Kids always think they've invented new ways to get away with stuff, but in truth, they just stumble across what others had already done.

The laundry room was the only window without secure bars, and he knew it. He knew the house parents were unable to see the last two bedrooms, as they were in the living room and kitchen. Those were the best rooms to sneak into the laundry room from, and then it was easy to slip outside. If he knew La Lechuza, she would be there waiting for one to stumble into her waiting talons.

As he rounded the corner, he saw the familiar feminine form looming outside the last bedroom window before reaching the laundry room window. Under the brightening morning sky, he could see that the sides of her head, where her ears were, were charred from either the vicious beating the sister had given her or perhaps from the music Papa played. Regardless, the fact that she hadn't seemed to hear him approach suggested that her ability to hear had been significantly damaged.

"That's right honey, Mimi is here. I've come to take you away, but you need to do exactly what I say, and you must hurry." Through the window, the owl witch said. "Go to the next room with the white machines. I've got a window open there. Crawl through the window and I'll take you away from here, but you need to hurry. There's not much time."

Devyn slid up next to her as she spoke to the child through the window. When she straightened, he swung the iron bar across, connecting with the side of her head. The bar struck, but it lacked any sparks or flames upon contact.

Staggering from the blow, she screeched at him. He reared back to swing again, but she backhanded him, sending him sprawling into the snow.

Talons erupted from her hands as she dove on to him, pinning him to the snowbank. The claws pierced his chest.

"Fool!" she screeched. "I don't know why I feared confronting you for so long. You do not know how to destroy me after all."

She raked one of her talons through his chest. To both of their surprise, no blood flowed. The wounds smoothly joined and stitched themselves back together like a zipper.

"How?" she questioned.

"I guess we all have our secrets." He replied while drawing the thirty-eight from his pocket and buried it in her side before pulling the trigger.

Her scream pierced the night as she rolled off him. In one fluid motion, she changed shape into the owl monstrosity that was her true form. Spreading her wings, she leaped into the air and took flight.

Devyn watched as she rose in the air. When the sun crested the horizon, she raised her arm to shield her face from the rays of light. She dove lower and landed on a boarded-up window of an abandoned church steeple. As the sun's rays raced towards her, she ripped the boards from the window and dove into the church just before the full brilliance of the sun reached her perch.

"I don't think that's going to be a pleasant resting place for her today." Devyn said to himself as he reloaded his revolver with more blessed bullets.

After picking up his iron bar from the snow, he made his way back to his car. As he pulled away from the curb and headed towards the church, he saw two city police cruisers pull up to the boys' treatment home. Even though the storm had ended, the slick streets were going to slow down emergency crews all over town.

Devyn stood in front of the abandoned church. The iron bar levered over his shoulder and his trusty revolver tucked in his pocket.

"Here goes nothing." He said as he walked up the stairs to the main entrance.

He grasped the doorknob to the church and found it locked. Not surprising or a big deal. Years of running the streets and escaping treatment facilities taught him a few things. After leaning his bar against the door frame, he pulled his lock pick set from an inside coat pocket. Using the L-shaped tensioner to apply pressure to the lock cylinder. Then he slid the triangle tipped rake into the cylinder and raked it back and forth across the top until he felt the pins stick into their home positions and the cylinder rotated open flawlessly. The bolt retracted and the door lock clicked, causing the door to swing open.

Upon looking inside, he noticed several intact stained-glass windows. Despite being boarded over, daylight still pierced the shadows through the gaps between the boards.

Feathers rustled overhead. Looking up, he could see he was standing under the choir loft. He recalled that the church steeple loomed above the main entrance. The entrance he had just walked through. He assumed the belfry was in the steeple and had an access point from the choir loft over his head. It wasn't the best position for him to be in.

Devyn wasn't sure how damaged Tuco's hearing was, but he would at least try to sneak up on her. He crept over to walk along the exterior wall with the most light coming through it. Maybe the light coming from behind him would hide him from her keen eyesight.

As he moved, he could hear the click of sharp points on wood and tile from overhead. He assumed she stayed in her monstrous form and prowled him from above. He paused just under the edge of the choir loft, where it joined the exterior wall. Taking the briefest of moments to allow his mind to clear.

"Look up!" the whispers echoed.

He snapped his eyes up in time for them to lock with the owl witch. Tuco hung by the talons on her feet. Her wings were spread partially. She braced one arm against the lower wall of the choir loft, while the other arm was pulled back with claws spread, ready to swing at his head.

His sudden appearance must have startled her because, for a split second, she froze in her attack. That gave him the chance he needed.

Shouting, "TuCo!" he swung the iron rod for the hand that braced her against the wall.

When the weapon connected with the witch, her hand burst into flames. She screamed as she flung herself from the loft, her attempt to take flight awkward and sluggish.

Leaping into the air, he swung again, repeating, "TuCo!"

This time he connected it with a wing that dipped low on a downstroke. Flames, sparks, and a resounding crack erupted from the wing as she crashed into one of the stained-glass windows, shattering it and dislodging the boards from the opening. Glorious sunlight bathed her. The feathers that covered her body smoldered before they ignited in tiny flames.

She screeched as she shielded her eyes from the purifying rays. Desperately, she writhed and tried to roll away from the window.

"Now! Pin her now!"

Devyn clenched his weapon. The rod was going to be a blunt spear, and bravely charged towards the witch. Before she cleared the beams of light, he yelled, "TuCo!" one last time and buried the iron rod through her chest and into the weakened wooden floor of the church. Flames and sparks spewed from her chest and cascaded down around them, igniting the dried wood of the building.

Holding his arms over his head, Devyn raced for the exit. As he reached the door, he risked a look back toward La Lechuza. Her screams and writhing had ceased. She laid still while her entire body burned to ash. Unfortunately, it appeared that the old church would also meet the same fate in ash.

Turning to flee, his eyes encountered the older sister's dark gaze. They showed no warmth or kindness as she pushed past him and looked into the burning building. Seemingly satisfied, she turned back toward Devyn and pulled the hourglass from a satchel that hung at her waist. She held it up and peered at something in the foggy glass.

"She thinks of breaking it."

"Please, don't." Devyn begged.

"Why shouldn't I?"

"I know what I did is unforgivable, but I want to do what I can to keep what happened to your sister from happening to anyone else. This," he gestured towards the artifact in her hand, "provides a means for me to do that. I'll be able to help more innocents for longer."

She considered his request for what he thought lasted a lifetime before handing the relic to him.

"I'll be watching," she said as she turned from him, "don't make me regret this."

"Thank you," he said, "Wait a minute. You hired me, but for the life of me, I can't remember your name. What is it?"

She turned and shot him the first smile he'd seen from her. It caused his heart to stutter.

"You will not trick me into giving you that type of power over me." She answered before turning and boldly walked down the street.

Walking to his car, he held the hourglass up and studied its cloudy glass and intricate chain wrapped frame as he said, "I have the time to learn your name, my lady."

The End

The Foxtrot Protocol

By K. Anders

I closed my eyes for three slow breaths to clear the fog of fatigue. At the end of the last breath, glowing crosshairs came to rest on Jerry's forehead. I'd already repeated the ritual three times, and my finger longed to feel the crisp break of a three-pound trigger.

This Op reeked of indecision. If someone wants a mark dead, they should be sure of it before they transfer a retainer fee to my account. That was the government for you, all cash—no cajónes. Which concerned me somewhat since a life hung in the balance.

I know what you're thinking: You're an assassin Eddie, what's one life to you?

I'm gonna tell you this once, so I want you to listen real good. Who knows the value of life better than the guy who's watched the light fade from hundreds of eyes? Unlike our street rep would have you believe—most good assassins don't enjoy killing.

Not that I have any problems putting down a rabid dog—metaphorically speaking. I can't do dogs. I tried once. When my Golden got hit by a car, I couldn't bring myself to press the bang switch. Had to take her to the vet. Human-trafficking scumbags like Jerry? I'd do him for free.

"Prodigal, this is Control. Crossroads is a green—"

Jerry's head jerked violently as a thousand-grain subsonic bullet slammed into his ear. In the same instant, the opposite wall became a Jackson Pollock painting. I took another cleansing breath and let the reticle settle on the wet bar where my secondary target had disappeared.

"Control, this is Prodigal," I subvocalized into my throat mic. "The Fat Man walks alone." A moment of silence went on forever while I waited for the radio operator to pass on my new orders. Alfie—or "Big Alfie" as his associates called him—had yet to peek his head out, and every second I sat here gave his thugs another minute to close in. My Russian VKS was suppressed, but given the nature of Jerry's last moments, my location would be easily triangulated.

"Prodigal, do you have a solution?"

"Negative, Control. The Secondary is dark."

"Prodigal, we need resolution."

Normally, I wouldn't mind giving a secondary target a few minutes to get antsy and pop a head up into my sights. But I was really exposed, and unless Alfie had a heart attack, he'd already be on the horn, calling in his cavalry.

"I can give you two minutes. Then I have to exfil."

"Baron says, 'If you want paid, you bag the big guy.'"

"You gotta be kidding me."

"Direct quote."

"I gathered that, Control." I flipped my mic to off before tying a string of four-letter elegance into a knotted paragraph of obscenities, curses, and threats that would have made me an honorary Drill back at Bragg.

Another thing you really need to understand about trigger pressers is this: no matter what you've seen in the movies, we are highly underpaid for the risk we take. Kamille and I lived frugally—if you ignored Jarrod's expensive private schooling. Even with our son's education costs, we could've retired two years ago. Then President Killjoy got elected, and the bottom dropped out of the economy. Like I said, it's not like we lived extravagantly, but unless we wanted to live out our days in Backwoods Indiana patching together a hundred-year-old farmhouse—or actually learn to grow corn—I needed to work a while longer.

So, here I lay, proned out on the most cliché contract of an assassin's life: The Last One.

A month ago, Kamille and I laughed about it over a bottle of Maker's Mark, joking about the wet work tropes in Hollywood. You know the ones: the employer doesn't pay up, leaves you in the wind, or goes after everyone you love...

"Not so funny now, is it Eddie?" I grumbled.

"Prodigal?" Funny thing about the voice on the radio, it didn't seem worried at all. Like a private army of mercenaries, closing in on their guy in the field was just another day at the beach.

I flipped the mic back on. "Copy, Control, I'll give the Fat Man what he deserves." I heard Baron say 'good man' in the background and I wanted to reach across that line, grab him by the neck, and rip the cocky paper-pushing bastard's throat out with my teeth.

"Roger that, Prodigal. Standing by for confirmation."

Eye back to the glass, I waited—doing my level best to dampen the voices telling me to bail *right-fricking-now* and put this part of my life in the rear-view. The voices were easier to ignore than you might think. The

OCD part of me couldn't leave a job half-finished, and the rest of me knew it was too late to bail without a fight. So... I might as well get paid.

Too highly disciplined or too scared to move, because not an ounce of Alfie's four hundred pounds plopped out from behind the bar. I turned the VKS sideways, pulled the magazine, ejected the heavy subsonic round in the chamber, and loaded a new mag with armor-piercing bullets. At two hundred meters, this load could pierce over half an inch of steel. I'd lasered the distance at six hundred meters, but I doubted Alfie bothered to reinforce his bar.

Exhale and press. A half-inch hole with splintered edges appeared in the wet bar. A moment later, Alfie's chubby leg kicked out from its hiding place.

"Concealment is not cover, dirtbag." I put a second round into Alfie's calf, disintegrating the heavily marbled meat. My shoulder absorbed two more jolts of recoil from the 12.7 x 55mm rifle, and his other leg slumped out from behind the walnut paneling. It disappeared in a flash of pink mist, leaving an expanding pool of crimson where it used to be. With at least one major artery in each leg piping the elixir of his twisted life into Rorschach's on the polished floor, I figured he'd be worm food soon enough.

Since the rifle couldn't be traced back to me or Uncle Sam, I left it behind. Not that it would take any real brainwork to realize I came on behalf of a three-letter agency from the good ole US of A and not the FSB. Russia wouldn't waste resources on human traffickers, but deniability is the holy grail of covert-ops, and it would do Americans no good to see a Remington 700 clone live on Al Jazeera tomorrow.

I crawled away from the island fortress and the remotely detonated C4 I'd planted in the guard house near the helipad at the top of the cliff. With any luck, all the earlier evidence I'd left on the four dead guards would be incinerated in the diversion. Efficiency of action. It's a thing.

So here is where it gets a little shaky, because when that explosion went off, the shock waves dominoed through the volcanic rock and started a small avalanche on my exfil route. Rather than a nice quiet walk in the park—if a painstaking two-day slog through snake, leech, and creepy-crawly infested southeast Asian jungle could be considered a walk—my escape turned into a haphazard series of leaps, tumbles and sprints into the canopy. AK47s accentuated the importance of speed, their supersonic projectiles snapping as they whizzed over my head.

I'd prepared a few remarks to thank God for their crappy marksmanship when something punched me in the back, and I stumbled to all fours. Look, lying in the prone position for hours with ceramic plates in your rig isn't super comfy, so I opted to leave that weight in my hotel. I know what you're thinking, not real smart Eddie. And now I find myself agreeing with your assessment.

A few more cracks popped around me, but the bullets thumped into the trees or splattered thick vegetation instead of my ass.

It might have just been the adrenaline shutting down my ears, but it seemed like the jungle absorbed the din of assault rifles—muting the chaos. Everything blurred together, as if I'd fallen into the impressionist world where Monet had learned to paint.

My hearing came back all at once, like a slap in the face. Chittering insects—louder than the shouting of angry henchmen—seemed to call out my position. Birds exploded upward in a brightly colored flare of betrayal. And the wet. Sweat and humidity condensed on my body like a second filmy skin. A reluctant heaviness settled into my bones, as if gravity had just multiplied by a factor of ten.

I cleared my throat of sticky phlegm and spit a wad of mucus tasting of spent gunpowder, blood, and anxiety. The instant it left my mouth, I regretted leaving a trace, but my hasty trail left shallow footprints in the soft earth, so fretting over a chunk of frothy pink saliva seemed pointless. Wits regained, I spent the next few minutes creating a false trail along the jungle's edge and then pushed deeper.

The goons decided to give chase, and it wouldn't be long before they caught up. I made the most of the little time I had looking for choke points to optimize an ambush. I'd left my sniper rifle behind because it would've slowed me down, but I still had a Krinkov in my pack and a CZ 75 on my thigh—each with three mags and a suppressor.

As good as a doorbell, another flurry of feathers let me know the Fat Man's mercenaries had decided to come calling.

"Dedicated, these sell swords," I muttered. Either their pay came from someone higher up the food chain, or the mercs took losing their principals personally. I put my money on the, well, money. You see, it's like I said—grunts like us just don't make that much. Ain't nobody risking their ass for a dead man if the checks won't cash. All that stuff about finishing the job for honor or reputation is more Hollywood bullshit. I mean, what rich dude still pays for killing the assassin after you let him get burned? None I'd ever met.

Once I thought it safe to use comms again, I'd have to let Command know a bigger fish still swam out there. But first, survival.

Ancient lava flows, probably as old as the island, had left a deep crevasse near the stream I'd been following. They made for a perfect ambush location. Stamping down the local flora in a conspicuous trail, I set a tripwire to one of my frags. Then I backtracked and made a second pair of tracks. These got concealed, leaving just enough sign for an astute tracker to pick up and set my last frag in a trap even I would have trouble finding.

Happy with the setup, I found an enormous tree for cover with a reasonably clear retreat on the opposite side. Dropping my pack, I collapsed against the thick trunk. A nickel-sized hole ventilated my ruck, but didn't pass through.

Thank you, Jesus! I was grateful for the save, but was loath to see what piece of vital gear had stopped the bullet. The Krinkov. Of course.

Bits of copper and lead fell out of a thumb shaped indentation in the short-barreled rifle's magazine well. Ruined. In another moment of stupidity, I let fly another stanza of poetic curses. I really should've written it down for posterity—it really was that good. But also loud, and I heard voices perk up when the goons zeroed in on my direction. Sure, that's what I'd wanted, but I'd also been hoping for a few more minutes to get ready.

If Kamille were here, she'd have said something about my big mouth getting me in trouble, and I'd remind her what else I could do with it. That's how we always ended up in bed two minutes after any argument started. Our therapist said it "fostered poor communication habits," but we'd made it to full retirement in this man's Army, through another dime on the outside with countless deployments, and we were still together— so what does he know?

Using the dense jungle floor as concealment, I slithered into position overlooking the kill zone of my crafty little ambush. I did a quick press-check to make sure the CZ had a round in the chamber. No reason it shouldn't, but a professional always double checks his gear. You should write that down. It'll be on the test later.

The mercenaries' clumsy charge through the undergrowth slowed to the occasional crunch of rotted deadwood, so I assumed they must have found the clues I'd left for them. Curiosity tempted me to peek around the tree and watch the fireworks, but I reminded myself that patience is considered virtuous for a reason.

The explosion never came, but the yelling arrived right on cue. Their AK47s open up like the opening day of deer season in rural Indiana, but none of their fire came anywhere near my position. It seemed like the goons were sending it all back down the trail the way we'd come. That's when the screams started in earnest.

I broke down and peeked, just in time to see a young girl sneaking into my kill zone. She had long dark hair and Asian features—all but hidden by a green hooded cloak. Notice I didn't say 'foliage' or 'OD.' Kamille wanted to break me of using Army colors to describe everything, so I settled on Forest Green even though it shimmered like high-tech reactive camo.

The girl ignored the obvious trap, instead creeping straight up the incline into my sights. In less time than it takes to spell "what the hell have I done?" she would trip the wire to my second frag.

"Pssst." I tried to whisper, but the warning sounded like a whistle on a freight train in my ears—even against the sound of dying men not fifty yards away.

It worked.

She looked up and gracefully stepped over the wire, offering a wry grin and a wink like she'd known where I put it the whole time.

Women.

Seconds later, she lay down next to me—looking out over the fatal funnel. Tugging at my sleeve, she pulled my attention away from the ambush zone. Two fingers pointed at her eyes, then toward the jungle followed by a motion of slitting a throat.

I nodded. I'm gonna stack 'em, alright.

Rolling onto her side, face resting on a palm, she said something that sounded Cantonese, but not enough like Cantonese for it to make sense. Either way, the dialect didn't seem right for a private island off the coast of Thailand.

"Yes. I'm going to kill them. Get down." I assumed the girl's meaning and motioned for her to put her head down. I didn't want to hurt a civie, much less a kid, but Kamille and Jarrod were at least a hundred names higher on my loyalty chain, and they needed me home. No way I'd die out here because a smartass kid couldn't sit still.

Lifted corners of a "bless your heart" smile called attention to her eyes. Pools of brown swirled with depth when she met my gaze. I had to revise my assessment—this was no child. The depth, joy, pride, mischief, and sorrow in that patronizing face reminded me of what my grandmother would call "an old soul."

"Get down," I said again—this time in Cantonese.

She raised an eyebrow in recognition. "*Something*-dead-*something*-follow me." She hopped to her feet and delved deeper into the jungle, motioning for me to join her.

On the teams, I'd been a Southeast Asia expert and spoke five languages pretty well. Cantonese? Not one of them. But I had passing skills—could say more than I understood—enough to know her dialect wasn't what they used in Beijing. I stayed put; glad she chose to leave before the enemy arrived.

She started in again when a blood-curdling scream reached a climax, then stopped abruptly—its echo moving inexorably onward like the ghost of a voice departing its shell of flesh.

"Already dead," the girl said—slow and loud—as if I were deaf. Or dumb.

I flinched at the clamor and waved her off. "Go!"

She signaled me again to follow. "Catch." She patted her chest. "Follow. Catch." Sweeping her hand back the way I'd come, she repeated, "Already dead. You. Come. Now."

If the enemy were all KIA, my original exfil plan might still be viable. I might even be able to sneak around the beach house fortress, dig up some intel about the higher-ups, and present it to Baron for a well-deserved bonus.

As if to laugh at me, a baying roar of something large and sure to have sharp teeth lifted over the canopy and three more answered its call. On second thought...

I told you so, embedded itself in her face with a smirk so powerful it instantly transcended our language barrier.

"Fine." But no way was I leaving live ordnance lying around. Thailand didn't need a trail of Uncle Sam's Blessings for kids to wander into. Understanding, she disarmed the second trap herself—so easily I wondered if she'd watched me set it up.

Deeper into the dense forest, we dove. The girl shimmied through bamboo and leapt over fallen tree trunks. I'd lose sight of her as she scouted ahead, then she'd silently reappear at my side with a big smile and pat me on the back like a champion horse. All this, and her leather boots never left so much as a dent in the soft earth.

Her cloak blended into the shadows, shimmering in the light as if changing to match—which I figured had to be the light playing tricks on my brain. Just like how the deeper we got, the brighter the flowers seemed to be. And how the whole place took on a soft glow like a fog in the morning—just before it melted away. I began to feel like I'd wandered into some kind of fairytale—the girl, a phantom, leading me to a doom of eternal sleep or some equally unpleasant fate.

Whatever she had in mind, her timing was impeccable. I'd made up my mind to turn around and take my chances with the mystery beasts when she announced our arrival and disappeared into the bush.

Except for the complete lack of sound, the clearing didn't seem any different from the rest of the last thirty-minute hike. No structures or evidence of a village spoiled the haven. My hand wandered to the butt of my pistol; the cold grip of lethality somehow comforting against the warm utopian setting.

My thoughts turned to Kamille and Jarrod. Financially, they'd be fine. I had a significant life insurance policy, but I knew Kamille would never forgive herself for giving me the green light.

Jarrod wouldn't blame himself though. He'd blame me. My son didn't know exactly what I did for a living, but as kids do, he knew dad did something dangerous and worried about me during deployments. Every time my wheels touched down, he asked me to get a new job. "As soon as I can," I'd reply. "Someone has to keep the lights on." Then I'd tussle his hair, and we'd both laugh, but neither one of us felt any better about my chances.

It's weird what you think about when it's all over, but I'm glad I thought about family. If anything separated those who killed for good or evil in the eyes of God, I think, in the end, maybe it came down to whether you were thinking about yourself or the people you loved when you got deep-sixed.

The girl stepped out of nowhere into my grill and all at once the world opened to me like a fog had been lifted. Brightly colored birds broke through the utter silence like shattering a stained glass window. Coming to rest on a nearby limb, they chirped at the girl as if they expected an answer.

Grinning widely, she whistled back.

Purple flowers as big as my face grew on vines, spiraling upward around enormous trees so coated in a velvet yellow moss you could hardly make out the pure white bark. At my knees, giant leaves swayed in the fragrant breeze like placid waves, glistening where the sun broke through the canopy to envelope the grove in gentle glowing light.

Dumbfounded, I looked to the girl, wondering if I should touch her—just to be sure this was real.

She grinned mischievously, and pointed skyward, following her finger with those too-wise-for-her-age eyes.

Above us, a ring of children stood on platforms hundreds of feet in the air. The narrow planks were connected by bridges, not much more than tightropes. Beyond the circle, cloth tents that might be silk reflected light and took the breeze—billowing like sails. The tents would have blown away except for slits cut out like ports in a shooting blind allowing the wind to pass.

Bewildered, I asked, "What is this place?"

"Home."

"Where are the adults? The parents?" I had a sinking feeling, I knew. These were kids who managed to escape from the traffickers and found each other in a sort of Peter Pan orphanage.

The girl lowered the hood of her cloak. When she did, long, pointed ears unfolded and wriggled with newfound freedom. "We are the parents, Child of Man."

I was getting used to being wrong.

If you expected the evening to pass like I'd been found by tiny talking bears living in an elaborate tree village and declared to be their god, you'd be mistaken. The day passed to starless night in solemn discussion.

At first, I had a hard time taking them seriously since their council looked more like a class of third graders than elders at least twice my age. I kept expecting to wake up and find I'd been captured and shot up with some psychedelic drugs. I've seen some crazy stuff outside the wire, but never in a million years did I expect to write an After-Action Report that read like a JRR Tolkien novel.

"He is a man—like those who steal our children. He cannot be trusted," the elf called Weaves With Metal said for what had to be the fiftieth time.

He opposed my presence here more strongly than any of the others, so I'd named him Blowhard. He took another drink of the sweet Elven wine we'd all been downing by the liter.

"Wa'an killed the slavers in the big fortress," my guide said… again. "I believe he will help us retrieve our children, should we ask."

She'd named me Wa'an after I told them my name was "Princess." Kamille called me that when I behaved with deliberate belligerence. For some reason, the crafty elf didn't believe me. Eventually, Catch As Catch Can gave up trying to wheedle out my real name and settled on Wa'an, which means "stubborn" in Cantonese. The moniker is probably her own version of "Princess."

In return, I named her Foxtrot after my FUBAR protocol, which meant I made it up as I went. As erstwhile prisoners do, I offered my help to Foxtrot in a plea to win my freedom. In an effort to seem trustworthy, I told them I'd get their kids back and make the bad guys pay. They didn't initially understand what it meant to go "Old Testament," but I eventually got the point across.

"He has the Old Blood," Foxtrot said. "There is still honor in him. How else could he come to The Land?"

"Thank you?"

Foxtrot spent the next half hour regaling the council—most likely for my benefit—with the story of how the elven children were led outside The Land by some elf-guy the called "Betrayer of Kin"—not his original name and not particularly creative in my opinion—and how he stole their kids into captivity with deceitful magic.

Apparently, only elves, some other things I'd never heard of—and didn't seem to have a translation for—and the very rare human could find this place, tucked away, hidden from outsiders by ancient spells. Foxtrot had been scouting the border when I'd stumbled in. She'd followed me until The Land said—her words, not mine—to approach the stranger and beseech his aid.

It sounded like bullshit to me, but the rest of the audience nodded like talking to The Land was an actual thing.

"If he did not have the Old Blood, if he were not worthy, would the Land not make it known? Would the—she said something-like-tigers?—let him live?"

My grandmother, the old soul, came from China, but after two generations of breeding with Americans, I was as Heinz 57 as the next Joe and looked like a well-tanned, dark-haired, green-eyed westerner. Still, Grams had been old-school, so maybe she'd gifted me some of this Old Blood to go with my daily Confucianism. If she did, and that's why those roaring things in the jungle didn't tear me apart, I owed the old lady one more debt.

I couldn't say when the meeting adjourned—but judging from my inability to keep my eyes open—I'd say... wee hours. Unlike my previous employers, the elves came to a unanimous and summary conclusion: I needed to cap the SOBs in The Outside, including The Banished—if I had the chance—and rescue the slaves. Pretty standard contract, really. Except, I did the job to avoid being eaten by tigers instead of cash. With those pleasant thoughts bouncing around in my skull, I crashed.

I woke up the next day with a headache to beat the band. A brass band. With lots of bass drums and cymbals. The little village rested blessedly, if not surprisingly, quiet. Birds sang softly, and I thanked the god of hangovers that the elves didn't keep a rooster. I don't know why it surprised me, but the others lay passed out on padded mats. I could appreciate a people who knew how to sleep-in properly.

I should have said "the others except Foxtrot." I could hear her lilting voice floating on the wind, tugging at me, calling me to her side. I walked the rope bridges—carefully holding on to the hand supports—until I saw her. Foxtrot brushed an enormous tiger—grooming it like you would a horse. I lost my shit and slipped—ending up like a piece of bait dangling over a bear trap a hundred feet in the air.

Sabretooth canines extended half a foot beneath the tiger's yawning maw. Its opal eyes never blinked as I clung to the rope for dear life. I didn't dare look away—even while Foxtrot got me back to firm footing.

"Wa'an, meet Leaps Gracefully." She handed me the brush and the tiger's eyes lost a bit of their tight distrust.

"Seems like Eats a Man Whole might have been a better name," I said sardonically.

The tiger snorted.

"Did he just laugh?"

"I think he likes you," she said, sounding relieved. As if meeting the magnificent creature had been the final test of my worthiness. A test that might have prematurely ended my last job as a culinary masterpiece.

I have to admit, it was a different way to vet your operators. Uncle Sam had two questions: Can and will you put bullets in bad guys? Yes? Welcome to the team!

Foxtrot handed me a lightweight leather saddle that strapped like a dog harness around the tiger's front legs. It stretched longer than the one she'd brought for herself—complete with an extra seat at the back. She saw me look at the smaller one and shrugged. "In case he didn't like you."

Lovely. "Can I drive?"

"Have you ever ridden a Gliding—that was the word I'd missed earlier—Tiger?"

I almost said, "Yes. Of course. Grew up on one." Just kidding. I did say that.

"I'm almost tempted to let you try." Foxtrot leapt easily into the saddle and held out a hand to help me board.

Ah, the irony.

Grace collapsed under my weight. Then hopped up and snorted in laughter.

"A fine joke," Foxtrot told the tiger, winking at me and patting his head. "Fly."

"Wait... What?"

Before I could say more, the tiger shoved off the platform into the air. Its legs spread out, stretching flaps of paper-thin skin like a flying squirrel. We caught wind and the gliding tiger earned its name. It floated on eddies of air around the canopy of trees standing hundreds of feet tall. Foxtrot guided the flight with commands and nudges until we landed a thousand yards away.

"Well, what do you think of him?"

"I have two words," I said. "Need."

Grace snorted again.

"So, the roaring you warned me about earlier?"

Foxtrot grinned sheepishly. "Leaps Gracefully. And his sisters."

"I thought as much," I said, shaking my head. I'd been played by the clever elf, but as much as I wanted to, I couldn't say 'no' to rescuing those kids. Kamille would never forgive me if I had a chance to save them and chose not to. No way could I keep this adventure under wraps. Whether she believed me or not? Different story.

"We'll drop you at the edge of The Outside," Foxtrot said. "You'll be on your own from there. I'm too old to leave The Land. I would not survive long enough to be of assistance."

"What do I do with the kids?" I asked—startled at the realization she planned to dump me off as soon as the tiger could get to the edge of the jungle.

"Bring them to the place where you entered the wood. I doubt if The Land will let you in a second time."

I felt my heart sink. I had no real intention of coming back for long, maybe only to show this place to my wife and son. How else could anyone believe me?

"I'll need my gear," I said. "What's left of it."

Foxtrot unzipped a small saddle bag and pulled out my pack. "I added food for your journey."

Don't ask me how my gear fit in the tiny space, I had no idea. Her other bag held my chest rig—complete with pistol and frags. Last, she pulled out my Krinkov. The short-barreled AK shone like new with a blue luminescence that swirled in the matte-black finish.

"Weaves With Metal fixed your weapon and added a charm. I don't know what it does; he wouldn't say."

"Tell him, 'Thank you,'" I said, admiring the handiwork. "And I apologize for calling him a Blowhard."

"Wa'an…" I could feel the air settle—as if the grove knew her heart and set the stage. The conversation had turned serious.

"Go ahead," I said, willing to answer whatever she asked.

"Why do The Outsiders take our children?"

My heart broke and the throbbing in my head I'd almost forgotten came back with a vengeance. "Probably," I said, loath to continue, "to mule drugs and—"

Foxtrot looked as if she might collapse under the grief, so I said no more. The truth haunted my eyes, confirming what she'd been afraid to accept.

"I promise," I choked out. "I will bring them back to you."

My body begged for quarter. The pounding in my head, now a dull ache behind scratchy eyes, made it hard to think. Rubbery legs made it hard to stand and fingers losing their dexterity made it hard to perform even simple tasks like dropping ceramic plates into a concealed plate carrier. Across the room, my king-sized bed in Bangkok's Hotel Indigo sucked at me like a vacuum—pulling me toward luxurious sleep.

But I had things to do, like call Kamille.

"Baby, it's good to hear your voice." We caught up on the mundane things a listener would expect to hear. Jarrod did well on a test and that sort of thing. "Oh hey, did Chuck pay me back for the bus fare?"

"I already spent it, sugar." She used our code phrase for 'the money is being laundered and hopefully becoming electronically untouchable to Uncle Sam,' my employer, who—too frequently—seemed to believe "he who giveth may taketh away at a whim."

For my part, I told her I'd finished the official job but couldn't leave yet. Not out of the woods. None of this could be said out loud lest I wake up dead. Such is the life.

We had the money. I could walk away right now. Forget about enchantments and elves. Go back to The World. Curl up in my own bed with Kamille. Work our own magic; make Jarrod lie awake wondering if his parents were gonna break through the upstairs floor of the old farmhouse.

But for the way Foxtrot's despair became hope when I'd promised to help.

My muscles ached as I stretched a clean black polo over my armor. I shoved a holstered CZP07 down the front of my pants and slung a beat-up leather ruck containing my shimmering Krinkov and a first aid kit over my shoulder.

Foxtrot gave me an address where the elves—it still felt weird to say—maintained a predictable presence on the mainland. Unfortunately, the contact could only be reliably found at night—which meant now, because I really didn't want to wait another day and have Baron begin to wonder why I hadn't come home. Handlers could be prickly if they even suspected a hitter had gone freelance.

Asiatique pulsed with life. The riverfront district was half mall, half street market, and half festival. I know that's too many halves, but listen, just because I can weaponize math, doesn't mean I'm good at it. Aromas of

Thai food, fireworks, perfumes, and sweat mixed together in savory harmony supporting a melody of commerce.

Vendors hawked, shoppers bought, and tourists gawked. Anything you wanted, needed, or craved could be acquired in this nightly ritual. I needed a performer at the famed Thai puppet show. I followed directions to the Joe Louis Theater and went in. On the stage, it took three puppeteers to employ a single four-foot puppet. Except for one of the troupe, who somehow managed to operate a large buffalo-hide ogre by himself.

When I got close enough, I saw why. Despite otherwise blending in as a human teenager, he had the age-old eyes I'd seen in Foxtrot and the Council of Elders. Elven dexterity, magic, or both made that puppet dance.

I stayed for the show, scoping out the theater for exits and finally hiding out backstage. When it finally closed, I followed the elf home and gave a street kid 500 Baht to deliver a message for me.

Fifteen minutes later, the two of us sized each other up over tea at a local dive. I looked enough like a native that we didn't stand out. He spoke Central Thai, one of my best dialects, but I spoke Laotian, which sounded close enough for him to understand. I played the part of a tourist to give any unwelcome listeners a reason for all the questions I asked about the layout of the city and its local flavor. I especially didn't want to look more military, police, or worse—a rival criminal enterprise looking for new territory—than I already did. Men accustomed to violence stand out. We move differently, act differently. Hell, even the way we survey our surroundings—casually taking note of anything which could help or hinder our purpose—is a giveaway to a fellow predator.

Voice Like a Quiet Grove insisted I call him by his adopted name, Sunan. I stuck with Wa'an.

"Listen, Wa'an," he moved his finger on the tourist map from one location to another, telling me about the city—what to see, what to avoid. "You just can't see everything in one week. Bangkok is over 1500 square kilometers. I'm telling you, Wat Pho is too good to miss!"

I felt the weight of his ancient eyes come to rest on my face and looked up from the map. Sunan's brow wrinkled in earnest concern as his finger tapped the King Power Mahanakhon building.

"It's your city," I said with a wicked smile. "Just point me in the right direction."

Just before first light, I quietly closed the secret underground door to King Power behind me. Stealth takes time. Bloodless stealth takes more. Without knowing how much of the temporal commodity remained, I'd already been a little louder and left more bodies in my wake than I'd prefer.

Most henchmen were just dudes trying to make a living—ignorant of their boss's nefarious dealings. But each corpse contained a wealth of evidence—just waiting for the right investigator to come along.

The keycard I took off the rent-a-cop opened an inside door where I found two more like him. Chest, chest, face and the first one dropped. Judging by the way my suppressed rounds reacted, the dead man had armor on, so my CZ found the second guard's nose to start with.

"You don't have to die," I said in Thai with as much guttural Russian accent as I could drip. "Open the door." My pistol didn't move as I nodded at the palm reader.

This level of henchman ranked above the last. Smarter. More plugged in. He knew what lay on the other side of the checkpoint and what awaited him if he let me by. I should probably just have shot him, and we both knew it. Still, I'm a step too far away for him to go hands on, too close for my bullet to miss his brain box.

It's like this, drawing a handgun and getting a good hit in under a second puts you in the top one-percent of trained gunslingers. It's possible this guy belonged to that group, but doubtful. With two pounds of pressure already applied to my trigger, it would take me 0.15 seconds to interrupt his cerebral function.

His only hope lay in mercy. Mine, or God's. He didn't strike me as a praying man.

The guard raised his hands and turned to look straight into the camera as he put one sweaty grabber on the scanner. It beeped and turned green—unlocking the heavy steel door.

"Good choice." I tossed him a pair of flex cuffs.

Bound, blindfolded, and gagged, I left him alive. Depending on what I found ahead, I might need him again.

I hoped my scrambler did its job on the camera. Even so, from here on out I could expect to earn my progress with blood, so I donned my chest rig and chambered a round in my short-barreled rifle. The guard's pistols found homes in my backpack, and I slung one of the AK 47s over my shoulder. All the rifle mags got stuffed in pouches and pockets.

I felt a lot more like the door kicker I'd been in Fallujah than the assassin I'd become. It felt... cleaner. But more dangerous. Like the first time Kamille kissed me after I told her I loved her.

My heart started to race, palms moistened in my tactical gloves. I'd almost died in Iraq doing this kind of work. After a month in a VA and six in rehab, I'd switched my Army MOS to "private contractor." It'd been a long ten years since I felt this unsettled about an op.

Not that toe tagging the top baddies one at a time is any safer, maybe just that the chances of sudden death seemed less... random. I don't know. It seemed like the right path for me at the time. The money also seemed a lot more important back then, than it did right now.

I used my space and angles to clear the next few rooms down the hall. Storage. Janitorial. More storage. Nothing a major corporation wouldn't have in its sublevels. Then I came to a sharp left turn in the corridor. It might have been the increasing smell of chemical sterility, the chill of air-conditioning on overdrive, or my highly developed sense of self-preservation and distrust of hospitals, but something turned my pre-battle jitters into full-on shakes.

In the old days, we had to bring bulky fiber-optics to show what my cell phone could see sticking out a scant half-inch. Two guards stood fifty-feet down the passage in front of a vault door. These were not rent-a-cops. These were real soldiers wearing full-body armor.

Getting close, Eddie. I pulled the pin on a frag and counted down. At the last second, I tossed the grenade around the corner and waited for the boom. The explosion reverberated through the floor—so loud in the enclosed space that my ears rang—even with electronic hearing protection.

Turning the corner muzzle first, I came face to face with one of the soldiers. He seemed much larger up close and didn't appear to be injured at all. Punching me square in the face, he knocked me reeling back into the hall. The extra AK went skidding away, but my suppressed Krinkov stayed slung around me. It only took a second to bring it to bear.

The huge armored merc walked toward me just as his buddy turned the corner.

Neither one is injured? With no time to worry about wasted grenades, I squeezed the fore-end of my rifle igniting the flashlight. The hot spot hit him dead center, so I pulled the trigger expecting a full-auto burst at ten rounds per second.

Click.

Remember when I told you a pro always checks? The whole movie of how I got here flashed through my head—ending with being so damn tired and amped up I'd forgotten to chamber a round when I pulled the glowing blue gun out my pack.

The huge dude—I assumed it was a dude, because I still haven't seen its face under the jet-black helmet faceplate—walked toward me with a little too much swing in the hips to be a six-and-half-foot colossus of a man. As if the guard could read my mind, their visor swooshed into the helmet.

A narrow green face grinned, tongue flicking out between rows of pointed teeth. Yellow eyes—slitted like a cat's—laughed at my impotence. A pug nose, right side pierced with a large ring, sniffed as if the creature wondered what I'd taste like.

"Oh, frag me…"

The beast caught me staring and kicked me square in the chest. I went sprawling ten-feet down the hall. At the end of the slide, I had the presence of mind to rack the bolt, turning the Krinkov from a high-tech club into a gun.

The monster didn't seem the least bit fazed as I shouldered the now loaded weapon. Its buddy joined it, opened its own mask and did the same sniffing thing with its nose. Judging by the second one, I'd been right about the first being female. This one towered over her, had a flatter face, meaner eyes, and a ridge of external bone running along its cheeks and jaw.

I hastily developed a plan to send half the thirty-round mag into the female and the rest into the big one. Since they didn't seem bothered by my gun, I assumed their armor must be impervious to bullets. I lifted the reticle to its face, but before I could pull the trigger, her visor slammed down and—I swear to God—she laughed.

I sent a half-second burst of hate, anyway. What else could I do?

Bullets slammed off her helmet, ricocheting past, as the armor deflected the stream of copper-coated lead.

"Raaaaaah!" I pinned the trigger against its guard, determined to empty the whole mag into her head. She stepped toward me, but her graceful gait was robotic and stiff. I kept shooting. The helmet frosted over like an arctic wind had blown against wet metal. Her visor cracked and split. The next flurry of bullets bucked through her skull, shards of bone exploding outward like icy shrapnel.

"What the—"

The male charged. If he hit me, his giant maul would shatter the meat inside my ceramic plates like hitting a walnut with a brick.

I swung the rifle in his direction and fired.

Ping, ping, ping, shunk.

The bolt locked open, gun dry. We both looked at the Krinkov swirling with blue runes. He tried to take another step, but Weaves With Metal's ice magic froze his suit and he staggered forward—trying to force the heavy battle armor to move against its will.

A second later, I slammed the bolt closed on a fresh mag, and three seconds after that his chest exploded out his back in spikes of icy innards.

I shook with adrenaline, staring at the beasts and the damage I'd done with my better-than-ever shorty. Usually, the silencer would be red-hot after two mags on full-auto, but a crystalized lace of frost kept it cool.

One look at the next door and I knew my gruesome task with these two had just begun. I loaded another AK magazine and let the Krinkov hang on its sling.

I'd need both hands to use my knife.

Almost too small to hold an amber monster eye to each monitor— deliberately placed six feet apart—I almost fell from the precariously balanced chairs, but I got it done. I nearly dropped the bloody orbs in disgust when I thought better of it. Baron may be interested in something like this, and what caught Baron's interest—he usually paid for. I wrapped the eyes in a bandana and stowed them in my pack.

The vault door finally finished groaning open, and I burst into a laboratory straight outta Hell.

A console of computers glowed and whizzed softly in the center of the large room. Cables reached out from a central stainless-steel tank toward four oversized beds like an evil brain stretching its tendrils. Two of the beds were empty. The others were occupied by another pair of the huge alien monsters. They wore nothing except compression undergarments to make their bodies available for the cables, monitors, and IVs stretching through the tank toward at least a dozen glass canisters lining the walls.

Inside each canister a childlike form floated in swirling psychedelic fluid, mouths open in a rictus, hands against their cheeks like they'd been the models for Munch's painting of the screaming man. I'd been wrong when I told Foxtrot her children were being used for drug mules or the sex trade. But who could have expected this?

The elves were being drained of... life? Of Magic? Was there a difference? The machine sucked their energy out to fuel these monsters.

What did you get yourself into, Eddie?

I nearly jumped out of my skin when the vault door slammed shut. I'd been so stunned sick by the tortured children, I'd forgotten myself. My eyes were angry slits and my mouth twisted with rage. I turned, hoping whoever closed me inside this depraved prison deserved to die, because I really wanted to kill someone right now. Not only kill, but rip souls from corpses and drag them to Hell just to see them burn.

I yowled in frustration, leveling my weapon. "Dammit, Sunan!" I yelled. "I almost freaking killed you." Growling, I went over to pick up the sleeping male creature's maul and start smashing. My rage had to go somewhere, and I had no idea how to safely remove the elves from their tiny cells. If I couldn't kill The Betrayer, I could at least end the suffering. Foxtrot would want that.

"Tsk, tsk, tsk. I can't allow you to ruin my work." A harsh, slippery voice seemed to come from everywhere all at once.

I looked to Sunan. He couldn't stop shivering, frozen at the horror— just as I'd been. It had to be so much harder for him. These were his people, maybe even his close kin. A child of his own? A tortured look distorted his soft artist's face as he looked over the console.

"You've already killed two of my favorite orcs!" the voice continued.

Sunan set a small sword on the console and began pressing buttons. Hope filled me. He might be able to save the elven kids! Then I'd kill whoever had taunted us and—

The elf's fingers flew across the keyboards with practiced ease. As if... As if—

"Raawwwr!" The sleeping orcs came to life.

I spun, loosing icy death at the huge male as fast as the Krinkov could cycle.

It turned to ice and shattered into a thousand frozen shards of meat, bone, and blood. "Not so tough without your armor," I snarled.

I turned to engage the female, but she'd already crossed the distance and knocked my enchanted rifle away with an easy swat of a claw-like hand. She shoved me with unearthly strength, and I stumbled back—landing hard against her partner's bed.

"No thanks. I'm not—"

The she-orc leapt forward, driving a punch like a jackhammer—barely missing me but crumpling the bed with the blow. She tore a cable loose and swung it toward me, snapping it like a whip, oily purplish fluid spewing to the floor. I stumbled again—falling to the ground, my heart pumping as I scampered back, looking for anything I could use as a weapon.

The Krinkov taunted me from three paces away.

I looked at the orc, calculating my chances. She sneered when our eyes met, flicking her head toward the rifle, daring me to try.

I drew a leg underneath myself, preparing to lunge.

She took a step toward my salvation and stopped. Raising an eyebrow at me, she ran her tongue over short, pointed teeth and licked her lips.

This is a game to her. I brought in my other leg.

She took another step.

I made to dive for the rifle, and so did she. Feint successful, I drew my pistol, lined the front sight up with her ribs, and pressed. It took an entire magazine of hollow point rounds for her to fall, but the shock on her face covered the price of admission in spades.

Sunan. I stood up slowly, aching everywhere as I walked toward him. Blood dripped from a wound on my right arm I hadn't noticed until now. It started to throb.

"Please," he said. "I had to. The Betrayer said he would kill them if I didn't help. I couldn't risk—"

I knocked him out cold with a left hook to the jaw. "How do these damn controls work?" I muttered. Probably should have asked that *before* I hit him.

A slow clap erupted from a now open door on the opposite side of the room. The ironic applause came from an oversized elf. Holy hulks, Batman, this guy must have taken the magic juice to get huge too. No wonder none of Foxtrot's people had seen him in years; no one could hide with a body like that. Whatever else happened, I had to kill him and destroy this place. If anyone ever found out how to replicate the lab, the elves would never see another day of peace.

"I see you have ice magic," he said, voice still echoing around the room from strategically placed speakers. "I've always preferred fire, myself."

"The psychos always do," I retorted, cracking my neck. I deliberately avoided looking at my pistol on the console as I waited for him to walk inside ten yards—the distance I knew I could hit him square in the heart without pausing to aim. If he could create fire the way my rifle made ice, I'd only have one chance.

He walked too slow. I had too much time to think about the shot and began to sag into post-adrenaline fatigue. Not to mention I hadn't really slept in two days.

I should just surrender, and everything will be—Wait, what? No! Those weren't my thoughts; the Betrayer was using his magic to screw with me. I reached for the CZ.

He'd seen it coming and blasted the pistol away with a tiny ball of flame. It sizzled on the ground, metal frame warped by the heat.

"Step away from the table, boy."

He seemed afraid of something I could do with the system controls, but I had no idea what. I held my hands up the same way he did, mimicking the way he'd moved just before he burned my gun out of my hand. I knew the ice magic came from my enchanted short-barreled rifle, but maybe he didn't realize I could cast no spells of my own.

Comply to buy time. I remembered my training, circling away from the control center, back toward the dead orcs and the true source of my magic.

The Betrayer chanted angrily, motioning his hands like a conductor—driving his orchestra into crescendo. On cue, tendrils of writhing flame sprouted from the dead goliath charing his massive body and gagging me with rancid smoke.

I cast a desperate, furtive glance toward my rifle and the wizard finally realized my intent. The gig was up so I launched myself into a full sprint toward the Krinkov. Unless I wanted to leave Kamille without a husband and Jarrod without a father, I had to get to my enchanted gun.

A second flame burst out of the female. It split into tentacles, each questing toward me like heads of a flaming hydra.

This is gonna hurt.

I dove—gritting my teeth in anticipation of the suck. The pain bit worse than expected. Flailing flame shot toward me. Cracking like a whip, it wrapped my ankle, sizzling and searing. The lick of orange agony circled my left calf, growing upward toward my knee. It sucked tight, not burning through and amputating my leg, but instead jerking me backward toward its fiery core.

My hands grasped madly for purchase, but the floor was slick with blood and melted ice. I kicked my right foot at the blazing lasso. A mistake. The rope of fire sprouted a new tendril, encircling my other leg. Already in agony, I hardly registered the new torment, but the smell of roasting flesh sent my brain into full panic mode.

The Krinkov, once inches away, grew further from my reach as The Betrayer's spell pulled me inexorably toward the orc's body, crackling and hissing as it fried.

Kamille's face appeared in my thoughts, the concern in her eyes as we said goodbye at the airport. The vague uncertainty—ever-present in my line of work—usually a dull ache behind my eyes throbbed. "Don't worry," I'd said. "Those tropes are just Hollywood bullshit. It's just another job."

"I know. Give 'em hell Eddie. I'm sure they deserve it."

And then some, I thought bitterly. I'd go to my grave confident the guys I toe-tagged in this op had it coming. I pictured my family and let go. I couldn't focus on getting free and keeping their faces in my mind—and more than anything I wanted my final thoughts to be of them.

Then the cinching fire at my legs slackened. It took a few seconds for me to register the change. And Sunan's voice—screaming at me to get up.

The Betrayer's focus switched in an instant. A burst of flame shot toward Sunan, but the inferno spread around him—as if striking an invisible dome.

I scrambled to my knees, pushing toward my enchanted rifle. The Betrayer screeched at Sunan in their odd Cantonese dialect. I didn't catch what he said, but I couldn't mistake the meaning. He. Was. Pissed. I barely heard the mechanical grating against my heart pounding in my ears.

The paradigm had changed.

Flames sprayed from The Betrayer toward the elven puppeteer. Whatever magic Sunan used to hold back the heat had almost burned out, but he kept his eyes on the console—using his last moments to get right with his kin.

My eyes focused on the back of The Betrayer's head through the red dot on my recovered rifle. Blood splattered the glass, but the dot still glowed.

My heart slowed, finger caressing the trigger—taking in the slack.

I sent a burst of fire through the silenced carbine. The Betrayer's head snapped forward, but his spells persisted. I reassessed and emptied the rest of the magazine into his torso. Without armor, the rounds zipped through skin and organs, freezing his body as they tore apart his flesh. Unlike the orcs, the heavy bullets passed straight through his unarmored chest—coating the wall behind him in crimson-stained ice crystals.

Adrenaline rush over, my pain kicked back in. Wobbling knees about to give way, I dropped onto the remaining bed.

"Wa'an!" Sunan yelled for me. But his musical voice faded like mist as my head hit the orc's pillow.

I jostled awake when the puddle jumper's landing gear touched down at Fort Wayne International Airport. The flights weren't bad, but I'd been so exhausted I wouldn't have known the difference. I half expected to find I'd dreamed the whole thing and about to start the job in Thailand.

Except for the jade figurine Foxtrot gave me—squeezed tightly in my hand.

Vague recollections of stealing a van, loading unconscious elves in the back, and speeding away to the sound of bleating police sirens were less convincing than the searing heat still present in my legs.

Between the elven wine—and the hallucinogens they fed me to control my pain—I remember the reunion with Foxtrot more like a fever dream than a memory. I recall asking if the kids would be ok and the reassuring smile on her face and long ears lilting gracefully as she nodded. Also, arguing with Weaves With Metal over who the enchanted Krinkov belonged to. I think it ended up in my luggage, but I wouldn't know for sure until I opened the Pelican case.

Fingering the jade figurine as I walked toward the luggage carousel, I longed for the good old days when Kamille could meet me at the gate with a deep kiss—promising a more intimate greeting behind closed doors.

Jarrod came running the moment I stepped through the security gate and nearly took me off my feet. My legs were getting stronger by the day but still unsteady. Foxtrot's healer said I'd regain full function, but he didn't know if the scars and burning sensation would ever go away—despite closing my wounds with a mix of poultices and elven magic.

When he let go, I gave Jarrod the luminescent green statue of a gliding tiger complete with a surprisingly good likeness of Foxtrot and yours truly perched on its back.

For Kamille, I had nothing. Only a smile built of joy, relief, and regret. If I never again have to witness an evil like the one I almost died trying to end, I could die a happy man. On the other hand, I'm not sure how long I can sit on my ass knowing people like The Betrayer are still out there, needing someone like me to put a bullet in their face.

"It's over," I said. "I'm done. For good."

She tried to smile back, but her eyes called me out. If Baron calls again, no matter how hard the job, no matter the risk of losing everything, I'm going back in. I have to.

The End

The Genuine Article

By: Eric Nirschel

Most cults are of the opinion that they're 'Indiana Jones and the Temple of Doom'. In reality, a vast majority are more like 'Manos: The Hands of Fate'.

Sure, they talk a good game. They've got their robes and sacrificial daggers; hidden pockets sewn into their sleeves for pouches of White Claudia, or Powder of Leng, or even vials of Black Honey. They may even have heard the slithering voice or the buzzing tree, but through it all, talk is just talk, and any berk can rattle his bone box.

When you've been playing the cosmic game as long as I have (too long), you get a feel for the genuine article. To save you the trouble: No, you don't know what I mean.

I'm sure you're thinking of the cutters ready to bleed for the old ones; the barmy bastards with names like 'Shammash-Ho' and 'Ik'lthan' on their lips, swearing loyalty unto the eternity box, writing vowels to the infinite. You are, and you'd be dead wrong. They're your talkers, your rattling bones. They mean every word they say; they're ready to bleed for the game, martyrs for the cause… and that's how you know they're imposters.

Don't follow?

You're probably thinking that the big sleep is the ultimate sacrifice, but you'd be wrong there, too.

See, in the game, you learn things. Comes with the trade. Whether you're a poor bastard who found himself on the wrong side of some ancient evil's little black book, nicked the wrong statue, or you're a lifer like me, you pick things up. Even if you don't want to.

It's not idle gossip, Jack, it's cigarette burns on your brain. You touch the infinite, and brother, it touches you right back. You see things. You *know* things.

It's easy to get yourself killed when you know the consequences of victory. When winning means the schizophrenic green sky opens up with the tentacles of a blind idiot god, or that the red message runs rivers from the gibbering mouths of stars set to devour the world, artillery and noisy death looks real fuckin' neato by comparison.

No, the genuine article is all about playing long ball. They don't throw their lives away because they know their lives are a gift in service of some higher power. They have a job to do, and the idea of not doing it is as foreign to them as the job itself is to you.

They're bloody halos. More often than not; we all are.

Like I said, the infinite doesn't let anyone slink away unchanged. The longer you're in, the more of it gets in you. You can't reason with them. They speak in ciphers and think in discordant dreams that would burn the soul from the uninitiated. They're not the players making the moves in the cosmic game, but they sure as hell aren't pawns. They keep the secrets and make damn sure the rest of us keep ours.

You want to know what's going on in my head, Jack? Why am I penning this little ditty if I know so much? It's because I just don't give a fuck anymore.

Maybe it's the drink, maybe it's the rage, but, brother, I can't be bothered to play the game by their rules now. Here's the dark of it: They cut me. They cut me deep.

See, I'm one of them. Or, I was, anyhow.

My family's name doesn't mean much these days. They're all locked away snuggly in the boneyard, now, and I haven't used it in years.

There's a lot of bad blood in that name and in me. I'm not just some basher from upstate, Jack, I'm the next of kin in a long, powerful line from the witch-cults of Europe. Sweden, Ireland, and America. Home is where the cult is.

They brought ancient rites with them and raised me to be one of their priests; a herald of the nameless days. I sang that song longer than I care to admit, and I cut some dark deals with ancient, evil things, but I dusted out the dark days when I met her.

It all sounds romantic and noir, but it's true.

Those were the bad old days. The eye for an eye days. I didn't let her in on the joke… I didn't want her voice on that bloody laugh track. Didn't want her to get a taste. She was my white spot in the blackness and I wasn't about to let the unknowable come to know her.

I was brutal. I was merciless. I killed, and brother, let me tell you, being on the other side of the exchange and tearing it all down felt better than any bargain I'd ever struck with any writhing god-thing. I burned it all down.

We skipped town. Three years. Best three years of my life. I was a damn fool. I should have known it wouldn't be that easy.

There's a stink that sticks to you. Once you cut a deal with the dreamers, it never leaves you, and others can smell it. They'll seek you out, either to convert you or kill you. There's no room for competition on the game board. New city, new cult. I wasn't about to pick up that dusty hymnal again. I'd done my time in the choir, sang that song too many times.

I bowed out. I left. They wanted me, and if they came after me, fine. As long as she wasn't in the way, I'd kill and I'd fight and I'd bleed until the stars burned out and I'd love every red second of it, knowing she was safe.

Only she wasn't.

They made her call me on the telephone. Made me listen when they cut into her. Four-hundred and sixty-eight miles between us, and all I could do was scream back. I listened while they worked. They worked, and they worked. There are fates worse than death in this whirling clusterfuck of a universe, and they made sure I knew she was getting one. I listened while she screamed, voice going plural as it came from a hundred new mouths. I knew there would be nothing to bury.

They went after her to get to me. They didn't want to chase me. They knew I'd go back, and I did.

So, here I am. Writing this in a liquor stained notebook in a shitty hotel room. I still haven't really gotten to the meat, though, have I? Why am I actually writing this all down? Maybe I don't really know. Maybe it's just to keep me from going insane, but I don't think so. I'm well past that now.

This is a big 'fuck you' to the secret keepers. I'm on the warpath now. They cut me, Jack, and I'm gonna cut back. I'm gonna throw the curtains wide and shine some light on this black spot, and it's gonna burn like a thousand suns. Show me that seedy underbelly, and I'll rip your fucking guts out. It's the bad old days all over again, and I'm gonna burn it right the fuck down.

I got my first real lead in a familiar place. Back in the day, the dark days, I'd had help. Underserved help.

The beau nasties from the Order of the Mysterium were dapper and charming, real upper-crust types, but each one of them was a black cat, hard-boiled and dark as midnight when the whispers got loud. They'd all been burned by the game, one way or another, and they circled the edges of the playing field, scooping up the wreckage, putting it together and puzzling it out.

They called themselves Curators; collectors of unspeakable things and unknowable secrets. Their retirement plan was shit, but giving the high-hat to the powers that be can be reward enough in and of itself.

When I—*we*—made our break, they anted up and pitched in when no one else would, gunpowder by the barrel and blood by the gallon. Molotov cocktails were our favorite drink. They didn't owe me a fucking thing. The debt was mine to pay, and still, they put some more on my tab. Hair of the Dog.

Every big city has its traffic; somebody's always on the lam and somebody's always chasing. Stare at the whispers long enough, though, and the cant comes through. It's all patterns. It looks like chaos to outsiders, but once you get the knack for it, you can pick up the late night reruns.

Those were your regular customers. Political office and corporate power structures are the perfect soft spot for lamprey-mouthed skags to worm their way in so they can smooth the comings and goings of less desirable business. The cult that gets its people into positions of power is the one that sticks around the longest; not all currency is coin.

Scribblers are usually low-level package boys in practice; they cook books, write favorable legislation, and close cases that might be best left open. Usually they're nothing more than bacon-faced diggers bought with promises of power and wealth. Weak motives for weak people. Easy to track, easy to squeeze.

The mark was an overfed Leatherhead and his big six; once I gave the muscle the bum's rush, though, the toady'd beat his gums trying to get on my good side. A fine darb of a gesture, but once I had what I needed, he was out with the trash, too. Joke's on you, Jack. I don't have a good side. This berk was posing as a mild-mannered antiquarian… quaint, but effective… and his goon was posing as the hired help, moving armoires every once in a blue moon to keep up appearances.

Antique joints are common in the business; nobody pays mind to oddball shit getting dropped off at all hours. A dusty old shop full of unwanted garbage rarely gets their shipments pinched. You could wheel in a full-blown sarcophagus stolen from some ancient temple and it would look on the level to most cutters on the street. Giant obsidian mirror inscribed with Antediluvian script? How *gauche*.

I waited until after dark to make my move; long coat, wide-brimmed hat, revolver in a shoulder holster, a knife on my hip, and a storm brewing on the edge of a jagged black city skyline. Hard-boiled, Jack. I wasn't planning on burning powder just yet. I wasn't playing button man on this one, and I wasn't planning on coming away clean.

The wind picked up, and the snow came down. The city was a tomb. White ribbon whips lashing lean asphalt scars. It was a night for bad tempers; chopper squads and hatchet men. On nights like these, the flatfoots and meat-wagons took their time and laid low. Tonight was a damn good night to get messy.

The joint was anything but Ritzy; a little hole in the wall on a tiny side street off a major one; the kind of shindig a berk would walk past a thousand times and never notice. That was the speed, Jack. Hide in plain sight. They knew who I was the second my shadow hit the doorstep. The muscle was up and moving before I'd cleared the door.

He was a heavy, squat grubber with pale, sickly skin and big, unwieldy looking shoulders. I pinned his make almost instantly; Congolese beast-man. The long arms and thin, almost slit lips would have been enough, even without the pallor. I could tell his black hair was dyed; pale silver was bleeding through like strips of ugly moonlight at the base of his clumsy part.

The Congolese ape-men dropped out of the game on a major scale more than a hundred years back after the N'bangu put the fade on them in a major scrap. Now the white apes were just hanging on, but sometimes they'd hire out their palookas as muscle to the other players, usually for something unsavory in return. They were fond of women, and it wasn't surprising that the ones they got kept pulling the Dutch act. You break it; you bought it.

He came at me high, big ham of a fist arcing wide and slow. I went low, dropping left to whip a spear hand into his groin, right where the leg met that hip socket. He lumbered, stumbling forward, but caught himself on the door jamb.

The ape-men made great brawlers, but nimble they were not. He wheeled, both lumbering arms on the backswing. I ducked again, and he blew down a china cabinet full of knick knacks for his trouble. The big six was made of stern stuff above the waist, but his legs were weaker, shorter. Mine were longer.

I snapped a kick out, the blade of my heavy booted foot slamming into the side of the ape's knee; I got a sick, wet celery crunch, and he roared like only an animal could. I jumped back before he could grab me on the way down; the only thing worse than his mitts were his teeth: long, thick, and yellow. The apes would bite if they got the chance, and if they got ahold of you, they'd turn you lank-sleeve with those chompers. The rest was applesauce, heavy boots and an ugly mug. The kind of party the meat wagon lives for.

The mark was too leather headed to run. The fat bastard was all wet, blubbering and whining even before I put the screws on him. He was quick to beat his gums. After I zotzed his bodyguard, he knew damn right well he wasn't making the break. He spilled the beans, and then I sent him to the boneyard with his pet ape. I choked the life out of the barmy fuck, and he died with a sputter that sounded like a Bronx cheer. I wasn't feeling generous.

My next big gig was across town. I still had no name to put on the face, but I knew where they were, and that was enough. It didn't matter what fancy title they gave themselves. They ran a club on the other side of town; a real dive joint full of dopers and drop men. Didn't matter how many hatchets they had in their deck, though. They were all on the chopping block.

Place was supposed to be a flophouse for jingle-brained artist types playing the mark. It fronted as a high-class goth club. Some kind of vampire bar. Fucking sanguinarians. Posers. Place was barely a step above a creep joint.

I could have taken a hack, but I let my dew beaters run the show. Subway wasn't far and the time I spent hoofing it would give my esteemed hosts time to get wind of their man ending up with a Chicago overcoat. I wanted them to be ready when the hammer fell. I wanted their look-outs and cutters just as much as I wanted the big cheese. When I started pumping lead, I didn't intend to stop.

The walk gave me time to think.

The dark city was a confessional and I could spill my guts to the shadows without the risk of judgement. If I'd been judged, it happened a long time ago.

Did it feel good to be back in? Yeah, I guess it did. I was a pushover, a poor sap stuck in the old times. It was easy to get back in the swing. Maybe too easy. A skid rogue like me, taking on the world? Yeah, maybe. Maybe I'd just had too much giggle water and was on track for a messy end. Maybe this was their plan, too. Get me riled. Get me careless. Get me mad.

Well, Jack, I aim to please. No time to find their angle. I'm a trigger man.

He'd been behind me for three blocks, collar turned up like Bela Lugosi in black and white. Couldn't see his face, but it was obvious he was a torpedo even without giving him the up-and-down. Remember what I said, Jack, it leaves a stink on you. You see them; they see you. He was a player.

I banked left, getaway-sticks taking me down into the catacomb beneath the city where the subway cars played ferryman and the river Styx smelled like stale piss. Cheerless smiles and empty eyes stared back from the far wall of the tunnel, wallet gods demanding you get down on your prayer bones and make offerings in paper and plastic. My tail wasn't far behind; that cold on the back of my neck wasn't just the snow.

He got close enough to whiff the eel juice on my breath before he made his move. He must've taken me for a mark, or maybe the mud-pipe had burned out too many of the bulbs upstairs. Either way, it was amateur hour at the laugh house, and the bartender was Mickey Finn. He asked me for a cigarette, so I lit him up.

I ducked just in time to avoid a swift backhand from the man in the high collar. In the buzz of the fluorescents, I got the make on his face, gaunt and terrible. The whites of his eyes were red, the iris night-black and shark-dead. The veins on his face stood out in regal purple, and there was blood on his lips. If the mug hadn't told the story, the whip-lash of black ichor from his hand would have. The lancing black mauler hit the pillar behind me with a whip crack and a shower of shattered tile.

These cutters were hitting on all eight, sending a Seeker of N'kai after me. They didn't come cheap. Ol' red eyes was only part of the problem. The slimy black thing slipping back up his sleeve was the other half of a duo, a formless parasite that fed on what was left of the man. When a seeker spoke, he spoke for two.

There was no Chinese angle for the formless spawn; no silver bullet or iron stake. You didn't put the fade on the spawn, you just cut on it until it took the hint. The berk it was riding, though, was another matter. He'd die if you hit him hard enough.

Another whip of acid black. I rolled, and it wrapped around the pillar, tearing more tile away and hurling it off into the dismal. I skinned my slug thrower and threw lead, thunder and heat in the cold dark. The seeker staggered, three large bores ventilating his chest cavity. Already I could see the onyx slime spilling into the holes, knitting them back together with new, putrid flesh. Spawn didn't let their hosts die easy.

The seeker listed to one side, tendrils leaping from his sleeve and pant leg to dance along the yellow and brown stained concrete, tiny clawed hands and gnashing teeth growing out of the slithering oil as it snaked toward me. As it grew closer, the tiny mitts of the thing grew into real grubbers, full sized arms out to wring my neck. I still had the bulge on this dropper… I knew more about it than it knew about me. My heater wasn't the only ace I had in the hole. The pouch was only the size of a silver dollar, but you know what they say, Jack, big things, little packages. I fished it from my pocket and threw it. It hit the concrete less than a foot ahead of the creeping death, a grey-red cloud of Nergal's rot growing wings. The primordial flesh bubbled and sizzled, and the black thread recoiled. I squeezed the trigger. Another three shots tore apart the knee and thigh of the seeker's left leg, and he made to topple, stumbling as the formless spawn convulsed, swirling into place to keep him standing on a rubbery tentacle appendage in place of a leg. I reloaded.

The hatchet man finally seemed to catch on that his pet ooze wasn't cutting the mustard, and his flippers made for his pockets. He was packing heat, sure as I was, but he hadn't counted on needing it. I aimed high.

The left half of his head disappeared in a haze of red, his bone box split near in half as his chompers rained to the floor. Tar leapt up the side of his neck as the spawn tried to hold what was left of the berk's skull together. He staggered backward, the tentacle desperate to compensate now for the missing leg and the lifeless other. I burned the other five slugs into his chest and the seeker of N'kai fell backward, sprawled onto the tracks. And me without a mustache to twirl.

I watched the patsy on the tracks for a long while through a haze of cigarette smoke. The spawn didn't make a move. Its disguise was dusted, and it knew I was no rube. The slimy bastards might not be the sharpest tacks, but this one got burned, and against me it just didn't rate. I watched it slink off into a storm drain just before the train made a messy entrance. One more twisted shape in the tunnels, one more nameless thing down in the dark. Think it's bad when they float down there, Jack? Wait 'till you peep what crawls. The train hissed to a crimson stop, doors creaking open on rusty hinges. All aboard, Jack, next stop, retribution. Make sure you got your ticket ready.

By the time I hit my stop, my flask was dry up and the cold was creeping in. Ducky. In the big game, you can always tell when something is coming. There's a song on high that nobody knows the words to. It sticks like a shiv in your gut and rolls into a long, bloody crescendo just before the bodies start to cool. The dreamers love a good nightmare. It's got a nice beat and you can dance to it. You can always tell when they're coming, and it makes your blood freeze. That's ok, though, Jack. It was a cold night, and I was colder than anyone.

Topside, the street was an empty trench from a war no one was fighting. Spent beer bottles craned their necks up through the drifting snow, dead soldiers hinting at things to come. The club was down two blocks on the right, and the red light from the grimy dime store novelty bulbs turned the snow into B-movie blood takes. The club thought it was hot shit, but it was just your typical dive. Leatherhead fringers who thought they knew the score would show up to dip the bill and pretend they ran with the nameless. For most of them, it was all a game, just playtime for bored salarymen and dormy housewives desperate to crush out on the 9-to-5. Some of them even took it a step further, making something of a hokey religion out of the vampire bit. They had no idea who was putting the Chinese squeeze on the club. '999' was emblazoned in black and gold above the door. A real gashouse.

I walked right in, playing it Bogart. My revolver was heavy under my arm, and the knife on my belt was just itching for a Harlem sunset. If there was a silver lining, the fog I was about to lay down would match the carpet; everything was the color of blood, already. I didn't even get to belly up to the gin mill before they had my make. There were only a few cutters in the joint, all done up in glad rags, there to play the part and keep up appearances. It was easy to tell they were in on the joke; under those cheap, frilled shirts and velvet blazers they'd be covered in tattoos done with sacred inks or carvings etched into their flesh on the wheels of Galgalim. One or two had the hazy-eyed look of Souvara addicts.

They drew on me, but not guns. I guess they took me for a pushover, or maybe they just liked the wet work. Whatever the thinking, they went for blades. They wanted to dance, and I was no stick-in-the-mud.

I pitched backward, away from the bar and toward one of the large, round tables with its faux black marble finish. Bottles of giggle water went sprawling, glass and cheap liquor sailing into a crimson night. A candle went wide, a small, sputtering flame leaping across a patch of battered carpet before fizzling out. I kept moving, the first goon trying to turn my skull into a canoe, but all he caught was tabletop. When he went high, and again I went low, leaning back on my heel and swinging upward with the butt of my gun. I made sweet chin-music, the sick crunch of shattering chompers gliding up my arm like a greasy commendation of a job well done. The mook reeled, rusty blood spilling over his pursed lips. Sorry, Mac, the bank's closed. I followed through, launching forward off my back heel, and burying my shiv in a souvara stained eye.

The next cutter tried to hook around the first, and caught me against the table, so I went over, diving like I was Chow Yun-Fat. I rolled, and made a knee just in time for him to reach me. This one was faster than I expected, faster than he should have been. No time to play the sheik. I made a clumsy, wide swing with my knife and caught him across the stomach, and he spilled the groceries, all sausage links and sweet breads.

The bartender blew the lid off the whole thing, coming up from behind the bar with a coach gun like John Wayne in a cow-town saloon, ready to drill me full of double-ought buck. Ventilation opened in my coat high on the shoulder and the wall behind me did its best impression of a black hole. My first big break since that nightmare phone call, dodging Chicago lightning only because the thunder god in question was a shitty shot. Joke's on you, Jack. Even with a shotgun, you still have to aim. I brought up my cannon, and I didn't miss.

The gunfire got their attention and a chopper squad dumped through a back-room door. They weren't in the mood to bump gums. They opened up, and I started singing in the rain, dancing between the drops. We burned enough powder to own stock, but they were no button-men. Something hot and sanguine engulfed my left arm, and my legs went out from under me like a stagehand with a crook was getting desperate to drop the curtain. There was a bullet in my gut, but that didn't stop me. They might have seen what I've seen, they might have done what I've done, but they weren't even one tenth as pissed off as I was. The storm subsided as fast as it rolled in. Five ugly, dark thunderclouds piled up near a door marked 'employees only.'

Somewhere in the distance, I could hear the siren song of the flatfoots finally rousing from their slumber. There was no way to know for sure if they were making tracks to my front door, but the timing was too conspicuous not to think so. It was easy to ignore a gunshot here or there, but when a pile of wooden kimonos all show up at once, even the doughiest desk jockey has to admit a cold night might just be heating up.

Things could have been going better. Sure, my kill death ratio was solid, but the job wasn't done. It didn't matter how many floaters turned up in the river tomorrow if the big cheese wasn't one of them, and I was. These low-level goons weren't the ones who ordered the hit. They were just dewdroppers and drugstore cowboys looking for an edge. I could mop them up later.

I was behind the Eightball, just like always, bleeding bad and laying beside a dead bartender, sipping on bottom shelf whiskey because that was all my blood-sticky mitts could reach. Your brain does funny things, Jack, when you lose a lot of blood. You get pensive and thoughtful. You think about the past, and my past was a flophouse for inner demons. Stare into that fog long enough and it turns dark, every time, until you find your memories are just a gaping hole. You can run from them, but they follow you, and eventually your only choice is to turn and face it. Looking into that hole wasn't much different from staring down the barrel of a gun and waiting for the flash. The flash of a smile you were never going to see again.

I must have started to pass out. The sirens were closer, a daemonic choir singing manic-depressive Christmas carols. If I didn't move, I was never going to. The vial had been sewn into the lining of my coat for the better part of six years, waiting for a chance to prove itself. Well, showtime, Jack.

If there was one thing about playing on the great game board is that, once you're on, it's impossible to get off. I found out the hard way. You couldn't hide. The great unknown has a lot of eyes, and you could only play the joker so long before you got shuffled back into the deck. It was time to play my hand.

The incantation came back to me like an old nursery rhyme, words not meant for human tongues gliding off mine with practiced ease. The room changed, the red light dimming like the color was bleeding from the world and the walls folding inward on themselves, trying to play the pyramid act. My eyes filled black, and the whispers choked my ears. Somewhere inside me, a door opened, and I summoned something through it. If I let it, it would wear my skin like a cheap suit. The slugs buried in me hit the carpet with wet thuds as my new roommate tried to repair the damage. I could feel things moving under my skin, and the whispers became wild screams inside my skull. The holes in me started to plug up with flesh that wasn't mine. I'd almost conjured it; the possession was almost complete. I drank the vial.

Tikkoun elixir was almost impossible to find, and I had no way of knowing if this vial was the real McCoy. The real thing was worth its weight in gold and emperors would sell their own organs for the stuff. There were so many wooden nickels on the market that trying to cop a real dose was like playing the Irish lottery, and yet... The screams in my head went from being merely insane to insane with rage. The thing I'd brought through from that other dimension to ours shrieked, and I went into convulsions as it started to die, its flesh dissolving like I was a cartel man making pozole. I vomited what was left of it into a chunky black puddle on the carpet, and the color seeped back into the world. I wasn't sure if it was really dead. With sirens closing in and that thing still twitching on the rug, I got moving.

One of the droppers who'd come bursting in like Sam Spade was still breathing, groaning on the floor as he tried to hold his guts in. He wasn't fit enough to make tracks, but he was fit enough to squeeze. He talked. Big cheese lived uptown in a mansion, but he'd never been there. The look in his eyes told me he was scouring his brain for more info, trying to buy more sand for his hourglass. I wasn't selling any.

In the back room, I found all the hallmarks of a classic drug ring. Mud-pipes and Mazuma scattered between stacks of light reading featuring titles like 'De Umbrarum Regni Novem Portis', 'The Magus', and 'Codex

Seraphinianus'. In the corner, jars of White Claudia sat patiently waiting for the next berk looking for a taste of the old ways, all blood and pus and dying screams. I knew already there would be no use trying to read any of the paperwork; it was all code fit for the headshrinkers. What I needed was directions, an address, and I found it on one of a handful of envelopes. A wax seal the size of a half dollar glared at me, a red eye held firm between barred teeth, ringed with symbols that made me feel like someone was groping around inside my skull. The seal had been removed from the envelope it was on, but when I gave the wastepaper basket the third, I found one with a red stain on it, and the return address read 'Clifton Heights' and the name 'Giorlando'. The letter inside was short and to the point, and, surprisingly, in plain English, and it fit with what the mook had told me.

"He's come back, as we expected. He knocked over the shop, and you know what that means. He'll be coming to the club next. Alano, take some men and handle it personally. Suffer no competition." -G

Donovan Giorlando. Big name. He was the law in town, big cheese DA, putting the pinch on every red hot and dope pusher in the city. No shock. To put the curse on someone the way they did, they needed the hookup, and he was the man to do it.

I'd heard the name once or twice back when I lived there, before it all went from bad to worse. Giorlando was your big-wig Harvey Dent, rolling into town all gangbusters, knocking down bindle punks and underbosses with practiced bravado. I should have had his make, then, but I wasn't playing the game; wasn't keeping an eye out for the big one. Giorlando was too good, too successful, all shark toothed smiles and tough talk. A little too charismatic and well connected for an assistant DA with no roots in this town. The shoe fit, though. He was the new bloody halo in town, and he was making nasty, rubbing out anyone he saw as a threat. His mooks sniffed me out. I wasn't on the payroll, and that made me a liability.

Giorlando was no bunny. If I didn't have his head under my arm by the end of the night, it'd be curtains for me and my little crusade. He'd have every gumshoe and bruno in the tri-state on my case, and then I'd have a little accident in my cooler right before the trial. It was now or never. No time for sleep. No time for doubt.

Funny. I remembered his face the second I read the name. I'd seen it in the papers, and it floated up out of the liquor fog like a mug shot from a prohibition era newsreel. It was two rusty gears locking into place. Tick tock, Jack, time's almost up.

The house on the hill was a monolith, a stark black monument against a wicked grey sky. The trees on the grounds shuddered in the wind, bone white and dead, as icy fingers curled around their trunks. Garden lights flickered, nervous, the falling snow making like the distant pinpoints of dying suns before the slinking black ate them up. Stars devoured by the void. You are all made of stars.

I could've said the size of the mansion surprised me, but it didn't. The low-level cutters were mayflies in the grand scheme. The bigwigs, the genuine articles, they were always putting on the ritz. There were always schmoozers and highbinders looking for an edge, willing to sell their souls, and who better to offer power unending than the ancient wizard with the blood of the gods flowing in their veins. Take a sip, live forever. Forever ain't what it used to be, Jack.

Neighborhoods like these ended up enclaves of screaming madness, ready to get hot the moment the time was right. Sacrificial lambs lined up for the slaughter. A father of four would start seeing green and take a pickaxe to the wife and kids. A gold-digger would get wise about the hubs' quiff and put two in them both. Overdoses and jalopies wrapped around telephone poles. A whole neighborhood cleaned out over the weekend, just in time for new lawyers, judges, and CEOs to move into those nice, big houses, and then it'd be time to meet the neighbors and cut some deals all over again.

None of that mattered to me. I was on a bender, blood drunk and over the edge. All screaming meemies and panther piss. I'd been awake for days, ossified and running on adrenaline, eating day-old sinkers and .357 caliber slugs. I wasn't there for the rubes who bought into the cult act. They cut a deal, and they paid for it. I was there for the man in charge, the big cheese. I was there for her.

I hit the ground running as I came over the wall, using a well-manicured hedge as cover, all the while wondering if anyone could see the monkey on my back peeking over. The weight was becoming too much, and my old demons were clawing up, ready to drag me down. That was definitely the place. The crawling prayer flowed in my veins, and it was just about ready to stand straight up and scream hallelujah. Rituals had been done there. Things had been summoned. Somewhere, down below, I'd find an altar stained with something that looked like rust.

The basement storm door had been sealed with a slab of heavy steel, bolted and welded. A keen-eyed jobbie would spot the faint etchings; words scrawled in Malachim and Enochian script, and other, older tongues. The slab was meant to keep things in, not out.

I circled around to the back of the joint, barely making the dropper standing on the back porch before his head swiveled my way. I played the plant and got out of sight just in time. The mug was a heavy hitter, tailored suit and artillery slung over his shoulder. It looked military, automatic. There would be more inside, ready to chew me up like hash-house eggs. I was too close to go down. I'd have to stay quiet, play the ninja. Calculate my moves with cold precision. Revenge, best served.

The mug turned his back to the wind, to me, and fished a lighter from his pocket. The drifting snow was dry powder, no crunch. Perfect for masking footfalls. My kung fu was strong. I buried my knife in his neck, in one side, out the other like a cheap Halloween gag. Trick or Treat, Jack. I chose Treat, and liberated him of his Chicago typewriter.

Once inside the kitchen, I closed the door behind me and locked it before fishing one of the last vials from my coat. Once upon a time, I could've replaced most of them on a whim, but by then I was an outsider playing an insider's game. The vials and powders I'd used were worth a literal fortune, and there was no replacing most of them. I dribbled a portion of the liquid onto the lock, and the metal began to dissolve, melting and seizing together. Only way through that door was to knock it down. It didn't matter if I couldn't replace the stuff. No one was leaving that mansion alive.

Most of the lights were off, but that was copacetic. I'd been carrying a torch since I met her, and it hadn't burned out, yet. Another hood was just inside the dining room, spooning the bar, wearing sunglasses in the dark to hide the wrongness in his eyes. The eel-juice went down smooth with a shiv chaser. I was a poet writing in shadows and blood, rubbing out Giorlando's goons one by one, filling my pockets with spare mags and guns as I went. I found a garrote on one of them, a fine silver string to lead a man from this world to the next. Another had a blackjack; brass knuckles, poison vials. Powder of Leng and Veridian sand. Each hatchet man I put down told more of the story. Dead men tell plenty of tales, Jack. Point of fact, once the dead start talking, they don't ever shut up. I knew from experience. The swanky mansion wasn't the only hint of wealth… each of Giorlando's goons was carrying a fortune in bad medicine.

It looked like I wasn't the only basher with a beef out there in the cold that night. Upstairs, I met two more goons playing sentry in the hall, rattling their bone boxes about the latest catch. Dame was supposed to be some kind of high-class escort… not high-class enough that anyone would notice she never left, though. I put the blinds on them with a vile of viridian I'd taken from the guards downstairs. Paralysis set in right away. That meant it was pure. I wondered if they'd used some on the dame. I played blood crow on the mugs in the hall and checked on the girl. Better if I hadn't. She was dead. I could tell by the empty, accusing stare in her eyes. It had been meant for the hatchet man who'd cut on her, but it worked just as well for me. Cheap tarot cards scattered on the floor, soggy and crimson, told the story in riddles. The note on the nightstand filled in the blanks.

"Make sure to observe all the tenets. I realize time is a concern, but a ritual failed is a ritual failed, regardless of cause. Incompetence is inexcusable. Too much is at stake to allow fear of one heretic to rush our hand. The girl must be disposed of appropriately to ensure the reagent is pure. Failure is not an option, Michael." -G

There wasn't much left of her for the eternity box. Pieces were missing. Reagents and spell components for the big nasty. If they put the fade on the girl here, that meant whatever back-room gospel they were singing was happening downstairs. I closed the door and got to thinking of a different girl. There's a rule about killing…that you're not supposed to make it personal. That it clouds your judgement. Makes you angry. Well, Jack, it was personal. Real personal.

Only place left to look was the belly of the brick beast. Somewhere down in the bowels of the manor, the high priest would be waiting. Giorlando was making a move. The song on the wind was getting heated, and the words were coming through in dribs and drabs. To a regular berk, it'd be a night too quiet, when it didn't feel right to talk loud and footsteps hung in the air too long. For those with the cant, it was loud as a freight train, and the whole world was tied to the tracks.

The basement door was just like the slab of steel outside, all fancy angles and pretty curves. The mash of wild writing faint enough to need cheaters to see was there for only one reason: To keep things in the basement from coming up for a nightcap. I opened the door and went down. Down into the dark of it.

The smell hit me like a point-blank shot to the face. A fifty-caliber bolt of lightning bored straight to the soul. Incense filled the air thick enough to make my eyes burn, faint trails whispering past like waves on a spectral sea. The incense smell wasn't the one that made me gag, though. There was another smell, something sickly sweet and corrupt, that made my skin crawl.

The basement was empty, scattered crates and a few wine racks long choked with dust. An extra leaf for the dining room table played the ghost, half draped in a white sheet. It was an act, trying to convince me the bigwig had made a clean sneak. I wasn't buying it. This might be Giorlando's house, but it was my clip joint, and I had bills to pay.

The fake wine cabinet slid aside with practiced bravado, revealing a long, rough hewn tunnel and two more of Giorlando's goons. There was no way to sneak past them, and they made me the moment the cabinet started to glide. I opened up with the rifle I'd taken upstairs before they could give me the bum's rush, filling those two goons so full of daylight they could melt the ice outside. The sickly sweet smell got stronger, as red confetti splattered the walls of the tunnel and acrid smoke drowned out the incense.

The tunnel was long and claustrophobic. Somewhere behind me, up in the mansion, I heard movement, and I got my wiggle on. There was no room left for dancing through the shadows and playing the ninja. It was time for thunder. Artillery and noisy death. My time. Her time.

The tunnel opened into a circular chamber with steel grates in the floor. I didn't bother to glom the holes; I'd seen their make a hundred times and knew the jakes in that hoosegow all too well. If the poor berks down in those holes had ever been human, they weren't anymore. As I passed overhead, their wailing was a cadence punctuating the past two days with a devil's wit, all icy pitchforks and bad ends. Clawed hands and writhing tendrils craning up from their earthen prisons beneath the heavy grates...once it was over, they could have me, for all I cared.

I felt it before I saw it. The whirling, drunken brew of forbidden things and ancient powers. Sick, greasy vertigo coiled in my gut, and the dimly lit walls seemed to pull back and away, falling off into some distant void. My thoughts echoed in my ears like drums in the deep, and ahead of me, out of that inky black, a man appeared before an altar.

I didn't need an introduction to know it was Giorlando. My gut dropped like an elevator with its cables cut, and I made his face even in the gloom. His mouth was a slit full of razors, and his eyes were like hot coals. The words he spoke were not meant for the mouths of men, and the altar before him was caked with remains of sacrifice, old and new. To make matters worse, I recognized the cant.

Something wet and sticky hit my right arm, and then my left. Another on my leg, my back... black worms, like leeches, careening in from the shadows of distant places, latching onto me, trying to hold me down so more could latch on. The man in the yellow robe was calling the black, summoning writhing death to drown me. The black wasn't one substance or thing, it was many... a mountain of lamprey-mouthed parasites that as much drowned their prey as devoured it. Maybe they were servitors from a parochial god, or maybe they were just a cheap trick of cosmic geometry... whatever they were, they'd put the rub on their mark in a minute, flat. I did the only thing I could. I pumped metal.

My first couple of shots went wide, but that was ducky. What I hadn't counted on was the muzzle flash. See, in the dark, the blast from a heater will light the room up real quick, and light doesn't play nice with things you summon from places where the sun is dead and the stars winked out a million years back. The teeth chewing at my flogger backed off, and I took the opportunity to steady myself. The goose in the gold robes grabbed air, as if I was in a forgiving mood. I wasn't. He opened his gob, and I shut it for him, a bullet tearing through his lower jaw and taking most of his tongue with it. Anything he could say now would just be bumping gums. There was nothing he could offer to make up for what he took.

I'd spent a lot of time, over the past few days, thinking of something to say. Everybody's got a great tough-guy line ready to go, but when it came time to play Bruno, there wasn't anything I could say to make things right. No punctuation on the bloodbath, no lullaby before the big sleep. All I could think of was her name… so that's all I said. I pulled the trigger. The room went white, and Donovan Giorlando's nose caved in, blowing out the back of his skull. He collapsed onto his altar. I let my finger slide off the trigger.

It was done.

I thought.

Revenge is a dish best served cold, Jack, and it ain't to enhance the flavor. When you're all worked up like a dope fiend on a tear, you don't think straight. You get tunnel vision. You get careless.

When the man in the gold robes hit the altar, it was like somebody turned a corkscrew on my head, and two days of cheap liquor and cheaper lives began to flood back to the fore. I peeped at the altar, and my blood went cold.

Obsidian goblet, white chrism, crimson tome… Donny G had been summoning something when I put the fade on him. I'd felt it when I arrived, and I'd gotten so lost in the pain and the rage that I blocked it out of my mind. The priest's blood oozed across the altar, and it began to dawn on me. That was what he'd wanted.

I'd been played. They had my make from jump. The phone call, the antique shop, the notes written in plain English when everything else was written in code. The button-men and two-bit mooks eager to spill the beans, keep me on the right track. It had all been to get me to that altar. I was spending orphan paper, too drunk on righteous fury and bathtub gin to realize it had been too easy, and now sacrificial blood was filling the cracks, drawing the shapes, signing the contract.

I felt it before I saw it. Something I had never felt before, something new, illimitable. Something that had no business in this world and yet, so sickeningly familiar that I almost couldn't bear to look. I was already addicted, and I hadn't even hit the pipe yet. I turned, and I got an eye full of the red god Giorlando had been summoning, the one brought into this world through Giorlando's final sacrifice. The sacrifice that I had officiated. I'd been raised to be a priest, Jack, and now I was, again. I looked on that god and realized the shape it took. The only thing I wanted in this world. I looked and it was *her.*

Looking back, now, I can't believe I'd been such a barmy fuck not to see it. I told you, Jack, it's not about the blood and guts. The chopper squads and button men are bottom rung. The real McCoy, your genuine article? They're all about the long con, and they never, never go to the boneyard without good reason.

I'd thought I'd gotten out, all those years ago. Burned those bridges and buried those bones, but once you're on the game board, you're on it until the game is done. The pieces don't make the rules, and anybody who tells you otherwise is selling static.

It's dark now, and I'm at peace with the things I've done. The things I'm going to do. It's all applesauce. Laying here, in the dark, with her beside me, I can't help but smile. She whispers things to me, Jack, shows me the things yet to come. Can't help it, I'm dizzy with the dame. She whispers with a hundred smiling mouths. Our children will be bloody halos. Our children will be the real McCoy. They'll be the genuine article.

Stray Imp Strut

By: Kortnee Bryant

Rosie saw the imp out of the corner of her eye and hit it with the fly swatter before she'd finished turning. It was hot pink with a purple ridge on its head that looked like a mohawk. It was also oozing lime green ichor on her counter.

She sprinkled salt on the mess before scraping it into the trash can. It could dissolve into neutralized demon dust in the plastic bag where it would be easier to contain, thank you very much. Now, she had to figure out how it had gotten in.

Imps were nasty little creatures; tenacious as cockroaches, hell-bent on destruction and mischief, and just smart enough to be a pain in the ass to catch. About the size of small field mice, they looked like a cross between a gecko and a monkey, with a touch of malevolent brimstone. Most of the time, they were a shade of gray-green, so the hot pink was new.

She grabbed a cigarette from the pack she kept on top of the refrigerator and the lighter from the junk drawer and took a long enough drag to blow smoke over the top of her counter. The imps' footprints caught the smoke and she followed the trail down the side of her cabinets to an odd patch of tile just between the kitchen and dining room.

More smoke around the floor showed that it had popped into her house on that tile and run almost directly into her fly swatter.

Rosie put the cigarette out in the sink and ran water over it until it was thoroughly soggy then dropped it in the trash can after what was left of the imp. Then she sat at her kitchen table and thought. Eventually, some of those thoughts made their way onto the notepad next to the landline phone.

Her one bedroom little cottage sat on a corner lot in a rundown area of the little town she'd grown up in. Still technically on the nice side of the tracks that had long since grown over from disuse, it was in almost the direct geographic center of town. Her second husband had called it the house that love built, usually while replacing a cracked tile or suddenly broken cabinet with one given to her by a friend. Usually while they were in the middle of their own repairs, and found themselves with extra and nowhere to put it.

In fact, almost everything in her home had a twin somewhere else in town. Some of the ladies at the quarterly church bake sale sniffed at her hand-me-down house but they'd all managed to hand her a spatula, or a ladle, or a lunch box when the others weren't looking. And Rosie had kept them and used them the way they were intended and didn't take disdainful looks too seriously.

She frowned at the patch of tile for a while longer then pulled her phone over and dialed a number she'd memorized decades earlier. It rang in another kitchen in a house the same shape and size as her own and was answered after almost a dozen rings. The voice that answered it puffed and wheezed like she'd been running to get to the phone and, to be fair, she had.

"Hello? Rosie? Everything okay?" Fred, short for Alfreida, asked.

Rosie chuckled. "I'm fine. I didn't mean to panic you by using the landline. Are you busy?"

"I was just finishing up in the garden," her friend said. "Do I need to come over? I need a shower but I can be there in an hour."

"Why don't you take that shower and I'll come to you," Rosie told her. "There's something I want to see on my way."

"Alright, there's lemonade in the fridge and I made a pie yesterday. There should be some of that on the counter if you get here before I'm done."

"Sounds good, I'll see you in a bit."

They both hung up without saying goodbye or otherwise indicating that they were finished talking. Mostly because they weren't finished, they were just continuing in another location. None of her husbands had understood the way the two of them talked but most of them had simply shrugged and let them be about it.

Rosie cleaned the rest of the dried imp ichor off her counter and hung her apron on the hook her first husband had put up for her a week after they'd gotten married and moved into the house together. Before they'd gotten married, she'd sworn she wasn't ever going to wear another apron again, directly after quitting her fourth job that required her to wear one.

An incident involving a new mixer, a bag of flour, and an enthusiastic but highly inexperienced brand new housewife had resulted in the apron hook and an apron with matching oven mitts. She'd pouted at the gift for a solid minute then pulled out her grandmother's cookbook and traced the symbols for blessing and protection on it with diluted lemon juice. She'd given it to a new mother who'd needed it just after Thanksgiving that year and he bought her a new one for Christmas.

They'd been divorced for almost thirty years and he still sent her a new apron set every Christmas. The packages were always infused with love, though it had changed and matured over the years.

The latest one was white with cherries all over it. It matched her favorite red flats which coordinated with most of her wardrobe.

She checked the high-waisted capri's she'd been wearing in various cuts since high school for dirt and brushed a stray piece of lint off the short sleeve cotton button down. In nearly forty years, she'd gained an inch or two in her waist and certain spots had gotten softer than they used to be but her figure still had heads turning. It was too hot for her usual black leather jacket so she slipped the notes she'd made into her back pocket.

Her keys were hanging on a hook by the door and she set the wards while she locked the door behind her. The vines around the door grabbed at her long, silvery hair and she wove them back into the frames that let them grow without digging into the brick walls. The latest notice from the city council about her jungle of a yard found itself under her welcome mat with the last three after she made a note of the name on it.

They'd be having a talk.

Her garage door slid open with a quiet that belied its carefully decrepit appearance to reveal one of her greatest treasures.

The cherry red 1969 mustang convertible had been a gift from her third husband. He'd completely restored it from the frame up, working late and taking extra jobs to afford the parts he put so much care and effort into. Every time she slid into the driver's seat, she could feel his arms fold around her.

He still insisted on doing all the maintenance on it and she wasn't about to argue with him over it. They argued over everything else, instead.

She took the long route to Fred's house, driving down streets half-full of abandoned houses until she saw what she was looking for. Curtains fluttered in an open window and a pale face tried to hide while she looked to see what kind of car was crawling slowly up the street. The yard was overgrown and the windows dirty but the door didn't look damaged.

Whoever was behind the face that was watching her had a key.

A chill ran down Rosie's spine with the faint whiff of sulfur. Most people wouldn't have noticed more than an unpleasant odor before it was gone but this was a smell she'd never forget. And while it could have come from anywhere, she knew it had come from the no longer abandoned house.

If all they'd managed to summon were imps, they were lucky. And they wouldn't be that lucky for much longer.

Rosie turned at the end of the block and headed towards Fred's house.

Where Rosie's house was a beautiful array of wild flowers and weeds, Fred's was surrounded by long garden boxes, each carefully labeled with support stakes where appropriate. The little bit of lawn she'd left in the center was carefully manicured and a healthier shade of green than any other lawn in town.

For some reason, Rosie always had the urge to go through the plants and move the labels around. It wouldn't have mattered, Fred kept a chart with where and when she'd planted each box, but it would make her feel better to create a little chaos in her friend's world.

She parked in the driveway behind Fred's old green truck and waved at the men on the porch. Fred's husband, Tracy, was holding their youngest grandson and talking to their son-in-law, Alex. A toddler sat in the doorway and jumped up to hold open for Rosie as she walked up the stairs.

"Oh, so you're the reason I can't finish off the pie," Tracy groused, then winked at her. "The men have been banished to the porch so you can finish off my pie and have your little hen party."

"I appreciate your sacrifice," Rosie told him. She turned to the toddler holding the door and thanked him with a ruffle to his hair that made him giggle. The door banged closed behind her and she headed for the kitchen.

Nicole, Alex's wife and Fred's second-oldest daughter, was bustling around the kitchen wearing the apron Rosie had brought over for her after her first child was born. She had her mother's pale cream complexion, though her hair was more strawberry blonde.

"Mama just got out of the shower," she said, pulling a plate out of the cabinet. "She should be out in a few minutes. Do you want a drink or somethin'?"

"I think your mom said something about lemonade," Rosie said. "Hand me a glass and I'll pour for all of us."

Nicole pulled glasses out along with the plates and served up the pie while Rosie poured the lemonade. She pulled the squeeze bottle of something purple out and showed it to Nicole.

"What's this?"

"That's the lavender syrup I told you I was working on," Fred said from the doorway. She was wearing a faded yellow cotton circle skirt and a cotton t-shirt with a dog wearing goggles and 'chemistry lab' on it. Her red hair was twisted up into a knot at the back of her head, though some wisps of the graying locks had escaped to wave around her face. "It works great with lemonade if you want to try some."

"Is this the final iteration?" Rosie asked, squirting some in her glass before handing the bottle to Nicole.

"Close," Fred said. "I think I'm going to tweak the recipe a bit more but it should be close. I've written up my notes on it already so the adjustments shouldn't take too long to record."

Nicole added the syrup to her lemonade and handed around the plates with pie as everybody sat. Rosie caught Fred's eye then glanced at Nicole with a slightly raised eyebrow.

"Nic's been copying out some of the family recipe's she'd like to try," Fred said. "And helping me preserve them before the notebooks disintegrate."

"And getting quite the education," Nicole said.

"As one does," Rosie agreed with a nod.

"So, what's so important you had to use the bat-phone?" Fred asked.

"Have you heard anything about Marianne Larson's family renting out her home? I haven't seen a for sale sign on it."

Fred shook her head. "I didn't know her kids that well. They were a decade behind me in school and moved out as soon as they could from what I could tell. Nobody's said anything about it, either."

Rosie nodded. "Well, I don't think they cleared much of it out when they moved her to the home and someone's managed to summon imps."

"Imps?" Nicole asked.

"Are you sure?"

"One hopped up onto my counter bold as brass," Rosie said. "Hot pink with a purple ridge but it was an imp."

"I didn't know they came in hot pink," Fred mused. "What do you think could cause that kind of color change?"

"It might have something to do with what she's using to summon them," Nicole said. "Grandma had something about color variations between imps they found in Europe and imps they found in Alaska. Of course, she didn't call them that but the descriptions match."

Rosie nodded. "Alright, I can see that. How much of your grandmother's notebooks have you read?"

"About half," Nicole said. "Give or take. Enough to know how to deal with imps, at least. She talks about them constantly."

Fred sighed. "They were a serious nuisance for a while. One of those new age books included a spell to bring yourself luck and visit misfortune on your enemies. Unfortunately, it didn't specify what kind of luck and it mostly summoned imps. Most people could only manage one or two but every now and then you'd get someone who could get a dozen or so. Or who was willing to try the same spell a few dozen times."

"Oh, I remember that one," Rosie said. "We got a rash of them through here for a while but I thought I'd found everybody who bought a copy of the book. I don't remember Marianne having any interest in that direction. Heck, I don't know that I could swear to it that Marianne could read. She wasn't exactly known for patronizing much beyond *Frank's* and the *Duck*."

Frank's was the local diner and the only real restaurant in town. Once upon a time, Rosie had worked for Frank as a waitress. She'd taken exception when he'd given her a pinch on her teenage'd ass and hit him with her tray. When he tried to fire her, the only patron in the restaurant had shown him the error of his ways. She was still fired but she ended up getting married to her knight in a black leather jacket six months later. He'd looked so sexy in his baby blue tux and blonde pompadour.

The Duck was actually *The Dead Duck* and it was one of the less reputable bars in town. The lights were dim, the drinks were cheap, and the furniture was bolted to the floor. There wasn't a one fight a night minimum but the patrons treated it like there was, just in case.

"I didn't know her that well," Fred said.

"Most people didn't. And her kids got out of town as soon as they were able. I don't know that they've even made an effort to get her house occupied or sold." Rosie shook her head.

"They may not think it's worth the effort. If it's the one I'm thinking of, it's pretty run down."

"It is," Rosie said. "But it was a beautiful little cottage back in its day. Marianne's Great Grandfather built it, I think. Or bought it just after it was built in the thirties. It has all the foundation issues those houses tend to have around here but it's solid enough that if Marianne took care of it at all, it's probably still in decent shape."

"Aside from the front half of the house trying to fall off when it's dry, which is more than half the year, and the back half trying to sink when it's wet," Fred said, her voice dry.

"It's solid, cool in the summer and warm enough in the winter, with a working fireplace and a yard," Rosie responded.

"And pipes that the Romans would have considered primitive."

Rosie and Nicole laughed.

"So, welcoming committee or concerned neighbors?" Fred asked. "Because I can't imagine you just letting the house sit with imps in it."

Nicole stood up and cleared the table while they talked. She pulled a basket out of her mother's pantry along with a loaf of bread wrapped in plastic and a container full of cookies. They went in the basket to be joined by a couple bottles of water and an envelope.

Rosie raised her eyebrow at Fred again and got a happy smile in return.

"I think we should be prepared for either," Rosie said. "And to be run off because they're not supposed to be there."

"One car or two?" Fred asked.

"Two, I think. I'll get her attention and you can wander in behind me."

Fred stood and put a few jars from her spice rack into the pockets on her skirt. "I'm going to grab some flowers from the garden for the basket."

Rosie stood up and headed for the front door. The toddler pulled the screen door open for her and nearly fell backwards off the porch in his enthusiasm. She caught his hand and pulled him and the door towards her, lifting him up in a turn that made him giggle before she deposited him in his father's lap.

"You are such a gentleman," she told him and kissed his forehead. "You must take after your daddy."

Alex grinned at her. "We're doing our best. Sometimes our enthusiasm gets the better of us."

"Heading out already?" Tracy asked, the baby asleep in his arms.

He'd gotten the extra large rocking chair he was sitting in specifically so he could hold his grandchildren and Rosie loved him for it. Tracy had worked hard most of his life and often came across as rude and a little rough. Anybody who saw him with his grandchildren knew it for the facade it was, though, and the gentle touch of his hands had soothed many babies to sleep over the years.

"The girls and I need to run an errand," Rosie said. "There's a piece of pie left for you."

"An errand, huh?" Tracy asked.

They shared a look and Rosie nodded. "We shouldn't be gone long."

Fred came out with a bunch of flowers in her hands, and some herbs to go with them. They were pretty and went nicely with the bread to give it a nice, homey feel. Nicole trailed behind her mother, waiting patiently for her to finish wrapping the flowers and put them in the basket.

"Dinner's in the fridge if I'm not back when you get hungry," Fred said, and leaned down to kiss her husband. Nicole did the same, with a gentle kiss for her son.

When she was younger, a brief pang of longing would have shot through Rosie at the sight. Not because she wanted either of the men, her type ran more towards brawlers and bikers, but because she could see the flare of love and devotion that enveloped the couples. However, she'd long made peace with who she was and the relationships she was destined for and could enjoy the reflected love from them without envy.

"Be safe," Tracy said, when they broke away and started to leave.

"Always," Fred returned with a smile.

The look Tracy gave her said he knew she was taking his wife and daughter somewhere dangerous and he'd hold her responsible if anything happened. They'd had the conversation that went with the look shortly after he and Fred had married and reached an understanding. Tracy wouldn't ever like their little hobby, as he called it, but he understood it was something that had to be done.

She tried to tamp down on the guilt that tried to surge in her gut when she got in her car. The imps had to be dealt with. Calling Fred was the right thing to do. Nicole would need to take the next step in her training eventually and imps were low risk. Of all of Fred's children, she'd been the one who'd shown the most aptitude and desire to learn.

And none of that combated the feeling that there was something darker than imps waiting for them in the house.

The curtains twitched again when she pulled up in front of the house. Brimstone floated on the breeze, stronger now, and the ice cold fingers of dread marched up her spine. She cut her engine and got out of the car, making a show of leaning against the bright red vehicle and studying the house.

A black cat, fatter than most strays tended to be, trotted along the sidewalk in front of the house with a hot pink body dangling from his mouth. He looked satisfied as only a cat can and Rosie made a mental note about finding out which pillow ended up with the dead imp before she focused her gaze on the door. The swirl of dust on the porch didn't match the gentle breeze against her skin.

Anyone who saw her would think she was disinterested, even bored, and waiting for something interesting to come along. Out of the corner of her eye, she saw Fred park at the end of the street. She waited until the driver's side door opened to approach the house. Loud comments about the state of the lawn and the utterly shameful condition of the paint and windows kept whoever was inside watching her. She could feel the weight of their stare as she approached and hoped Fred managed to stay out of sight until the last possible minute.

With a loud knock on the door, Rosie put on her best old woman who is an upstanding citizen of the neighborhood voice. "Hello!" she called brightly.

The door creaked open an inch and a pale young woman stared at her with a combination of anger and disbelief. "Go away," she hissed.

"What was that, dear?" Rosie asked, leaning forward. "I'm having trouble hearing you, I just wanted to introduce myself since you seem to be new to the neighborhood. I'm Miss Rose Hawthorne but everybody calls me Miss Rosie. What's your name?"

She leaned her shoulder against the door and watched the young woman's face as she struggled with the sudden weight.

"Go away," the young woman said louder. "You can't be here!"

"Did I bring beer?" Rosie asked, her eyes widening in feigned shock. "Why, what an impertinent question to ask. And are you certain you're old enough to be drinking beer? Where's your mother? I'm going to have a word with her about how rude you're being."

"You can't, she's not here, and you shouldn't be either," the young woman said, and tried to shut the door.

Rosie put more weight into her lean and the door flew out of the young woman's hand. Rosie caught the young woman's hand before she could fall back and pulled her onto the porch, straight into Fred's warm and inviting smile.

"Oh, you must be the new renter!" Fred said happily. "We were just coming to drop off some goodies and see if you needed any help getting this lawn in order. I know it's such a mess and it's always a hassle moving into a new house when it hasn't been taken care of."

The young woman gaped at Fred and took the basket Nicole thrust at her.

"Here, we'll help you take it to the kitchen and get set up," Fred said, and pushed her around and into the house.

The three women followed and closed the door behind them.

"I'm not-" the young woman started. "You can't-"

She was painfully young though Rosie guessed she was technically an adult. Her face was pale in the sense that she didn't get a lot of sun but her dark brown eyes were sunken and the skin around them was slightly gray with fear and stress. When it was styled, her dark brown hair was probably long and spiky down the center with a close-cropped undercut that suited her. Right now, though, it was scraggly and unkempt.

"Oh, honey, you look like you haven't slept in a week," Fred said, tilting the young woman's face up to look at her. "Did you have any help getting moved in?"

Before she could answer, a lime green imp with a turquoise ridge jumped into the basket and started cackling.

The young woman stared at it in horror before Rosie reached out and grabbed it by the scruff of its neck.

"What are you using to get such bright colors?" she asked, ignoring the imps screeching while she examined it. "I thought you'd only managed the pink."

It twisted and tried to bite her and Rosie flung it hard against the wall. It hit with a wet squeak and slid to the floor, leaving a trail of ichor behind it.

"Do you happen to have any salt?" Rosie asked.

"I brought some," Fred said, and handed her a shaker from her pocket. "I wouldn't trust what's in the house right now."

Rosie nodded and went to deal with the imps' remains while Fred and Nicole bundled the young woman off to the kitchen.

The house was dark and in desperate need of a good scrub. It was obvious that nobody had been inside since they'd moved Marianne to the assisted living facility. Most of the furniture was still there complete with cigarette stains and musty throws. She wouldn't be surprised to find closets full of clothes and a lifetime of clutter.

When she got to the kitchen, Fred and Nicole had the young woman sitting at the table with the bottle of water and container of cookies open in front of her. Her hands shook as she set the water down on the table and took a deep breath.

"Are you Marianne's granddaughter?" Rosie asked, sitting at the table. "You look a little old to belong to her oldest child but you look just like her when she was younger."

The young woman nodded. "I found out a few months ago. Mama was adopted but I took one of those tests to see if I could find my dad or if I had any family besides her."

"And you found Marianne," Rosie said.

"I just wanted to get to know her, you know?"

Fred reached out and took the young woman's hand. "We understand. Family's important. But why did you stay when you realized there wasn't anybody here?"

"I didn't have anywhere else to go," she said quietly.

An imp leapt onto the table in front of Rosie and stuck its tongue out at her before screeching and trying to jump away. It met with the sole of a red shoe and went flying into the wall behind the sink.

"Where did the imps come from?" Rosie asked while she walked over to sprinkle the imp with salt.

The young woman flushed. "I found a book and it seemed okay. I thought it would be, like, venting to the universe or something."

"Who were you cursing?" Nicole asked. "Boyfriend? Stepdad? Family? Friends?"

"All of the above," she muttered.

Rosie sighed heavily and sat down. "What's your name?"

"Hailey," she said.

"Well, Hailey, we're going to have to talk about how you managed to summon the imps the way you did but first, we're going to have to get rid of them. How many came through the portal when you did the spell?"

Hailey shrugged. "I don't know, I didn't notice any at first."

"What do you mean 'at first'?" Fred asked.

"I mean they didn't show up right away but every couple of days I'd notice new ones."

Rosie and Fred exchanged a glance.

"Can you show us where you did the spell? I just want to see what symbols you used," Rosie lied.

As soon as she asked the question, the air in the house shifted and the floor shook.

"I used the ones in the book," Hailey said. "Do y'all get earthquakes here? I didn't think you did but that sure felt like one."

"It sure did," Fred said. "And no, we don't. Spell. Now."

The speed with which Fred went from gentle, friendly mother figure to cold, hard, and demanding authoritarian shocked Hailey. Rosie had seen it before but always stood in awe with the way the subtle shift in posture and demeanor made her friend a foot taller and infinitely more frightening.

"In the bedroom in the hallway," Hailey said, shrinking in on herself.

The three women were out of their chairs and moving down the hallway before she'd finished speaking. When they opened the door, the smell of sulfur was almost overwhelming, the heat intense.

The room was swarming with imps in a rainbow of neon colors. They scratched and pulled at the walls and floor boards, occasionally coming away with long splinters they dragged to the glowing hole in the middle of the room.

An ancient box of crayons lay spilled in the corner and the largest imps she'd ever seen were dragging them around the symbols on the floor, following the pattern carefully with different colors until the glowing hole shuddered and grew.

The house rocked again and paint rained from the ceiling only to be swarmed by the imps and thrown into the glowing hole which glowed brighter with every chip.

Rosie stepped into the room and grabbed the first imp she could catch. She threw it into the hole. It screamed and chittered and popped back out angry and trailing smoke.

"I think you pissed it off," Nicole said from the hallway.

"Search the house for the rest," Fred said, and slammed the door before her daughter could step into the room.

With the ease of years of practice, Rosie sketched a quick seal over the door. Nothing was getting in or out until she released it.

"I thought you were going to let her learn," she told Fred.

"She did learn," Fred responded. "I don't want her near a portal that size yet."

"We're going to need a third eventually."

"Not her. Not yet."

Rosie nodded and turned to the imps that had started to swarm them. She stomped and kicked as many as she could and their tiny claws and teeth burned where they managed to dig into her skin. Any she could grab hold of got thrown against the wall, the crunch and drip of ichor painting the room in a horrible, terrifying lime green.

She didn't have enough time to salt the remains but she didn't need to. As the imps died, they dissolved and their ashes were sucked into the glowing hole in the middle of the room, which shuddered and grew while the house rocked.

More imps popped out of the portal, bigger than the last, and came straight for her. Rosie looked around the room, frantically searching for something she could use to fight them off. It had been ages since she'd needed to carry anything larger than her fly swatter.

Her eyes lit on an old baseball bat in the closet and she started towards it. One of the big imps bit hard on her ankle and she kicked at it, trying to ignore the hellfire burn that raced up all the nerves in her leg.

"Fred, we have to close that portal," she called to her friend. She glanced over to see her friend batting at the imps crawling up her skirt while she made notes in a tiny pocket notebook.

"They changed one of the symbols," Fred said. "I have to work out the counter for it but it's one I've never seen before."

Rosie grabbed the bat and hit the next imp coming for her legs. It chittered and screeched but didn't die. The house shook and she fell hard against the wall. Fred wasn't much better, her notebook was clenched in her hand but she'd dropped her pencil and one of the imps was running with it towards the portal.

With a fencing lunge, Rosie managed to bat it away from the portal but the parts of her that crossed the circle screamed with fire and heat.

A clawed hand reached out of the portal and tried to grab her bat. She pulled it back just in time but the demonic chuckle that rang through her ears told her she wouldn't be able to do it again.

"Fuck it," Fred said, and started kicking at the imps with the crayons. They were getting bigger with each circle they drew, the malevolent intelligence in their eyes increasing with each completed ring.

She took the crayons, plucking them from their grips as they fell away stunned, then off the floor.

The house shook again with the deep, rolling motion that told them it wasn't just the house that was rocking.

Fred knelt and started to draw the counter-symbols over the ones she recognized. Rosie stood next to her and put her bat to work as well as she could. Her reflexes had slowed over the years and more imps got through but Fred didn't stop working.

With the first counter, the heat in the room eased, and the imps screeched. They rushed Fred and jumped at her, pulling at her hair and biting her arms. Rosie smacked and threw them, sending as many flying into the walls as she could, and Fred did the same until she could move to the next symbol.

The big imps attacked and Rosie stood between them and her friend the best she could, shifting and moving to keep her body between Fred and the imps. Until she realized she was being herded.

Her heel landed on the circle and fire scorched up her back before she rocked forward and out again. The imps laughed and chittered and pushed while she kicked them away. A demonic laugh rang through the room and she spun to face the portal.

Something was watching her.

The face filled the portal; dark gray skin with an evil smile and hate-filled eyes that flickered with reflected fire and heat. It opened its mouth and a long, forked tongue spilled out to lick its lips.

A familiar heat pooled low in her belly and Rosie swallowed hard. She clenched her fist around the baseball bat, the weight a reminder of where she was and what she was doing.

"Naughty witch," the demon rumbled. "I can taste your desire from here. You know how I can use your magic, the dark delights that are possible. Open the circle, let me out, and I will show you ecstasy you've never imagined."

Rosie's mouth went dry and she had to fight her body to keep from taking the step that would move her into the circle. Into the grasp of the clawed hand she could see reaching for her.

A cold spray of lavender scented water hit her in the face and she jerked back. Fred sprayed her again and pulled her away from the circle.

Before she could thank her, Fred moved to the next symbol. The imps were less aggressive now, cowering back when Rosie kicked at them, and she knew the first two counters were working.

She grabbed one and threw it into the portal. It exploded into a spray of dust and ichor at the edge and she grinned. They ran from her, scrambling away from the destruction they saw written in her face.

Fred finished the third counter and moved to the fourth. The imps were scrambling at the door, desperate to get out and into the world to wreak the havoc that their tiny brains craved.

The demon continued to rumble temptation at her but it was muffled, remote. Whatever power he'd had to influence things in their world had been diminished with the third and fourth counter symbols.

What imps were left cowered in the corners while they contemplated the last symbol and the demon mocked them from within the portal.

"It's like they spelled the formula wrong," Fred said.

"Can we fix it and then counter-sign that?" Rosie suggested.

Fred shook her head. "The misspelling changes the meaning entirely. I'm going to need time to study it."

"We can't just leave a portal to hell open in the middle of an abandoned house," Rosie protested.

"No, I know," Fred said. "But it's stabilized and not growing. If we clean up the imps and keep the door sealed, we should be able to buy some time to get it closed."

Rosie nodded. "Alright, let's start with the imps then we can let the girls in to help clean up."

They chased and squished the imps, sprinkling salt as they went, until the room was coated in a fine layer of ichor and demonic dust. Rosie found an empty box and created an imp trap to catch any that had managed to hide in a dark corner or closet.

When she took the seal off the door, Nicole burst into the room to throw her arms around her mother and scold her for locking her out. The love and affection between the two women was so obvious it hurt and Rosie turned away to find Hailey staring at the portal in fascination.

"Did I make that?" she asked softly.

"Part of it," Rosie told her. "And you're going to help clean it up. Did you guys find any cleaning supplies?"

Hailey shook her head. "A couple brooms but most of the bottles were empty and probably no good anymore anyway. How am I going to help clean it up?"

"First you're going to grab a broom and start sweeping up all the dust," Rosie said. "Then you're going to bring the book you used to the kitchen so I can beat you with it."

"What?" Hailey asked, shocked.

"You can't beat the baby witch," Fred scolded.

"I can when she summons a demon without being able to put it back," Rosie protested.

"I didn't mean to," Hailey said. "Really, I didn't know it would do that."

Rosie sighed and she suddenly felt very old. Every cut, bite, ache and bruise made itself known. "And you didn't have anybody to teach you any better either, did you? Alright, no beatings, but you're going to clean until I'm satisfied and then we're going to start with the basics."

Hailey nodded and scampered off to get a broom.

"How old is she?" Rosie asked Nicole. "Tell me you got some information out of her."

"Eighteen as of last week," Nicole said. "And she's been on the street for a couple years with a home life I wouldn't send my worst enemy back to. Even if she was exaggerating some of it, it's still bad."

"She can't stay here," Rosie said. "Not with a portal to hell in the guest room."

"I'll take her home with me," Fred said. "And get her started on the fundamentals."

"Fine, I'm going to go sit down for a minute. Let me know when it's cleaned up enough to leave." Rosie passed Hailey in the hall and grumbled.

The kitchen table was the same one she'd sat at decades ago when she'd come to see Marianne after her aunt had passed. She'd been young, cheerful and brittle, with no real idea of where she'd come from or what she was doing. The subsequent decades had seen her meander through life, bumping from man to man and drink to drink, with an early decline and weak relationships with all of her children.

Rosie could have kicked herself for not knowing about a child that had been given up for adoption.

The other women joined her in the kitchen later, chatting happily and drawing Hailey out into the sunny, family feeling that radiated from Fred. They'd grabbed her bag from the bedroom she'd been in and it was depressingly small and empty. It wouldn't stay that way for long, Rosie knew, and she could already picture the black skirts and lace gloves the young woman would favor.

"Are you coming over for dinner?" Fred asked after they'd finished warding and sealing the house.

"No, I need a shower and a drink," Rosie said. "Give my love to Tracy and the babies."

Fred herded her charges into her truck and headed home while Rosie sat in her car and ached. She was getting too old to go toe to toe with a demon any more. And this one hadn't even made it through the portal.

She closed her eyes and let out a deep breath. The symbols on the floor nagged at her brain and she ran through them and what they meant until she got to the last one. The formula, as Fred called it, was wrong for summoning imps but it was perfect for creating a personal gate for a demon.

It wasn't naming a creature type, it was naming a demon. A very specific demon. One she'd tangled with before.

"Son of a bitch," Rosie said as her eyes flew open. She knew how to close the portal.

Everything in her wanted to go home, take a long soak in a hot bath, and pour herself a glass of bourbon. Everything hurt. Her hair ached.

But she couldn't walk away. Not yet.

It was dangerous to leave a portal to hell open, even with the doors sealed against intruders. The very presence would eat away at the seals until it started to infect the rest of the neighborhood.

She had to close it now.

With a groan, she got out of her car and walked up to the front door. The seals parted under her hands and she knew they'd already been worn away from the inside.

The demon had pulled back on purpose.

The evil chuckle that filled the room when she walked in filled her with dread and a certainty that she'd been right.

"The naughty witch returns," the demon said, his lips twisted into an evil smile. "I knew she couldn't resist me."

"Cut the crap," Rosie snapped. "I've turned you down every time you've tried to get at me and it's getting old."

"You've turned me down, yes," the demon said. "But don't tell me some part of you doesn't thrill at the offer. You know exactly how much pleasure I can give you, what kind of power I could fill you with, and the temptation grows with every year."

"It gets older with every year."

"I see the silver in your hair, naughty witch, feel the ache in your bones. I can make you young and beautiful again, take away every ache that comes with the passing years. You know the joy that comes with submission, the power I can share."

"I have earned every gray hair I have and pain is a part of life. There is nothing you can offer me, demon, that's worth the price."

"Are you sure?" Its voice rumbled through her and she felt her feet moving towards the portal. "I can give you a taste of what's to come. Put your hand through the portal and I'll let you feel everything I can do to you."

Heat blasted against her skin and she watched her hand as though it wasn't hers. Flame licked along her fingers and wrist as it passed the barrier and he grabbed it in his own clawed hand. His forked tongue licked along her palm and wrist and she felt her body writhe with pleasure. A sharp claw pressed against her palm and she yanked her arm back, cutting her hand on the claw.

He hissed in displeasure and licked the drop of blood off his claw. She cradled her injured hand against her chest and snarled.

Rosie stalked over to the final symbol and knelt next to it. "I said no, asshole," she said, then pressed her bleeding palm against the symbol.

He shouted in anger, then disbelief, as the portal shrank then popped out of existence.

The last of her energy drained out of her into the floor and she sagged, her head bent while she waited to recover enough to stand up and walk to her car.

It hadn't required blood to banish him last time, and she worried about what the next one would take.

After long minutes, she pushed herself to her feet and stumbled out of the room, and then out of the house. She had a bath and a bottle of bourbon waiting for her and she intended to enjoy both.

Shock n' Awe

A Misadventure of Braxton Hicks
By William Joseph Roberts

I'd gotten lucky so far on this run out west. It was the middle of February in Colorado and the weather really wasn't all that bad. I had to go all the way up into Wyoming to take care of a skinwalker sighting that turned out to be nothing more than a false alarm.

And since I was already kinda in the area, I didn't see any point in wasting the trip, so I decided to swing south and head toward Colorado Springs. I'd heard from a few folks back east that an old friend of mine from the deep south was running her own restaurant out here now, and I wanted to stop in to pay her a visit, and hopefully get a belly full of her cooking.

A few years back, Mandy wanted to go to New Orleans for Mardi Gras, so we did. As usual, things went sideways, and we ended up chasing down a small coven of witches who'd tried to re-establish their name and position in the city's dark-side hierarchy.

While there, we met Bernadette Boudreaux. She was one of the best damn Cajun chefs I have ever had the pleasure of knowing. And her food was so good we'd eaten at Bernadette's restaurant every night while in town, even though some of that trip was still a tad bit fuzzy. When we weren't chasing witches and vamps, we were having fun and drinking way too much.

Well, just before heading out on this trip, I'd found out that Bernadette had taken up a job in Colorado Springs as the head chef for Spring Orleans. And a great big bowl of her gumbo was screaming my name after the long cold hours on the back of my bike.

Even though I'd gotten lucky on this run and the temperatures hadn't been stupid-cold, it was still a little chilly at interstate speeds. There had been a bit of snow here and there, but if you bundled up well enough, that wasn't a problem.

I pulled up and parked along the street in front of the restaurant. The joint had that quaint little bistro look on the outside, with wrought-iron tables and chairs. I could see a six-man band through the front window that played a Dixieland tune for patrons.

I shut off Jonie, my newer Harley-Davidson Road King, dropped the kickstand, and stretched, popping things back into place. After being in the saddle for the last hundred miles or so, things had gotten a little numb.

Riding through these mountains was a beautiful experience like nothing we had back east. Maybe if I'd gone to Europe, I could find something close. Wouldn't that be a hell of a trip?

I tucked my gloves into my pocket, strapped my helmet to the bike, and made my way inside. A number of heads turned, looking in my direction. It might have had something to do with the kutte and full riding leathers.

The rush of heat from the room on my cold chest when I opened my jacket was something amazing. I hadn't realized how deep the cold had gotten until that moment.

"Well, I'll be, if it isn't Braxton Hicks," I heard shouted from the kitchen area in the back. I stepped past the hostess, who stuttered an unsure *sir* and headed toward the voice. Sure enough, there was Bernadette, a big bright smile on her face that seemed to gleam as bright as the large diamonds she wore in each ear.

"I thought that was you," Bernadette said as I approached the back counter. "Heard you pull in on that bike of yours. What in the world brings you this far west?"

I shrugged. "Heard you were out here working your magic. Figured I'd swing in for some of your finest while I was in the area."

"Well, you just in time, Boo. You pull you up a seat there and take a listen to the band while I get you some grub. I know exactly what you want." She smiled, laughed, and slapped me on the arm.

"You sure about that?" I asked. "There are an awful lot of things in this world that I want," I said with a wink.

She let out a hysterical chuckle. "It is good to see you again, Braxton. You sit'n I'll bring something right out."

Two pints of a dark beer arrived moments later. I wasn't sure what they were, but beer was beer, and the darker, the better, in my opinion. The first sip was a wonderful thing after a long haul on the back of the sled in the middle of the cold Rocky Mountains of Colorado.

I took a sip of what I guessed was a nutty brown ale, then pulled off my jacket and stretched again, trying to get the blood flowing to my extremities. I'd barely taken a good long draw of the beer before Bernadette returned with a bowl full of crawdads, crab legs, andouille sausage, shrimp, potatoes, corn on the cob, and a small bowl of her amazing gumbo.

It smelled wonderful.

From behind her back she produced a small bowl of hot garlic butter, and from her pocket came a bottle of hot sauce labeled *Worst Nightmare* that she placed on the table in front of me.

I looked up at her and smiled. "Yeah, you might happen to know a little about what I want."

"I know your taste buds, Boo. But this one will light you up. It'd light fire to Satan's asshole if'n he ain't careful."

I looked at the innocent-looking bottle and nodded. "So, what you're saying is that this might actually be a challenge for me?"

"Might be," she said, then chuckled.

"Then I graciously accept."

"Thought you might." She slapped me on the back and headed back toward the kitchen. "You just let me know if you need anything else."

I didn't hesitate and dug into the meal. I'd be damned if it wasn't good. There wasn't anything like properly done crawdads, even if I knew they were frozen and shipped in. The middle of Colorado in the dead of winter was not the easiest place to get fresh mud bugs, not to mention the shrimp and crab legs. But you can get away with that, as long as you season them right.

I was in hog heaven. I had no idea where I was going to be laying my head for the night yet, but wherever it was, a food coma would follow close behind because the grub was just that damned good.

I sat there and ate until I'd gotten more than my fill. Hell, I didn't even bother to ask what the cost was going to be. Bernadette knew how I'd grown up, and there's one thing about growing up poor. Once poor, you're always thinking poor. Just one of those things that becomes a habit, so I knew Bernadette wouldn't rip me off too bad.

By the time I'd finished my third bowl and 3rd beer, I was done and throwing in the towel. I sat there for a while just watching the other customers and listening to the band play several ragtime tunes I hadn't heard in a while.

"So what do you think, Braxton?" Bernadette asked, returning from the kitchen with another beer in her hand. "Do you reckon these Rocky Mountain folk even know what good Cajun is?"

I smiled, picking my teeth with a crawdad claw, then let out a long, drawn out "nope." She laughed. "But anyone exposed to your grub is in for one heavenly treat."

"That just makes my heart happy to hear you say that. I've been out here for nearly a year and it's hard to tell if they know what they are talking about or if they're just blowing smoke up my ass because they'd eat at the Big Easy Grille once before and they consider themselves *experts*."

"Well, I'm glad I could be of service." I held up what was left of my beer in toast, then drained the glass.

"So what else has been going on besides keeping the populous of Colorado Springs supplied with fine Cajun cuisine?"

"Oh, not much. Basic stuff really. Trouble from the Air Force Academy brats on occasion, and of course we have the Space Force here now."

I let out a chuckle. "Guess we're going to finally get some space Marines."

"Just maybe," she said with a giggle snort.

"I'm telling you, it's gotta be," someone across the room insisted. We both turned to see a larger guy, animatedly talking to two men sitting in one of the booths along the far wall.

"And then there's that," Bernadette said.

I shook my head in confusion and turned back to her. "And that is?"

"There's been some happenings around town. Most folks think it's all insurance scams and the like. There's been several unexplained fires and electrocutions around the Knob Hill area. And him right there, mister bigshot, thinks he knows everything about everything when it comes down to dat there Tesla fella."

"You mean like Tesla the cars?"

"No dummy. Tesla. As in the engineer and inventor. The one who came out here way back when to do his research."

"Really? Well, now that's something," I said, then tried to listen in over the noise of the restaurant. Sure enough, Bernadette was right. The guy was going on about this fire and that fire, then about one of the strange electrocutions where the victims looked like someone had grabbed onto a live high-voltage wire and been burnt to a crisp.

I chuckled and looked back to Bernadette. "Is he sure it wasn't just spontaneous combustion from all of the…" Bernadette slapped the back of my shoulder and laughed.

"Don't go giving him any new ideas. You finish up your drinks. I have a kitchen to run. Just let me know before you leave."

"Well, I can go ahead and get my tab now."

"No, no, no," she said, placing her hand back onto my shoulder. "I'll have none of that. You're a good, honest man and you give me a good honest opinion. I think that's worth at least one meal."

"You aren't going to let me argue about it, are you?"

She smiled wide, shaking her head. "Damned right."

I nodded. "I'm much obliged, Bernadette."

She smiled and went on back to the kitchen while I sat sipping on the beer, enjoying the music from the small band. It was getting harder and harder to ignore the conversation on the other side of the room, though. The guy kept getting louder and more animated the longer the conversation went on.

I didn't know a whole lot about Nikola Tesla, but I did know of the name. The animated guy kept on about the fires and how there was nothing to cause ignition in those areas, or how surveillance video was nonexistent for over three blocks surrounding each site because something had fried the nearby security cameras.

He concluded there must be something else unexplained going on, but he just couldn't pinpoint the cause or the source and that he was going to get to the bottom of it whether the two men helped him out or not.

This guy must have been desperate. You'd have to be completely clueless to miss the passive-aggressive BS he was forcing into the conversation.

I thought about it for a long minute while I sipped at the beer. I didn't have anything else better to do at the moment, and there could always be something to this thing, so I dialed up Mandy, my research assistant, IT department, and best friend, all wrapped into one.

"Hey hot stuff," I said when I heard her pick up on the other end. "What trouble are you getting into tonight?"

"Upgrades to the county server and a pint of rocky road." I could hear her licking the spoon after another bite. "You didn't call me just to chitchat, Brax. So spit it out. What do you want?"

I could already tell she was in the kinda mood that I really didn't want to test my luck with, so I just hurried and got to the point. "I'm in Colorado Springs and have possibly come across an incident. You ever heard something causing random fires and unexplained electrocutions? And there isn't any video evidence because the cameras have apparently been fried."

"So, some sort of EMP?"

"What's that?"

"Electromagnetic pulse, but generally those are only generated with a nuclear blast."

"Well, there are several military bases nearby," I said. "Could something have come from there?"

"Doubtful. There's too much danger to the civilian population. But then again, that hasn't stopped the government before."

"Okay, well, is there anything in the database that fits the description?" I could already hear her fingers clacking away at the keyboard.

"Huh," she mumbled.

"Got something?"

"Not really. The best I'm coming up with is a fire elemental, but that doesn't explain the electrocutions." I could still hear her fingers clacking away at the keys. She hadn't given up yet. "There is a chance that it could be a Jinn, or well, any other creature that can cast or control lightning."

"Well, that makes for a fun day, doesn't it? Would something like this have a finder's fee?"

"Possibly, but you know how this works. You must have some kind of physical, testable proof if not a specimen."

"Let me see what I can come up with. I can probably find some kind of shiny lamp to stuff a genie into and get it back to the labs."

"I don't think that's how it works, Braxton."

"Well, why not? It works in the movies."

"It's a movie…" she started to say, then let out a frustrated huff.

"Don't worry. I'll figure something out," I said, then hung up and continued listening in on the guy across the room as he talked.

The guy was starting to sound frustrated the more that he talked to the men at the table. They didn't look like they wanted to hear anything he had to say. And by the way that they watched the room, they were probably detectives or plain clothes cops if not part of the government element here in town.

The guy let out a huff and turned to leave, making his way around the tables as he headed for the door.

"Hey, buddy," I said as he passed by. He stopped and did a double take, unsure if I was talking to him or not. "Sit down. Have a beer with me."

Suspicious, he glared at me. "And exactly why do I want to sit and have a beer with you?"

"I overheard a little of your conversation and I'm interested in hearing more." In a split second, I knew I'd probably made a big mistake. The guy's eyes were as big as saucers. I pushed the chair on the other side of the table out with my foot, and he excitedly sat down across the table from me.

"You ain't from some government agency or something, are you?"

"Not really…" He looked taken aback and about ready to leave. "Let's just say I'm an independent contractor. The government hires me to take care of the weird things that pop up. You're going on about weird stuff. So what's the skinny? I overheard you talking about fires, electrocutions, and burned-out electronics."

"See, that's just it." This guy went into a full-out shamwow stance. You could tell he was all-in on whatever it was he was getting ready to spill to me. "These random fires have been happening around downtown, where Nikola Tesla's old lab used to be. I swear it has to be connected somehow, because there's nothing else connecting any of the fires or electrocutions. They keep happening, but there isn't any video evidence or witnesses to any of the deaths."

"How many have there been?"

"Three deaths from electrocution, and about a dozen injuries from the fires and smoke inhalation. One firefighter was burned pretty badly, but he'll make a full recovery."

"How do you know the deaths were from electrocution?"

"From the coroner's reports," he answered. "Burn marks across their bodies that only correlate to being in contact with high voltage power."

"You saw the coroner's reports?"

He suddenly sat bolt upright and stared back at the men he'd been talking to earlier. "Um… Why would you ask something like that?"

"Considering this sounds like an ongoing case, those files wouldn't be available to the general public yet."

He looked nervous and started to stand.

"Whoa, man. Where you going?"

"I'm not sure this is a good idea."

"Why's that? Cause I'm asking questions? I'm curious, and want to know what I'm getting myself into before I jump in feet first."

He let out a calming breath. "I just know some people, okay?"

"Okay. Cool. I feel ya, man. That's how I manage to get most of the info I get on jobs. I either know someone, or I know someone who knows someone. Was there any other evidence of foul play of any kind?"

He shook his head. "Nothing."

"Sounds like it might be a fun little mystery. Can you show me where the incidents took place?"

"Yeah. We can do that."

"You eat yet?" I asked.

"No, I was just about to go get something."

I waved down one of the waitresses. "Get him whatever he wants and bring me the check."

The guy smiled real big and cocked his head to the side. "You sure about that?"

"Absolutely," I said and extended my hand across the table. "The name's Braxton. Braxton Hicks."

He took my hand and gave it a hearty squeeze. "Connor O'Tool," he replied.

"It's a pleasure to meet you, Connor."

We sat for a while longer as he ate and I had myself another of those nutty brown ales. While he ate, he regaled me with the glory and knowledge of all things Nikola Tesla, the scientist's experiments, and everything that happened here in Colorado Springs. I never in my life thought that anybody could have as much information in their head as Mandy, but this guy could easily give her a run for her money.

He was the proverbial bible on everything Tesla. From his early beginnings to his death in poverty, and you could tell he wasn't just one of these batshit crazies. He was passionate to the point of obsessive about the way that man had been treated and how his designs had been confiscated, stolen, or destroyed.

A lot of it screamed conspiracy theory, but after some of the stuff I'd seen over the years working for the government, you never know what might actually be true.

Connor continued on during the meal, telling me about the first reported fire in a warehouse that had been abandoned since the 70s, and the property had been in an airship status all these years, so nothing had been touched on the site for decades.

"Two of the most recent electrocutions," he continued, "happened in the park on top of Knob Hill, where Tesla's lab once stood. The victims, a young couple, had been out for a picnic in the park according to their friends and family. Their hearts stopped with no explanation other than a few scorch marks similar to electrical burns. There had been no storms to speak of, no lightning, and no power lines even remotely nearby."

He leaned onto the table and lowered his voice. "Unless, of course, the military had some kind of secret weapons testing going on that no one knew about, there wasn't any other explanation."

If I could get a look at the sites, I might spot a clue that normal law enforcement would miss and think nothing of. Then maybe I could get an idea of what I might be dealing with.

"Do you think we could get a look at that warehouse that burned first?" I asked.

Connor's eyes went wide with excitement, and he stuffed the remainder of his sandwich in his mouth. He nodded and mumbled a *yes* through the mouthful of food.

"We can maybe do that. I know a guy who could probably get us in."

"What about the other sites?"

I started plugging the addresses into the map app on my phone just to see if there was any sort of pattern as he listed them off from memory.

Once I typed in the last entry, I zoomed it out, but it just looked like random points surrounding the initial site at the warehouse. I turned the phone around and showed it to Connor.

"Oh, holy shit!" He yanked the phone out of my hand and stared at the screen, mumbling to himself.

"Okay? So I'm guessing that's supposed to mean something?" I asked.

"You don't see that?"

"See what?"

He took a screenshot of the map, then brought up the photo and drew a curved line starting at the warehouse that connected each of those points.

"Do you see that curve?"

"Yeah. It's a spiral."

Connor let out what sounded like a slightly maniacal laugh. "It is, but it's so much more than that. It's the golden ratio, known by most as the Fibonacci Sequence. Tesla based almost all his developments on the golden ratio or the numbers three, six, and nine."

"Okay? So what does that mean?"

"That there is a damned good chance all of this weird shit is connected back to Tesla in some way. I just don't know how, yet."

"How can we prove it?" I asked.

"I wish I knew," he said, staring off in thought.

I downed my beer and then dropped some cash on the table for the waitress. "You ready? Let's go take a look at this warehouse."

A quick word with Bernadette scored me parking out back of the restaurant for the bike so no one would mess with it and I jumped in the truck with Connor.

Connor called his buddy that worked security in the warehouse district while we drove and got the combination to the building.

"They got really lucky that fire didn't burn up anything important. My buddy said this place has been untouched for decades. It must have become a catch-all for someone at one point, because of all the extra junk stored there. Luckily, the fire only damaged a small section at the back of the building, and mostly just burned up some empty boxes and crates."

Pulling up to a dilapidated, metal-sided building, Connor reached into the back seat and retrieved two large Maglite flashlights.

"There hasn't been power in this building in decades, so we'll probably need these," he said, testing each of them with a click of a button.

The place was absolutely massive—lots of old industrial equipment scattered here and there in several states of disarray. Nothing seemed to be assembled. It just looked like piles of junk, for the most part. The deeper we went into the building, the older the equipment and items seemed to get. It was like the building was a time capsule of the Industrial Revolution, and we were traveling back in time the further we went.

As we continued, we began to see small boilers, stacks of locomotive parts, and what looked like mining equipment shoved into a corner and left to rot for eternity.

"Oh, hey, look at this," Connor said, pointing at one particular piece of equipment.

"It looks like the bucket off of an old steam shovel," I replied.

"It must have been used in the mines back in the day. And that over there," he said, pointing across the bay. "That looks like an old military transport from the 30s."

He was like a kid in a candy store, and I couldn't blame him. I mean, I loved old equipment. Just part of being a mechanic, I guess. I could spend days in here poking about and exploring if left to my own curiosities, but we had an investigation to take care of. The thought of getting caught here in a snowstorm before I could get out of Colorado Springs really didn't appeal to me, either.

As Connor dug around in another bin of miscellaneous parts, I took a left turn through a doorway into the next bay. In the far back corner, stacked in over a dozen rows of five deep, were these strange metallic cylinders made of copper or bronze, that resembled a copper-top battery like you'd find at the store, but large and more steampunk looking. Several of them had recent scorch marks, like the marks left by high voltage arcing.

I worked my way back to the stack to get a better look, and found one of the cylinders cracked wide open. It looked like it had swollen and ripped along the weld seam of the cylinder. Whatever happened had managed to melt a section out of a stack of train wheels sitting next to the cylinder, as well as the wall at the end of the building. Shattered glass and melted metal slag littered the floor next to the wall.

I'd seen a lot of equipment in my days, but I'd never seen anything like this before. Granted, it was old tech, and old tech was a forgotten knowledge. As technology advanced, we forgot the old ways. Hell, with all of today's advanced computer technology, you'd think it would be easy to work out how things were done before. Then because the know-how from the 60s got lost somehow, the eggheads have forgotten how to put a man on the moon.

"Hey, Connor. Do these things look familiar to you?"

Connor scuttled through some other industrial gear stacked on the other side of the bay and stopped dead in his tracks. "Holy shit!"

He scrambled, getting past all the other stuff, and pushed past me to get a better look at them, laughing a happy little laugh like a maniacal madman.

"Do you know what these are?"

"Nope. Not a clue," I replied. "Kegs for a steampunk frat party?"

Conner turned and glared at me with a serious, *don't fuck with me* look.

"Not even close," he said.

"These look like the descriptions of the original capacitors that Tesla had designed and used at his testing facility for his wireless transmission of power. They were designed to retain energy gathered from the aether and used to boost the transmission signal."

"Okay, I could see where the cylinders resembled a capacitor off of a circuit board."

"Yeah, exactly," Conner said excitedly. "Only these would be about a million times stronger, though. Like if one of these babies were to blow, the amount of power that would go out would be insane."

"Enough power to melt hardened steel and shatter glass?" I asked, pointing at the train wheels and the hole burned in the warehouse wall.

"Without a doubt," Conner replied, nodding as he examined one of the steel wheels.

"Could these really still be holding a charge after all of these years?"

"I wouldn't think so. I mean, they shut down the lab in 1904, and dismantled it to pay off his debts."

"Do you think one of these things rupturing could do the kinda damage you're looking at there?"

Conner nodded. "Oh, without a doubt. Tesla was playing with voltages so high that it could easily vaporize anything that got in the way."

He stood up and looked around, confusion danced across his face.

"What's wrong?"

"This could have easily caused the fire, but the fire wasn't in this part of the building. It was on the west side of the warehouse. It also doesn't explain the electrocutions," he added.

I pointed up to the hole in the wall. "What if whatever it was that was in there escaped?"

Conner grabbed a metal rod laying nearby and tapped at the cylinder that had ruptured.

"Are you sure that's a good idea?"

"I don't know," he said. He shined his light between two of the cylinders and knelt down to get closer.

"What is it?" I asked.

"It's some of Tesla's old equipment. See right here," he said, pointing at a small plate on the side of one of the cylinders with his flashlight. He read the markings. "Manufactured for the Tesla Experimental Station, by Hensley Station Manufacturing, Richmond Virginia, 1900."

Connor stood and set the rod across the top of several cylinders, causing a big, beautiful blue arc of electricity to shoot out, knocking him backward. He slid several feet before crashing into a stack of crates at the end of the narrow path.

"Conner," I shouted, rushing over to him. The arching blast had left black scorch marks across his heavy brown leather jacket, burning through in several places. I shook him and he moaned.

"Perfect, you're still alive. I really didn't want to dig a hole this late at night."

He coughed and shook his head, trying to get up and get his bearings.

"Hold on, dude. Don't get up yet. Give your senses a second to come back. That thing zapped the shit out of you."

Connor's eyes suddenly went wide. That's when I noticed the flickering electric blue glow that seemed to be coming from behind me. Still kneeling, I pivoted on my heel to find a small humanoid-shaped thing that flashed and arced. It looked like one of those lightning balls that you find in a Science Museum, but humanoid-shaped and small.

"What the hell is that?" I asked Connor. He shook his head slowly, at a complete loss for words. He mumbled, trying to get something out resembling a coherent sentence, but it only sounded like gibberish. Connor worked his mouth, trying to form words around what sounded like a swollen tongue.

"I'll take it, that wasn't part of Tesla's experiments and isn't a good thing," I asked, turning to look back at him. "We should go." He nodded emphatically.

I grabbed him by the front of his jacket and yanked him to his feet. "Alright then, we gotta go." Pushing him ahead of me, we headed toward the direction we'd come from.

Glancing back, I saw the creature was following us. Small arcs of electricity lanced out, striking at the building's girders and other bits of equipment as it passed by.

The electrical tendrils sparked and scorched surfaces where it touched like when striking a welding arc.

"Is there any chance that your buddy Tesla trapped that thing in one of his capacitors?" I asked, pushing Connor faster and faster toward the door.

"I… I don't know. Maybe? I don't remember hearing of anything like this in Tesla's experiments, either."

"Well, sometimes things don't get documented 'cause they're too fucking weird."

We rounded a corner into the next bay and stopped for a moment to catch our breath.

"It's possible," Connor gasped. "The government confiscated a lot of Tesla's work early on when they shut the project down. And there was this huge rivalry between Tesla and Thomas Edison, to the point that Edison sent his goons out to bust the place up and steal whatever research they could."

Connor froze, his face going ghostly white. "If I just let that one out, then that means there are two of them things on the loose."

"Okay, Mister Wizard, how do we stop something like that?"

Connor looked at me in disbelief and slowly shook his head. "I have no idea."

"Okay, stay here." Rushing back to the doorway we'd passed through, I peeked around the corner and spotted the creature slowly making its way toward the opening. It seemed to be examining everything as it moved. I took out my phone, snapped several pictures that I immediately sent to Mandy, and hurried back to where Connor rested.

"Okay, so how would Tesla have dissipated a massive amount of energy quickly?"

"He'd have grounded it," Connor answered. "Or you'd place it into a container designed to handle that much voltage."

"You mean like the one that you just broke open?"

"Yeah," he said, letting out a reluctant sigh.

My phone dinged. Mandy replied on it, and I followed with another quick message, to contact the US Marshal's office for Colorado Springs to activate me and show me on a case.

"What are you doing?" Connor asked.

"Agent things."

I didn't even bother to look for a reply. I just shoved the phone back in my pocket and moved further down the bay and away from the arcing electrical strikes.

"If the other one started here and followed that spiral to the park, do you think this one will do the same?"

"Possibly if they follow the same kind of pattern, but I don't know. I've never seen anything like this before."

"Neither have I," I replied. "So, if that's the case, where would the next spot be?"

Connor rattled off an address from memory, followed by several others.

"Okay, cool," I said. "That means we might have time to prep and figure out what we're doing with this thing. What would be the easiest way to send this much power to ground? Or could we quickly get hold of something to contain it?"

"No idea," Connor said, shaking his head as he turned to face me.

"Don't look at me, dude. I am not an electrical engineer. I'm just a grease monkey."

"What if we can't stop it?"

"Don't start that 'woe is me' bullshit. We can't let this thing get out of here and harm the populous. Did you see any other Tesla stuff in the building?"

"Maybe. There were a few pieces of old equipment that could have come from the lab, but it didn't really amount to much."

"Think we could use any of it to trap this thing?"

"Maybe? It would be nice if we had a Faraday cage. That might trap it."

"Faraday cage? What's that?"

"It's a cage that only allows certain wavelengths through the gaps in the cage. It's one way to shield yourself from EMP strikes."

"What would something like that look like?"

"About maybe that big," Connor said, pointing at something covered in tarps at the far end of the bay.

We rushed over, fumbling with the dry, rotten canvas straps that held the tarp in place.

"Oh my God," he gasped, revealing a large wire mesh cylinder a few feet in diameter and maybe eight feet tall. "I can't believe this has been hiding here this whole time."

"So, this is what you were talking about?"

"Oh, yeah, absolutely."

"Okay, so how do we use it to catch that thing?"

"We could use waveguides or grounding rods to guide it into place."

I turned and glared at him. "Do you have either of those things?"

"No."

If I didn't think fast, we were about to end up extra crispy. I glanced around, but it all just seemed like useless junk to me. Then a thought struck me when I looked up.

"You said they cut the power in the warehouse. What about the water?"

"Doubtful. I wouldn't think they'd be allowed to shut off the water because of fire codes and all."

"Well, what if we flushed it?" I asked, examining the sprinkler system stretching across the bay.

"Maybe," he said. "But it could just as easily electrify everything in this building that the water touches if you did that."

"Okay, so we don't want to be in here when we set it off. But do you think it might work?"

Connor thought for a moment. "It's possible. Water and electricity don't mix."

"Well, I don't have any better ideas, do you?"

He shook his head. "Not really."

"Alright, now we need a game plan." I hurried to the next doorway, looking for a way to manually activate the sprinkler system—some kind of valve, or a pull handle. There was no guarantee that the water was even on, but it was all I had to work with at the moment.

The thing continued its slow march through the building, arcing its way through the stacks of materials still heading our way.

I continued through to the next bay. This section of the warehouse was two to three stories tall, with large overhead cranes and an upper-level office box that overlooked the entire bay.

"Let's see if we can't drive that thing into here," I said to Connor. "We might be able to hide up there in that office. See if you can find any rubber matting lying around and carry it up there."

I hurried to circle around through another opening to the section of the warehouse we'd found the capacitors in and found the emergency release valve for the sprinklers. With a quick crank of the handle, a downpour rained down from above. I continued to the next bay, opening the valve there, before cutting back through to the larger bay where I'd left Connor searching for rubber mats. I found him waiting at the top of the stairs to the dock office when I returned.

"Okay, sprinklers are working. Hopefully, that'll keep the thing from retreating. Any luck finding something to insulate us?"

"Yeah, the office is already lined with rubber flooring, and I found these, he said, holding out a set of rubber cleaning gloves that I guessed could easily reach my elbows when I pulled them on."

"That'll have to work." I took the stairs two steps at a time, then took the gloves offered by Conner after reaching the surrounding catwalk. "Did you find the emergency sprinkler release?"

"Yeah, just on the other side of the dock box," Connor said, pointing toward the door on the other side of the small office.

Sizzling electrical pops of blue arcing tendrils preceded the creature as it entered the far end of the bay through the doorway we'd originally passed through.

"Alright, get ready. We're gonna short out this little son of a bitch before it can do any more damage. Just don't touch anything metal when I kick over the sprinklers."

Searching, I looked for something to tie around the valve, so I could open it from the relative safety of the office. It was a long shot, but I was counting on the rubber matting inside the office to be enough insulation to keep us from frying like a chicken in a microwave.

Finding an extension cord, I wrapped it around the valve handle and stepped back into the office, standing roughly in the middle of the room.

"Ready?"

"Ready as I'll ever be," Connor answered.

I pulled, but nothing happened.

Tugging first, I pulled again with the same result, but then it suddenly broke free and the cord went slack.

"Okay? What happened?"

I stepped back to the door and examined the valve from a distance. The release handle had moved, but the thin steel cable that ran from the wall to the ancient valve overhead had snapped halfway up.

"Dammit."

"What?"

"The cable snapped," I replied.

"Can you fix it?"

It looked like the cable had just snapped where it had corroded through over the years. Quickly I found an old barrel that I rolled over to the wall and climbed up on it so that I could reach the valve.

"Stay where you're at," I shouted back over my shoulder. Grabbing the release handle of the valve, I dropped, letting all of my weight pull on the release handle.

It popped and creaked at first, then stopped. Still hanging, I kicked and jerked at the handle. Finally, my efforts were answered by the rush of water passing through the valve into the sprinkler pipes overhead.

Bright electrical arcs flickered, lighting up the warehouse. The hairs on the back of my neck stood up straight. Tendrils of lightning struck all around the far end of the bay where the creature had entered.

"That can't be good," I mumbled to myself. Letting go of the handle, I dropped to the barrel and leapt. Electric tentacles arced around me as I soared through the air, falling toward the steel grading of the catwalk. If it wasn't for the fact I was probably about to die, I'd say it was the coolest *superhero* like scene I could ever hope for. But then I realized I was going to fall a few feet short of the office door.

The world around me exploded in a cacophony of light and smoke when my boots struck the grating. An awkward numbness, like when you stick your finger in a light socket, or accidentally touch the prongs when blindly plugging something in, hit me. I continued forward, rolling headlong into the open office door, where I tucked in my knees and rolled up into the fetal position.

A sudden explosion, like a bomb exploding nearby, rocked the foreman's office. In the distance, car alarms screeched and warbled. Connor let out a laughing scream as blue and purple lights strobed, lighting up the warehouse like some sort of techno rave party.

Slowly, the popping arcs of flashing lights died down. Cautiously, we rose up and glanced out over the bay through the office windows. Moments passed without another sound beyond the shower of sprinklers flooding the building.

Connor broke the silence. "You think it's safe?"

"I don't know, but there's only one way to find out." I looked around the room for anything metal that I could toss out onto the catwalk and test it for current. Leaned in the corner behind the door was a short section of threaded pipe that I chucked out the door. It bounced end first on the grating and tumbled its way down the wet metal stairs.

"Nothing arced," Connor shouted. "It might be safe after all."

"Maybe." There was no telling how long it would take before somebody would come along and find us. Only Connor's security friend even knew we were out here. So either we waited or someone had to give it a shot.

Reluctantly, I took a step out onto the catwalk, testing my luck.

Nothing happened. "I think we're good," I said, turning back to Connor, then hurried out onto the catwalk. Looking in the direction of where the creature should have been, there were scorch marks all around on the concrete and equipment along the aisle down the center of the bay.

The creature wasn't anywhere in sight. Then a tiny glimmer of light winked to life where it should have been. It was like a speckle of stardust floating there, struggling to hold itself together. It flickered and glowed once more. Weak arcs of electricity licked out like the creature was the core of one of those novelty lightning balls. It flashed again, then faded away, dissolving into the darkness to a tiny pinprick that vanished without a trace.

"You don't see that every day," Conner said then slapped me on the back of the shoulder.

"Nope," I agreed. "The worst part is going to be writing the report for my superiors. But if I'm lucky, I'll score a little pay out of it. I did get picture evidence that it existed. One down, one to go."

"I don't know that we'd have to worry about the other one."

"Why's that?"

"Because of the massive snowstorm we had a few days ago. There haven't been any other incidents since then. The storm wasn't anything out of the ordinary for around here, but if the creature was caught outside in the storm, I bet that would have been enough to short it out, just like we did with the sprinklers."

"Sounds as feasible as anything else to me," I said.

Connor hurried down the stairs to the warehouse floor. "Let's get out of here before the cops show up."

"Right behind you." We made a beeline for the door and hauled ass for his truck. "I'm wet and cold, but I could really go for a good beer right now."

"I know the perfect place. Do you like fish and chips?"

"Who doesn't? Do they have stout on tap?" I jumped into the truck.

"They do, and it's a great local brew."

"Sounds like a plan to me."

He chuckled, then started up the truck and shifted into gear. "Jack Quinn's it is then. The best Irish pub in Colorado Springs."

A Pawn's Promotion

A Finn Rhodes story
By Philip K. Booker

My heart sank with each echoing clang of the aluminum plate as it bounced along the smooth concrete floor of Scenic City Brews. It felt like it was screaming, *"Look at this Loser!"*

What's worse, it had taken the still-steaming pair of pepperoni and mushroom slices with it on its flight to the floor.

Smooth going, Phineas. There goes your chance to leave a business card behind later.

I mean, first impressions matter. Coming-off like a fumbling klutz hardly screams competence when you're presenting yourself as someone who you'd trust with taking care of their business during a biohazard event.

I eased off the tall stool with a wince. My ribs had nearly healed from the beating I'd taken in October. They apparently felt the need to remind me that *nearly* was not the same as *healed*. It's not like getting frog-stomped by a giant faerie-dog is something you forget easily. Besides, I still had my right arm wrapped in a long-arm cast until my appointment with the doctor this week; another of my consolation prizes from my fight with Uther.

"Oh, Hon! Here, let me get that," the kindly waitress with the short muddy-red curls said as she hurried up to the high-top table where I'd been sitting.

The large ramekin of marinara that had come with my dinner had splattered across the floor, highlighting the death of my pizza with a saucy, blood-like splatter. In my head, I ran through the steps I'd have used to handle the decontamination of said blood-splatter.

Man, I *really* need to get back in the field. I'm losing it.

Bio-remediation—better known as crime-scene cleaning, but it covers more than that—is physically demanding work. It's not something that one can expect to handle when you're in bad shape. It can be hours of back-breaking work in miserable conditions. And I love doing it. I feel like I'm making a difference in the community and in the lives of our clients. We help safely erase the traces of what is, arguably, the worst day in someone's life. However, until the doctors cleared me, my cousin and business partner, Nic, was having to handle the labor on his own. We'd been able to make-do, mostly. Our mutual friend Jeremy had been willing to chip in on a couple of jobs that'd demanded heavy lifting. Meanwhile, I'm stuck running ops and billing, hating every second. Give me fieldwork over paperwork any day.

The waitress told me she'd rush two replacement slices out to me, and I thanked her before trying to shrink into obscurity from the other patrons who could eat without knocking their food onto the floor.

As promised, they soon presented me with another plate of pizza. I gave myself a little clumsiness insurance with a damp napkin under the plate. Nic had shown me the trick which he'd picked up while serving drunks in several area bars while attending college at UT Chattanooga. In his words, I was so pathetically bad at using my left hand to eat after I got out of the hospital; I made the drunks look good. Weeks later, I was still not great, but I had thought I'd improved. My former pieces of pizza begged to differ, though.

I nursed my Coke, attention absently drifting between the bank of muted televisions over the bar. The talking heads on ESPN were busy speculating over who would come out on top in this year's college football playoffs. Literally no one on the panel thought my old alma mater, UT Knoxville, had a chance of making it to the championship game, but I still believed the Vols could surprise everyone. If nothing else, the boys in orange and white had bragging rights over Bama; which made me smile just thinking about it. The Vols had struggled badly while I'd been a student there, so it was refreshing to see them listed as a Top Ten team.

A young wisp of a woman, in a short skirt and one of the black Scenic City Brews tees that all the staff wore, breezed by and set another stack of napkins on the edge of my table. Her bright purple hair was curled along the back of her neck and it obscured her face, but I was sure I hadn't noticed her moving about until just now. The tee was easily two sizes too big for her. Without turning to attend to anyone else, she left the building.

Huh. Weird.

I glanced at the stack of off-white napkins and noticed the sheet on top had words on it. Scrawled in hurried black writing:

Finn—meet me outside. We need to talk.

My stomach sank a little. Only people I'm familiar with call me Finn, and this was the first time I'd been here. And it's not like someone could have spotted my car or our decommissioned ambulance, jokingly dubbed the Blood Bus, since I hadn't driven either vehicle since my injuries. Instead,

I just rode CARTA to get around Chattanooga, or let Nic handle the driving.

I flagged down the waitress to settle my tab and get my pizza to-go and left her a larger than usual tip, for having to deal with my mess.

The late-December air bit at the exposed skin of my face when I stepped outside. My nose instantly ran in protest at the chill. Between my loose olive-drab coat—the only one in my closet that fit over this damnable cast—and the heat coming off the pizza box, I was warm enough. Still, I pulled the navy-knit cap I'd brought with me over my head. Our company name, Chatt-Decon, embroidered on it in bold white lettering.

I paced through the cramped little parking lot that sat next to the bar but didn't see any sign of the purple-haired woman who'd left me the note.

"Bang! You're dead," came a voice from behind me, with an accompanying poke in my back.

"Son of a—!" I hollered, heart leaping in my chest. I wheeled about, trying to check my would-be attacker with my cast.

Instead, my cast whooshed through empty air and I lost my food to the forces of gravity for the second time this evening. Before the box could hit the ground, though, a swift hand rescued it from its certainty of sidewalk-doom.

"Whoa! Easy there, Finn! It was just a joke," said the woman with the purple-hair as she knelt—well below my attempted swing—my pizza box deftly held in one hand.

I blinked, finally recognizing her voice and something in her face.

Her hair was longer than when I'd last seen her; more than I would have thought possible. It had been an icy-white pixie cut a couple months ago. Her eyes had changed color again, nicely matching with the purple of her hair. A hint of a shimmer lit off them. I used to write off her rotating eye colors as contacts; not anymore.

"What the hell, Amy!"

"Sorry. I didn't mean to freak you out," she said as she stood up and handed me back my dinner. "I just needed to speak to you."

Fully standing, she was about five-foot-nothing. My impression of the t-shirt had been right. It practically swallowed her thin body whole. A gray skirt peeked out below the t-shirt, along with a pair of stretchy denim leggings and a pair of thick-soled combat boots. Though the boots gave her some extra height, she was still easily a foot shorter than me. I might have missed her with my swing, even if she hadn't ducked so quickly.

"You know where I live," I replied coldly.

"Yes," she hesitated.

"But you didn't want to risk running into Nic."

Her eyes fell to her feet, and she shuffled her pair of knock-off Doc Martens against the bits of dirt and ground glass in the parking lot. I'd guessed right.

"I can't face him right now. Not until I can figure out how to explain."

"You mean explain how you're a *faerie*, and only got with him so could you spy on me for Uther," I said with as much acid in my voice as I could muster. "*Yeah*, I see that going over really well." She'd met my cousin three years ago, and they'd been in a hot-and-heavy relationship since then. That was until a couple months ago, when the proverbial shit hit the fan and years-worth of secrecy went out the window with it.

"*Half-fae!*" she said defensively, louder than she'd probably intended. She looked around the parking lot cautiously before continuing. "Just like *you* are, Finn."

That'd been a moment worthy of the Maury Show. I'd never known who my father was. So, after my mother mysteriously disappeared following a car accident when I was just a year old, my aunt and uncle raised me alongside my cousin, Nic. Skip forward twenty-four years and I end up discovering that not only are faeries and other creatures of myth and legend *real,* but my dead-beat dad is among their rank. It was something I was still trying to come to terms with.

"But unlike me, *you* knew that already. *You* knew who you were, knew who *I* was, and lied about it."

She looked truly hurt by that. "I didn't lie—I just didn't tell you the truth. Meeting your family wasn't accidental, and I *was* initially using my position to give reports on you to Uther, but I developed genuine feelings for Nic. I never meant to hurt him—or you. I swear it. I *love* him, Finn."

My scowl softened. I couldn't help but feel she was being straight with me. In three years of knowing her, I couldn't recall ever hearing her say those words to Nic. Sure, they'd exchanged substitutions, but never the Dread-Three.

I swore under my breath as I pinched the bridge of my nose, "What do you want?"

She looked relieved, like I'd removed an enormous weight from her shoulders. "I'm parked around the corner. I'll explain on the way. Just don't think you're bringing that pizza in my car; eat it now or dump it."

I'd like to think knowing someone for three years is long enough not to have to worry about being set up for an ambush, but that set my Spidey-Sense off. Even excluding my recent discoveries of the unbelievable, being raised by a cop taught me that straight-up ordinary people are capable of astounding levels of deceit. And the Fae can make the most accomplished con-artist look like a rank amateur. Luckily, the Fae are beholden to Old Laws and, even if to a lesser extent, so are their less-pure offspring.

"Before I go anywhere with you, I need your sworn oath that I'm not being led into a trap and that you mean me no ill will."

Her body stiffened. "Are you serious? We're wasting time here, Finn."

"I'm deadly serious."

Her mouth drew into a hard, thin line before she spat at my feet. "Fine!" She wiped her mouth with the back of her hand and took a deep breath. Her voice took on a faint thrumming quality as she spoke: "I swear on my blood and power, that I am not leading you into a trap, and that—other than a swift kick in the balls, I intend to give you for this—I, Amy Lester, bare you, Phineas Rhodes, no ill will."

I could feel she meant every word, too. Almost reflexively, I felt a phantom twinge between my legs.

"You're an ass," she said to me. "You know that, right?"

"Yeah, but it never hurts to be too careful."

"Oh no, it's gonna hurt later," she said, pantomiming a punter's kick in her boots.

True to her word, there wasn't anyone waiting to jump me when we got to the lot where she'd parked her sporty little hatchback Subaru. The cramped alleyway we had to walk through, nestled between the twelve-stories of polished white stone edifices of the James and Maclellan Buildings, would have made an ideal ambush location. Thankfully, a web of encased Edison lights strung across the alley kept my paranoia from running amok. I advise against trying to inhale a box of pizza when you think there's a chance of being jumped; it's terrible for your stomach.

I had waited until we were in the confines of her car before trying to extract more information. "Okay, spill it."

"Grouchy much? I said I'd tell you, didn't I?" She paused and sniffed the air, her nose crinkled. "What's that smell? It's like beer, fryer grease and—*Beltane's Fire*—is that *vomit*?" Her face twisted in revulsion as she brought the bar's shirt up to it. "Oh, *hell no!*"

She leaped out of the car, leaving the door wide-open behind her, I noted with a frown. She whipped the offending article off in a flash and flung it atop a nearby dumpster.

I'd like to say Amy's lack of regard for proper attire was shocking, but frankly, I was just thankful she was wearing a bra tonight. It wasn't always the case during the time she'd stayed over at our apartment. However, I was more concerned that she'd attract the attention of the cops if they saw her walking around in a state of undress. Word would undoubtedly get to Uncle Robbie, who served as a sergeant for the CPD in this part of the city, and I didn't want to have to explain why I was with my cousin's half-naked ex in a darkened parking lot.

Nic might be clued-in to the weirdness of the world, but we had avoided revealing the truth to either Uncle Robbie or Aunt Jackie out of concern for their mental well-being. And although my girlfriend, Keira, was intimately in the loop regarding the world of the Fae, I doubted she'd take the news well either. And since she is also my rehabilitation trainer, I had even more reason to want to avoid relationship trouble.

It ended up being a moot concern. As soon as she'd torn the bar's ill-fitted shirt off, I could see the gray skirt had really been a sweater she'd tied about her waist. She undid it and threw it on. I could have written that off as not really paying attention to what she'd been wearing, but her hair had changed too. In an instant, it had reverted from the wild shade of electric purple to the icy white it had been the last couple of months she'd lived with us.

She strode over and fished through the drivers-side door panel, pulled out a small tube of body spray and danced through a copious cloud of the stuff. When she climbed back into the car, she smelled like a blend of cucumber and melon and the scent wove about the interior as she cranked the engine and turned the heat on.

She nodded, testing herself against any lingering smells with a sniff to "So, uh," I motioned to her changed appearance, "that was all a Glamour?"

She nodded, testing herself against any lingering smells with a sniff to each of her arms. "Unrelated odors can ruin even quality Glamours. That's why I nicked the t-shirt instead of just using a Glamour. Less taxing, and it added a sense of authenticity to the construction. Nothing conjures memories better than the sense of smell. That's also why I'm adamant about keeping my car so clean."

She wasn't wrong, and I noted her car was practically pristine. "Nic left a takeout bag from Krystal's in the *Blood Bus* last month; the cab smelled like onions and mustard for a week."

"Ugh. I used to tell him he couldn't eat anything from there if he wanted to get lucky that night."

"I… I really don't need details of y'all's sex life. It was bad enough being in the same apartment some nights," I said while conjuring enough mental-bleach to banish memories of grunts and moans from across the hall. A few shakes of my head finished the brain-scrub, and I returned my attention to matters at hand. "So, why do you need my help?"

"Actually, the Court is calling upon your service."

"Screw that! We're done here," I said, reaching for the door latch.

It locked as I pulled it.

"Finn, you need to hear me out," she said, her finger on the auto-lock button on the driver's side panel.

"What—what do you think you could *possibly* say to me that would make me get wrapped into the affairs of your Court? The Duke declared I was free to live my life if I kept my head down. I'm fucking Switzerland to you guys."

"*You* are…" she said, biting her lip. "The safety of your family *inside* Court, however, is reliant on the stability of the Duke's power."

There was an unspoken hint in her words that suggested she knew more than was common knowledge. Crap. My hand fell from the door handle.

"The Duchy is vulnerable to displays of weakness right now. This might be one of the other players in the region testing the strength of His Grace's control. The importance of image in fae society can rival the darkest corners of Hollywood or Washington. It's *because* they do not consider you part of the Court that the Duke needs to get you involved. It reflects strength if he's able to be seen as moving you around the chessboard and we succeed."

"What are we dealing with?"

"Gremlins."

"Oh, come on! You know I love that movie; please don't kill my childhood!"

That might have gotten a dumbfounded look from any other member of the Court of the Valley, but Amy had spent years among us mere mortals and had become a huge movie buff.

"Same mischievous, destructive nature; without the Xenomorph eggs or the watery multiplication. There's a small contingent of gremlins living in Helen, Georgia—we think they're drawn to the kitschy Bavarian feel of the town. Nasty little creatures, only about two-feet tall, but they travel in packs, causing mayhem whenever they get bored. And they get bored easily; like European Soccer Hooligans with short-man syndrome. Anyway, I guess they're done with Oktoberfest and decided to take another shot at our Duchy again."

"Wait, again?"

"Remember that controversy at Volkswagen with the Passat Diesel a few years ago? They were responsible for the initial equipment design failure. Management tried to cover it up afterwards, but yeah, it involved gremlins. Uther led the effort that ran them out of town last time, but…"

"He can't because of me. Is that what you're telling me?"

"Well, you *are* the reason they banished him."

"They banished him for being a psychotic asshole!" I held up my arm. "I'll be damned if I shed a tear over him being gone."

"Be that as it may, Uther was willing to hit the frontline against them before. Gremlins are creatures of the modern world's influence. Iron doesn't affect them like it does to us, and they have a real connection with electricity. They feed on it and can manipulate it, to a degree."

That was a kick in the pants. Iron served as one of the most consistent weaknesses of the fae. Even half-breeds, like Amy and me, could have an allergic reaction to the stuff if it were pure enough. Cold Iron—iron that is prepared and wrought in special low-temperature techniques—can be lethal to fae. I'd gotten knocked into a chunk of the stuff during my fight with Uther, and it had left me with a wicked burn on my hand; but it had saved my life.

"So, do we know how many of these things we're dealing with? Or even where to find them? Chattanooga's big enough as it is, but doesn't the Duke control a chunk of the surrounding area too? That's a lot for you and me to cover on our own."

"It is," she said nodding, "but if quests were easy, there'd be no glory in them."

"Oh, that's dirty… using my own D&D line against me."

"And you thought I wasn't paying attention," she said with a sly smirk. She popped the car into reverse and angled out of the tiny private lot and turned south onto Chestnut Street. "Anyway, I bribed a small contingent of pixies from Cloudland Canyon to be on the lookout for them and report their movements northward to me. And they did," she let out a sigh, "but they lost sight of them when they passed Finley Stadium—the lights were too distracting. That was about an hour ago, so I'm thinking they're still in the City Center district, but no further than the North Shore."

A much smaller search area to be sure, but it was still roughly four square miles of city to cover, and the area with the highest building density in the city.

"So, it's up to us to find them again. What then?"

"Break up whatever crap they're trying to start here and send them packing. Or," she said, locking eyes with me as she pulled to an intersection. "Or we kill them."

"Just like that?"

"Just like that," she answered firmly.

Gulp.

It turns out we didn't have to go too far to find signs of their passing. Just before we got to the Convention Center, we came across one of CARTA's free-to-ride electric shuttles broken down on the side of the road. The back-end of the bus had a gout of smoke pouring out of the mangled cooling vent behind the back tire. The driver was using a small extinguisher at the vent, trying to prevent a flare-up.

As much as I hated to face the icy night air again—my hands were just starting to regain feeling—I rolled the window down to eavesdrop on the situation. A handful of passengers were milling around the sidewalk, staring at the mess or holding animated conversations on their phones.

"This mangy-looking dog ran right out in front of the bus!" One bystander said into his phone, a panicked-looking elderly man with a balding pate and a green and silver chevroned sweater. "No way the driver can swerve, so he hits the damn thing. Then three more of the things jump out from behind that big glass number on the corner." The Merrill Lynch

Building, I noted. "And they chased the bus, smashing into the back of it until the first one popped out the other side—and the stupid thing got back up and ran off with the rest of them!"

Amy and I glanced back at each other.

"Sounds like our boys," she said, pulling past the bus and turning back toward the North Shore. "They're still moving this way."

"Yeah, and one of them just shook off being run over by a thirteen-ton bus," I noted. "Do you have something bigger than that in the trunk I don't know about?"

"We don't need anything so dramatic. They're hardy little monsters, but only to a point. It probably only took a glancing hit from the bus and rolled with it. They can be killed."

"Good to know this isn't a complete suicide mission," I said, rolling my eyes.

"I've got a pair of new swing-sticks in the back," she said with a wicked grin. "They're even better than the last set I had, nigh indestructible."

I raised my arm, waving it back and forth for emphasis. "Uh, hello? You want me to go walking through downtown Chattanooga—at night, mind you—with a cricket bat and a broken arm? You've lost every bit of your mind. There's no cop in this world who would see me and not know that I was looking to cause trouble."

"And they'd be right. You *are* looking to cause trouble," she shrugged as she edged up Broad Street slowly.

"There are no words," I said, stunned by her glibness.

"That is why you shouldn't *be* seen. These are dangerous creatures, Finn. They won't go down without a fight, and it is sure to cause a scene. You will need to spin a Glamour to hide your appearance, since you are intent on living a *normal* life."

"You say it like it's a bad thing."

"Not bad, just weird. Like choosing to walk when you have wings."

Huh. "Anyway, I don't know how to do all that... fae stuff," I said, gesturing weakly.

She laughed. "It's much more instinctual than you'd believe; the straightforward stuff, at least. Like what Ronan showed you."

"When he tried to *drown* me!"

"Sometimes you have to push the baby bird out of the nest," she shrugged again. "Look, I'm not saying it was nice, but you're still here. You've got to will yourself into looking different. Even if you can only make a relatively minor change, it could be enough to mess with the cameras around here."

I hadn't even stopped to think about cameras. Modern cities have cameras everywhere. There's a billboard I saw once that said you're never more than three feet away from a spider, and as much as that made my flesh crawl, truthfully, cameras are giving arachnids a run for their money. Most commercial buildings use a video security system to monitor their entrances. Then you have all the mandatory cameras attached to ATMs and traffic cameras. Even dashboard cameras were becoming more common in civilian vehicles for security and for evidence in traffic disputes. And then you have the fact that most people walking around have a camera attached to the phones in their pockets.

I suddenly felt incredibly exposed.

If this went sideways, even if we managed to find and thwart a pack of bus-shrugging hobgoblins, my entire livelihood could be in ruins if I couldn't pull off what sounded like the equivalent of Faerie 101.

Fuck me.

My world shrank in on me. My heart pounded in my ears like a drumline.

"Hey, Finn! Yo, man!" She shook me from the driver's seat. "*Phineas! Snap out of it!*"

I gasped for breath and hunched over and closed my eyes to ground myself. "I—I'm okay," I lied. Instantly, a thick, coppery taste filled my mouth. It ran over my tongue and I choked back the taste with a grimace. It wasn't real—I knew that—but that didn't stop it from feeling like I had a mouth full of blood. Stupid Fae Geas.

"Remind me to start up a cash poker game with you, because you really suck at lying."

Still leaning over, I raised my left hand high enough to flip her off.

"Cute. Come on, we don't have time to waste on you being a worm. So what? Your arm is in a cast. It's almost time for you to take it off anyway, and you've got more than one arm. You haul tainted materials out of houses wearing a glorified garbage bag all day. This is nothing."

"PPE suit," I said, turning to her.

"Whatever. I tried one on once and nearly had to cut it off to get out of it after only a few minutes."

"You what?" I said, suddenly furious. "I pay for those suits! They're not toys!" The suits might be disposable, but I couldn't afford to piss the cost away for her to mess with them.

She grinned, "Snapped you out of it, though, didn't I?"

"You suck."

"Please… you wish. Besides, Keira would kill me."

"*W—what?*" My face burned with a flash of heat as I caught her words, and I turned away from her to hide my reaction. A frantic mess of strobing lights in one of the Electric Power Board's Christmas windows caught my attention. "Ugh, I'm pretty sure that might qualify for what we're looking for." An animatronic Santa in the holiday window was actively committing a lewd act on the display's Mrs. Claus, which was sure as heck not how it was designed.

I pointed out the display to Amy, and she swerved quickly across Broad Street onto MLK, then deftly swung into an empty curbside spot in front of the building.

"Crash course in Glamour," she said to me as she cut the engine. "Get a picture in your mind. The clearer you can imagine it, the better. Picture it over your body, like a mask or makeup, and then pull the image out and over yourself like a blanket."

I tried thinking, picturing someone else in my head; to control my breathing in the panic that was still dancing in my gut. I was about to break into the main office of one of Chattanooga's most prestigious businesses to stop an invasion of creatures most people considered pure fantasy. I could only picture the look of disappointment in my uncle's eyes. He and my aunt had raised me since I was a small baby, and I couldn't stand the thought of breaking his heart.

The skin on the top of my hands darkened from my ruddy tone to a smoky brown hue. In shock, I shook the image away quickly, recognizing my uncle's features forming in the effect. My stomach lurched at donning magical Blackface, let alone smearing my uncle's good-name.

"That was… interesting," Amy said, observing me. "The addition of the dress-blues was a nice touch."

"I wasn't trying to make myself look like Uncle Robbie," I said, ashamed by what I'd done, but a little exhilarated that I'd managed anything at all. "You said you had a set of cricket bats in the back?"

She nodded in the affirmative. "Yeah, why?"

"You've really watched *Shaun of the Dead* too many times."

"Watch your mouth," she said defensively. "That's not possible."

I took another breath and closed my eyes to focus. I felt the energy move over my body. It was light, like a feather at first; then it felt more substantive, like the feel of latex paint when it gets on your skin.

"He's not even in that movie," she said, as I felt like I'd gotten it right. "And Vinnie Jones was a footballer, not a cricket player. Nerd-card revoked, Finn."

I pulled the passenger visor down and examined my work in the mirror. It wasn't an exact match, but I looked enough like a younger Jones, circa *Lock, Stock and Two Smoking Barrels* perhaps, that I felt sufficiently unrecognizable.

"Match the weapon to the persona," I said, startled to hear my voice come out with a similar, glottaling accent as the actor had used, with my own unaltered voice echoing within my head.

Amy beamed, "Now, say *I'm the Juggernaut, bitch.*"

"Piss off," I said as I reached over and opened the passenger door with my good-hand.

"Oi," she barked, snapping her fingers. "Lose the knit-cap! It's got your company logo on it!"

"Oh, right." I chucked it into her floorboard.

In the time it took me to straighten out and face Amy, she'd popped the rear hatch of her Subaru open, and had adopted a frizzy nest of tangled brown hair bound in a loose elastic tie, and was wearing an old camo BDU jacket. She handed me one of the bats; its handle covered in a red threaded coating and the blade made of a hefty black material. It probably was as durable as she'd said. I tested the feel in my good-hand; which was weird. The thing was solid; probably over three pounds and nearly three feet long. The raised spine of the bat had the words "Liverpool Assassin" printed on it.

"Really?" I said as I examined the bat. "That's a bit much, even for you."

"What do you want?" She said, joining me on the sidewalk, "It's sturdy, hits like a truck and it's street legal."

"For now," I muttered. "How do you want to handle this, then? This office is closed on the weekend." This close to the building, it hurt to crane my neck enough to take in the whole of the structure. It's an interesting design; eight-stories of glass and steel, with a smooth red granite façade.

"Well, they had to get in there somehow," she said with a shrug and walked up to the main entrance.

"As if—" I began, but was struck dumb when she tugged on the front door and the damn thing opened without a fuss. What's more, I couldn't hear an alarm either.

"*Whatever, Alicia,*" she said with an exaggerated Valley Girl inflection and then gestured me inside. "Don't look a gift horse in the mouth."

EPB had spent a ton of money in the mid-2000's updating their system into the fiber optic Smart Grid. Designed to remote-read new Smart Meters, reroute the flow of power during outages and paved the way for them to offer high-speed internet to their customers, with speeds of up to 25 Gigs.

I would be a pissed off Cord-cutter if these gremlins screwed up my internet. And yes, I can hear how bad that sounds.

Upon entering the building, we stepped lightly across the marble flooring of the lobby, using the columns as cover as we moved toward the Broad Street facing windows where the holiday display had been. A thick black curtain, with the words *We Are Gig City* printed on it, hung across the windows. We crept to the edge of the curtain, bats at the ready, and wordlessly counted in unison.

One. Two. Three—Go!

I whipped the curtain back as Amy spun in, ready to deliver a hurt to whatever was on the other side with her *Liverpool Assassin,* and then froze.

"It's gone…" she said, defeated.

"What?" I asked in surprise, as I rolled under the curtain to join her. "Where could it have gone? It was just there."

Sure enough, the animatronic Mrs. Claus remained slumped over the torn Naughty List, but Santa was nowhere to be seen.

"It's still riding the Fat Man," she said. "It couldn't have gotten far."

As if on cue, something ripped through the curtain and forcefully jerked me back through the fabric and out into the lobby. My bat skittered out of my hand as I went.

The booming voice of Santa rang in my ear as the display piece shook me about with unbelievable strength, shaking me like a rag-doll. "*Ho-Ho No!*"

Each shake jerked my neck around painfully, and the world danced wildly.

"*Finn!*" Amy yelped in surprise as she dashed after us, but had to reverse course as the hefty curtain broke free of its moorings and fell on top of her.

I struggled to pull free of my thick coat which Santa had grabbed, but I couldn't free my right arm when my cast got caught in the twisting fabric. I fell to the floor with a thud, painfully jerked about by my still bound arm.

The Santa gleefully kicked at me from my prone position, peppering each hit with a *Ho-Ho-Ho*. I did my best to deflect its blows away from my ribs with my free limbs, but I was fading fast.

"*Hey Kringle!*"

I risked a glance to see Amy standing angrily behind my attacker, who had stopped its rain of kicks long enough to turn and face her.

"Silent Night!" She swung the heavy bat and cracked Santa in the face with the flat striking edge. Its head came clean off and sailed across the lobby.

The hold on my jacket fell away, and I dragged myself to my feet with a groan; shakily untangling myself from the remains of my jacket.

The headless Santa shook a little and, to my surprise, a scrawny, impish creature with dark leathery skin crawled out of the chest cavity. It glared at Amy and hissed with contempt.

She didn't miss a beat and brought the bat back around, this time with the thinner edge of the bat's blade. She caught the creature in the throat and its head snapped backwards with a wet *crack*.

"See?" she said between heavy breaths. "They're not so tough."

"Fine," I wheezed. "Next time, *you* can be the punching bag." I rolled my shoulders around, testing them for muscle tears. Satisfied I'd not destroyed weeks of PT progress, I carefully checked over the rest of my body. Other than a few understandably tender spots on my legs and arm, I hadn't collected too many fresh injuries.

"But you play punching bag so well," she said as she retrieved my dropped bat and handed it to me. "Seriously though, Finn, am I going to have to teach you how to fight? A cop who looks like he could bench-press my dresser raised you. Didn't you and Nic ever come to blows when you were kids?"

"Fighting family members is different. Most people aren't trying to kill each other when you're growing up. Plus, I beat Uther."

"You got *lucky* with Uther," she said dismissively. And she wasn't wrong. "The Court may think you pulled off some amazing victory against their former General, but I saw what happened. And besides, that gremlin damn near turned you into a fleshy stocking for its chimney just now. I need your help, but only if you can man up and snap out of whatever is holding you back."

That stung.

I glanced over to the body of the gremlin limply draped over the headless Santa. The ink black skin of the creature was already beginning to show signs of decomposition, which was startlingly fast. Perhaps that was why there's little-to-no proof of the existence of fae creatures. Amy didn't even pay it any notice. I would have to remember to pick her brain on the topic some other time, when she might be feeling a little more charitable.

"Alright," I said with a sigh. "They were all together—or at least mostly—when they were coming this way. Why stop here? Obviously, that one was having a laugh while playing guard duty. But what purpose does it serve to hit the Power Board?"

"They thrive on causing trouble and breaking down machinery."

"Yes, but why *here*? They could cause trouble anywhere in the city. You said they're supposed to be testing the Duke's control and influence in the region, but it's not like the Court is reliant on electricity. So *why here?*"

"We know they're in the building, Finn. I don't have to know why; I just need to find them and kill them."

"Fight smarter, not harder. We need to know why they'd want to screw with the Smart Grid here. If they shut things down here, it shouldn't take long to reroute things from another branch. That's theoretically the way they built it."

The lights flickered above us.

"Basement," we said in unison, and made our way to the stairwell.

In covering cleanups over the years, I've had to become familiar with how many electrical systems work so I can cut the power and properly remove any contaminants as needed. Usually that's in residential homes, but I've had jobs in a few commercial properties where I've had to do the same. Never have I had to work around something as complex as a city utility. Using those other jobs as a guide and—to my shame—that scene in Jurassic Park where Hammond is guiding Dr. Sattler to restore power to the Island, I thought it made sense to follow the conduit lines down to the basement. That's where most power systems are, right?

Well, that was before it dawned on me the massive number of computers needed to maintain and control something like the Smart Grid. I'd like to say that this thought occurred to me quickly, but really it kicked into gear moments after we heard a desperate scream coming from the floors above us.

Amy and I dashed up the stairwell, trying not to dwell on the number of floors we were slogging up, but to pinpoint where the commotion had come from. We were just about to round another flight of stairs, when we heard a sudden thud against the door we'd just passed. Amy opened the door and found an unconscious black man in a security guard's uniform. We pulled him into the safety of the stairway corridor with us. He looked to be in his mid-forties, his face and chest covered in bites and scratches. I checked his vitals.

"Is he still alive?"

I nodded. "Yes, but he needs a doctor." I handed her the wadded remains of my jacket. "Press that against that neck wound and hold it there."

"What are you going to do?"

"Play bait and try to figure a way out of this."

"You can't be serious," she said.

I winked at her and then went through the door.

Fight smarter, not harder, I'd said. Yeah, I'm smart… S-M-R-T.

What I *am* is fast. And while I am faster in the water these days than I am on land, I've still been running since I was in grade school. Admittedly, I will never outrun someone like Usain Bolt, but then again, I'm not racing Usain Bolt. I am racing a bunch of knee-high gremlins with sharp teeth and bad attitudes.

Had I been a little less concussed after my fight with the Santa-riding gremlin, I might have made the mental note that the ugly little critter had a set of little leathery wings on its back. That little nugget altered my previous advantage over the creatures.

After pulling the injured guard into the stairwell with Amy, I'd entered the server room of EPB HQ. Fluorescent lighting ran the length of the massive room, giving it a sterile soullessness. The flooring panels had a hollow sound to them, and I imagined they had cables running under them for easy routing. Hundreds of fans whined from the hefty racks that were filled to the ceiling with rows and rows of computer servers. These machines made it possible for the company to control and remotely monitor all six hundred square miles of the utility's service area. Only a row beyond the doorway, I caught sight of one gremlin clinging to the rack with its claws and staring intently at a terminal computer. Now, I'm not some kind of luddite. I was raised around computers and can get around on them well enough. But I'm all but certain this *thing* was confidently navigating the company's programs as it clicked around on the touchpad of the terminal computer with its other foot. Whatever it was doing, I knew I needed to stop it. I shot through the door.

"Batter up!" I shouted as I slammed the bat's flat end over the thing's skull. I didn't get the same neck-snapping satisfaction as Amy had downstairs, but it went careening into the wall and fell motionless to the floor. Not bad for one-hand.

"Who da man? I'm da man!" I roared in triumph.

Don't look at me like that. I got knocked around earlier.

And that's when another half-dozen of the creatures popped their heads out from the other aisles.

So I ran.

And, well, they flew.

Like I said, I'm fast. While that's great when you're outdoors or on a track; when you're in a giant enclosed computer room, it's only good for so long. Specifically, until you run out of space to run.

I passed the door I'd taken to get in the server room; I couldn't lead the gremlins back to Amy and the guard. There was no way that we'd be able to carry him down the stairs with those creatures on our heels. I made it to the end of the corridor, and noticed another door. Unfortunately, it opened inward and I couldn't just burst through to safety.

By the time I got the door open, one of the gremlins was practically on me. The little monster bounded off the corner at the end of the hall and launched itself at my face. I threw my casted arm in its way. It flailed wildly at me with its claws as it clamped onto my cast with its needle-like teeth. Together, we rolled into the other room and I wedged the bat in between the handle and the door, keeping its friends from joining us.

One on one, I had an advantage against my attacker, making up in mass for what I lacked in ferociousness. It desperately bit and tore at me. A claw flew at my left eye. I spun about and felt my cheek erupt in searing pain as a pair of claws tore it open.

Furious, I slammed my plaster-wrapped arm, which it still clung to, into the floor repeatedly. Each blow drove the gremlin's skull into the ground, and my cast against its jaw. The creature's jaw split apart and shattered sometime around the fourth blow.

I didn't stop. I couldn't.

Every bit of anger I'd felt since October came pouring out of me. I'd risked so much to find my mother, to discover the truth about who my father was. To learn all about my family, and by extension, maybe learn more about myself. The truth had been a lot. More than anyone should have to confront in such a brief time. And now I was being dragged full-on back into things because these little ugly leathery Tasmanian Devils picked a fight with the local Court!

By the time I stopped, its head looked like a watermelon that had picked a fight with a mallet. The blows broke my cast at the elbow, leaving it in two jagged pieces, letting me move my arm and bend it for the first time in weeks. I was covered in a black, viscous mess. It smelled awful, like burning hair doused in bile and cat piss. I was going to incinerate these clothes and scrub myself raw if I got out of this alive.

Which returned my attention to the present; the other five gremlins had not sat quietly outside the door as I beat their compatriot to a bloody pulp. Instead, they'd busily ripped away at the door and the surrounding wall and were quickly coming close to finishing that job. Apparently, witnessing portions of my overkill had whipped them into a fury.

It'd been one thing to take on a single gremlin, particularly as it had confined itself to one place of attack. Five…? That was going to be more than I could manage. A fact not lost on them, either.

I quickly scrambled about the room, looking for something of use. I was in an engineering room, with spools of wiring and tools lining the walls.

Nothing that I thought I could use before one of those creatures finished breaking through, I guessed. I risked another glance back at their frenzied efforts; it couldn't hold much longer. Then I saw the fire extinguisher behind the door.

I ripped the extinguisher off the hook and yanked the safety pin free from the lock just as the first of the gremlins cleared enough drywall to get its wings through behind it.

Hitting it with a blast of CO_2 in the face, I followed it up with a boot to the head; stunning it. I sprayed the other four gremlins with the icy mixture. Catching my breath became harder with each blast of the oxygen-robbing chemical.

When I'd emptied the canister, I slammed it down on the gremlin that I'd stunned. Its head exploded in a shower of viscous ick, covering my clothes.

I was definitely burning everything.

I pried a few more chunks apart on my cast for greater flexibility, including at the wrist and palm. The remaining chunks could continue serving as a makeshift bracer.

"It's showtime," I said, trying to psych myself up. Then I yanked the cricket bat out from the door and charged into the gauntlet with my best attempt at a war-cry.

With a kick of the door, I barreled out of engineering, smacking one of the remaining gremlins with the door. I caught another one that had taken to the air by hurling the empty extinguisher at it. Without the added weight, I took up the cricket bat with both hands and ran like hell for the doors that led back to Amy. I liked my odds of finishing this with the two of us.

I didn't risk a glance back, but I could hear chittering screams of anger and flapping wings behind me. I had their full attention.

"Amy!" I yelled down the corridor, a thunderous *clang* echoing with each footfall against the floor panels. "Coming in hot!"

Ninety feet to the door, I told myself. *Third Base to Home.*

Closing the gap, the door popped open and Amy stuck her head out. Judging by her reaction, I was right to feel confident. She spun her bat and prepared to swing away.

Then the floor panel in front of me flew up and caught me in the gut, as a pair of gremlins chittered maniacally below it.

The air shot out of me. My forehead bounced off the other side, and I fell ass-over-head down the back-end of the panel and into the subfloor.

Smack! Crack! Amy's bat sang out above me, but I couldn't see what was happening.

The subfloor wasn't deep—maybe four feet. I needed to get up and move, but between the ache in my gut, the ringing in my head, and the excruciating manner of my landing; I couldn't. My ankles now wedged above my head, I realized sorely.

Finn the Human Pretzel—get your tickets now!

There was something else. What was it?

Think.

What else?

And what the *hell* was that chittering sound?

Aww Crap.

Have you ever been unnerved by the shine of an animal's eyes at night?

As we generally consider humanity to be the apex predator in most modern environs, it might be a creepy sight, but not something the average person worries about. Go on a stroll out into any considerable woodland, forest or mountain range, some place nature still calls the shots, and that fear ramps up real fast. It's been my limited experience that the denizens of the Fae Wylds couldn't give a rat's ass about your perceived position on the food chain.

A point made abundantly clear as two pairs of eyes beamed menacingly in the subfloor's darkness. They chittered at each other as they cautiously bobbed their heads and snapped their jaws, moving ever closer to me. Each of their small leathery bodies, no more than thirty-inches tall, were tensed and getting set to attack. They pulled in their wings against their backs, little bony protrusions capping their joints. Similar bony spurs protruded from their knees and at the tops of their skulls. Each hand had a pair of fingers and thumb capped with wickedly sharp claws. Their feet bore three digits as well, and a clicking hind claw on the heel.

"Uh… Amy! I could use some help down here!"

Crack!

"Busy at the moment," she answered. Her running footsteps pounded overhead, dropping little motes of dust below.

"About to be eaten down here! Can't move! Amy!"

"What? Shit!"

Smash!

I twisted and pulled to break loose, but couldn't wrench the heavy panel off my legs. My neck and shoulders cried out as the wires and brackets in the subfloor cut into them. I weakly swung my bat at the pair of stalking gremlins, but they danced easily out of the way and continued to get closer, threatening to flank me.

"Watch your feet!"

Huh?

The panel, which had been pinning my ankles overhead, rocketed back enough for me to pull my legs free. I rolled clear of the gremlins and flailed in the darkness with my bat. It connected with something, but only barely. I had to get out of here. I pushed on some of the heavy panels above me. They wouldn't budge. I must have rolled under the racks.

"*Aziz*, Light!" I hollered as I swung about my darkened periphery. Being hunted by creatures who could see me when I couldn't see them was making me crack.

A panel—probably the same one that had trapped me before—shifted about six feet to my left.

"You are *such* a *nerd*!"

Light poured back into the under-chamber. I caught sight of the gremlins just as they were charging me. I swung as hard as I could with the bat and caught one in the neck; knocking it into the other. A wet *snap* sound accompanied the hit, and its head almost spun around completely. I made a note that their necks must be a weaker point in their anatomy.

The second of the two shook its head and righted itself. I couldn't stand upright with the cramped space, so I bolted after it like a gorilla and slammed my club down over its back in an instant, driving it to the ground. Huddled over it, I grabbed the blade of the bat with both hands and drove the edge as hard as I could into its neck and nearly decapitated the damn thing.

It was over.

Alarms started screaming all over the building.

Dammit! What now?

Amy's head popped through to the subfloor. "Time to go, Finn!"

"No shit!" I yelled as I made my way out to her. "What happened?"

She pulled me out, and we hurried to the stairwell. "Remember how I said that gremlins have a connection with electricity?"

"Vaguely."

"Well, they were probably using their connection to prevent the alarms from going off. When you killed that last gremlin, the connection stopped."

"Great. The cops will be all over this building any minute now. There's no way we can make it out of here without being seen."

She nodded and snatched the cricket bat out of my hand. She wiped the thing down quickly and chucked it into a small opening at the base of the next flight of stairs, and then did the same with hers. "New plan. Knit a Glamoured uniform like his together. We're gonna have to carry the guard out anyway," she said, gesturing to the man I'd nearly forgotten about in all the chaos. His bleeding had stopped, which was good, but he was still out cold.

"No way this works." Nevertheless, I added the uniform to my current Glamour. Pressure behind my eyes roared to life, making them water.

"Not bad," she said with approval. She duplicated the image as well and we used a pistol-belt carry to move the guard down the stairs.

Blue strobing lights reflected throughout the lobby as we left the stairwell. She nodded reassuringly to me and said, "Just keep your head down and leave the talking to me."

She waved to the cops peering through the glass doors, and we continued shuffling toward them. "We need an ambulance! He—some kind of weird animal got in the building and attacked him!" It was unnerving how easily she spun that story. I mean, *technically* she wasn't lying, but I knew I'd have blown it.

The urgency of the situation seemed to convince the officers, and they took over care of the guard. We slipped away as soon as the chance presented itself. I didn't know what the guard might remember, but took comfort in that it wouldn't be us.

Duke Cailean was pleased with the results of the mission. It had been messier than he'd have preferred, but he assured me that my independence from the Court was certain and would continue to be recognized; so long as he reigned. The distinction left wiggle room for him to drag me into his game of chess again as a pawn. Frankly, I was too exhausted to argue. Between the physical abuse and the mental strain in using the Glamour, all I wanted was to crawl into bed and sleep for a week. I'd damn sure put up a fight if it became a habit; even a Pawn can ascend to positions of power.

My broken cast jangled about like the world's ugliest set of armbands as I reached into my pocket to turn my phone back on. The load screen cast an eerie blue light about the still quietness of the Battlefield's wintry air.

"Get Nic to cut the rest of that cast off when you get home."

"*Geez*—Wear a frickin' bell if you're gonna sneak up on people." I hadn't heard Amy come out of the faerie trod beneath Wilder Tower. "You could just come in when you drop me off."

"Even if I were headed your way, I'm not ready to face that drama yet. I've had enough fighting for one evening. I've got to go settle my debt with the pixies in the Canyon for the assist tonight."

"Wait, how am I supposed to get home?"

"You could call an Uber, or just start walking." She was enjoying this. "Maybe one of the Patrol units will see you on your way out of the Park."

"You're a riot. Ha-ha."

She shot me a look that said she wasn't messing with me and reached into her car and grabbed the knit-cap that I'd left in it. "So you don't get too cold." She walked it back to me, tossing it at my face in the final steps. As I caught the hat, she finished closing the distance between us and planted her boot right between my legs.

Fire tore through my already weary body, searing every nerve from the point of impact up to my teeth. I fought hard not to puke on the spot, but tasted the bile in my mouth.

Not missing a beat, Amy caught me as I crumpled forward, bracing me with her shoulder and cradling my head with one hand.

She spoke into my ear, "I like you, Finn. Really, I do. But never force me into an Oath again. I'd hate to have to *really* hurt you."

With a level of gentleness incongruous with the savage kick, she guided me to a nearby slab of stone and helped me sit. "I'll see you around," she said as she climbed into her car and drove off.

Taking a minute to ensure the waves of nausea had passed, I unlocked my phone and debated who to call. Absentmindedly, I leaned against my knuckle and was reminded that I'd gotten up-close and personal with the business-end of an angry gremlin; I would probably need stitches too. I'd have everything I'd need to clean myself up at the apartment or the office, but I'd need some help with that. Letting Nic cut the plaster off my arm was one thing, but I'd be damned if I would trust him with a needle and thread. My options weren't plentiful. In the end, I knew who I trusted most.

"Keira? I'm sorry it's so late. Listen, I need a few favors. I—I'll explain later, I promise. How comfortable are you with sewing?"

Keira took me to the office, so I could get cleaned up and grab some clothes that didn't scream horror movie survivor. She did a truly amazing job patching me up, and after bringing me back to my place where I had to explain *everything* again to Nic, they let me get some rest.

That afternoon, I woke to hear that a three-block area of Chattanooga had lost all power about the time of our showdown. During the outage, someone had raided an antiques dealer's safe and stolen a collection of old manuscripts, and maps of the Tennessee Valley. The dealer had been translating the manuscripts and maps, revealing a vast series of unknown caverns and tunnels in the area.

I wondered if that had been the reason for the gremlin attack on EPB. And if so, what secrets could those documents hold?

I had a bad feeling I would find out soon enough.

The Legend of Black Cats

A Chronos Chronicles story
By Shami Stovall

"I'm so excited to be on my first ever case," Bree said, smiling ear to ear.

Adair Finch parked his Toyota Celica on the side of the road. The quiet city of Modesto was sleepy most months, and September was no different. It was hot—it was always hot in the central valley of California—and the trees had already begun to shed their leaves, coating the sidewalk in oranges and yellows.

After a long exhale, Finch turned off his vehicle. "Most PIs don't call their assignments *cases*. You sound like a Saturday morning cartoon."

Bree opened the passenger side door and leapt out. She had all the energy, and attention span, of a thirteen-year-old girl. Probably because she was one.

"Okay, where do you think our evil spirit is?" Bree couldn't stop smiling. "Should we just start questioning all the neighbors? Oh! Can I take notes? I brought a notebook!"

Always prepared, Bree showed off her black backpack. It matched her black hoodie, and her dark jeans. She looked like a young witch, even if she didn't like being called that. The only thing vibrant and bright about her was her blue eyes, that sparkled with delight, no matter the time of day.

Bree opened her pack and withdrew a binder that had star constellations on the front. Then she pulled out a pen with a pumpkin.

"Can I say I'm your assistant when I question people?" Bree asked.

Finch stepped out of the car and slammed his door shut. "You *are* my assistant."

"I know, I just don't want you to get grumpy when I tell everyone." Bree gathered up her pack, closed the door, and practically leapt around the Toyota. "Okay, the facts of the case are—"

"We don't call it a *case*."

"—we're being paid to investigate the strange occurrences on Maplewood Drive." Bree tapped the pumpkin pen to her lower lip. "A strange spirit or creature has been causing disturbances in the neighborhood, and they're getting worse and worse."

Finch smoothed his coat. It was hot, but he didn't care. He liked his coat—he wore it everywhere.

"The last occurrence was a BBQ that exploded." Bree spoke with a matter-of-fact tone, as though she was in a dramatic TV show. "The man at the grill was injured and sent to the hospital. The local witch, who lives on this street, said magic was involved."

"Yup."

Finch turned his attention to the neighborhood. Maplewood Drive was boring. No dog barks. No people taking a walk. There were plenty of vehicles parked on the side of the road, and some faint music playing from people's backyards, but other than that, nothing to remark on.

The houses were all a single story, and likely built forty years ago. Chain-link fences were the norm, but despite their low-class appearance, everything on the road was well taken care of. The people in this neighborhood still cared, unlike most of Modesto, which was affectionately called *Meth-desto* by the local law enforcement.

"The strange occurrence before that was someone's dog drowning in a pool." Bree actually frowned after repeating that information. "The witch said magic was involved then, too."

"Yeah, I read the same email," Finch said with a sigh. "Look, we're being paid to figure out what's doing this, and potentially more if we can stop it. Okay? Let's start with the most suspicious house and work our way from there."

Bree glanced down the road. Most of the houses were painted white or blue. Some had American flags out front.

"None of them looks suspicious," she whispered.

Finch pointed to a house four down. "That one is the most suspect."

Bree crossed her arms. "Ya know, in school, our teachers tell us to *show our work*. You should tell me why it's suspicious, that way I know, too."

After a short exhale, Finch gestured to the chimney. Gray smoke billowed up into the sky. "It's a hot day. Why is that family burning things? Plus, we know for certain they're home, so we should start there."

"Okay! Let's go."

Finch pulled out his phone.

5:10 p.m.

He marked the time and then motioned for Bree to get close. She already knew what he was going to do, and even offered her pumpkin pen for those purposes. Finch took it, and wrote a symbol on the back of Bree's hand: three lines down, and one across, so that it looked like three lowercase Ts.

It was the Mark of Chronos.

"Now we're all set," Finch stated.

Bree gently touched the mark on the back of her hand. "Do you think *I* could make a pact with Chronos one day?"

Finch pointed to the house. "Let's just focus, all right? I want to figure this case out before it gets dark."

With a snort, Bree wagged her finger. "It's not called a *case*, isn't that what you said?"

He frowned as he headed for the sidewalk. Bree giggled the whole way to the suspicious house. There were no decorations for the fall season—only dusty circles on the front porch, as though something had been recently taken away.

Bree jumped in front of Finch before he could knock on the door.

"I'll do all the questioning, okay?" Bree held herself straight. "I want to solve this."

With a sarcastic wave of his arm, Finch motioned to the door.

Bree knocked as hard as she could. Afterward, she shook her hand out and rubbed her knuckles. She had clearly knocked *too* hard.

It only took a few seconds before a man answered. He opened the door wide, and stared out with a bewildered expression. He was overweight—close to three hundred pounds—but wore it well, since he was so tall. His face was puffy and red, and his eyes had acres of bags underneath.

Finch figured the man hadn't slept in a while.

"Hello?" the man asked.

Bree stood on her tippy-toes and held her notebook up and ready. "Hello! My name is Bree Blackstone, and I'm a private investigator."

"You look a little young," the man muttered, his eyes narrowing. They were bloodshot.

"W-Well, that's because I'm in training. And right now, I'm here to figure out who has been disturbing the peace of your quaint neighborhood."

The man shifted his weight from one foot to the next, frowning. He was rather pale—except for the redness on his face—and his eyes were a light green. His expression seemed set to a permanent state of *sad.*

"I don't have much to do with the neighbors," the man said.

Bree held up her notebook. "Can I get your name?"

"Uh… It's Ron. Ron Shabord."

"Excellent." Bree wrote that down. "Ron—why are you burning things? I see smoke from your chimney, and that's really odd."

Finch pinched the bridge of his nose. "Real subtle," he whispered under his breath.

"I'm burning things I don't want anymore," Ron said, half closing the door. "Look, I need to keep cleaning. Why don't you—"

"What're you burning?" Bree slid closer to the door. "You don't need to burn things you don't want. You can give them to charity. That's what my mum always said."

Ron—who was clearly not having this conversation—tried to shut the door. Bree shoved her foot in the way before it closed, but then she yelped and leapt backward. Her little sneaker was no match for the door.

Concerned, Ron opened it halfway again and muttered an apology.

"Look," he said, firm this time. "I'm burning old photographs of me and my wife. Ex-wife. I don't want them, and I doubt Goodwill wants them, either. Goodbye."

Ron slammed the door.

Bree stood still for a couple seconds, and then glanced over at Finch. "I think he's hiding something."

"All he's hiding is an alcohol problem," Finch quipped. "And he's doing it poorly."

With a sheepish expression, and a flutter of her eyelashes, Bree hesitantly asked, "Can we try again?"

"You want to question Ron a second time? Why? That wasn't enough misery for one day?"

"I think I felt… magic in his house, ya know?"

Finch hadn't been paying much attention. Perhaps there was? The neighborhood was rather devoid of it, but if there was a chance they could find something magical, he supposed it was worth a second glance.

"I have a plan this time." Bree tapped her notebook. "Please? I think I know exactly what to do."

After rolling his eyes a second time, Finch activated his magic.

The world froze around him. All the leaves hung in midair, the faint music stopped in the distance, and the world was paused. Then the color drained from everything, melting away until it was a world of black and white. Finally, the objects melted, too, disappearing into a swirl, leaving Finch all alone in a void of white space.

When he blinked, he found himself back on the sidewalk near his car. Finch stood next to Bree, right where he had marked the time.

5:10 p.m.

Bree held out her hand so Finch could redraw the Mark of Chronos. Once finished, she smiled' You have to follow my lead," she said.

"All right," Finch muttered.

Once they arrived at Ron's house, Bree poked at Finch's arm until he knocked.

Ron answered, the same sad expression he wore before.

"Hello?" he asked.

"Hello!" Bree smiled up at him. "I'm selling girl scout cookies!" She had raised the pitch of voice so that she sounded just a tad bit younger. Then Bree motioned to Finch. "Normally, my mommy would help, but she… left… so it's just me and my dad now." Her last few words were accompanied by an exaggerated downward shift of her voice, practically depressed.

"We need to get you acting lessons," Finch whispered, more to himself than to her.

Then he snapped his attention to her. He *wanted* to remind her that he was only thirty-seven, and that he wouldn't have a thirteen-year-old daughter, but he held back.

Despite her cartoonish-levels of acting, Ron seemed moved by her statement. His eyes grew glassy with a sheen of water, and he nodded once.

"I'll take some cookies," Ron managed to choke out.

Bree nodded once and then fumbled around as she attempted to write that in her notebook. With an adorable frown, she asked, "Do you mind if I use your table to write down your information?"

"Uh, sure." Ron stepped aside. "The kitchen is right here. I'll take two boxes of Thin Mints."

After giving Finch a subtle smirk, Bree hopped inside and made her way over to the kitchen table.

The house was definitely owned by someone who had just gone through a divorce. Half the furniture was missing, there were no photos on the walls, and everything smelled of dust. Finch followed in behind Bree, keeping his eye out for anything that might be magical.

"Told you I had a plan," Bree whispered to Finch as she slowly made her way into the kitchen.

Finch was impressed—now they just needed to find something of interest.

The kitchen table was a sad little circle big enough for three people, max. The chairs were rickety, and Finch suspected this had once been outside furniture.

Bree sat down and began writing a little list. "Two boxes…" Then she eyed Finch and glared.

She clearly wanted him to do something.

Ron walked into the kitchen and sighed. "Maybe make it *three* boxes of Thin Mints."

While Finch was tempted to make a joke, his train of thought was completely interrupted when he spotted a black cat sauntering into the kitchen from the living room. To a normal human, it was just a normal black cat—short onyx fur, and bright yellow eyes—but Finch knew better.

"That's it," he blurted out.

Bree and Ron both whipped their heads in the direction of the cat.

The feline froze, its ears erect, its tail straight up.

"That's just *Smudge*," Ron said, dismissively waving away the comment. "He's my cat. I got him just recently. I, uh, was lonely."

Smudge took a step backward, his pupils shrinking to tiny slits as he stared at Finch.

"That's no cat," Finch said as he stepped around the kitchen table.

Bree leapt from her chair. "Oh! Really? What is it? A spirit? *A demon*?"

"It's just a cat," Ron said, baffled.

"It's an *oozla*," Finch said. "A creature born from a murder."

When a human loved a cat, and cherished it, a special kind of magic was born. However, if that cat were ever murdered, the shadow of the cat absorbed the magic, and the despair, and became an *oozla*. And whenever oozla were nearby, terrible things happened. The magic that poured from their black fur was that of bad luck and misfortune.

Which was why the myth of black cats being unlucky spawned. Oozla were always black, just like the shadows they were born from.

It was the same with the *barghest*. A barghest was a black dog born from the love and despair of a beloved dog being murdered. And just like the *oozla*, all black dogs were seen as unlucky.

The keyword for both oozla and barghests was *murdered*. The cat or dog in question couldn't just die of natural causes—they had to be killed in an intentional, and malicious fashion.

Bree's eyes went wide. "Wait! My mum told me all about oozla. Sometimes witches keep them as guard animals, to bring misfortune to whoever visits them."

"I said it's just a cat," Ron said, louder than before. "And I think you two need to leave."

"Not without the damn feline," Finch said as he stomped around the table.

Smudge, the oozla, hissed and then whirled around. He ran down the hall and Finch gave chase. As he went, he felt his anger building. The little oozla was causing so much trouble in the neighborhood that innocent people were being harmed. He couldn't allow this to go on any further.

Hot air rushed through Finch's lungs. He was not only bonded to Chronos, but also to Ke-Koh, the Ifrit of Rebellion, which gave him access to magical fire.

And oozla died pretty quickly when on fire.

Smudge darted into a bedroom, through a barely cracked open door. Finch slammed through it, embers on his breath. He glared as he scanned the room, and immediately spotted the long black tail of oozla as it slipped under the bed.

Finch stomped over, grabbing the bed-frame, and lifting it into the air, before hissing with pain, and dropping back into place. A nail had been sticking out of the wooden frame, and he had pierced himself on it.

How unlucky…

The powers of oozla were quite potent. If Finch didn't catch the creature soon, the misfortune that befell him would only get worse.

Before Finch could light the whole room up with fire, Ron grabbed his shoulder and yanked him around.

"You can't have my cat!" Ron shouted; his face redder than before. "Get out before I call the cops!"

Bree stood in the doorframe of the bedroom; her blue eyes wide. "A-Adair. Let's just try again. Don't hurt him, okay?"

Ron's grip on Finch tightened.

Torn between just fighting his way through this and doing things the way Bree wanted, Finch forced himself to calm down. Once his concentration was back where he needed it, Finch rewound time.

Everything froze. The colors slipped away. Then everything melted.

Finch opened his eyes, and he was back on the sideway.

5:10 p.m.

Bree gasped. "We did it!" She bounded around Finch for a moment, clearly giddy. "Okay, we found an oozla. That's a big step. We've almost cracked this case—I'm so good at being a private detective! Did you see that? First house? Super subterfuge? Did you see it?"

"I saw," Finch drawled.

He ran a hand down his face and tried to clear his thoughts. They couldn't chase an oozla forever. The bad luck would hound them and make it nearly impossible to catch.

Finch knew he would have to kill it fast.

"Okay, I have another plan," Bree said. She tugged on Finch's coat sleeve. "C'mon! We have to slash Ron's tires."

Holding back a chuckle, Finch allowed himself to be dragged along. "We're going to *what?*"

Bree brought him to the car out in front of Ron's house. Just like the inside, the vehicle seemed half empty and sad. Bree pulled a pocket knife from her backpack and then handed it to Finch with a gleeful smile.

"Can you do it?" she asked.

"Of course." Finch went to the two back tires and—after some effort—managed to jab the knife into the tires. The hiss of air told him the job was done.

Bree pointed to the house. "Okay, once Ron runs off, we have to get inside and grab the oozla before he comes back. Got it?"

Finch had agreed to let Bree handle the investigation, so he just nodded. In his mind, it would be far easier to just sneak into the house at night, or when Ron was at work, but he didn't mind humoring the girl. If she wanted to bust in, metaphorical guns blazin', he was going to let her have her fun.

With a snicker, Bree ran to the front door. She pounded on it with the side of her fist. "Hello!" she called out. "Does someone live here!"

The door flew open, and Ron wildly glanced around until his eyes settled on Bree. "What's going on?" he demanded.

Bree pointed at his car. "Someone was slashing your tires! We tried to stop him, but then he just ran off down the street!" She gestured down Maplewood Drive.

"*What?*"

Ron stepped outside and slammed his door shut behind him. Then he hurried to his car, saw his tires slashed, and promptly pulled out his phone as he hustled down the way Bree had indicated. While he was distracted,

Bree grabbed the front door handle and turned. Unlocked, obviously—Ron hadn't locked it on his way out.

She slipped inside, and Finch followed afterward.

While this wasn't the way *he* would've handled things, he had to admit—he was having fun.

Once inside the house, Bree hurried into the kitchen. Sure enough, the little oozla, Smudge, walked in. His yellow eyes went wide the instant he spotted them.

"There you are, you little devil," Finch said.

Smudge took a step back and then arched his back. "What's a pair of warlocks doing here?" he asked, his voice rather deep for how small he was.

"We know what you've been doing," Bree said, pointing at the black cat. "You're under arrest!"

"Private investigators don't arrest people," Finch muttered under his breath.

The oozla didn't stick around. He turned on his four pawed feet and took off down the hallway, just like before. Finch leapt over the table and gave chase, with Bree close on his heels. Since Finch knew which room the oozla was heading to, he picked up the pace and slammed through the bedroom door at nearly the same time as the cat.

Diving for the feline, Finch managed to grab his back leg before the cat got under the bed. The oozla hissed and screamed, and then reached back and started clawing Finch's hands.

"Ow! *Fuckin'* cat! Ow!"

Despite the claws and teeth, Finch forced himself to stand. He held the cat by both legs and Smudge thrashed wildly, hissing and spitting with all his might. Oozla had plenty of magic, but it wasn't in a direct fashion. Their misfortune only happened to the environment around a person.

Finch concentrated on his connection to Ke-Koh, and the palms of his hands began to glow.

"*W-Wait!*" the oozla hissed. "Don't!"

Perfectly prepared to cook the evil creature, Finch ignored Smudge's pleas.

The front door opened. Then it closed.

Everyone froze. Bree, Finch—even the oozla.

"That's my human," the oozla whispered, his claws deep into Finch's hands. His yellow eyes narrowed. "He's a sad sack, but he's *my* sad sack."

With his tail, Smudge pointed to the bedroom window.

"It's not locked. You can get out of here without hurting my human."

"You care about Ron?" Bree furrowed her brow.

Finch didn't care about any of this. He *did* need to get out of the house without harming a magicless human, though. He hurried to the window and then gestured for Bree to handle it. She grabbed the bottom and pushed it up, the *squeak* of the movement just a bit too loud.

"Hello?" Ron asked from somewhere else in the house. "Is someone here?"

He sounded out of breath. Finch wondered how far the man had run.

Without waiting a moment later, Finch leapt out the window, the oozla still clutched tightly in his hands. Much to his misfortune, he landed outside in a rosebush; the thorns digging into his flesh as he slid down the dirt. The sting was enough that Finch sucked in air through his teeth—but he never let go of the damn cat.

The oozla snickered a *hiss-hiss-hiss* laugh at Finch's pain.

Bree climbed out afterward and carefully stepped down. Then she shut the window. Another *squeak*.

It couldn't be helped.

Finch forced himself to stand and then ran from the side of the house to the sidewalk. Bree kept his pace, and even motioned to the Toyota. They took off, the animal still in their grasp.

When they reached the vehicle, Finch had to let go of a single leg to fish out his keys. The oozla thrashed again, hissing and clawing, shredding his knuckles clean of skin.

Finch grunted as he took a seat in his car, careful not to let the cat anywhere near his lap. He pressed Smudge against the top of his steering wheel, trapping the feline in place.

Fire built in Finch's hand, and the singed hair stank up the car in an instant. While he knew he would damage his vehicle if he used too much, he didn't care. Blood was weeping from his torn-up hands, and it was getting all over his coat and jeans.

Bree grabbed his arm and then yanked his elbow. He jerked his attention over, and she pleaded at him with large eyes.

"Wait! Maybe we can… talk to him?" Bree asked.

Finch already knew where this was going. His fire receded, and the cat in his hands growled something fierce, but it slowly stopped fighting so much. With his fangs sunk into Finch's wrist, Smudge turned his yellow eyes to her.

"You said you knew what oozla were," Finch said through clenched teeth, the sting of his injuries flaring through his arms.

Bree nodded. "Yeah, but… Don't you think it's so sad? The poor oozla didn't have a choice that it was born."

"Remember why we're here? Remember the man whose BBQ exploded?"

"But Smudge loves Ron, and didn't want us to hurt him."

Smudge slowly pulled his fangs from Finch's flesh. Then he laid his ears back. "Love is a strong word."

"You still cared!" Bree glared at Finch. "We can't just kill him. We should… save him, too! Maybe we can give Smudge to a witch who needs him. That way he won't hurt the magicless mortals here."

Finch took in a deep breath, and then exhaled. This was Bree's case, after all.

"Fine," he eventually said. "*Fine*. If you want to take the damn oozla somewhere, we will." Finch pulled it away from the steering wheel and then offered the cat over to Bree. "But you have to hold him."

She hesitated. For a long moment, Finch thought she might not take the oozla, but then Bree pursed her lips together in a straight line, and held out her hands. Finch passed over the creature, prepared to rewind time if it started savaging her.

But the cat didn't.

Smudge rested easy in her arms before he started licking the burn mark on his back leg. After a few licks, he laid his ears back and glared. "You were going to cook me!"

Finch started the car. "It would've been quick."

"Still!"

Bree gently patted his head. "It's okay. Don't worry, Smudge. We'll take you to a witch. Maybe one of my mum's old friends."

The little feline relaxed a bit in Bree's arms. "Really? You two are… going to help me?"

With a dramatic nod of her head, Bree smiled. "Of course. That's what we do. We help people."

"That's not really the job description of a private investigator," Finch muttered.

"Well, it is in *my* description." Bree snuggled the cat close. "We're good private investigators that make everything better wherever we go, and we're going to start by helping the poor little oozla. Okay?"

Finch let out a long sigh. He supposed he knew this was coming.

"What about Ron?" Smudge tilted his head. "He's sad. And I mean that in more ways than one. He needs something to care for, or else he might stop caring altogether."

Sometimes, Finch couldn't believe how many things he needed to save. With a long sigh, he said, "We'll get Ron a puppy. And also a therapist. And maybe a few rounds of speed dating."

"Really?" Bree perked up in her seat. "You mean it, Adair? We should definitely do those things. Ron needs it!"

Finch slowly turned his car and headed out of Maplewood Drive. "I mean. But first, let's get this damn oozla out of my car before we get ourselves into a fatal accident."

We hope that you enjoyed this title and look forward to many more to come. Please, leave us a review! Reviews matter to all of our authors.

And don't forget to check out the latest edition of *Car Wars*

http://www.sjgames.com/car-wars/

Or the other amazing titles from
Steve Jackson Games

http://www.sjgames.com

…or the latest in the Car Warriors: Autoduel Chronicle fiction series.
https://threeravenspublishing.com/car-warriors-autoduel-chronicles/

Take a look at some of our other award-winning series at
https://threeravenspublishing.com/series-universes/

Visit us at https://www.threeravenspublishing.com and sign up for our newsletter for the latest and greatest news on upcoming titles and events.

Other series and titles you might enjoy.

DECLAN FINN
DECLAN FINN
DECLAN FINN
DECLAN FINN
Demons are Forever
Honor at Stake
Live and Let Bite
Good to the Last Drop
The Dragon Award Nominated Series
FREE on Kindle Unlimited!

AVAILABLE ON
AMAZON
JOINT TASK FORCE
13
HOLDING THE LINE
BETWEEN HEAVEN AND HELL

MYSTERY,
MAGIC &
MAYHEM
WITH A TWIST
OF ROMANCE
J.F. POSTHUMUS
ON AMAZON
FIND ME
B.C.N.T.
BIOLOGIC   ENHANCED   NASCENT   TALENT

THE RAVEN
AND
THE CROW
MICHAEL K. FALCIANI
FIND ME
ON AMAZON

STARFLIGHT

IT CAME FROM THE
TRAILER PARK

3R
Three Ravens
Publishing
Are you looking for fun, new fiction?
The FEATHER and the LAMP
L.N. Hunter
TRAILER PARK
JONATHAN MABERRY
LEGENDS
A JOINT TASK FORCE 13 ANTHOLOGY
Edited by
William Joseph Roberts
Philip K. Booker
CROSSWAYS
THE WAYMAN CHRONICLES
MICHAEL J ALLEN
THE RAVEN AND THE CROW
DARK STORM RISING
J.F. POSTHUMUS
STAFF OF CHAOS
The Written Word Will Never Be The Same…
https://www.threeravenspublishing.com
Veteran Owned and Operated

You can also keep up to date with our latest release announcements on Scifi.radio and get some of the best fandom programing on the planet.

Scifi for your Wifi

And don't forget to check out our other Sponsors and Affiliates

A southern Appalachian jewel for craft beer lovers, Buck Bald Brewing offers something for everyone. With delicious, locally brewed beverages from across the spectrum, Buck Bald Brewing offers craft brews that are consistently amazing.

From the dark and smooth Shesquatch Scottish ale, to the intense hops of Hippibilly IPA, to the puckering sour of the blackberry and cinnamon in Berry My Heart at the Trailer Park, and more than 60+ rotating brews, you'll find what you're looking for and more.

With smiling faces behind the bar ready to help you find your next favorite brew, a constantly rotating selection of delicious craft beverages, toe-tapping tunes always playing, and the biggest games on TV, you can kick your feet up in either Copperhill, Tennessee or Murphy, North Carolina and immerse yourself in the Buck Bald Brewing experience. So, come out, fill a pint, fill a growler, and fill your mind at your new favorite family-owned craft brewery.

To discover more visit us at buckbaldbrewing.com or follow us on Facebook @buckbaldbrewing and @buckbaldbrewingmurphy.

Vesper Wren's
TRAILER PARK
PIXIE
PUNCH
• A PEACH STRAWBERRY SELTZER •
BUCK BALD BREWING

BRAXTON
HICKS
MIDNIGHT MOCHA MILK
STOUT
BUCK BALD BREWING